UNDER OATH
by Shelby Yastrow

"I'm going to ask you to find in favor of the Waltons, and that won't be easy for you. You're going to have to decide that a doctor was negligent, and there are still people who don't believe that doctors make mistakes. But they do, ladies and gentlemen, and the evidence in this case will convince you that Steven Sinclair *did* make a mistake."

Charlie looked intently from juror to juror and then slowly nodded as if to say, "I trust you to do the right thing."

As he walked back to his seat at the counsel table, he caught Lew Beck's eye and winked. *Top that, you son of a bitch.*

UNDER OATH

SHELBY YASTROW

A Bernard Geis Associates Book

DIAMOND BOOKS, NEW YORK

This book is a Diamond original edition,
and has never been previously published.

UNDER OATH

A Diamond Book / published by arrangement with
the author

PRINTING HISTORY
Diamond edition / May 1994

ISBN: 0-7865-0005-0

Diamond Books are published by The Berkley Publishing Group,
200 Madison Avenue, New York, NY 10016.
DIAMOND and the "D" design
are trademarks belonging to Charter Communications, Inc.

PRINTED IN THE UNITED STATES OF AMERICA

10 9 8 7 6 5 4 3 2 1

To our children, Sara, Phil, and Steve, to their spouses, Bob, Ellen, and Arna, and to the grandchildren they've given us, Ellen, Levi, Erin, Adam, and Noah.

ACKNOWLEDGMENTS

I'd like to express my deep appreciation to Dr. Ernest Weis and Zel Pyatt who collectively and patiently gave me a crash course in genetics and answered my endless questions about the mysteries of chromosomes, and to Dr. Lee Yosowitz, Dr. Joseph Burke, and my nephew, Dr. Edward Yastrow, for their help in guiding me through the other medical jungles I encountered in the writing of this book.

And I'd never forgive myself if I didn't publicly thank Richard Schultz for double-checking the accuracy of my courtroom scenes, Lori Hoye for her help on the geography that plays such an important part in the solution of my story, and Barbara Peters (proprietor of the Poisoned Pen bookstore in Scottsdale, Arizona—the greatest haunt in the world for mystery buffs) for her many useful suggestions.

Deceive not thy physician, confessor nor lawyer.
George Herbert, *Jacula Prudentum,* 1651

Isn't the best defense always a good attack?
Ovid, *The Loves,* c. A.D. 8

PART ONE

THE TRIAL

ONE ═══

"MR. MAYFIELD?"

"Yes, Your Honor." He pushed back his chair and lifted his tall, overweight frame, careful to move slowly at first to hide his jitters, to get the feel of the moment. Doin' this for thirty-six years, he thought to himself, and it still gives me the heebie-jeebies. He lumbered over to a spot several feet from the lectern that faced the jury. He wouldn't need a lectern, just as he wouldn't need notes. He knew his cases too well to need notes. He ran his fingers through his thick gray hair and looked from juror to juror with eyes that other trial lawyers would have killed for—sad and droopy, like a Saint Bernard's. Honest eyes. "Trust me," those eyes said.

"Ladies and gentlemen," he began in his slow, deep voice, "my name is Charlie Mayfield. My driver's license says Charles, but even my teachers never called me that. I'm a lawyer, born right here in Chicago, and I've been here my whole life. I practice in my own little firm with a couple of young lawyers to help me."

He took a step closer to the twelve people facing him and then half turned away from them and motioned with his arm toward a handsome couple seated at the plaintiffs' counsel table. "I represent Tracey and Lawrence Walton, the two people you see sitting over there. Tracey and Larry were husband and wife until a year ago, but now they're divorced. Nevertheless, they're acting together in this lawsuit—a lawsuit they filed for them-

3

selves and for their daughter, Angela—Angel we call her."

The lawyer looked from juror to juror—he had this knack for making each one of them think he was talking only to him or her. Then he shook his head sadly and sighed. "I've been talking to juries for nearly forty years now, and this is the first time that I have been unable to find the words to describe my case. I'll do the best I can, but if I fall short, well, I hope you won't hold it against my clients—particularly Angel.

"Angel was born in 1988, four years ago. We can't have her here every day during the trial, and you'll understand why when you meet her a day or two from now. I'll just tell you that she's very sick—she's about the most pathetically sick little girl you'll ever see—and leave it at that for now."

Mayfield had wavered throughout his preparation of the case as to when, and how, he would first let the jurors learn of Angel's illness. It wasn't until late the previous night that he'd finally decided not to go into the details of her condition during his opening statement. And once he made the decision, he knew it was right. Better impact on the jury to have the mother tell 'em, he thought. That'll get more sympathy. Then, when they're softened up, I'll have Angel wheeled into the courtroom. Play it right and that'll be the end of the case. Charlie Mayfield had known from the get-go that this trial would eventually boil down to "our word against their word" and that sympathy would tilt the balance his way. "No way," he had told the Waltons, "that those twelve people are going to be able to look Tracey in the eye and call her a liar after they see what she's living with. And that's just what they'd have to do to go against us—call her a liar. No way."

Now he put his hands in the pockets of the well-worn navy blue suit he pulled out only for jury trials. Like many litigators, Charlie believed that jurors might be put off by a lawyer who wore a different well-pressed tailor-made suit every day—the kind he wore when he wasn't in court. He shuffled back and forth in front of the jury box, looking at the floor as if he were trying to think of what to say next. "What do we have here?" he asked of no one in particular. "We have a couple who, five years ago, were blessed with the wonderful news that they were going to have their first baby. They had wanted this child, and then God smiled upon them. During the next several months they would buy a home with a yard, and they would convert a bedroom into the nursery that would be Angel's. They took a class together on natural childbirth. They selected names for their new baby— Angela for a girl and Daniel for a boy. And they told everyone of their happy news. Everything was good."

Mayfield stopped pacing, turned to face the jury, and placed his large hands on the low partition that separated him from those who would soon be deciding his case. "But even before they bought a house and redid a bedroom, before they chose names, and before they counted their blessings, Tracey Walton did something else." Mayfield turned and walked over to the opposite counsel table. There he stood and pointed—actually pointed—at an almost frail man with thinning hair that was somewhere between blond and brown. Five years earlier he had looked too young to be thirty-eight, but now he looked too old to be forty-three. "She became the patient of Dr. Steven Sinclair, the man you see sitting there with his lawyer. He's an obstetrician. He's supposed to take care of pregnant women and deliver their babies." Although the doctor was sitting at the table reserved for the defense, he looked totally defenseless with Charlie Mayfield glaring down at him.

Apparently reluctant to get into a stare-down with the man with the trust-me eyes, but not knowing what else to do, Steve Sinclair leaned over to whisper a few meaningless words to his lawyer, who was sitting at his right.

Charlie Mayfield, satisfied that he had shown the jurors that pointing a finger at this doctor was easy to do, walked back toward the jury box. Experience had taught him the importance of positioning—being in the right place and facing the right direction—when presenting a case to a jury, but whatever position he chose, he always worked his way back toward the jury as often as possible. "Hell," he'd often say, "I'd climb right up there into the box with 'em if the judge'd let me. I want 'em to think I'm one of them, and I want 'em to see the case through my eyes."

"Now," he was saying, "you're going to hear two different stories about what went on in Sinclair's office." He had deliberately chosen not to refer to the defendant as Dr. Sinclair, except when he could do so sarcastically. Why show respect for the man whose carelessness had hurt his client? If he didn't want the jury to respect the guy, why should he? "Tracey Walton is going to get on that witness stand over there, and she's going to tell you, *under oath*, that she told Sinclair about her fear, her terrible fear, of having a baby that wasn't perfect. She and her husband wanted this baby, and they didn't want anything to go wrong. Now," he added, stretching out his arms, his palms up, "I know that every mother worries about this. It's only natural." He glanced at the jurors who were mothers—he knew who they were from the jury selection process. Their expressions confirmed the point, as he had known they would. "But," Mayfield continued as he moved over to stand next to Tracey Walton, "this woman's fear was even stronger than that of most mothers. She'll tell you it was constantly on her mind. And you'll believe her, ladies and gentlemen, because it's the truth."

The jurors, for the first time, studied Tracey Walton. They could see that she was tall and well proportioned. She was thirty-one years old, had long reddish-brown hair, and was even more stunning now than when she was elected homecoming queen at her high school fourteen years earlier. Her steady gaze showed the courage that had impressed everyone who knew what she'd been going through, but the nervous wringing of her handkerchief betrayed her anxiety. Her former husband, sitting by her side, appeared to be a few years older than she. He, too, was tall and handsome.

Back to the jury box. "What did she do about her fear? She did what any one of you would have done. She told her doctor about it, and she asked him to take every precaution. 'Please, Doctor,' she said, 'do every test, so if there's a problem we can treat it. I don't want to find out later that I could have avoided it by taking some medicine or by taking better care of myself.' She even asked him to do a special test—they call it an amniocentesis, and I want you to remember that—which would tell them if the baby had certain abnormalities."

Now Charlie looked at Sinclair again. "And what did the good doctor do? I'll tell you what he did. He shrugged her fears off with a 'Don't worry, my dear,' and went about treating her as if she was just another customer at the counter waiting for her number to be called."

"Objection!" Sinclair's lawyer was on his feet. "I'm sorry, Your Honor. I don't like to interrupt counsel during opening statements, but Mr. Mayfield is going too far. He's already gone out of his way to prejudice the jury against Dr. Sinclair, and now, before any evidence is in, he's implying that my client treats his patients like customers at the corner deli."

Charlie Mayfield started to reply, but Judge Horace Grubner held up a hand. "Your point is well taken, Mr. Beck." He looked at Charlie. "Mr. Mayfield, try to save your characterizations of the evidence. Otherwise," he added with a smile, "you won't have anything left for your closing argument."

Charlie was satisfied. True to form, Judge Grubner had effectively sustained the objection, but he had done it in a way that wouldn't hurt the plaintiff. In fact, his warm smile when he spoke to Mayfield, and the casual way he handled Beck's objection, had told the jury that ol' Charlie wasn't really that far off base and that Beck was petty to object. Vintage Grubner! Charlie knew that Horace Grubner, before being elected to the bench, had been a plaintiffs' personal injury lawyer, and it wasn't any secret in the courthouse that he still leaned over backwards to favor the plaintiffs in injury cases. The fact was that he did his best to be fair, but years of fighting defense counsel and insurance companies seemed to have tainted his vision of impartiality. If a fair trial meant giving a little boost now and then to the plaintiff to offset what he saw as the deceit and tightfistedness of the defense, then so be it.

Mayfield grinned to show the jury that the ruling didn't mean a thing. "Thanks, Your Honor." Then he slipped neatly into his serious manner.

"As I was saying, and you'll hear testimony on this, Sinclair did not respond to Tracey Walton's pleas. He even refused to do the one test, the amniocentesis, which could've put her mind at ease or"—and here his eyes took on a whole new dimension of sadness—"could have told her what was in store for her and her husband." He paused to let that sink in. "He told her that such a test entailed—wait till you hear this—that it entailed a minor risk." Another pause. Then a roar: *"Minor risk!* Can you imagine that? That he'd subject her to nine months of worry and fear? And that he'd sentence poor little Angel to a lifetime of helplessness? All this to avoid a 'minor risk'? Steven Sinclair was not *avoiding* risk ladies and gentlemen, he was *incurring* risk." The trust-me eyes looked at each of the jurors, who were hanging on every word. "He gambled on which risk to take," Mayfield added in a soft whisper, "and he lost."

Now the lawyer pulled at his ear and looked squarely at Steve Sinclair. "What kind of 'minor risk,' *Doctor*? Isn't it a fact that thousands of amniocentesis tests are done every day? Haven't hundreds of your own patients had this very test? Has *any* of them ever had a problem with it? That so-called minor risk didn't stop you before, did it? I'm going to call you to the stand, *Doctor,* and I'm going to ask you these questions. So think about your answers. The jury will be eager to hear them. They'll want to know if that so-called minor risk was worth the sentence you handed down to Angel Walton and to her parents." Mayfield wasn't asking rhetorical questions; he had already asked Dr. Sinclair these same questions at a pretrial deposition, and he knew the answers were just what he wanted.

Now he moved back to stand beside Tracey, placing a fatherly hand on her shoulder. "What did this dear lady do when her doctor ignored her urgings? Did she simply sit back and continue to worry? Not on your life. She asked Sinclair if there were other tests she could have, less risky than the amniocentesis, to quiet her fears. And guess what he told her? He told her that he could perform a very simple test right there in his office, totally risk-free, which would tell whether an amniocentesis should be done. This is called an AFP, or alpha-fetoprotein, test. It's nothing more than a simple blood test. If it shows normal, then fine, no amniocentesis is needed. But if it shows high or low, then he'd know that there could be a problem and that the amniocentesis should be given. So, after hearing this, Tracey asked Sinclair—this man sitting right there—to do this AFP test. Well, he did do it all right. He gave her the test. But *then* guess what he did. He misread the results of the test. *He actually misread them!*" Mayfield shouted, pounding his fist on the railing that separated him from the twelve jurors. "*Can you imagine that?*"

Charlie then looked from juror to juror, all the time shaking his head sadly. "Sinclair said the test results were just fine, that there was no problem. But there *was* a problem, ladies and gentlemen. There was a problem, *and he missed it.* It was as plain as the nose on my face, and he didn't see it. And," he added in a whisper, "guess what." He paused for effect, then slammed the railing again. "Angel was born with a terrible defect that he would have seen if he'd been paying attention. *That's what!*"

Charlie then held his arms out and said, "And if all that weren't enough, this *doctor*—this man sitting over there—failed to give Tracey Walton *another* test, a test that's very common, painless, and risk-free. It doesn't even pose a *minor* risk," he added, throwing a look of disgust at Steve Sinclair. "It's called a sonograph or, more commonly, an ultrasound. You'll hear evidence in this case, crystal clear evidence, that an ultrasound should be done on *all* pregnant women. But did the good doctor sitting over there do an ultrasound in this case? The answer is no! And did he have a good reason for not doing it? The answer is *still* no. And would such an ultrasound have detected Angel Walton's condition?" Charlie allowed an expression of blatant hostility to cross his face as he stole another look at Steve Sinclair. "The answer is yes!" he hissed.

He wheeled around and pointed his finger at Sinclair. "You, *Doctor* Sinclair, refused to give one test, neglected to give another test, and misread a third one, and the jury will soon see the consequences of your negligence."

With that, Charlie Mayfield walked back and stood at his counsel table, going through the motions of examining a few documents. When he felt sure that he'd given the jury enough time to digest his last points, he turned. "Before I sit down, I'd like to address two questions you may be wondering about. First, you're probably asking what the doctor's records say about the things I've been telling you. You've all been to see doctors, and you know how they write everything down. Did Sinclair write down that Tracey asked for the amniocentesis? Did he record her anxiety and her fears? Well, I'll tell you right now that his records don't say anything about the amniocentesis. At least *now* they don't."

From the corner of his eye, Charlie saw Beck start to rise, but he was a split second too late; he quietly sat down, apparently electing not to call attention to the insinuation that Sinclair had altered his records to cover up a mistake.

Charlie ignored him and went on with his opening statement. "And let me tell you what Sinclair's records say about the ultrasound he never gave." His voice now rang with incredulity. "Sinclair's records say—at least *now* they say—that he wanted to do an ultrasound but that Tracey—listen to this—that Tracey refused. *Re-*

fused! Can you imagine that—that she would have refused a painless, risk-free test that could have given her the assurance she was begging for? You'll decide who's telling the truth, and you'll decide how reliable Sinclair's records are.

"On the other hand," Mayfield continued, "his records *do* show that he did the alpha-fetoprotein test. There's no hiding that, because there's a record of it at the laboratory where the blood was sent. And he will admit to you that he misread the test results. He'll actually *admit* it because he *has* to admit it. He can't deny it. You'll see and hear the evidence. It's too clear to deny. So you know how Sinclair tried to get out of this thing, ladies and gentlemen? I'll tell you how." Charlie spun around and walked over to stand behind Tracey. Placing his large hands on her shoulders, he spat out the words: "He blamed it on her! That's right. You'll hear him claim that it was all *Tracey's* fault because she supposedly gave him some wrong information, that it's *her* fault that she has an incurably ill child." He sighed as if he had just passed judgment on an ax murderer. "I can't explain it. Maybe *he'll* be able to."

He moved back to the jury box. "The other question you may have is this: What would Tracey and Larry have done if the amniocentesis had been done and they had discovered Angel's problem early on? Was the condition one that could have been treated? No, unfortunately it was not. They would have sought an abortion. Now I know," he said, holding his palms out as if he were about to stop a freight train, "that abortion is a touchy subject and that each of you may have strong views about it one way or the other. But when you were questioned at the beginning of this trial, each of you said that you believed abortion was appropriate in certain cases. And when you see Angel Walton, and when you hear the evidence about her condition, I'm sure you'll agree that this is one of those cases."

Actually, Charlie would have preferred if the jurors never saw Angel. It would have been much easier for him to talk about abortion if she remained a faceless child they had never seen. But he had to convince them that she was totally nonfunctional, that she could do nothing for herself, and that caring for her was a terrible burden for even the strongest of parents. And the best way to do that was to let them see her.

In a quiet, serious voice, Charlie said, "We all have a job to do here. Mine is to represent the Walton family, Mr. Beck's is to defend Steven Sinclair, and Judge Grubner's is to make sure that we follow all the rules. But your job, ladies and gentlemen, is the hardest one of all. Your job is to sort out all of the evidence and then deliver a verdict. I'm going to ask you to find in favor of the Waltons, and that won't be easy for you. You're going to have to decide that a doctor was negligent, and there are still people who don't believe that doctors make mistakes. But they do, ladies and gentlemen, and the evidence in this case will convince you that Steven Sinclair *did* make a mistake."

Charlie looked intently from juror to juror and then slowly nodded as if to say, "I trust you to do the right thing."

As he walked back to his seat at the counsel table, he caught Lew Beck's eye and winked. *Top that, you son of a bitch.*

TWO

LEWELLEN BECK ROSE to his feet as soon as Charlie Mayfield sat down. "Your Honor?"

"Yes, Mr. Beck?"

The defense lawyer tilted his head toward the clock on the side wall. "It's eleven-forty, Judge. With the court's permission—"

"I understand," Judge Grubner cut in. "This is a good time to break for lunch." The judge knew that it wouldn't be fair to force Beck to start his opening statement and then interrupt it in the middle to call a lunch recess. And to defer lunch until Beck was done would also be unfair; no lawyer wanted to talk to a hungry jury.

A break for Beck, Grubner thought. Now he gets extra time to reshape his opening to respond to everything Charlie brought up. He would even things by adjourning court for the day after Beck's opening statement, giving Charlie extra time to prepare his first witness after hearing what Beck had to say. "Let's try to resume at one-thirty," he said aloud.

Then he swiveled his seat to face the jury box. "Ladies and gentlemen, you are not to discuss this case, neither anything you've heard here this morning nor any views or opinions you may already have formed. This applies to conversations you will have with your fellow jurors and to conversations you may have with your friends or family. You can talk about anything else you wish—the weather, your children, your jobs—but don't talk about this case until it's over. If, by chance, the case is reported

13

in the newspapers or on radio or television, pay no attention. You are to decide this case *only* on the basis of the evidence you will see and hear in this courtroom and on the instructions I will give you when it's time for you to deliberate. Nothing else."

Grubner spun around, nodded to his clerk, and disappeared through the door behind the bench. His bailiff pounded a gavel. "Court's adjourned."

Lewellen Beck and Steve Sinclair shared the descending elevator with four or five strangers. While the other passengers occupied their time watching the numbers flash above the doors, Beck stared straight ahead. His jaw was pulsating from the gritting of his teeth.

About halfway down, Sinclair leaned toward him to say something, but the lawyer stopped him short with a slight shake of his head. "Careful where you talk," Beck explained when they walked into the lobby. "Never know who the hell's listening."

"Son of a *bitch*!" Beck bellowed as he and Steve Sinclair entered his office in the tower of One North LaSalle a few minutes later. He threw his briefcase at his couch, already crowded with files, papers, and law books. "One son of a bitch knows better, and the other son of a bitch lets him get away with it." His secretary, setting a tray of cold cuts and fruit on a corner table, didn't even blink at his thunderous shout.

Beck's stoic behavior all morning, lasting through the elevator ride and the three-block walk back to his office, suddenly gave way to this burst of pent-up temper. Circling his large office in frustration, he continued to inveigh against Charlie Mayfield, Judge Grubner, and even Tracey and Larry Walton. "Goddamn pack of thieves, every one of 'em. A cabal, that's what it is. A fuckin' cabal." He stopped and ran his hands through his neatly trimmed salt-and-pepper hair. "How the hell we gonna fight it?"

His secretary was obviously accustomed to these

tirades, which occurred only in his office, never in court where he tried not to let a judge, a jury, or especially the opposing counsel see him lose control. It was not unusual for trial lawyers to have dual personalities. Charlie Mayfield, a devotee of the Chicago Symphony and the Lyric Opera, preferred to be seen by judges and juries as simple and unsophisticated. And Lewellen Beck, a man often given to outbursts of temper and profanity, assumed a sedate, unflappable posture in the courtroom. Their different styles served each of them well.

"Remember your ulcer, Lew," the secretary said as she gestured toward the tray of food. "Settle down and have some lunch. You've got a long afternoon ahead of you."

"Okay, Tess," he said with an embarrassed grin, his mood changing in a wink. "At least I know *you're* not out to get me." If Lewellen Beck had an ulcer or any other malady, it was well concealed by a lean, muscular body, glowing complexion, and lightness of foot. His legal career had been punctuated by many noteworthy accomplishments—teaching, writing, and winning lawsuits—but none gave him greater pride than his having won the over-fifty division of the Illinois amateur tennis championship the previous summer. He waved his client to the table. "Let's have at it, Steve. We don't have a lot of time."

As Steve Sinclair reached for a couple of slices of whole wheat bread, he asked the question every client asked every lawyer at the end of every court session. "How do you think it went?"

"Pretty much as I expected," Beck replied, stabbing at some melon and pineapple chunks. "Charlie didn't say anything that surprised me."

"That's a relief. When we got back here you acted like—"

"Nah," the lawyer interjected. "Don't pay any attention to that. Sure, Charlie pissed me off with some of those cornball tricks of his, but as I said, it was exactly what I expected. Remember, I've watched him work for over twenty years, and we've gone head to head maybe a dozen times."

The doctor wanted to ask several more questions. He made a mental note never again to be annoyed when a patient seemed too curious. "What about the judge?" he inquired.

"Aye," Beck said, holding up his fork, "there's the rub. He's a plaintiff's judge, no question about it, but I never thought he'd just sit back and let Charlie get away with that crap."

"What could he have done?"

"He should've stopped him in his tracks. If he'd done it just once, Charlie would have gotten the message. Like when Charlie kept calling you 'Sinclair.' Grubner should have interrupted him and said something like, 'This is a court of law, Mr. Mayfield, not an alley or a football field.' That's all it would've taken. The old bastard knew that Charlie was off base, but would he do anything about it? Hell, no. That would've made poor Charlie look like he was breaking the rules."

Beck chewed on a carrot. "So the old bastard lays it all on me. He puts me in the position of having to object. Tries to make me look like a crybaby hiding behind technicalities. He knows juries hate interruptions. I have to make a decision: Do I sit back and take this nonsense or do I jump up and down like an asshole?"

As he shook his head Steve could sense Lew's frustration. "The one time I decided to draw the line is when Charlie pulled that bit about your treating Tracey like a customer at the corner deli. Remember? So I stand up and object, and what does Grubner do? He doesn't even give me the courtesy of sustaining my objection. No sirree. He simply wiggles a finger at Charlie and reminds him to save it for closing, and then he laughs about it—actually laughs—to let the jury think that I was making a big deal out of nothing."

None of this was making Steve Sinclair feel better. Even though he carried insurance that would pay whatever the Waltons might be awarded—well, at least up to five million dollars, but no one believed the case was worth *that* much—*he* was still the one who was on trial. The jury was going to decide whether he was a responsible doctor. His reputation, all he had worked for all these years, was on the line. And now he was hearing that the guy who was out to get him was getting all the breaks. Not good. "Well," he said, groping for some consolation, "maybe this afternoon the judge will give you the same breaks."

"Don't bet on it." Beck chuckled. "He thinks that we guys who work for insurance companies are cold-blooded monsters, that we get our kicks from seeing cripples beg for coins on street corners."

Steve was sure the remark was meant as a joke, but somehow he missed the humor.

"How do you think it went?" Tracey Walton asked as soon as she and Charlie Mayfield sat down at the Metropolitan Club, a private restaurant on the sixty-seventh floor of Sears Tower. The views of the city were spectacular on this bright spring day, but Tracey wasn't interested in the scenery. Larry Walton, who had some business calls to make, had begged off the lunch.

"How do I think it went? Perfect," Charlie replied, "absolutely perfect. I was studying the jurors' faces when I hinted at Angel's condition, and I'm sure they'll understand when you testify that you would have had an abortion."

Tracey's jaw tightened. "Do I really have to get on the witness stand and say that?"

"Absolutely! If they think that you would have had Angel anyway, even knowing she would have Down's syndrome, then they'll think you're no worse off now than you would have been if Sinclair hadn't blown the diagnosis. And if they think that, they won't give you any money. Sinclair didn't cause the problem, he just didn't discover it; but if you wouldn't have done anything even if he *had* discovered it, then his negligence didn't hurt you." Charlie reminded her that during the initial questioning of the jurors they had all agreed that in some cases abortion was justified.

He knew the abortion issue was upsetting to Tracey, and he wanted to get off the subject. After asking her what she'd like to drink, he hailed a passing waiter and ordered sparkling water for her and a martini for himself. "I have two rules," he said after the waiter left. "One: I never drink at lunch if I have to work in the afternoon. And two: I reward myself with a drink if I did a good job in the morning." His client smiled politely. "Anyway," he added to assure her that his having a drink wouldn't jeopardize her case, "I don't have to do much this afternoon. Just sit back and watch Lew try to climb out of the hole I dug for him. The judge is going to recess court for the day after Lew's opening statement, and I won't start calling our witnesses until tomorrow morning."

Tracey noted, as she had so many times since her introduction to the mysterious world of litigation, how lawyers always talked about their cases as if that's what they were—*their* cases. Never *your* case, or even *our* case, but always *my* case. And it was Lew Beck who was in a hole, not Steven Sinclair. "So," she asked, "you feel good about the way it's going?"

"Oh, sure I do, Trace. Couldn't have gone better. Of course, I knew what I was going to say before we got in there. I'd never ad-lib an opening or closing," he said, reaching for a roll. "But this one just seemed to go right. I could see the jurors were hanging on my every word. It's a funny thing, but sometimes I prepare right down to the smallest detail, and I even rehearse it to make sure it's just the way I want it, but then I do it and, damn, it just doesn't come off—the jury doesn't seem to buy it. Other times I go in there not quite satisfied, not quite ready, maybe a little flat, and guess what. A grand slam."

Then Charlie reached across the table and touched Tracey's hand with his. "Listen, Trace, I might've overplayed that business about your anxiety over having a healthy baby. It's just that I want those twelve people to get a sense of what you went through."

"Well, certainly I was concerned. I mean——"

"Sure you were, but we have to make sure they think it was more than the normal apprehension of an expectant mother. Can you keep that in mind when you get on the stand, Tracey?"

She studied her hands for a moment. Then she looked up at her lawyer and nodded.

Tracey glanced around the dining room, aware that she and Charlie Mayfield were a study in contrasts. She sat erect in her chair, hands quiet on her lap and feet flat on the floor, watching her lawyer, who kept looking around, checking his wristwatch, folding and unfolding his napkin, and waving at friends, and all the while keeping the conversation going without missing a beat. Was this his normal manner, she asked herself, or was he especially keyed up because of the trial? She found herself comparing him to her father. Both were sixtyish, successful in their different fields, fiercely competitive whether at work or on the golf course, and bursting with nervous energy. In fact it had been her father, Bernard Benedict, who insisted that Tracey consult with his good friend Charlie after Angel's birth. Yet, there were marked differences between the two men. Bernard Benedict's manner was guarded and dignified; Charlie's was informal and casual, even hokey. Benedict was quiche with a light chardonnay; Charlie was bratwurst with a can of beer.

Tracey had a special relationship with her father. When she was an infant her mother had been killed in a head-on automobile collision during a blinding rainstorm. Bernard Benedict had never forgiven himself for letting his wife go out alone in the storm; his atonement was to be the very best father, and mother, he could possibly be to his daughter. He never missed a teacher's conference or a school play, chaperoned more than his share of parties, and played chauffeur more often than any of the other parents. Although he had his share of lady friends and would have been regarded as a good catch by any of them, he had never seriously considered remarriage.

As Tracey matured into a beautiful and sophisticated young woman, she began to play a role in the family construction business that had been started by her grandfather and was now run by her father. Those who knew the Benedicts did not think it odd that this very feminine person could succeed in a business dominated by tool-wielding men wearing hard hats; they would have been surprised if she had *not* gone to work with her father after earning her M.B.A. from Northwestern.

Although Benedict Construction was a large and well-established business, its growth and profits over the past few years had been disappointing. Both Tracey and her dad hoped that she would be the shot in the arm the business needed. She started work the day after graduation and poured all of her energy into the enterprise. Even after her marriage to Larry Walton, a young partner in an architectural firm, and after Angel's birth, Tracey worked long hours at the office, entertaining business associates and serving as hostess and escort for her father. That had always been a sore spot with her husband, and she knew that their friends had speculated that Tracey's devotion to her father and the company was the main reason their marriage foundered.

". . . But I can't say I'm excited about your husband," Charlie was now saying, as if he'd read her wandering thoughts. "I can't figure the guy."

"My ex-husband," she corrected, returning her attention to the conversation.

"Whatever. He doesn't seem to have his heart in the case. The jury's going to pick up on that, Trace. If they sense that Angel's father is not serious about this thing, that he doesn't want to rip the throat out of the doctor who's responsible for this, then they'll get the idea that maybe Sinclair didn't do anything wrong. And if that happens, we're dead."

Even Tracey knew how critical a client's behavior in

the courtroom could be. A smirk, a scowl, a look of boredom or embarrassment—any of those reactions could mean disaster when seen by a jury groping for an excuse to go one way or the other. She watched as Charlie tore a roll in half and reached for the butter.

"Look," he said, "I know you'll be just fine, but Larry is a question mark, and that scares me. I hate surprises, Tracey. I'd rather deal with a problem I know about than worry about whether I have one. Why in the hell is Larry so negative? He's got a lot to gain here and nothing to lose."

"I've told you and Daddy a thousand times that Larry can't see Angel's problems in terms of money. He thinks that personal injury cases are"—she searched for an inoffensive word—"unseemly." She didn't tell Charlie that Larry Walton believed personal injury lawyers were unscrupulous vultures who preyed on the misfortunes of others and earned unconscionable fees that, in the end, were paid for by the public through higher insurance premiums.

"And anyway," she added, "he's never been all that sure that Dr. Sinclair did anything wrong. He calls the whole thing an act of God, and he feels that if we sue anyone it should be the Man Upstairs."

Steve Sinclair, still seated in Beck's office, was fretting. He had never, until that very day, been inside a courtroom, but his sixth sense warned him of unseen dangers. He was, at least, thankful that he carried malpractice insurance, and he was grateful that his insurance carrier had hired and paid for his lawyer, but he hated to be reminded that Beck was working for the insurance company and not for him. Beck assured him that it didn't make any difference, but lately Steve hadn't been so sure. He recalled the confused settlement negotiations that had preceded the trial. It was Mayfield and the Waltons on one side, and Beck and the insurance guys on the other. *Nobody asked me what I wanted. Nobody cared about my reputation as a doctor. And nobody cared that I would be financially ruined if a jury gave the Waltons more than five million bucks.*

His reverie was broken by a slap on the back. "Okay," Lew Beck said, "let's get back there and see if we can stop the bleeding."

THREE ═══

CHARLIE MAYFIELD'S COURTROOM style was deliberate. His folksy manner, his speaking without notes, his almost disheveled clothing, and even his use of "Charlie" instead of "Charles"—all of it was calculated to invite the jurors to identify with him and believe what he told them. Charlie wanted them to see him as a dependable man. "Follow me," he seemed to say to them. "Take my hand and I'll show you the way. I won't let you make a mistake." For Charlie it usually worked, and those trust-me eyes helped.

Lewellen Beck, on the other hand, took pains to appear to be all business. He wore handsome tailored suits to complement his no-nonsense, by-the-book trial technique. He would let Charlie Mayfield sway juries with charm and trust; Lew Beck would do it with logic and reason. While Charlie worked on their hearts, Lew worked on their heads. Each had an enviable record, but Charlie was better known because he was a plaintiff's lawyer; large verdicts attracted more attention than not guilty verdicts.

"Good afternoon, ladies and gentlemen," Lew Beck began. He spoke in a matter-of-fact voice while standing erect behind the lectern. If the jurors were blindfolded, they might think they were in a classroom listening to a lecture. Beck had decided on an opening statement that would preview the way he would handle the whole case. He would stick to the facts and present them in an unemotional staccato manner. "My name is Lewellen

Beck. I'm representing Dr. Steven Sinclair." He turned to Steve, who nodded to the jurors. "Dr. Sinclair is a physician, a specialist in obstetrics and gynecology. His job is to heal, and he does it well. He has been admitted to the staff of each of four hospitals in Chicago. He teaches a course at the University of Illinois Medical School. As you will learn, he has earned a position of respect and esteem in his profession. He has been asked to chair several committees of the state and national medical associations. He is"—and here Beck slowed his speech for emphasis—"an excellent doctor, a model for his profession."

The lawyer removed his Ben Franklin glasses and, placing an elbow on the lectern, leaned forward a few inches. This was about as dramatic a gesture as Lew Beck ever made in a courtroom. "Is it possible for a doctor with those credentials, with that record, to make a mistake?" he asked. "Of course it is. Doctors aren't gods. They're people, just like you and me."

There, I put it right there on the table, he thought to himself.

"That's right," he added, "doctors can make mistakes like the rest of us." He paused for a beat. "But the fact that Steven Sinclair *could* make a mistake doesn't mean he *did* make a mistake. Are we clear on that?" He paused for several seconds. "Are we *absolutely* clear on that?" he repeated, looking from juror to juror long enough for all of them to nod their understanding.

Satisfied, Beck put his glasses back on and shuffled through his note cards. Unlike Charlie Mayfield, he did not hesitate to use notes. Sure, it was impressive to watch a guy like Charlie waltz around the courtroom, hollering and weeping, but this wasn't a contest in the performing arts. Beck saw it as a contest in building a case and, like any good builder, he occasionally checked his blueprint to make sure everything went in the right place and nothing got left out.

"I agree with one thing Mr. Mayfield told you this morning. He told you that when we're all done putting our evidence in, and when it's finally time for you to make your decision, you'll have to decide who's telling the truth, Steve Sinclair or Traccy Walton. One of them will be lying to you, ladies and gentlemen—lying to you *under oath*—and you'll have to decide which one it is.

"Did Tracey Walton give Dr. Sinclair some wrong information, and is *that* the reason we're all here today? She says no; Dr. Sinclair says yes. The records bear him out.

"Did Tracey Walton request that an amniocentesis be done? She says yes; Dr. Sinclair says no. Again, the records are on Dr. Sinclair's side. If she had made such a request, which she didn't, he would have made a note of it in her record.

"Did they *discuss* an amniocentesis? Sure they did. They had the same discussion Dr. Sinclair has with *all* his patients. He explains what the test is, when it's used, and when it isn't. As you will learn, the test is not without its dangers, and therefore it isn't used unless there's a reason—a clinical reason—to use it. In this instance there was no reason for the test, no symptom or signal that called for it.

"Did Tracey Walton voice her fear of having an imperfect baby? Yes, she probably did. But again, every pregnant woman has that fear. Didn't *you*?" he asked, looking directly at each of the women jurors who he knew had children. "Were her fears any different— or any worse—than yours? No, of course not."

Lew Beck had one more question to pose. It was about the most bothersome aspect of the case. He knew this would be the pivotal issue, and he knew it was his weakest link. "What about the alpha-fetoprotein test? The one that's commonly called the AFP test? Was this test done on Tracey Walton? Yes, it was, but not because she asked for it. It was done because Dr. Sinclair *always* does this test; it's his standard procedure." He took a deep breath before making his next statement. "Did Dr. Sinclair misread the test, as Mr. Mayfield suggested this morning?" He paused to scan the jurors' faces. "Yes, ladies and gentlemen, he did." Several members of the jury reacted to this statement, this confession, with visible shock. Beck held up a hand, his palm toward the jury. "But let me tell you *why* he misread it. He misread it because of that wrong information Tracey Walton had given him." Then he leaned forward again. "And *that*, ladies and gentlemen, is why we're all here."

He riffled through his note cards before finding the one he needed. "Mrs. Walton had been a patient of Dr. Sinclair's since 1985. She saw him about this pregnancy for the first time in August of 1987. August seventeenth, to be exact. She told him she had started her most recent menstrual period on July fifth, and he wrote that down. Based on that information, Dr. Sinclair calculated the age of the fetus at approximately six weeks, because the gestational age—that is, the age of the fetus—is always measured from the date of the onset of the last menses— menstrual period. Remember that, ladies and gentlemen. The pregnancy is measured from the date of the last period—not from the date the baby was actually conceived.

"Based on the information Tracey Walton gave him, Dr. Sinclair scheduled the AFP test for October twenti- eth. He was very careful about selecting that date because the best time to give the AFP test is during the fifteenth or sixteenth week of gestation. But you will learn from the evidence—and this is the crux of the case, ladies and gentlemen—that the fetus was *older* than he was led to believe by *at least three weeks*. That's because Tracey Walton's last period did *not* begin on July fifth, as she told Dr. Sinclair; it began in mid-June—at least three weeks earlier."

He looked up from his note card. "Is it important that Dr. Sinclair believed the fetus was only six weeks old when it was really more than nine weeks old? And that they did the alpha-fetoprotein test when the fetus was more than *eighteen* weeks along, though he thought— because of what Mrs. Walton told him—that it was only *fifteen* weeks along?" Beck took a sip of water, not because he was thirsty but because he wanted to give the jurors time to absorb the facts he had just recited. It was crucial to his defense that they understand this.

"Yes, ladies and gentlemen, it *was* important. I'm not going to give you all the details right now. That information will be part of the evidence you'll be hearing. But I'll tell you this much: The AFP test measures the amount of alpha-fetoprotein in the mother's blood. An abnormally high or low reading is a clue that something is wrong. That tells the doctor that he should do some further testing—specifically an amniocentesis, which is more reliable. But the amount of alpha-fetoprotein in the mother's blood does *not* stay the same throughout the pregnancy. It increases. So when the doctor interprets the results of the test, it's important—very important— for him to know *precisely* how far along the pregnancy is at this time. As it happened, Tracey Walton had a very low amount of alpha-fetoprotein in her blood, considering she was nearly nineteen weeks pregnant at the time of the test. But it was a *normal* reading for a mother in her fifteenth week, which is what Dr. Sinclair thought. And," Beck again reminded the jurors, "he thought that because that's what Mrs. Walton had told him. So, when he read the results of the test, he naturally thought the alpha-fetoprotein level was normal and therefore did not order the amniocentesis."

For the first time since he'd started talking to the jury, Beck moved away from the lectern. He walked over to a point near the corner of the jury box. "Why did Tracey Walton give her doctor the wrong date for her last period? Why did she tell him that her period began on July fifth, when it actually started about three weeks earlier, in the middle of June? Certainly this misstatement could not have been deliberate. She'd have no reason to lie about something like that, and I'm not saying that she *did* lie when she gave Dr. Sinclair that date. I'm saying only that she made a mistake. A mistake she'll have to live with, bless her soul, every time she looks at her daughter. But it was *her* mistake, ladies and gentlemen, not Dr. Sinclair's. True, a doctor has other ways to estimate the age of a fetus, but that early in the pregnancy, no other way is as reliable as counting from the date of the last period. And who would know that date better than the mother?"

Lew Beck shuffled through his note cards again, and by now everyone in the courtroom knew it meant that he was about to change the subject. "Now let's talk about the ultrasound, sometimes called a sonograph. This was the other test that Mr. Mayfield said Dr. Sinclair failed to give to Mrs. Walton. It's true the test wasn't given, but that was not because of any negligence on the part of Dr. Sinclair. Far from it. The evidence will show that he *tried* to schedule Mrs. Walton for an ultrasound test, but that she kept putting it off. First she said she was too busy; then she said she didn't want the test because her insurance wouldn't pay for it. That information is all right there in her record. So the failure to have the ultrasound, ladies and gentlemen, was *also* the fault of Mrs. Walton, not Dr. Sinclair."

Lew Beck knew that Charlie Mayfield had an uncanny sense of the dramatic. Charlie hadn't told the jurors the details of Angel's condition, and Lew knew why: The old bastard wanted to save it for the perfect moment. Beck decided to bring it out now and take away a little of the drama. Mess up Charlie's game plan.

He carefully wound a rubber band around his note cards and put them into a folder. "Angel Walton is a terribly sick child," he said soberly. He moved a few paces so that he stood directly in front of the jurors. "She's severely retarded, she has serious heart defects, and," he added softly, "she may not live much longer. She suffers from a condition called Down's syndrome."

Beck scanned the faces of the jurors. "How is it," he asked, "that God can let something like this happen to an innocent child? None of us is smart enough to know the answer to that question. But," he said, holding a finger up, "we do know that it's God's will. And we also know that nothing is going to happen in this courtroom—there is nothing you can do—that will make Angel well."

He walked over to the plaintiffs' counsel table and stood directly behind Tracey and Larry Walton. "My heart cries for these two parents, just as it cries for their little girl. They don't deserve this tragedy." Then he moved toward Dr. Sinclair and, still speaking to the jury, looked down at him. "And my heart cries for Steven Sinclair. He doesn't deserve this either."

FOUR

"YOU HOME?" STEVE Sinclair shouted as he entered his Lake Shore Drive apartment.

The response came from somewhere down the hall: "No."

He smiled as he loosened his necktie and headed for the kitchen.

"And don't bother going into the kitchen to get a drink," came the distant voice. "I have all the fixin's back here."

He did an about-face and started toward the back of the apartment, knowing he'd probably catch hell. When he walked into the den he raised his hands in mock surrender. "I know, I know, I didn't call. But it wasn't because—"

"Can the crap, Doc," Molly interrupted from the sofa where she was lying and reading a newspaper. She was petite and had fair skin that seemed even fairer because of the contrast with her pitch-black curly hair. While she could hardly have been described as beautiful, no one could deny that she was fetching. Since she had an upbeat, happy-go-lucky personality, her present testiness was all the more apparent. Without looking up from the newspaper, she pointed toward a pitcher of margaritas on the buffet that doubled as a bar. "Nice and sour, just like my disposition."

"Thanks for having a real drink ready," he said, sidestepping her thrust. "Wine just wouldn't have done it tonight." He made a ritual of salting the rim of the glass

30

and pouring the drink, knowing that as soon as he sat down he was going to catch hell.

She didn't wait. "No fucking—" She grimaced and started over. "No bloody phones in the courthouse?" she asked, her nose still in the newspaper. "Couldn't have been a bloody phone strike. Mine was working." Steve knew that Molly O'Connor was trying to break her habit of using foul language, a habit she'd acquired growing up with four older brothers and with a Chicago cop for a father. Her proclivity for four-letter words hadn't been a problem for her earlier; in fact, it had been a trademark in which she took a perverse pride. But since she had become an account executive at an advertising agency, she had been not so subtly reproached once or twice. Some of the stodgier clients, it was suggested, might be put off by an attractive woman whose language could make a sailor blush. She'd told Steve that "Fuck 'em" was her first reply but, since dumb was something Molly O'Connor was not, she had resolved to clean up her act. Her language never bothered Steve or her other friends, but she'd admitted that she lacked the discipline to use one vocabulary in her social life and another at the office. So she was making a valiant, if not altogether successful, effort to be careful even in her private life. Her usual substitute adjective, when she remembered to use it, was "bloody."

"Yes, Molly," Steve answered, gently shoving her feet off the sofa so he could sit down, "there are phones in the courthouse, and yes, they were working, but I decided to torture you by not telling you what was going on all day."

"Very funny," she mumbled, again burying her nose in her newspaper.

"For cryin' out loud, Molly, give me a break." He heard his voice rising. "It's not like I was sitting there all day with a secretary and nothing to do but make phone calls. We only got a couple of ten-minute breaks all day, and after going to the john and checking with my office—remember, Molly? I'm a doctor? I have sick patients?—I somehow didn't have the time to call my girlfriend to tell her I was getting my ass kicked." He angrily plopped his feet on the coffee table and took a large swallow from his drink.

Molly, perhaps remembering how seldom he lost his temper, decided to back off. "That bad, huh?"

He shrugged without looking at her. "You decide. Tracey Walton's cornball lawyer said I refused to listen to her cries for help, that I refused to give her routine tests, that I—let's see—oh, yeah, and that I fraudulently altered my records. And when he said that I treated the plaintiff like a customer at the corner grocery, the judge just laughed."

"He actually *laughed*? Why, that rotten . . ." Molly suddenly threw her paper aside and buried her head in her hands.

Steve heard a deep moan. "What is it?" he asked, alarmed that she might be in pain.

Still speaking into the palms of her hands, she replied, "I can't think of a clean word to describe that bloody mother humper." Then she rose up, put her hands on Steve's cheeks, and drew his face close to hers. "You don't deserve this. You really don't."

"Which is exactly what my lawyer told the jury this afternoon."

Molly reached for her purse and looked at Steve as she fumbled for her pack of cigarettes. "Just one?" she pleaded.

Steve had told her how much he hated for her to smoke, and she generally respected that by not smoking around him—and certainly not in the apartment. But this seemed like the right moment to make an exception.

He nodded reluctantly.

She blew him a kiss as she walked to the window and opened it a crack, letting a gust of Chicago's wind whistle into the room. Lighting her cigarette and inhaling deeply as she looked down at the Outer Drive and the Oak Street beach, Molly asked the same question she had put to him at least a dozen times during the past few months. "How do you feel about Beck now?" she asked. "I mean, now that the trial has started and you've seen him in action, are you comfortable with him?"

When Steve didn't answer, she turned around. "It's a fair question, isn't it?"

"Sure it is," he replied.

"So?"

"So, I'm hesitating because I don't know how to answer it. I don't know how I feel about him. He sure seems to know his stuff, no question about that. And he's a good guy. I like him, and I think he likes me."

"But?" Molly prodded.

"But . . . I can't put my finger on it, but something bothers me. It's like— I feel as if he's not telling me things. I know that sounds crazy, but . . . Aw, hell, Molly, I don't even want to talk about it." He studied the white rim of salt on his cocktail glass.

"C'mon, Sinclair. Don't cut me out of this, and don't go climbing into that cocoon of yours. I'm sure you don't have anything to worry about, but as long as you *are* worried, I want you to be able to talk to me about it." When she called him Sinclair he knew she was serious— not as serious as when she called him Steve, though—or, in a real knock-down-drag-out fight, Steven. Usually it was Doc, Buster, Mac, love, or brother. Once, after they made love, he'd boasted that she had called him God. To which she had replied, "I wasn't talking to you, Mac."

"It isn't crazy that you have that feeling about him," she said, "but I'm sure it's nothing to fret about. I mean, do you tell your patients everything you know about them? 'Gee, Mrs. Schwartz,' she said, mocking his deeper voice, 'I saw the weirdest little thing when I was looking up your what's-it.' C'mon, Doc, you don't tell your patients everything that crosses your mind. That doesn't mean you're not taking good care of them, and it doesn't mean that Beck isn't taking good care of you."

"I know all that," Steve responded, "but this is different. I have this feeling that he's not all that concerned about me. I mean, I know he wants to win the case, but it's like he wants to win it for himself and for the insurance company, not for me."

"I take back what I said a minute ago." Molly sighed. "I think you just might be crazy after all. My God, you're his fu— his bloody client. Of course he cares about you."

"That's just it. I'm not one hundred percent sure that I *am* his client. Not really."

She flipped her cigarette out the window. "You better run that one by me again."

Steve suppressed a reprimand for the discarded cigarette. "Remember," he said instead, holding up his empty glass and nodding toward the margarita pitcher, "I didn't exactly pick him to defend me. My insurance company did that. That's the way it works. It's just like your car insurance. If you get sued for running over someone, your insurance company hires and pays a lawyer to defend you. So who's the client," he asked rhetorically, "you or the insurance company?"

"What's the difference?" she asked, handing him his refilled glass. "And who cares? It's their money."

"But it's my reputation that's at stake here, and I'd like to know that my lawyer is thinking about that as much as he's thinking about the insurance company's money."

"But your reputation won't be hurt by what any jury does. Nobody pays any attention to these cases, Doc, and even if people hear you lost, they'll just think the jury wanted to give a sick kid some insurance money."

"Well," he said, "there's another thing. My insurance policy is for five million dollars. What if the jury brings back a verdict for more than that? I'll have to pay the difference."

"*More* than that!" Molly exclaimed. "More than *five million bucks?* You are definitely certifiably whacko, Sinclair. You're looking for ghosts. First of all, you are *not* going to lose this case. And even if your lawyer screws it up or the jury feels sorry for the kid, five million'll be more than enough to settle it."

"That's what Beck says, too. He keeps telling me not to worry, but——"

"But nothing! Just take his advice and stop eating your heart out. Now put on your jacket so we can go out and get something to eat."

Bernard Benedict signalled the headwaiter. "May we sit on the veranda, Curtis? It's a beautiful night and we could use the fresh air."

"Certainly, Mr. Benedict. As you wish."

As Bernard Benedict and his daughter were shown to their table on the spacious patio, they exchanged greetings with several of the other club members along the way. Both were popular at Butterfield Country Club, where Benedict had been an active member for more than thirty years. Tracey had virtually lived at Butterfield during the summers of her childhood. It was an ideal place for a motherless child whose father's business required that he spend weekdays in his office or on a job site. When she was too young to be left alone, she went to the club with her nanny, but in the evening and on weekends, and at any other time when he could escape from his business, her father had stayed close to his little girl.

Bernard Benedict was a strong and versatile athlete as well as a successful businessman who had passed those attributes on to his daughter by dint of hard work. He had taught her to swim before her fourth birthday. Later he'd spent countless hours helping her develop a solid tennis stroke and a sound golf swing. And still later he had taught her the construction business, literally from the ground up.

Benedict had fought conflicting emotions after Tracey's marriage to Larry Walton. He was delighted with Tracey's happiness—he neither expected nor wanted her to stay single on his account—but he knew he was losing his best friend. Sure, they'd still be close, and she'd continue in the business, probably even after she had children, but their relationship would never be the same. He had liked

Larry, whom he had known and worked with even before Tracey met him. But was Larry Walton strong enough to match the daughter that Bernard Benedict had raised to be tough and independent? Were the young man's shoulders broad enough for Tracey to lean on if she needed to? Benedict's fears had turned out to be well founded; when she finally did need that shoulder, after Angel was born, the son of a bitch had crapped out on her. Larry couldn't take it, the coward. So he turned his back on his own child and left the onerous care and immeasurable grief to her mother and grandfather.

"Beautiful sight, isn't it?" Benedict asked, gesturing toward the eighteenth hole, its long, bending fairway skirting a pond and then rising to meet an elevated green surrounded by majestic oak trees. "Don't care what anyone says, it's the best damn finishing hole in the Chicago area, maybe the whole damn country."

Tracey smiled warmly. "Daddy, I have walked down that fairway with you at least a thousand times, and we've sat on this patio even more often than that, and at none of those times—not even once—have you *not* remarked that that's 'the best damn finishing hole in the whole damn country.'"

Her father laughed. He leaned forward and put his huge hands around hers. "It was torture for me in there today, pumpkin, sitting there in the back of the court-room, helpless, while you were up there all alone."

"Larry was there."

"Oh, please! I almost puked, seeing him up there trying to make people think he gives a damn about you and Angel."

"Now, don't go working yourself up. You've never understood Larry, that's all."

The waiter brought their drinks—red wine for her and scotch with soda on the side for him. "I'll never figure it out," Benedict said as he poured a small splash of club soda over his scotch. "The guy walks out on you and Angel, he gives you hardly any money, and you treat him like he's entitled to some respect. Me, I wouldn't waste another minute on him."

"Daddy, we've been through this a hundred times. Larry has not turned his back on Angel and me. He made a generous settlement when we got divorced, and he still sends me extra money whenever he can. And don't forget, he agreed not to take a cent from the lawsuit. Anything he gets goes to us."

Benedict watched as Tracey stared wistfully at the eighteenth green, a hint of tears showing in the corners of her eyes. "Aw, pumpkin, you're not still carrying a torch for him, are you?"

She shook her head emphatically. "No, Daddy, I'm not carrying a torch for him. I'm glad he's out of my life, and I'm just as glad he's staying out of Angel's. But I don't hate him, and I won't sit here and listen to you tear him apart."

"Why'd he leave, Tracey? You've never told me, not really. You've only given me the standard line about each of you wanting to do your own thing, whatever the hell that means."

"We just fell out of love. That's all there was to it."

"That's *not* all there was to it. I think I know what happened, and I think I know why you won't tell me about it."

She looked startled and began to say something, but Benedict held his hand up. "Let me finish. I've come this far, so I might as well get it out. Larry is telling people—you know, it gets back to me because we do business with the same crowd—he's telling people your marriage failed because you were spending too much time with me and the business and not enough with him. And that you were always off entertaining the people we did business with. Now, Tracey, if that's the truth—"

"It isn't the truth," she interrupted. "Please, Daddy, don't think that's why we broke up. You and the business had nothing to do with it. Larry and I are just . . . well, different. We didn't like the same things, we didn't read the same books, and we didn't even have the same friends. None of that really bothered Larry, but it wasn't what I wanted in a marriage. We kept drifting further apart, and if he chooses to blame the business it's okay with me."

"Different books? Different friends?" Bernard Benedict shook his head and sighed. "In my day people needed stronger reasons to split up, especially when they had a child. What's the *real* reason, pumpkin?"

Tracey Walton nodded toward the last foursome of the day trudging up the eighteenth fairway. "You know, Daddy, that might just be the best damn finishing hole in the whole damn country."

Beck heard the voice of a secretary: "Mayfield and Associates."

"Charlie Mayfield, please."

"I'm not sure he can come to the phone. He's been in court all day and—"

"I know, ma'am. This is Lew Beck. I think he'll want to talk to me." It was after six o'clock, but Beck knew his opponent would still be in the office. Late hours were unavoidable for a lawyer during a trial, particularly a plaintiff's lawyer who would begin to present his evidence in the morning.

A few seconds later Charlie's voice came booming out of the phone. "Lew. Long time no see—not since this afternoon, anyway."

Beck had to smile. Good ol' Charlie would never let an adversary catch him sounding weary or dejected. He knew that his supreme confidence and good humor could disarm the enemy—even an enemy who thought he had drawn blood. And both knew that Beck hadn't drawn any blood today—at least not Charlie's. "Listen, Charlie. I know you're busy getting ready for tomorrow, but I think it'd be worth your while to meet with us before court in the morning, or even tonight if you have an hour or so."

"Us?"

"One of the guys from North American Casualty

happens to be in town. He'd like to meet you, maybe find a way to settle this thing."

"Just happens to be in town, huh?"

"Well, maybe—"

"Lew, don't ever try to bullshit a bullshitter. We both know the guy flew in special. He probably thinks I'm looking for an excuse to settle and if he offers me a few extra bucks I'll grab it and run. If that's the case, Lew, you tell him to climb back on that airplane and get the hell out of my way. I got a case to try, and I can't try it while I'm wasting time with those tight-ass insurance guys."

"C'mon, Charlie, talk to him. If you don't like what he has to say, just tell him, and that'll be the end of it."

"Okay, Lew, but only for you. I know you handle a lot of cases for North American, and I wouldn't want them to think you can't even get me to a meeting. My office, eight tomorrow morning."

"Thanks, Charlie."

"And, Lew?"

"Yes."

"Tell him I don't want to be insulted with another one of their horseshit offers. I got a good case. You know it and they know it. So let's not pussyfoot around."

Molly and Steve were not alone as they strolled along Michigan Avenue. The first warm days of spring in Chicago always brought out the walkers, and this marvelous April evening, with the wind tamed after a fierce winter, seemed to suck people out of cabs, buses, and apartments. They were coming home from their offices, window-shopping, walking to or from dinner, or just plain strolling.

When Steve and Molly had left Pizzeria Uno, the restaurant that had put the famous Chicago Pizza on the map, Steve instinctively started to hail a taxi. Molly grabbed his arm and said, "Hey, Doc, let's walk. It's too nice a night to waste."

"All the way? I have to conserve my strength for the courtroom."

"Some doctor." She laughed as she took his hand. "C'mon, the exercise is good for you, and we'll be at your place in half an hour." Molly had more or less moved in with him several months ago, but by silent agreement they referred to the apartment as Steve's. She was still on a lease for the place she shared with two other women and where she still kept most of her belongings. She and Steve both knew that when that lease was up there would be a day of reckoning; to arrive at your boyfriend's place with a suitcase is no big deal, but to move completely out of your own home represents a whole new level of commitment. And while their relationship had developed to the point where there was little they couldn't discuss, the apartment arrangement was the one subject they both ducked.

There were differences between them—differences that required each of them to make adjustments, differences that had to be dealt with. She was thirty-three; he was forty-three. She was gregarious; he hated crowds and had few close friends. She had previously had a long, serious romance but had not yet married; he had suffered through a short but unforgettably miserable marriage that made him balk at the prospect of a repeat performance. The one factor that overshadowed these differences was obvious to those who knew them: They were in love.

Walking hand in hand along that section of North Michigan Avenue known as the Magnificent Mile, Molly sensed that Steve was slipping back into his pensive mood. His eyes didn't move from the sidewalk in front of him, and her questions and comments were met with uh-huh's. During dinner she had been able to steer the conversation away from the lawsuit, but she knew his mind had drifted back to the courtroom.

"Okay, pal," she said, slipping her arm into his, "I know you too well to believe you're wallowing in self-pity. You've got something on your mind, something you want to do. Right?"

"I don't think it'll change anything, Molly, but it might help clear up a few questions for me."

"Hey, that's what you need. Just tell the guy—what's his name? Beck?—just tell him you have a list of questions and you want some god— some bloody answers."

"No, I think I want to do something a little different. I'd like to talk to Phil."

"Phil Ogden?"

"Yeah."

"Can you do that? I mean, he's not really your attorney, at least not in this case."

"Molly, do you have any idea how many people ask me about their medical problems even when I'm not their doctor?"

"Sure do. And I know how much you hate it."

"Well, Phil does do some legal work for me, and he's a good friend. I don't think he'd mind. I was thinking of calling him when we get home and ask if he'll meet me for an early breakfast. Even if he can't see me for a day or two, or even if he won't see me at all, I'll feel better for trying."

"Then I think it's a good idea," she said, holding him a little tighter. "But after you call him, will you try to forget about judges and juries until tomorrow? I have something in mind for us, and it doesn't have a lot to do with law. In fact"—she giggled mischievously—"it might not even be legal."

"One condition."

"Name it, Doc."

"Brush your teeth, rinse your mouth, and gargle. You sneaked a cigarette back at the restaurant, probably when you went to the john."

"May thou goest forth and fornicate thyself."

Bernard Benedict opened the passenger door for Tracey, and then walked around to the driver's side where he slapped a few bills into the parking attendant's outstretched hand.

"Thanks, Mr. Benedict. Have a good evening."

The black Mercedes had passed quietly along the tree-lined drive from the club and then onto Midwest Road before Benedict spoke. "Why don't I take you downtown to my place, honey? Then I'll drive back to Burr Ridge and stay with Angel. She'll be just fine with me and the nurse, and you won't have to get up early and fight traffic in the morning." After Tracey started college, Benedict had sold their large home in Hinsdale and bought a spectacular condominium on one of the uppermost floors of Water Tower Plaza, only a short drive from his company offices in an industrial park southwest of the Loop. As convenient as this was for him, he would never have done it before Tracey went off to school. The city was no place to raise a young girl, he believed, especially when one had a large home and a wonderful country club in the suburbs.

"Thanks, Daddy, but I'd better go home. Dave Roberts is stopping by to pick up our bid on the Civic Center remodeling job, and I want to double-check the numbers before I give it to him." Roberts, who headed a large civil engineering firm, was the chief outside consultant to the city of Chicago on construction and engineering projects, and he was also a confidant of the mayor. If a contractor wanted to do business with the city, Dave Roberts was the man to know. "The bid was due today," she explained, "but Dave knew I was in court all day and said that it would be okay as long as it was in his hands before midnight. He said he was going to be out west tonight anyway—right near Burr Ridge, in fact—and he volunteered to pick it up."

"Aw, pumpkin, don't knock yourself out over a crummy little job like that. Let someone else get it—someone who gets a bang out of throwing up a bunch of partitions and making sixty offices where there used to be thirty. Who needs it?"

Benedict was glad that Tracey didn't remind him that *they* needed it. Business had been slow, and small jobs were filling in the gaps and keeping the crews and office staff busy.

"It's only a complimentary bid," she said. "The mayor's already told Dave to award the job to a black or Hispanic contractor, but he needs a few other bids just to make everything kosher."

"Then why are you going through all the trouble of double-checking the numbers when you should be getting rested up for tomorrow?"

She smiled. "I have to make sure that our bid is so high that we don't get the job. Anyway, we have to play ball with Dave whenever we can, and I'm happy to help him with the small jobs if he'll help us get a few of the large ones."

Bernard Benedict pursed his lips. "You know I don't like that kind of monkey business, Tracey. I know everybody does it, but—"

"But nothing, Daddy. There's not a contractor in the city who doesn't give complimentary bids. You're just upset because Dave is involved."

"I admit that I've never cared for the guy. He's a damn good engineer, but I don't like the way he's always sucking up to the gang at City Hall. He's a political ass-kisser, and I've never trusted those kinds of people."

Benedict had a well-deserved reputation as a tough, astute, and scrupulously honest businessman who neither gave nor asked for political favors. But he allowed a broad leeway to his daughter, who would eventually run the business on her own, and the issue of a complimentary bid wasn't important enough for him to overrule her, especially in the middle of the trial. He decided to get off the subject. "Well, just the same, honey, I'd feel better if you went downtown and got a good night's sleep."

"Listen, Daddy, if I spent the night downtown, Sinclair's lawyer would probably know about it by morning. I can hear him now: 'She doesn't even care enough about that child to stay with her, ladies and gentlemen of the jury. She'd rather stay in her father's sumptuous condo downtown where all the action is.'"

Benedict laughed at her imitation of Beck; she really *did* sound like him. "He'd never know, honey."

"Don't be so sure. Charlie told me from the day he took the case that I should assume I was being followed at all times."

"What? What the hell's that all about?"

"I guess it has something to do with my credibility as a witness. I'll be testifying about how hard it is to take care of Angel. You know, dealing with her retardation and heart problems, her inability to communicate, her medicine—everything. Well, they'd love to have some detective discover that I don't do any of those things, and that instead I'm gallivanting around Rush Street. And Charlie said I'd have to be even more careful since the divorce."

"Makes me sick the way some people make a living."

"It's true. He told me about a case he once had when he was a young attorney starting out. His client was suing because he supposedly broke his back in an industrial accident. He claimed he'd never work again, that he'd be a cripple for the rest of his life. So Charlie goes to the insurance company and says—and these are his words—'My guy is so incapacitated that he can't even lift his weenie to pee.' The insurance men sat there politely and listened to Charlie go through this whole thing, and when he finished"—Tracey laughed for the first time all day—"they showed him movies of his client bowling just the week before."

"Good ol' Charlie," her father said. "He likes to play the clown, but he's as smart as they come."

"I hope you're right, Daddy. He's a lovable man, like a big teddy bear, but I'm not sure he's the right lawyer for this case."

Benedict took his eyes off the road and looked at his daughter. "What do you mean, pumpkin? He's the best."

"Well, I know he wins a lot of cases and gets a lot of publicity, but this one is different. Usually he's representing some poor person against a big company, and he makes the jurors feel like Robin Hood, taking from the rich and giving to the poor. But here he's representing Tracey Benedict Walton, former debutante, daughter of Bernard Benedict whose name is emblazoned across half the construction sites in Chicago. And we're going against a young, innocent-looking doctor. The jury won't be told that he has malpractice insurance. They're not supposed to know about it."

"Don't you worry about Charlie. I've known him for years, and, even so, I checked with other attorneys before we hired him. He's been a winner for a long time, and he's beaten the best."

"And there's another thing," Tracey added as if she hadn't listened to her father's assurances. "Most of his cases deal with a specific accident—somebody crashes or something breaks—and the only question is who caused it. There's nothing complicated about it. But my case gets into chromosomes and genetics, things a lot of *doctors* don't even understand. It's very technical; I hope he can handle it."

"Well, that goddamn Sinclair couldn't handle it, that's for sure."

FIVE

AT EIGHT SHARP Lewellen Beck was ushered into Charlie Mayfield's office. With him was a heavyset man who immediately began looking around the room as if he were about to put in a bid for the furniture. Lew nodded when Charlie, his phone cradled under his chin, motioned for them to sit in the chairs pulled up to a large round table by the window. He held a yellow pencil between his teeth and was riffling through a thick file while he listened to his caller. Suddenly he opened his mouth and dropped the pencil.

"Look here, my friend," he barked into the phone, "it's your case. If you want to take a puny settlement like that, it's up to you. . . . Sure, it could be a couple of years before we get to trial, and if we settle you get the money right now, but that's no reason to take . . . You're damn right I want to try the case. I don't think we should let those bastards off for peanuts, not after what they did to you. . . . Okay, you think about it and get back to me."

He slammed the phone down and said to Beck, "Poor guy's out of work and has a family to feed. So the insurance company figures he's hard up for cash and they wave a few bucks under his nose hoping he'll take it and run."

Beck knew Charlie was saying all of that for the benefit of the man he'd brought to the meeting. In fact, the thought crossed his mind that there wasn't even anyone on the other end of the line. "Well, Charlie," he

46

said with a smile, "we're a bunch of pricks and that's the way we work. You should know that by now."

He motioned toward his companion. "Charlie, this is Duane DeLuca. He's a claims manager for North American Casualty."

The man was short and fat, one of those overweight types who go around with beads of sweat constantly on their foreheads and upper lips. His girth was accentuated by a bold plaid suit and by an oversized knot in his bright tie that was pulled down a full two inches below the loosened collar of his shirt. The long hair on the right side of his head was combed over his shiny crown in a ridiculous attempt to hide his baldness. And his clothes reeked of stale cigar smoke.

Charlie offered a halfhearted handshake. Beck knew that his opponent had learned to despise everything about insurance men except the checks they reluctantly wrote when they had to. And this one, Beck himself could see, was a real lulu.

After a few amenities, Charlie got right to business. "Okay, Mr. Paluka, Lew here tells me you'd like to take another shot at a settlement, but first I'd like to ask—"

"It's DeLuca, with a *D*."

"Excuse me. DeLuca. But before we talk numbers, I think I should ask why Dr. Sinclair isn't here."

Beck started to answer, but DeLuca held up a stubby hand. "No reason for him to be here, Mr. Mayfield. He's—"

"It's Charlie, with a *C*."

The fat man smiled. "Dr. Sinclair isn't here because *we're* here. That's why he has insurance."

"But he's only got five million coverage," Charlie pointed out. "Wouldn't he want to be—"

"And your case isn't worth five million," DeLuca interjected. "It isn't worth half that, Charlie, and you know it, so Sinclair isn't at risk. It's only *our* money we're talking about."

Charlie sighed. "Here we go again. You insurance guys are something else. You've probably never been in a courtroom, let alone tried a case, and I'll bet you didn't even look at this file until we picked a jury. But here you are telling me—and I've lived with this case for nearly four years—telling me what the jury's going to do. Okay, Mr. DeLuca, if I've got such a lousy case, why did you fly clear out here from Boston? You could've told me that on the phone."

"Now wait a minute," Beck interceded, "no one said you had a *bad* case. If we thought that, we wouldn't have made our last offer—which, frankly, I thought was generous."

"Ha!" Charlie blurted out. "You call that an offer?"

"It was over two million dollars. Two-point-two to be exact."

"Which leaves my clients with less than a million and a half after my fee, and less than *that* after expenses. Once they invest it they'll net—what?—not even a hundred grand a year. Shit, that'll hardly cover the nurses."

"But," DeLuca observed, "if their child dies in the next year or two, and that's a real possibility, they'll have a million and a half to piss away on themselves."

Charlie Mayfield looked at the insurance man with blatant disgust. "Maybe they should smother the kid now, huh? Save a lot of money."

DeLuca nodded. "I guess I had that coming, but the fact is, if the Waltons lose the case, they won't have anything."

"Okay, gentlemen, we've played around long enough. It's getting late and I have work to do. Our last demand was four and a half million, and we're sticking with it—for now. But once I wheel that kid into the courtroom, all bets are off."

"But, Charlie—"

"No deal, Lew, and that's final. Now, if you gentlemen don't have some green to throw on the table, I suggest you leave. I have a case to try."

"Okay," DeLuca said, "here's what we can do. This is a take-it-or-leave-it offer, Charlie, so—"

"Yeah, sure, so was the last one, and the one before that."

The insurance man was on his feet. "Now, wait a goddamn second, here! I've been listening to you spouting off since we walked into this office. You've insulted my company, my ethics, and my intelligence. Save your bluster for the jury. If you don't want to accept my offer, then say so, but don't try to wipe my nose in it. And don't sit there and try to sell your case to me."

DeLuca sat down, put his elbows on Charlie's desk, and held up his index finger. "First, you're banking your entire case on the testimony of a rich bitch. She won't get any sympathy from the jury, not when we're done with her. And they won't feel the least bit guilty about finding in our favor because they'll know damn well that she and her ex-husband already have enough money to take care of that kid." He held up another finger. "Second, your Mrs. Walton gave the doctor the wrong date for her last period. Maybe she made an honest mistake, but it's right there in her record and it explains why Sinclair misread the results of the alpha-fetoprotein test. Third, she was the one who screwed up by not having an ultrasound. Sinclair tried to schedule one, but she was either too busy or too cheap to take it, and that's *also* in the record. And finally," he said, holding up a fourth finger, "what are your clients going to tell the jury they would've done if the doctor *hadn't* misread the test, if he *had* diagnosed the kid's problem? They planned to get an abortion! Go ahead, Counselor, have the parents testify that they were willing to murder their kid, and *then* see how much money they get."

Duane DeLuca began to put his papers back into his briefcase. Without looking up, he grumbled, "However, and in spite of my own feelings about the case, my company is willing to make a token increase in our offer—"

"Save your tokens for the bus," Charlie Mayfield interrupted. "Now please get the hell out of here."

SIX

NURSING A CUP of coffee in a corner booth that gave him a clear view of the door to the Courthouse Cafe, Steve was trying to figure out exactly what to ask Phil Ogden, who had graciously agreed to meet with him before court convened. He couldn't expect him to second-guess Lew Beck's trial strategy, since Phil didn't know the details of the case, and since Steve wasn't sure what the strategy was. What he really needed, he admitted to himself, was encouragement and a shoulder to lean on. Beck might well be a successful trial lawyer, he thought, but a warm bedside manner was not among the skills one needed to represent insurance companies.

He raised his arm to get Ogden's attention when the lawyer and another man came through the door. There wasn't anything remarkable about Phil Ogden's appearance, but Steve knew that women found his angular jawline and sensitive eyes appealing. His dark hair, which always needed a trim, didn't seem to detract from his appeal.

Phil smiled warmly as he approached the booth. "Hope you don't mind that I brought Tom along," he said as he extended his hand.

Steve knew that Tom Andrews had been Phil's law partner ever since they'd finished a celebrated probate case a few years earlier. They hadn't been on the same side, but they'd quickly come to admire, respect, and trust each other and had decided to combine their small individual practices.

"Of course not," Steve replied, shaking the other man's hand. Two years earlier Steve had retained Phil Ogden to handle his routine legal work—a lease, a will, and the usual business forms. He had met Andrews through Ogden, and he genuinely liked the six-foot-three-inch lawyer who had started his career defending other blacks who lived on Chicago's South Side and who were charged with rent delinquencies, paternity claims, child support arrearages, and street crimes.

The two lawyers slid into the booth opposite Steve and, after ordering coffee, listened without interruption while Steve told them about the case.

"First of all, I'm not a trial lawyer," Ogden said after Steve finished speaking. "When I argue with another attorney," he added with a grin, "I prefer to have a desk between us. And while Tom here does quite a bit of trial work, he's never handled a medical malpractice case. Second, even if we had more experience in the area, we'd be in no position to predict whether you'll win or lose. That depends on a lot of things we don't know. But it all boils down to one question: Were you negligent? If the jury believes you were, then you lose; if they don't, you win."

"But what constitutes negligence?" Steve asked. "Beck gave me the legal definition, but I want to make sure I've got it straight."

"You'd be considered negligent if you hadn't exercised the care normally exercised by physicians in like circumstances. Now, remember, Steve, that's a shorthand definition, and it leaves a lot unanswered. For example, a specialist is held to a higher degree of care than a general practitioner. And a doctor in Chicago or New York is generally expected to give a higher level of care than some sawbones out in the sticks."

Steve smiled wryly. "Well, since I'm an obstetrical specialist in Chicago, I guess a lot is expected of me."

"That's right," Tom Andrews offered, "but no more than what is expected from other obstetrical specialists in Chicago. Mayfield will put one or two obstetricians on

the stand to testify that they would've done the amniocentesis, or that they would've read the results of the
alpha-fetoprotein test differently. In other words, they'll
say that they would've somehow detected the child's
condition. Then you could be in trouble. But I assume
that your lawyer—Beck? Is that his name?—has a few
of his own expert witnesses lined up to testify that they
would've done exactly as you did."

Steve frowned. "Are you guys telling me that this
whole thing rides on whether the jury believes our
doctors or their doctors?"

"Well," Tom Andrews answered, "that would be the
case if your doctors were totally believable and theirs
weren't, or vice versa. Then it would be easy for the jury
to decide. But it never really works that way. The experts
chosen to testify are usually good witnesses—persuasive
and believable. But they give contrary opinions, and by
the time they're done the jury isn't sure which ones to
believe. It's all very confusing to them, especially
because medical testimony gets very technical."

"So what happens?"

"So the jurors end up making their decision on other
grounds, like whether they trust one lawyer more than
the other, or whether they like you more than the child's
parents."

"Oh, Christ," Steve sighed, "so it turns into a popularity contest. That could be bad for me."

"How so?"

"Because I'm kind of a plain guy, but those parents—
they look like the king and queen of the junior prom. And
their attorney, hell, he's already got the jurors eating out
of his hand." Steve reluctantly accepted that the jury
might not warm up to him. He realized that he was rather
standoffish, and that his soft voice might be interpreted
as equivocal or doubtful. Not good for a witness.

"Well," Phil said, "there's no question that Charlie
Mayfield can play to a jury. He's a master, and here he's
got a case where he can generate a lot of sympathy for

that little girl and her family. Let's face it, sympathy means a lot."

Steve had a feeling that his depression was written all over his face. His whole career, everything he had studied and worked so hard for, could be lost, not because of medical or even legal reasons but because of emotional considerations. "I guess I should have studied charisma instead of anatomy in med school."

"Hey, you haven't lost this case yet," Andrews said, "not by a long shot. It's hardly begun. And anyway, the award is the insurance company's problem, not yours."

"That's what everybody tells me, but—"

"I know, I know, you're worried about your reputation but, hell, Steve, plenty of successful doctors in this town have been sued for malpractice, a lot of them more than once. Comes with the territory."

"I know all that, but I'm also worried about whether I've got enough insurance."

"What do you have?"

"Five million."

"*Five million?*" Phil laughed. "What the hell are you worried about? How often do you think juries give anything *near* five million dollars? Oh, sure, there have been some larger verdicts than that against doctors, but only where the doctor did something really reckless, like amputate the wrong leg or prescribe the wrong medicine or get caught trying to phony up a patient's record to cover his ass. But never in a close case, or where the only issue is whether the doctor exercised good judgment— and that's the most they could accuse you of."

"But they said the mother asked for an amniocentesis and that I refused to give it."

"From what you told me there was no medical reason to do that."

"And they claim that I misread the results of the alpha-fetoprotein test."

"But only because you misjudged the age of the fetus, and *that* was because the patient gave you the wrong information about the date she became pregnant. At worst, it's a judgment call. No problem. At least not one worth more than five million dollars."

"She denies she gave me the wrong date."

"But isn't it right there in her record?" The question came from Tom Andrews.

"Sure it is, Tom, but they'll say that I misunderstood her or that I wrote it down wrong or maybe that I confused the information with data from another patient. And there are two even bigger problems."

"Which are?" Phil asked.

"One, that I should have done a sonograph—an ultrasound test. That would've given me a picture of the fetus and very likely would've told me that I had its age wrong. And the fact is, it just might've told me that the child had Down's syndrome."

"Why *didn't* you do it?"

"I tried to. I don't do ultrasounds in my office, and I couldn't get Tracey Walton over to the lab to have it done. She's a busy woman, and there was always a reason she couldn't be there. She even said something about wanting to save the money. The test wouldn't be covered by her insurance because there was no indication that she had a problem at that time. In any event, I didn't press the issue. I know that some obstetricians do ultrasounds in every case," Steve added, "but it's still not considered a standard procedure by the profession."

"What's the other problem?" Tom Andrews said.

"Her lawyer is saying that I phonied up my records to change the date of conception, to conceal the fact that she supposedly asked for the amniocentesis, and to show that I tried to schedule an ultrasound test." Then, knowing that his fear was written all over his face, he looked at Phil. "Aren't these the kinds of things you were talking about a minute ago—where a doctor phonies up his records to cover his ass? And isn't that the kind of case that could move a jury to award a lot of money?"

Phil Ogden nodded uncomfortably.

"More than five million?" Steve pressed.

His friend didn't answer.

SEVEN ═══

CHARLIE MAYFIELD HAD long wrestled with the hodge-podge of pesky logistical problems that surround trials, like making sure that witnesses were available when needed and that necessary documents were always at his fingertips. But one of the most irksome for him was the problem of finding a place in the courthouse where he and his clients could talk privately during court recesses or in the moments before a session began. Last-minute questions and instructions were crucial and required at least a modicum of privacy. Yet, in Charlie's experience, very few courthouses had convenient facilities for this purpose.

In the Cook County Courthouse, where Charlie tried most of his cases, there was but a single conference room annexed to each courtroom—hardly adequate, since there were at least two opposing teams in every case—and these tiny rooms were used for everything from meetings with clients to storing coats. Consequently, the corridors outside the courtrooms were dotted with hushed little meetings of lawyers, witnesses, clients, and even family members. Witnesses were rehearsed, documents reviewed, settlements negotiated, pep talks given, and important facts double-checked, all in whispers amid throngs of others doing the same thing.

On this, the first morning of testimony in the case of *Walton v. Sinclair,* Charlie was huddled in a corner at the end of the corridor with Tracey and Larry Walton. Although the three of them were standing close enough to one another to be dancing, Charlie was talking directly to Tracey, and if a passer-by happened to be listening he might have thought he was in a locker room before the big game or backstage at the theater just before the opening curtain.

"Okay, Trace," Charlie was saying, "you're gonna go in there and knock 'em dead. Just remember what ol' Charlie told you. Watch me closely when I ask you a question, but try to look at the jury while you're answering. They'll know you're telling the truth if you can look 'em in the eye while you're talking. Now, do you remember how you're going to answer questions?"

She nodded while chewing nervously on her lower lip. "Short answers—just yes and no whenever possible. And I'm not supposed to volunteer information."

"Right. If I want more I'll ask a follow-up question. Beck'll do the same when he's cross-examining you. Don't help him. Make him work for everything he gets."

"But I'm supposed to look cooperative, as if I'm not hiding anything."

"Right again. Don't forget, you're a lady. I want those jurors to love you, and they won't love a feisty bitch. Don't worry about him getting tough with you. He's too smart to do that in this kind of case. Okay, now tell me, how quickly are you going to answer the questions?"

"It depends."

He smiled. "On what?"

"On who asks them. Yours I answer as quickly as I can. But I wait a few seconds before I answer his."

"Good girl. When I'm doing the asking, I want your answer out before Beck can object. Once you've replied, he's too late 'cause the jury already heard your response. But when *he's* got you on the stand, I'll need time to object before you answer a question he shouldn't have asked."

"Will a few seconds give you enough time?"

"Plenty. I'll probably know before he's even done with the question. When you've done this as long as I have, Trace, it becomes automatic—like a reflex." He snickered. "Hell, every once in a while my wife will be asking me a question and I catch myself about to object."

Then Charlie stepped back and looked Tracey over from head to toe. "Uh-huh, good dress." He was thinking that it wouldn't look too expensive to the ladies on the jury, but it would make her figure look great to the men. "And not a lot of makeup. That's good."

"It's the same makeup I always use," she said with a slight edge to her voice.

"But the jewelry," he continued, not paying attention to what she had said, "it's too much. Take off the necklace or the pin—I don't care which—and that ring on your right hand."

She stole a glance at her ex-husband and then took a deep breath, as if silently counting to ten, before she reached up and unclasped her pearls.

Charlie smiled broadly and gave Tracey an exaggerated wink. "Okay, kid, let's get in there and go to work."

Heading toward Judge Grubner's courtroom he put his burly arm over Larry's shoulder. He knew it would be risky not to put Larry on the stand—the jury might get the wrong message if the father didn't testify—but he was worried that Larry's testimony would do more harm than good in view of his attitude toward the case. Charlie still wasn't sure how he was going to solve the problem. "Listen, Larry, we'll lead off with Tracey; then maybe we'll put you on the stand near the end of the case."

Larry Walton stopped walking. "Charlie, may I say something before we go in there?"

"Sure." Christ! Charlie said to himself. What's coming now?

"Tracey told me what she said to you—that I was against filing suit—and that's true. I don't have much respect for a system that puts a price tag on broken bodies. But now we're here, and Angel's still my daughter. If this case can mean a better life for her, then I want to do whatever I can to help. And if that means testifying, then that's what I'm willing to do."

Charlie looked him square in the eye. "Can you put

your hand on the Bible and swear to God that Steven Sinclair is responsible for your daughter's condition and that he should pay you millions of dollars for that?''

Larry hesitated. Finally he answered, "I hope no one asks me that question."

While Charlie was going through his countdown with Tracey, Lewellen Beck was giving a last-minute pep talk to Steve Sinclair at the other end of the corridor. Steve, who was normally composed, obviously had the jitters, and Beck didn't want his client's nervousness to betray itself in his voice and manner.

"I want you to keep this in mind, Steve. You didn't screw up with Tracey Walton, and we're going to convince the jury of that. You did nothing wrong. You're a good doctor, the best, and you didn't make a mistake. Got that? Now I want you to go in there and *look* like you didn't make a mistake." Beck held up a finger. "That doesn't mean I want you to seem cocky or arrogant, but you can't go in there looking like a scared rabbit. The jury'll see that, and they'll figure you have something to be scared about."

"I'll be okay, Lew. I don't feel any different than you would if you were going in for surgery. You do *this* every day, I do *that*."

"I suppose, but if I were about to be cut open, I wouldn't have to think about making an impression on anyone. You do." Beck put his hands on Steve's shoulders. "I know you'll be okay. You'll be great. Just relax and leave the driving to me, okay?" He lightly patted the side of his client's face.

"All right, Steve, a couple of last minute things," Beck added. "They go first, and Mayfield told the judge it would take him three days to put in his case. That means he plans to finish Thursday afternoon, but it usually goes slower than we plan, so I'd guess he'll finish sometime Friday. In fact, I'll try to slow him up a little—I don't want him to finish before Friday afternoon."

"Why's that?"

"If they finish late in the day on Friday, Grubner'll probably adjourn until Monday morning. That would give me the weekend to review all their evidence and fine-tune our side of the case. We have to be able to rebut everything they put in. But until then we won't have a hell of a lot to do except listen and get ready. And you're going to have to help me do that."

"Me? How?"

"First, Tracey will testify to her version of everything you and she talked about. What she said about the date of her last period, that she expressed fear about having an imperfect baby, and that she specifically asked for an amniocentesis. I want you to listen closely; maybe you'll hear something we can use to trip her up. Second, there'll be a lot of medical testimony. I'm pretty good with that stuff, but you might have to translate a few things for me as we go along."

Steve was bobbing his head up and down; he seemed glad to know that he might be able to help.

"Now," Beck said, "when you want to tell me something in there, write it down. I brought a stack of note cards for you. We'll go over them whenever there's a break. But if you think something is really important, hand me the card right then. Don't wait, even if you have to nudge me to get my attention. You'll have to play that by ear."

"Is it okay for us to talk in there? I mean, if I want to whisper something to you—"

"It's better than okay. I want the jury to see that you're part of this defense. That you're fighting because you've been falsely accused. God helps those who help themselves—so do juries. I want you to look busy in there."

Beck checked his wristwatch. "It's about that time, but there's one more thing. And it's damned important." He looked at his client to be sure he was listening. "People can get very emotional in a courtroom. You'll find yourself hanging on every word, every nuance. And it's only natural that you'll react when you hear anything that could have a bearing on the outcome. But," he said

sternly, "keep your reactions to yourself. I don't want to
see you slap your forehead or make a face when Tracey
or Charlie says something you don't like. It looks
juvenile, and it could draw attention to something dam-
aging that the jury might otherwise have missed. And
when *we* score a point—if I get Tracey to trip all over
her testimony or, better yet, to change it—I don't want to
see you gloat."

Beck knew he would have to handle Tracey Walton
with kid gloves. She was a mother with a tragically ill
child, and he couldn't treat her disrespectfully in front of
a jury. When he challenged her testimony, he'd have to
use a stiletto and not a meat ax. It was delicate work, and
he didn't need his client interfering with gestures the
jurors could see. "But," he added with a grin, "however
serious things seem to be in there, if Grubner cracks a
joke, I want you to laugh!"

The lawyer checked the time again and then said,
"Steve, you're going to love me and hate me ten times a
day until this is over. You'll want me to ask the witnesses
a thousand questions that I won't ask, but I know what
I'm doing. Just be sure of this: I promise to break my ass
to win this thing."

"And I promise to be on my best behavior," Steve
replied as he shook his lawyer's hand.

When Steve Sinclair walked into the courtroom that
morning, he glanced over at the spectator section to smile
at Molly, who had taken the morning off to give him
moral support. He paid little attention to the short, fat
man in the plaid suit who was dabbing his forehead with
a handkerchief. But he did recognize the tall, aristocratic
man in the well-tailored blue suit who was scowling at
him, just as he had four years earlier in Tracey Walton's
hospital room.

Bernard Benedict.

EIGHT ===

TRACEY WALTON SAT down and surveyed the courtroom. She noticed that the two rectangular counsel tables had been placed parallel to each other, the narrow ends facing the front and rear of the courtroom. Each bore scratch marks from the metal studs of thousands of briefcases placed upon and dragged over their surfaces. At the front of the spacious, unadorned room was a broad, elevated bench where the presiding judge would sit. On either side and just below it at floor level were two smaller desks, one for the clerk and the other for the court reporter with her stenotype machine. Both were already seated.

The empty jury box was off to one side, and Charlie Mayfield and Larry were seated with Tracey at the table closest to it. She knew that Charlie had purposely chosen one of the chairs that faced the jury so he could maintain eye contact with the jurors throughout the trial. He'd told her that he wanted to observe how certain bits of evidence registered on them, and that he knew they would identify better with him if they could see his face during the highs and lows of the trial. He had asked Tracey to sit next to him and had placed Larry across from them with his back to the jury.

She noticed that Lew Beck and Steve Sinclair were already seated at the other counsel table, Beck at the narrow end facing the front of the courtroom and the judge's bench. Tracey could see that Beck likewise had a clear view of the jury, but she sensed that he would be far more interested in watching the witnesses.

She glanced up as the paneled door behind the bench opened, and Judge Horace Grubner, robes flowing, strode to his high-backed chair and stood behind it. He was a thin, cadaverous-looking man whose expression and demeanor accurately reflected a coldness that was inconsistent with his sporadic attempts at humor and his unfulfilled wish to be liked and more respected by those who came before him. Charlie had told Tracey that Horace Grubner never found, but continued to grope for, the right balance between solemnity and affability. His hawk eyes took in the entire courtroom, in which everyone had risen, before he nodded to his bailiff.

The elderly bailiff rapped his gavel loudly. "Court's in session," he intoned. "Honorable Horace Grubner presiding. Please be seated."

As Tracey sat down, she looked over her shoulder at her father, seated in the second pew. She smiled nervously and felt reassured when she saw him wink and give her a thumbs-up sign.

Judge Grubner spent several moments arranging papers on his desk. Without looking up he announced, "*Walton versus Sinclair.* Do counsel have anything before we bring in the jury?"

Charlie and Beck rose and stated that they were ready to proceed.

"Fine." Grubner again nodded to his bailiff who quickly stepped out of the courtroom and returned less than a minute later, trailed by twelve people.

Tracey studied them carefully, knowing these were the twelve who would decide whether her daughter's disability was a result of Steven Sinclair's negligence and, if so, how much money he should be made to pay to compensate her.

When they were finally seated, Judge Grubner nodded toward the plaintiffs' counsel table, and Tracey turned toward her lawyer. Charlie, wearing the same baggy suit he'd had on the day before, stood up. "The plaintiffs will call Tracey Walton."

Tracey walked to the witness stand, an enclosed seat

behind and slightly above the court reporter, and next to and slightly below the judge. She stood as the clerk administered the oath, then took her seat and looked out at the courtroom with an expression that she hoped concealed her nervousness.

"Tell us your name, please," Charlie asked. He spoke casually, and Tracey knew he was trying to make her feel at ease.

"Tracey Benedict Walton." The strength of her voice surprised her.

"And you live in Burr Ridge?" When she nodded, Charlie said, "You must speak up, Tracey, so the court reporter can record your answers." Charlie had told her he would address her by her first name. He'd said that "Mrs. Walton" was too formal to elicit the empathy he wanted the jurors to feel for her.

"Yes, I live in Burr Ridge."

"Where is that?"

"In the western suburbs."

"Are you employed?"

"Yes, sir. At Benedict Construction Company." Charlie had told her not to volunteer that she was executive vice president of the company.

"And you are the mother of Angela Walton?"

"Yes, sir."

"You call her Angel?"

"We do, yes."

"And for the record, you, Angel, and Larry Walton, her father, are all plaintiffs in this case. Is that right?"

"Yes."

"How old are you, Tracey?"

"Thirty-one."

"And Angel?"

"Four. She was four last month."

"Is she your only child?"

"Yes, sir."

"And Larry's only child?"

"Yes."

"And where is Angel now?"

"Home, with a nurse."

"All right, Tracey, we'll get back to Angel in a few minutes. But first I'd like you to tell the jury about your visits to Dr. Sinclair. He was your obstetrician, the doctor who saw you when you were pregnant and who delivered Angel, correct?"

"Yes, sir."

"And is that Dr. Sinclair, sitting there next to Mr. Beck?"

"Yes." She didn't look directly at Steve when she answered. She knew what this lawsuit could do to his reputation, and in spite of her problems she felt a twinge of guilt for putting him through it. But she was doing what she must, and though she'd had doubts at the beginning, her father had none at all.

"Suing the son of a bitch is too good for him," Bernard Benedict had said over and over again. "They should tear up his license and then make him take care of babies like Angel for the rest of his life."

In a way she owed it to her father to pursue the suit. He was footing a good part of the staggering bills—the medical insurance and Tracey's divorce settlement didn't begin to pay for everything, even with an extra check now and then from Larry, and she was one of the few people who knew that Benedict Construction was having financial problems. Bernard Benedict was overleveraged at a time when the entire country was going through an unexpected construction slowdown. He was having trouble servicing his debts, and the banks were reluctant to extend his loans.

In short, he and Tracey needed the money from this lawsuit to meet Angel's enormous expenses. And of course Charlie Mayfield had gone so far as to imply that filing the suit was a moral and social obligation. "That's why doctors carry malpractice insurance, Tracey, because they commit malpractice," Charlie had said. "And if patients don't do anything about it, those doctors will keep on leavin' sponges in people and sawin' off the wrong leg."

Tracey saw Charlie glance at the jury box and then turn back to her. "Tell us the first time you saw Dr. Sinclair."

"It was in 1985."

"And when did you first see him about this pregnancy?"

"August 17, 1987."

"And you saw him several times between then and the time Angel was born?"

"Yes."

"On each of these occasions, Tracey, did you tell him of your fear that—"

"Objection!" Lew Beck was on his feet. "Leading the witness."

Horace Grubner, whose seat was turned so he could watch Tracey while she testified, nodded to himself as if replaying the partial question in his mind. "Sustained."

"I'll rephrase it," Charlie said. He seemed satisfied that now Tracey knew what he was looking for. "Did you make a point of bringing up any particular subject during those visits?"

"Yes," she answered quickly, remembering Charlie's instructions about not giving Beck time to voice an objection. She also remembered his asking her to overplay her anxiety.

"And what was that?"

"Well, I had this fear that there would be a problem with the baby. I told Dr. Sinclair to give me every possible test so I could be assured. I just couldn't—"

She stopped in mid-sentence as Charlie held up his hand. "We'll get to all of that, Tracey. But first I want to ask you why you had that fear. Had there been previous problems with birth defects in your family? Or Larry's?"

"No, there hadn't," she replied. "There was no particular reason for my anxiety. I suppose I was being foolish, but as it turned out—"

"We understand," Charlie said before she finished her answer, reminding her that she should not volunteer information. If a question called for a yes or no answer, that was all he wanted. "Tell the jurors whether you asked Dr. Sinclair to give you any special test."

When she heard the words "Tell the jurors," Tracey's memory flashed back to Charlie's insistence that she look at the jury when she answered. She shifted slightly in her seat and said unequivocally, "I asked for an amniocentesis. In fact, I asked him for that several times, starting with that first visit in August."

"How did you know about amniocentesis?"

"Oh, I think every pregnant woman knows about that test. It isn't unusual."

"Okay. And did you have that test?"

"No," she answered grimly.

"Why not?"

"He said—"

"Who's 'he'?"

"I'm sorry. Dr. Sinclair said there was no reason for me to have the test. I asked him whether there was any reason for me *not* to have it. He told me that amniocentesis involved a minor risk."

"Did he tell you what that risk was, Tracey?"

"I remember him saying there was always a possibility of an infection when using needles. I told him I'd gladly take that risk, but he still wouldn't do the test."

Charlie seemed satisfied with her testimony thus far. Tracey knew she was expanding on some of her answers, but she was trying to do so in a completely natural way that would enhance her credibility. She knew her voice sounded confident, but the vulnerability she wanted the jury to see was there too. And she had expressed her fears about having a defective baby exactly the way Charlie had asked her to.

"All right, Tracey, that's enough about the amniocentesis for now," Charlie said, walking over to stand close to the jury so that it would be easier for her to look at them when she answered his next questions. "We'll have other witnesses come in later to tell the jury more about that procedure, but now I'd like to ask you about another test—the alpha-fetoprotein test. Do you remember that?"

"Yes, I do. After Dr. Sinclair assured me that there was no reason to do the amniocentesis, I was still worried. So I asked if there were any other tests that could detect a problem, and he mentioned the AFP."

"Did Dr. Sinclair do the AFP test on you?"

"Yes."

"When?"

"In October 1987. October twentieth."

"By the way, Tracey, how is it that you remember these dates?"

"I record all my appointments, both personal and business, in a calendar, and I file those calendars at the end of each year. I reviewed my 1987 calendar before testifying." She didn't say that Charlie had her go over these dates so many times that she could have recited them in her sleep.

"Tell the jury what you had to do for the AFP test."

"Nothing, really. I just went to Dr. Sinclair's office and his nurse drew some blood. I guess they sent it to a lab."

"What, if anything, did he tell you about the results of the test?"

"He called a few days later, as I recall, and said that everything was normal, that I had nothing to worry about."

"Did that ease your fears?"

"Well, sure, but deep down I still had some apprehension. I knew I'd never relax completely until I saw a healthy, happy baby."

Now Charlie moved over to the witness stand and stood next to Tracey, facing the jury. "Now, Tracey," he said as if he were chatting with someone in his living room, "let's go back to that first visit in the doctor's office in August of 1987. Do you remember him asking you questions, and you giving him answers, to determine just how far along you were at the time?"

"I do, yes."

"Tell us about it."

Tracey squinted, as if she were trying for the first time to recall a conversation that had taken place nearly five years earlier. In reality, she and Charlie had gone over this particular conversation at least a dozen times—and as recently as fifteen minutes before she took the stand. "He asked me the date I started my last period. I told him it was in June, mid-June, somewhere between the tenth and the fifteenth."

"How do you know that? As you're sitting here today, how can you remember what you told him? Do you record the dates of your periods in your calendar?"

"No, Mr. Mayfield. I know that some women do that, but I don't. However I do know from my calendar that I was in Dr. Sinclair's office on August seventeenth. I recall his explaining to me that the pregnancy is measured from the date the last period started, and that based on what I told him he—and I remember this very clearly—he estimated the baby to be about nine weeks along. So I *must* have told him my last period started in mid-June."

Charlie started to ask another question, but Tracey said, "And there's another reason I remember the mid-June date."

"And what's that?"

"My periods have always been very irregular. When I was late in July, I really didn't give it much thought. But when I hadn't had my July period by early August I started to feel hopeful. Then, on August eighth, Larry and I took a short vacation. We were gone for a week—that's in my calendar. I hadn't said anything to him yet because I wasn't sure I was pregnant and I didn't want to get him excited for nothing, but while we were still out of town I called Dr. Sinclair's office and made an appointment for August seventeenth, the Monday after we got back to town. Since I'm positive that I called him between August tenth and August fourteenth—those were the only days his office would have been open during our vacation—and since I certainly wouldn't have called until I was at least three weeks late, it would confirm that I must have started my last period in mid-June."

"So," Charlie said while looking directly at the jurors,

"since you called Sinclair's office while you were on vacation during the second week of August, and since you remember calling him when you were at least three weeks late with your July period, you must have had your June period, which was your last one, in the middle of June. Is that your testimony?"

"It is."

"And that's what you told him, isn't it? He asked you when you started your last period, and you told him it was in mid-June. Right?"

"Right," she agreed.

Charlie seemed satisfied that he had driven the point home. He put his hands in his pockets and shuffled toward the jury box. Facing the jurors, his back still to the witness stand, he asked, "Then how could it be, Tracey, that his records say your last period began on the fifth of July? That's several weeks later than you're telling us now."

"I have no idea. He certainly didn't get that date from me."

The lawyer spun around. "And how can we be sure you're telling us the truth?"

This was the question she was waiting for, the one she and Charlie had gone over time and time again. "As I said earlier, Mr. Mayfield, I know I called the doctor's office for the appointment while we were still out of town on our vacation. I specifically remember that. And I know we were on vacation during the second week of August—that is in my calendar. Now, if Dr. Sinclair's records are to be believed—that I started my last period on July fifth—it would mean that I called for the appointment almost immediately, just a few days after being late with my August period. There is simply no way I'd have called that soon. It would have been foolish, knowing my history of irregular periods. No, Mr. Mayfield," she added with finality. "I know that I was further along than that when I called his office."

"So if his records say July fifth, they're wrong. Is that— Wait a minute!" Charlie exclaimed as if he had just thought of something. "Tracey, do you remember *seeing* him write that July fifth date down in your file when you were there in his office?"

"No, I don't."

"Then he could have written it in later, couldn't he?"

"Well, I guess so," she answered, as if the thought of an altered record entry had never occurred to her.

Charlie glanced at the jurors, blatantly calling their attention to the innuendo, then moved back a few paces and shifted to another line of questioning.

"Incidentally, Tracey, do you know what a sonograph is? It's usually called an ultrasound test."

"Yes."

"And what is it?"

"It's a test they give pregnant women. It's like an X-ray of the baby."

"And did Dr. Sinclair do a sonograph, an ultrasound, on you?"

"No."

"Did you *ask* him to, like you did with the amniocentesis?"

"No, but only because I didn't know then what I know now."

Tracey glanced at the defense table and saw Steve Sinclair lean over and whisper in Beck's ear. The lawyer nodded and made a note which he underlined heavily.

Charlie turned to face the bench. "Your Honor, before I get into a new line of questions, I wonder if you'd indulge me with a short recess."

"Ten minutes," Horace Grubner announced to the entire courtroom.

NINE

"DON'T HASSLE ME, Doc. I need it and I'm going to have it." Molly O'Connor lit a cigarette, inhaled deeply, and then blew out an endless stream of blue smoke. "Besides," she added after a second or two, "with all the smoke out here you'll never know the difference."

"So what do you think?" Steve asked as they walked along the corridor outside the courtroom.

"Hey, what do I know? I'm just a dumb advertising type."

"Be serious. Tell me how you think it's going. If you don't want to tell me what *you* think, tell me what you think the jury thinks."

"Okay." She took another drag from her cigarette. "First of all, I've never seen a real trial before, only the stuff they show in movies. But *this*! It's rough, Doc. They actually go for the throat. I mean, that Walton dame and her mouthpiece—they're like Bonnie and Clyde. They want more than your insurance. They won't be satisfied until they have your balls."

"That's reassuring."

"Well, you asked me and I'm telling you."

"You're right," Steve said impatiently. "Go on."

She flipped an ash into one of the many butt-filled ashtrays that lined the corridor. "Let me put it this way: That Tracey dame is doing her thing very well. The jury has to be thinking that either she's telling the truth or she's the greatest actress in the world."

"What do *you* think?"

"C'mon, Sinclair, that's not fair."

"Why not?"

"Because I *know* you! You're too careful to make a mistake like that, writing down the wrong date, and I know you'd never change your records just to cover up. But those jurors—God, what do *they* know? All they have to go on so far is that woman, and they have no reason not to believe her."

Steve leaned back against the wall and closed his eyes.

"Now listen to me," Molly said. "I'm on your side, and don't you forget it. But think about it. Why *would* she have called for that appointment when she was only a few days late, a week at the most? That's no big deal for a woman, especially one who has irregular periods." Then she suddenly snapped her fingers. "Hey, maybe she's lying about that! Maybe she *didn't* have irregular periods!"

Steve sighed. "They *were* irregular. She told me that long before she became pregnant. I wrote it down in her record."

They stood in silence for a while. Finally Steve said, as if to reassure himself, "But she *must* have given me that July fifth date. I wouldn't have made it up. Maybe she made a mistake, but she *must* have said it."

Molly reached up and gently put the palm of her hand against his cheek. "You're grasping at straws, Doc. You know there's not a woman alive who can't tell you when she had her last period, even if she doesn't have it written down in a calendar."

"Okay," Steve challenged her with a forced smile, "let's test that. When was yours?"

"I've been meaning to tell you about that, sport. It was seven weeks ago." She paused, and then added, "Just kidding," before turning to head for the ladies' room.

Bernard Benedict was waiting for Tracey when she came into the corridor. "You were great, pumpkin, just great," he said as soon as he saw her.

She smiled and took his arm as they started to walk.

"Thanks, Daddy, but this is the easy part. When we go back in there we'll be talking about Angel, and you know how tough that'll be for me."

"I know, but you'll be just fine."

"And then there's the cross-examination."

Benedict stopped and put both hands on Tracey's shoulders. "Honey, you just stick with the truth in there, like you've been doing, and everything will be all right. Isn't that what I taught you when you were a little girl?"

"I know, but those lawyers have a way—"

"Don't even think about that. Lawyers can only trip up liars, not people who tell the truth."

"Charlie, can I see you for a minute?" Duane DeLuca asked as Mayfield came out of the men's room.

"Sure, but we have to make it fast. I don't want to keep Horace waiting." Charlie used the judge's first name as if he and Grubner were buddies.

"This won't take long. Listen," the insurance man said, dropping his voice so he wouldn't be overheard. "I just called the home office. I think I can shake a few more coconuts off the tree, but I have to know if you'll come down."

Charlie smiled to himself. DeLuca had heard Tracey's testimony and panicked. "How many coconuts?" he asked, heading back toward the courtroom.

DeLuca was in a bind, and both of them knew it. By coming back to Charlie so soon after their early morning meeting, during which Charlie hadn't budged, he was admitting that he was nervous. And that told Charlie that DeLuca hadn't been serious when he spouted off about what a weak case the Waltons had. Charlie almost felt sorry for the guy, but now that he had him in a hammerlock, he wasn't about to release the pressure; on the contrary, now was the time to squeeze a little harder. "Look, Duane, it's too late to play games. Suppose you just give me a realistic offer. Not a token like the settlement you were talking about this morning. If it has a nice ring to it, I'll talk it over with the Waltons, and we'll either take it or leave it. Then neither of us will have to waste any more time."

They were nearing the courtroom door, and Charlie deliberately refused to slow down. He wanted to force DeLuca to make a decision: either to stonewall until the Waltons came down below the four and a half million, or to throw his maximum offer out on the table, or to compromise by offering only part of it for now. Charlie suspected he'd choose the third alternative—the partial offer—even though it was getting late for the bit-by-bit game. Insurance companies knew that if they kept adding to the pot while the plaintiff stood pat, the plaintiff would get the message and continue to stand pat.

"Well, here we are," Charlie said as they reached the courtroom door. "See ya around."

DeLuca grabbed his arm.

Charlie's eyes twinkled triumphantly. "What's your number, Duane?"

The insurance man hesitated an instant too long. "Two-seven."

The twinkle disappeared. "Like I said, Duane, see ya around."

As Charlie entered the courtroom he heard a desperate voice over his shoulder. "Hey, where ya goin'? I just offered you another half mill—"

Charlie let the door swing shut and cut off the rest of the sentence.

TEN

"**YOU'RE STILL UNDER** oath, Mrs. Walton," Judge Horace Grubner said as Tracey took the witness stand. "Do you understand that?"

"Yes, sir." She sat down, put her purse on the floor next to her, arranged her skirt, and then looked at her lawyer.

Charlie had decided to change the pace of her testimony. Earlier, when he was trying to nail down specific facts—dates and conversations—that were sure to be contested by the defense, he'd wanted short, concise answers. He had led Tracey carefully through that testimony, building step by step, fact by fact. But her remaining testimony would play more to the jurors' emotions than to their logic, and Charlie was sure that Lew Beck wouldn't even try to contradict it. So he decided to give Tracey center stage; he would stay seated at the counsel table and ask broader questions that called for longer answers.

"Tracey, please describe Angel for us, as she looked when she was born."

Tracey beamed. "I'll never forget how beautiful she was when I first saw her in the delivery room. She weighed nearly eight pounds, and she had a full head of dark hair. Her skin was smooth—you know, none of those wrinkles that a lot of babies have at first. Angel seemed like a perfect name for her, even though we'd picked it before she was born."

"And when did you first notice that something was wrong?"

Charlie saw that Tracey stiffened ever so slightly. He knew that those first few hours after she had learned of her baby's problem, and its hopelessness, had been the hardest. Thinking about it in private had to be tough enough for her, but talking about it in a public courtroom would probably be next to impossible.

"I didn't notice anything at first. I mean, not with Angel." She was speaking softly, almost in a whisper. "But the people in the hospital were acting strange, and before that first day was over I had a feeling that something was the matter. Then they said that Angel should stay a few extra days for some tests. It was then I knew something was—" Tracey's lips trembled as she reached into her purse for some tissues.

"What did they tell you, Tracey?" Charlie asked gently.

She took a deep breath. "At first they talked only to Larry, so I didn't find out for sure until he told me. He came into my room and lay down next to me on the bed. He held me tightly, and he was trembling." With that, Tracey broke down, just as she had each time she'd told Charlie about it in his office. Whether it was the realization of Angel's terrible illness or the way that Larry held her, it was a scene she just couldn't relive without losing control.

Judge Grubner looked concerned for her. "Would you like a short break?" he asked Charlie.

"Thank you, Your Honor, but I believe Mrs. Walton would like to get this over with as soon as possible." He walked over to the witness stand. "Can you go ahead, Tracey?"

She nodded. "Yes, thank you. I'll be okay." She dabbed at her eyes and nose with the tissues.

"What disease were you told Angel has?"

"Down's syndrome."

"Now, Tracey, I'm going to ask you to describe Angel to the jurors. Tell them about her condition. I know this is hard for you, but we have to do it." His voice was soothing, and he used it like a balm to ease her pain.

"Her heart is malformed. That's common with many Down children. And she's retarded. For me, that's the worst part—looking at Angel and knowing she'll never have a normal life, never understand what the world is all about or what it has to offer little girls. It's so hard—"

Charlie held up hand. "Excuse me, Tracey. When you use the word 'retarded,' what do you mean, exactly?"

"I mean mental retardation. Severe mental damage. Angel is not a slow learner. She does not have a lower than average IQ. She is a child who will never grow up, even if she lives. She has very little mental capacity— much less than most other Down children, and her condition is getting worse. Every day she grows more distant and drifts deeper into her own little dark world."

"Is there anything else you can tell the jurors to help describe Angel's condition?" Charlie prodded.

As distraught as Tracey was, she obviously recognized Charlie's cue to talk directly to the jury. "She has all the physical abnormalities that accompany Down's syndrome. I didn't notice them at first because they're not very obvious in a newborn—not to someone untrained like me." She told them of her child's misshapen head, the lack of muscle tone, the short neck and legs, the narrow palate, the small hands with the oddly curved fifth fingers. She described how Angel, like other Down children, had a flattened nasal bridge, a thick tongue, slanting eyelids, and a mouth that hung open. But, she told them, these abnormalities were not the main problem; it was the retardation that was so impossible to accept, even after four years, and the heart defects that would probably end Angel's tragic little life within the next few years. Tracey explained to the jury that some Down children escaped the cardiac malformation and lived into adulthood and even old age. But Angel would not be one of those.

Charlie moved toward the far corner of the jury box to begin a new line of questioning. "Going back to those first few days, Tracey, when you first learned of your child's condition, did you ask the doctors what had caused Angel to be like this?"

"Yes, I—"

"Was Steven Sinclair one of those doctors you met with?"

"Well, he was there at the hospital every day, and spoke with me, but he wasn't one of the doctors taking care of Angel."

"I see. Do you recall any conversations you had with Sinclair about Angel at that time?"

"Yes, I recall one conversation very clearly."

"Tell us about it."

"It was in my room in the hospital, a few hours after Larry told me that our baby was not normal, that Angel had very serious birth defects. Dr. Sinclair was standing next to my bed and was acting very strange."

"Strange?"

"Yes. He seemed uncomfortable and nervous."

"Could it have been guilt?"

"Objection!" Lew Beck exploded. "Your Honor, Mr. Mayfield is trying to put words into the witness's mouth. I've been sitting here very patiently, not wanting to interrupt Mrs. Walton's testimony in spite of the way Mr. Mayfield is playing to the jury's emotions. But to suggest the word 'guilt' to the witness in her description of my client is just too much."

"I agree," Judge Grubner said. "The objection is sustained, and the jury will disregard Mr. Mayfield's last question." He looked at Charlie and added, "You know better than that, Mr. Mayfield. Guilt is something to be decided by the jury, not by you and your witness. If the jurors believe that Dr. Sinclair was guilty of malpractice in his treatment of Mrs. Walton, they'll let him know soon enough."

Thanks, Horace, Charlie said to himself. Between you, me, and Beck, we've now said the word "guilt" four times in the last thirty seconds. Better than I could have done with my one question to Tracey!

Aloud he said, "I apologize, Your Honor. I guess I'm the one who's guilty." That made five!

"Let's go back to that visit with Dr. Sinclair in your hospital room," he said to Tracey. "You said he was standing next to your bed?"

"Yes. As I started to say, he seemed so uncomfortable that I took his hand and indicated that he should sit down on the edge of the bed. As I think back, it was as if I was trying to console him, to put him at ease, because he acted as if the whole thing was his fault."

Charlie noticed that Lew Beck started to rise, but apparently thought better of it. After being slaughtered with "guilt" a moment ago, he probably didn't want to meet the same fate with the word "fault."

"I remember," Tracey was saying, "asking Dr. Sinclair if there was anything we could have done—*should* have done—that would have prevented this from happening. He said that the only way we would have known for sure is if we had done the amniocentesis."

Still addressing Tracey, Charlie turned to face the jury and repeated, "If he had done the amniocentesis, you would have known about Angel's condition right at the very beginning. Is that what he told you?"

"Yes."

"And what did you say to him?"

"I don't recall. My mind went blank when I heard that. To think that I had asked for that test and that he had refused to give it to me, and now . . ." Unable to finish the sentence, she reached for another tissue and used it to dry her eyes.

After waiting for her to compose herself, Charlie said, "Tracey, when you spoke with the other doctors, did they tell you what had caused Angel's condition?"

"They told me that Down's syndrome is caused by an extra chromosome. Sometimes it's inherited—one of the parents might be a carrier—and sometimes it just happens by itself when a baby is conceived. I don't know if I understand it well enough to explain—"

"That's okay. We'll have someone else explain those

technical things to the jury. Did the doctors tell you if *Angel's* condition was inherited or if it just happened all by itself?"

"It just happened by itself. They said it occurred *de novo*—that means it was a spontaneous mutation. It happened at the moment of conception."

"Tell us what else the doctors said."

"Well, most important—at least to me at the time—was their assurance that I did not cause the disease in Angel. I mean, it wasn't as though I took the wrong medicine or smoked or took drugs or anything like that. I don't do any of those things, except to drink a glass of wine now and then. Then they told me about the disease—the symptoms and what we could expect."

"And what was it they told you?"

"That Angel would be mentally retarded, very badly. They called it dementia. Then they told me about her heart. They said that when the heart is malformed, as Angel's is—" Again she stopped to fight off the tears.

"Take your time, Tracey. We're almost done."

"Angel's heart could give out at any time." Tracey said this quickly, obviously trying to get the words out before she fell apart.

"Did the doctors tell you how long they expect Angel to live?"

She nodded her head. "Probably not more than a few more years." The tears were flowing freely now, but Tracey seemed determined to finish. "And of course Angel can't walk. She can't even stand up. And when she tries to speak, her—" But she couldn't finish after all. She buried her head in her hands to muffle her sobbing.

This time Judge Grubner didn't ask if Charlie wanted a short break to give Tracey a respite from this ordeal. "Fifteen-minute recess," he announced.

Fifteen minutes later Tracey was composed and back on the witness stand.

"Just a few more questions," Charlie assured her. He'd decided to let Beck be the heavy and keep her up there.

He then led her through the day-by-day care and attention a Down child required. The jury learned the details of carefully monitoring Angel's heart medication and seeing to her personal hygiene, they heard about the child's problems in learning and the frustration of trying to communicate with her, and they became aware of the strength and courage needed to deal with the knowledge that this nightmare would only get worse.

Charlie knew that the jurors would never forget the grief that this dread disease could visit upon a family. They would realize that it wasn't the child's abnormal appearance, her inability to communicate, or even her fragile heart that were so impossibly difficult to deal with, although those conditions would have tested the mettle of the strongest parents; it was the voids that lay within the misshapen head of the child named Angel.

"I have one more question, Tracey."

She took a deep breath, knowing what that question would be.

"If you and your husband had known, at the time of the alpha-fetoprotein test or shortly thereafter, that your child would have Down's syndrome, what would you have done?"

"Objection!" Lew Beck announced from the defense counsel table. "The question calls for conjecture, Your Honor. The witness can't be permitted to testify as to what she might have done five years ago under circumstances that she didn't become aware of until later. At best she would be guessing what her state of mind would have been. How could I cross-examine that?"

"May I be heard, Judge?" Charlie asked.

"Go ahead, Mr. Mayfield."

"It's true that Mr. Beck's objection would have merit if Mrs. Walton had to guess at the answer to my question. But she doesn't need to guess. If you'll indulge me for another question or two, I can establish that."

"Subject to that, I'll overrule the objection."

Charlie turned back to his witness. "Tracey, how do

you know what you would have done if you had known about Angel's condition?"

"Larry and I had discussed it many times, and we were in full agreement that—"

"Objection!" declared Lew Beck. "The question only calls for how she knew, not for what they would have done."

"That's correct," the judge said, "but I'm sure that would be Mr. Mayfield's next question. I'm going to let the witness testify on this. You may finish your answer, Mrs. Walton."

"Larry and I agreed that if we found out that our baby would have a serious birth defect—one that would rob her of a happy and meaningful life—we would terminate the pregnancy."

"You mean that you would have had an abortion?"

"Yes," she replied softly.

Charlie thought about Duane DeLuca's warning that the jury would hold it against the Waltons if they testified that Tracey would have had an abortion. He glanced toward the back of the courtroom and caught the insurance man's eye. *Okay, fat-ass, there it is. Now we'll see who's right.*

Then Charlie turned back to address the judge. "With the court's permission, we'd like to reserve the right to recall Mrs. Walton later when we put in our evidence on monetary damages. We thought it would be easier for the jury and the court to hear all of that evidence at the same time."

"I shouldn't think that would be a problem," Judge Grubner replied. "Mr. Beck?"

"That would be fine."

"Then this would be a good time to break for lunch," the judge said. "The jury will remember my admonition from yesterday about discussing the case. Court stands adjourned until one-thirty."

Charlie Mayfield knew that the power of a witness could not be measured only by his or her answers to questions. Intangible elements such as eye contact with the jurors, a sincere voice, and showing the right emotion at the right time—those were the things that made the testimony credible to the twelve people who would ultimately decide the case. Those were the things that distinguished the best, most trustworthy witnesses, and those were the things that Tracey had been doing to perfection. He knew that she had pierced the hearts of the jurors. They saw her as courageous, capable, and totally believable, a tower of strength, but no less grief-stricken than any of them would be.

Earlier Charlie had been worried that the jury might see her as a part-time mother who hired nurses to care for her child so that she could wheel and deal as a business executive, but he wasn't worried about that anymore. He had been watching the jurors while they were watching Tracey, and he could see that they embraced every word she said. When she left the witness stand and passed before the jurors, they smiled sympathetically at her. It was all they could do not to reach out and comfort her.

Better yet, Charlie knew that he had put Lewellen Beck squarely behind the eight ball. If Beck challenged an appealing witness like Tracey Walton, he could lose the jury; if he didn't, he could lose the case.

Checkmate!

ELEVEN

THROUGHOUT TRACEY WALTON'S testimony that morning, Lew Beck had been concentrating on two things: how to deal with the cross-examination that afternoon, and how to deal with the short, fat insurance man who had sat anxiously in the back of the courtroom.

Now, during the noon recess he and Duane DeLuca were eating sandwiches in Beck's office and reviewing the morning's testimony. Finally Lew said, "Duane, we have to talk about the settlement. Things are going on that piss me off."

"Tell me what they are."

"For one, I don't think it's right for you to negotiate directly with Mayfield. Early this morning, in his office, that was okay because I was there, but he told me that you cornered him during the recess and upped the offer. You know how that makes me look?"

"I was going to tell you about it over lunch, but you beat me to it. Anyway, what's the difference whether it's you or I who does the offering?"

"The difference is that I'm the one who has cases with Charlie and every other plaintiff's lawyer in Chicago. I lose all my negotiating credibility as soon as the word gets out that the guys from the home office will come out and sweeten the pot. Hell, Duane, next time I tell a guy that I just made my last offer, he'll tell me to shove it and then wait for you to fly out here and make him a better one. I'll have a hell of a time settling cases after this."

"I understand," DeLuca said. "I'm not trying to screw

you up with the plaintiffs' bar. In fact, I hadn't even *intended* to increase the offer to Mayfield; I was just trying to feel him out—find out if his four and a half million figure is etched in stone. Before I knew it, I took us up to two-seven."

"*Two-seven!* Jesus Christ, Duane, you threw another half million in the pot? I thought the company set a limit of two-five on the case and that we had only another three hundred thousand to play around with. That's what they've been telling me for the past six months."

The insurance man pretended to study his half-eaten sandwich. He had guilt written all over his face.

"Okay," Beck said angrily, "that brings us to the other thing that's been on my mind. I've been sold a bill of goods about what the company's willing to settle for, haven't I?" Getting no reply, he pointed a finger at the other man's chest and said, "C'mon, Duane, don't just sit there. Level with me."

"Now, don't get excited, Lew. There's nothing unusual about this. Lots of times we don't tell our attorneys how much we're willing to pay to settle. Some of those lily-livered defense lawyers out there, as soon as we tell 'em we're willing to go as high as, say, five hundred thou, they run over to the plaintiff and offer it. So we tell 'em the limit is maybe two or three hundred thousand. If the plaintiff won't accept that, and we're getting close to trial, then maybe I'll come out and offer three-fifty or four. I wouldn't go the whole five until I knew— absolutely knew—that I had to."

"Well, I'm not one of those lily-livered defense lawyers. I've done a hell of a good job for North American Casualty and for every other carrier I represent. Nearly all my settlements are for less than my authorization. Damn it, Duane, I try to protect your money like it was my own."

"I never said you didn't, Lew, but I don't make the rules."

"Maybe not, but I'm asking you to break them right here and now. I want to know how high the company is

willing to go. Not what they told me before trial, and not
what you offered Charlie this morning, but the whole
figure. What is it, Duane?"

"For cryin' out loud, Lew, you're trying to put me in
a box. I work for North American. They pay my salary,
and if they tell me not to give you the number, what the
hell am I supposed to do?" He searched Beck's eyes for
a clue that the lawyer understood his predicament, but all
he saw was contempt. "All right, all right," he finally
said, "but only on the condition that you don't make any
offers to Mayfield without my knowledge."

Beck nodded. "And you agree not to make any more
offers behind my back."

"Agreed."

"What's the figure?"

"Four-point-two."

"*Four-point-two?* Are you telling me that you had
another two million in your pocket and you never told
me about it? What the hell kind of game are you guys
playing?"

"Look, Lew, I was only—"

"Don't give me that 'I was only' shit. Do you realize
what you've done to my credibility with Judge Grubner?"

"Grubner? What's he have to do with this?"

"We had two pretrial conferences to talk settlement;
the second one was just two weeks ago. Grubner got
Charlie and me together and really hammered us. He
wanted us to get rid of this thing. That's when Charlie
came down off his five million figure—until then he'd
been insisting on the whole amount of the policy—and
I went from two to two-point-two. Then Grubner asked
Charlie to step out of the room, and when he had me
alone he asked me to tell him, off the record, just how
high we could go if we absolutely had to. 'Don't shit me,
Lew,' he said. 'Give me your highest number so I'll
know whether we should continue to try for a settlement.' He promised me he wouldn't tell Charlie the
number, so I told him."

"What'd you tell him?"

"I told him two-point-five. I said I was holding back the last three hundred thousand until Charlie made another move. Grubner couldn't believe that was all we'd pay for a case like this, but I assured him that I was being honest with him. Now what the hell will he think of me when he hears that you went to two-point-seven less than two hours after Charlie called his first witness, or when he hears that the company is willing to go to four-point-two. Christ, Duane, I lied to the man by almost *two million dollars!*"

"I'm sorry about that, but—"

"*You're* sorry? Grubner has a grudge against defense lawyers as it is. Now he'll have a good excuse never to trust me again. You guys really put me in the shit house."

After an uncomfortable silence the insurance man tried to change the subject. "How do you plan to handle the Walton lady's cross-examination?"

Beck wasn't happy to change the subject. He had been betrayed by North American Casualty, and he was irate. Nevertheless he outlined his general strategy for Tracey Walton's cross-examination. "I'll have to be damn careful," he concluded. "The jurors love her, and if I rough her up they'll jump out of the jury box and poke my eyes out."

He finished his sandwich and scowled at DeLuca. "Listen, Duane," he said, "I want to come back to the settlement for a minute."

"Sure, Lew, go ahead."

"Well, since the company is actually willing to go to four-point-two, that means we're only three hundred thousand apart. I'll bet that Charlie would come down that much to settle right now."

"I agree, Lew, but if we play it right, I think we can get him down below four, maybe even three-five. We've still got a few days to work on him before this thing goes to the jury. Why blow our wad now?"

"Two reasons. First, he's killing us with Mrs. Walton. He knows it, and he knows we know it. If the rest of his case goes as well for him, he'll have no reason to come down. Hell, he's liable to withdraw the four-point-five and go back up to the policy limit.

"And that brings me to the second reason: Steve Sinclair. He won't be a strong witness. Right after the case was filed we gave him the standard letter advising him that his policy was for five million dollars and that if the jury brought back a higher verdict, he'd be responsible for the excess. We told him he had a right to retain his own lawyer to protect his interests, but of course he didn't. Doctors hardly ever do in these cases. So I figured that if the jury *did* come back with a big number, it would be tough luck for him."

"So what's different now?" DeLuca asked.

"What's different now is that you're telling me the company has been willing to pay four-point-two. Mayfield would probably have taken it, but we've never offered it to him. Instead, we're playing around trying to get away for less than we think the case is worth—in other words, in order to try to save a few hundred thousand for ourselves, we're putting Sinclair at risk for everything over five million."

"Tough titty." The insurance man shrugged. "If Sinclair wanted more insurance, he should've bought it. Why in the hell should we offer over four million to settle? The worst that can happen is we pay the five, even if the jury brings back a giant verdict. But hell, Lew, you might still win this thing, and then we'd pay nothing. So why give away four when we can't lose more than five? Screw Sinclair."

Charlie had invited Tracey, Larry, and Bernard Benedict back to his office for lunch. He figured Tracey could relax for an hour and a half after her morning's ordeal, and he would have a chance to tell them about his encounter with DeLuca.

"So anyway," he was saying between large bites of his roast beef sandwich, "the insurance guy corners me when I come out of the john, and he tries to play the old insurance game—'We can go up if you'll come down, but you have to come down first.' Well, I told him, we weren't coming down, but if he made a realistic offer I'd mention it to you. I thought he'd tell me to go to hell, but damn if he doesn't grab my arm just as I'm going back into the courtroom and throw another half million at us, just like that."

"Does that mean they're up to two-point-seven million dollars?" asked Bernard Benedict.

"Yeah, so far."

"So far? You think they'll go higher?"

"Hell yes," Charlie said confidently. "And that was before they heard the rest of Tracey's testimony. Believe me, Bernie, she was dynamite."

"And we're still demanding four and half million?"

"Right, but we all agreed we'd take four."

"Why don't we just come out and tell them that?" Larry Walton asked. "Maybe they'll pay it and we can put an end to all this."

"Because as soon as I say we'll take four million, they'll think that's only a first move and that if they wait we'll come down further."

"Can't you tell them that that's as low as we'll go?" he asked.

The lawyer laughed. "Sure, but they'd never believe it. First of all, in this business *everyone* says their last offer is the furthest they'll go. Second, I already told them that we wouldn't go below four and a half. The longer we stay there, the more they'll believe that maybe, just maybe, ol' Charlie is serious, and that if they want to settle they'll have to come to me."

Tracey let her frustration show. "We have to trust that you know what you're doing," she said, "but all this gamesmanship worries me. I'd hate to lose a good settlement just because neither of you will be honest about how far you're really willing to go."

Charlie put down his sandwich. "Listen, Tracey, this is your case—yours and Larry's. I'm just working for you, but I've been through these negotiations a thousand times, and I know what I'm doing. We've got these guys scared to death. They're desperate and they'll keep after me to settle. I'll know when it's the right time to come down. But in the meantime I don't want you to lose faith, either in me or in the case."

Larry changed the subject. "Charlie, we believe you when you say that Tracey is making a good impression on the jury and that the case is going well, but the fact remains that we still have to give the jury some reason to think that Dr. Sinclair was negligent. If we can't do that, they might not give us a thing, no matter *how* much they feel sorry for us."

"Don't you think I know that? We're in this together, Larry. The more you get, the more I get, so I have as much reason as you do to squeeze the last dime out of these jokers." Charlie was referring to his one-third contingent fee arrangement. If he could hold out for the entire four and a half million, he would pocket a cool one and a half million and the Waltons would get three. But even if they settled for less, Charlie knew that he would do just fine, thank you, so he had plenty of incentive not to turn his back on a settlement and then lose the case.

"But don't go thinking I've slammed the door on anything less than four and a half," he said. "Uh-uh. I specifically told this DeLuca guy that I'd talk to you and Tracey about any realistic offer he made; that was my way of telling him that we weren't necessarily married to the four and a half million."

"Do you think he understands that?" asked Bernard Benedict.

"Sure he does. Listen, this guy knows the game; he's been playing it a long time. But I still think they'd be smarter to let Lew Beck handle the settlement talk. I believe the person who tries a case ought to be the one to settle it; he knows it better than anyone in the world—the strong points *and* the weak points. Besides, Lew's an expert negotiator and he'd do a better job than that dip they sent out here from Boston."

Charlie took a huge bite from a pickle and held up the

uneaten stub as he made another point. "And I'll tell you something else: I'll bet you anything that they're not telling Lew how much they're actually willing to pay. They're afraid he might tell Sinclair."

Larry said he didn't understand.

"If Sinclair knew they were willing to pay more than they've offered, he could raise holy hell," Charlie explained. "You see, he's responsible for everything over five million dollars, so he wants to see this thing go away. He couldn't care less whether they settle for two or four-point-nine—either way he's off the hook. But if they screw up the settlement trying to save themselves a few bucks, and then the jury comes back with more than five million, he could claim deliberate misfeasance and sue to make them pay the whole amount. That's why they don't want him to know their top figure, and they have to keep Lew in the dark, too, because he has a duty to tell Sinclair everything he knows. Technically, Sinclair is his client, but the goddamn insurance companies never look at it that way."

TWELVE ══

IN SPITE OF Charlie's encouragement, Tracey was a nervous wreck when she resumed the witness stand after the lunch break. During the morning session she had been questioned by her own lawyer, and they had repeatedly gone over those questions, and the answers to them, beforehand. But there was no good way to rehearse a cross-examination.

"Mrs. Walton, you realize you're still under oath?" This from Judge Grubner.

"Yes, sir."

"You may proceed, Mr. Beck."

Lew Beck rose and walked briskly to the lectern. He wanted the jury, and Tracey Walton, to see confidence written all over him. He had to give the impression that he had a good case and that none of Tracey's earlier testimony bothered him in the least. And he wanted to cap off that first impression with a solid opening question, a real zinger that Tracey and Charlie wouldn't have anticipated and that might throw her off balance. Beck sensed her nervousness and wanted to keep her on edge.

"Mrs. Walton, when were you and Mr. Walton divorced?"

It worked. Tracey flinched and looked at Charlie for help.

"You needn't look to your lawyer, Mrs. Walton. Just answer the question."

"Last May."

"And what was the reason for the divorce?" Beck had

taken her pretrial deposition before the divorce and therefore hadn't asked her about it previously. However, while subsequently interviewing other potential witnesses, he had heard enough to suspect that the divorce might have had something to do with her job; he knew she spent countless hours working or entertaining business contacts. If he asked the right questions the jury would start to see Tracey as a part-time mother and full-time executive, more concerned about her career than her family, someone who hired nurses to see to the needs of her retarded daughter.

Tracey saw the trap and tried to sidestep it. "Larry and I were having problems even before Angel was born. Our marriage just didn't seem to be working. We thought maybe having a baby would bring us closer together, but it didn't turn out that way. Angel's condition only added to the strain. We finally got divorced when she was three."

Beck was not satisfied with that answer. "*Why* wasn't the marriage working, Mrs. Walton? Did it have something to do with your job at Benedict Construction?"

"Of course not," she snapped. "Many women have careers and happy marriages."

"But you didn't. And I'm asking if your work created a problem for you and Mr. Walton."

"No, it didn't."

Lewellen Beck was persistent. "Mrs. Walton, aren't you the executive vice president of the Benedict Construction Company?"

"Yes."

"And isn't it a fact that you leave for your office every morning by seven, that you hardly ever come home before seven at night, and that at least once or twice a week you have dinner with business associates? Isn't that true?"

"Yes, but I never neglected my—"

"No one is accusing you of neglect, Mrs. Walton."

"And this isn't a divorce case," Charlie Mayfield said sarcastically from his seat at the counsel table. "If you want to retry *Walton versus Walton,* Mr. Beck, you're in the wrong court at the wrong time. This case is *Walton versus Sinclair,* and I suggest you get on with it."

Irritated by the interruption, Beck spun around to glare at Charlie. "I'll ask whatever questions I—"

"Gentlemen, gentlemen," Horace Grubner said sternly, "remember where we are. I will not tolerate a shouting match between counsel. Mr. Mayfield, if you have an objection to Mr. Beck's line of questioning, then address it to me."

"All right, Your Honor. I object to his questions about the marriage and divorce of Mr. and Mrs. Walton. They have no relevance to the issues in this case."

"I'm not sure I agree, Mr. Mayfield." The judge looked at Lew Beck and said, "But since the witness has now answered those questions, Mr. Beck, I suggest you move on to something else."

Beck nodded. Just as well, he thought. The jury got the message about Tracey's career and work schedule, and that was all he'd been trying to bring out. Further questions about the divorce would risk giving the impression that he was browbeating her, and that was something he had to avoid at all costs.

He turned back to face Tracey. "Mrs. Walton, you testified this morning that you would have had an abortion if you and your husband had known of Angel's condition. That would have been almost five years ago. As you sit here today, how can you say for sure what you would have done at that time?"

"As I said this morning, my husband and I had discussed it many times. We agreed that if we ever learned I was carrying a child with a serious defect, we would terminate the pregnancy."

"But some defects are more serious than others, isn't that right?"

Something in the question triggered an alarm in Tracey's mind. "I don't understand the question."

"Well, you wouldn't have run to an abortionist if you

were told that your baby would have six toes on each foot, would you?"

"Of course not," she snapped, indignant that Beck would equate such a condition with Down's syndrome.

"So you would have been willing to accept *some* defects. Is that what you're saying?"

"I find your questions distasteful, Mr. Beck."

Beck was worried that the jury would agree with her, but he had to walk the tightrope a little longer. "I apologize, Mrs. Walton, I really do. But I'm just trying to find out how serious a defect would have to be to cause you to make the decision to abort. Let me try it another way." He pondered for a moment, then asked: "Wouldn't you agree that some birth defects are even more serious than Down's syndrome?"

"I suppose."

"Well, isn't it a fact that some of them will cause a child to be stillborn or to die soon after birth?"

"Yes, I believe there are some like that."

"Now, Mrs. Walton, when you were on the stand this morning, didn't you testify that many Down children survive into their teens and even into adulthood?"

"Yes, that's true, but—"

"And some can even live to old age?"

"Yes, but Angel's condition is more serious than most. She's not expected to live that long."

Lew Beck held up a finger. "But you couldn't know that until after she was born, could you?"

Tracey saw where he was leading, and she began to tense up. "I don't understand."

"Well, if Dr. Sinclair had diagnosed Down's syndrome before Angel was born, you still wouldn't have known how serious a case it was. Isn't that right?"

Charlie rose to object. "Your Honor, Mrs. Walton isn't a doctor. How could she possibly know whether the seriousness of this condition can be ascertained before birth?"

"I'll withdraw the question," Beck said before the judge could rule. Then he turned to Tracey. "If you had been told that Angel would have a relatively minor case of Down's syndrome and that she could be expected to live to old age, would you still have aborted her?"

Charlie saw that Beck was painting Tracey into a corner. He had to try to help her. "Objection!" he shouted from his seat. "He's asking the witness what she would have done if she knew something that she didn't know."

Judge Grubner shook his head. "But Mr. Mayfield, you yourself asked her on direct examination whether she would have had an abortion if she'd known she was carrying a Down fetus. I see no difference. Overruled." He turned to Tracey and said, "Please answer the question, Mrs. Walton."

She hesitated for what seemed an eternity. She knew that if she said she would have opted for an abortion regardless of the seriousness of Angel's condition, she would sound heartless. Finally she replied in a voice that was barely audible. "I don't know."

"And what if you had known that she would live for at least four or five years," he asked, his voice rising, *"which is in fact the case?"*

Confused, she whispered, "I'm not sure I can answer that."

"Thank you, Mrs. Walton. That's all I'm trying to establish—that you're not really sure what you would have done."

Beck could enjoy a moment of relief. He had made his point, but in fact it was a small one. He still had to explain why Steve Sinclair had failed to diagnose the condition. That was really what the trial was all about.

Okay, Lew, he said to himself, let's try to trip her up on the dates. "Mrs. Walton, I'd like to direct your attention to that first day in Dr. Sinclair's office. What was that date again?"

"August 17, 1987."

"Thank you. By the way, that wasn't the first time you saw Dr. Sinclair, was it?"

"No. I had seen him once or twice for routine checkups. The gynecologist I had previously used was quite elderly, and he retired. I believe that was in 1985. A friend recommended Dr. Sinclair, so I had my records sent to his office."

Charlie was fidgeting in his seat. He could see that Tracey was unnerved by all the questions about the divorce and her job, and all that business about abortions. She'd forgotten what he told her about short answers. She should've just answered no. Now Beck had some other things to ask about.

"Who was the friend who recommended Dr. Sinclair?"

"I don't recall," she replied quickly.

Charlie was on his feet to object to the irrelevant question, but she had already answered. He sat back down. Damnit, now Tracey was forgetting to delay her answers. Lew was getting to her.

"Mrs. Walton, you testified this morning that you told Dr. Sinclair on August 17, 1987, that your last menstrual period was in mid-June, or about two months earlier. Is that correct?"

"Yes, it is."

"Isn't it possible that you were mistaken, and that you told him it was in early July? July fifth, to be exact?"

"No. Absolutely not."

"How can you be so sure?"

Tracey reiterated her earlier testimony about waiting until she was about three weeks late before calling Steve's office while she was on vacation, and then not seeing him until she returned home. "No, Mr. Beck," she concluded, "I never mentioned July fifth to Dr. Sinclair or anyone else. I told him mid-June, period."

Nearly everyone in the courtroom, including Lew Beck and Horace Grubner, laughed. It was comic relief from a tense situation. At first Tracey seemed startled to hear the reaction to her answer, but then she obviously realized what she had said and shook her head with an embarrassed smile.

Beck waited until the murmur of laughter trailed off before he asked his next question. "Then how is it, Mrs.

Walton, that Dr. Sinclair wrote down in your record that your last menstrual period was in July, not June?"

"I suggest you ask Dr. Sinclair that question. Maybe he had me confused with another patient."

Beck had made a mistake by giving her an opportunity to take a free shot at Steve. She was quick, and he'd have to be careful not to give her that kind of opening again.

"Mrs. Walton, you testified that you didn't have an ultrasound, right?"

"That's right. Nor the amniocentesis."

"Well, let's just stick with the ultrasound for now. Do you recall any conversations with Dr. Sinclair about having it done?"

"No, it was never mentioned."

"Why didn't you ask him to do it?"

"Because at the time I didn't know much about it."

"Now, I find that hard to understand, Mrs. Walton." Beck consulted a note he had made during her direct examination that morning. "You testified this morning that you knew about amniocentesis because it isn't an unusual test. You said that every pregnant woman knows about it. But you say you didn't know about ultrasound. That's also a very common procedure, isn't it?"

"As I said, Mr. Beck, I vaguely knew that there was such a test but I didn't know what it was for. And Dr. Sinclair never brought it up."

Beck looked at her suspiciously for several seconds. "Isn't it a fact, Mrs. Walton, that Dr. Sinclair wanted you to have an ultrasound, but that the test couldn't be scheduled because of your busy schedule, and that—"

"No, Mr. Beck," she interrupted, "that isn't a fact."

"—and that you even told him you'd rather not spend the money for ultrasound, since your insurance wouldn't pay for it?"

Tracey laughed bitterly. "Ask yourself, Mr. Beck, why in the world would I refuse to have an ultrasound? It only takes a few minutes, it's risk-free—it's even safer than an X-ray—and it's painless. To suggest that I was trying to save a few dollars—why, that's ludicrous, and I resent it.

I was very concerned about my baby, and if I had thought an ultrasound or any other test could tell me there was a problem, I'd have run to have it done."

Lew Beck had to admit to himself that her answer made a lot of sense. There really *wasn't* any logical reason for her not to have had the test. But Sinclair's records, which were in his own handwriting, clearly showed that the failure to have the ultrasound was all her own doing. Was it really possible that Steven Sinclair could have altered those records?

THIRTEEN ════

MOLLY HAD SAT through Tracey Walton's cross-examination but left the courthouse during the afternoon recess. She had explained to Steve that she had to get back to her office and that an evening meeting would keep her from having dinner with him.

"You're not mad, are you, Doc?"

"No, of course not. You've got work to do. I'm just glad you were here for Tracey's cross-examination."

"It looked to me like your lawyer did a good job," Molly lied. In fact, it seemed to her—and probably to everyone else in the courtroom, including Steve—that Beck hadn't laid a glove on Tracey. Sure, he had momentarily rattled her with a few questions, but it hadn't come to anything. The critical parts of her earlier testimony—the date of her last period, her demand for an amniocentesis, Steve's failure to do an ultrasound, and the condition of her child—remained undisturbed. Indeed, the cross-examination gave her the opportunity to repeat many of those things for the benefit of the jury, and if anything, she left the stand as an even more credible and sympathetic witness than she was after her direct examination.

"Don't forget," Molly said as she stood on tiptoe to give him a kiss, "there's soup in the freezer and leftover turkey in the fridge."

Steve smiled and told her not to worry, he'd be fine, but the thought of going home to an empty apartment seemed altogether depressing.

• • •

When court reconvened after the recess, Charlie called his first expert witness to the stand.

Dr. Cynthia Caruso was one of those perfect experts that trial lawyers tried to keep on tap. She spoke directly to the jury, her voice was confident, and she used language everyone understood. Better yet, she had a friendly smile and an expression that radiated sincerity and warmth.

Charlie first had her tell the jury of her impeccable credentials. She taught and practiced pediatrics at the University of Chicago School of Medicine, and had written two books and several papers—all greeted with acclaim by the profession—on the diagnosis and treatment of genetic birth defects. She was on numerous professional panels and served as a consultant to other practicing pediatricians.

Dr. Caruso explained to the jury that, although she was not Angel Walton's physician, she had reviewed all of her medical records and personally supervised an extensive physical and mental examination of the child. This, she said, was done at the request of Mr. Mayfield in order to present her testimony.

"And now, Dr. Caruso, is there a name for Angel Walton's condition—her illness?" Charlie asked.

"Yes."

"And what is it?"

"Technically, it's trisomy twenty-one syndrome, but it's more commonly known as Down's syndrome, named for Dr. John Down, a London physician in the nineteenth century."

"In terms that a lay person could understand, Doctor, what causes that disease?"

"Down's syndrome is caused by an extra chromosome, specifically an extra twenty-first chromosome. Most people have forty-six chromosomes, but a Down patient has forty-seven."

"And again, in terms that we can understand, can you tell us something about this disease?"

"Surely." Dr. Caruso shifted slightly in her seat so she could face the jury before giving her answer. "It wasn't too long ago that Down patients were referred to as Mongoloids, mainly because of the shape of the eyelids and nasal bridge. In fact, at one time they were cruelly referred to as Mongoloid idiots." She glanced over at Tracey and Larry in silent apology, then went on to describe the other symptoms of the disease, most of which the jury had heard when Tracey testified.

"What is the frequency of the Down's syndrome, Doctor? How rare is it?"

"The frequency rises dramatically with maternal age, that is, the age of the mother. But for all live births, including mothers of all ages, the odds are about one in eight hundred. It occurs more often than that at conception, but about two-thirds of the fetuses with that extra chromosome self-abort."

"What is the life expectancy of a Down child?"

"Those Down children who develop severe cardiac malformation, as Angel Walton has, seldom survive into their teens. The others often live into adulthood, and some even to old age. On the other hand, survival carries the curse of intensified mental deterioration."

"Are you saying that they start out retarded and that the retardation gets worse as they get older?"

"Definitely. And coupled with that, Down patients mentally age at an accelerated pace and may develop the symptoms of advanced senility and even Alzheimer's disease by their thirties."

"Do Down children walk and talk like other children?"

"They will learn to walk, yes, but usually not until they are two to four years old. As a rule, they don't begin to speak until they are between four and six, and when they do speak it is generally with pronounced speech impediments." The witness held up a hand. "May I add something, Mr. Mayfield?"

"Certainly."

"Angel Walton's symptoms are more serious than most. She's four and still isn't able to walk."

"Dr. Caruso, how can you be sure that that is the disease Angel has? How do you identify Down's syndrome?"

"Well, a trained physician or clinician will usually begin to suspect the presence of the disease, even in a newborn, during a visual examination. The physical anomalies I described before—the abnormal palate, nasal bridge, eyes, and tongue, and the brachycephalic head shape, short and broad, and even the shape of the fingers and toes—are all visible and consistent with the disorder. But we can positively diagnose the disease through karyotyping."

"Karyotyping? What is that?"

"Chromosomal analysis. We can actually examine and analyze chromosomes from a microphotograph of a single cell."

"You mean," Charlie said in a surprised voice, "that you can actually *see* chromosomes? And take pictures of them?"

"Oh, sure." Dr. Caruso smiled. "And we can tell which are which by looking at such features as their length and shape. You see, each chromosome is made up of two segments connected by something called a centromere, and the overall size and configuration of chromosome thirteen, for example, is different from that of chromosome eighteen. Also, the chromosomes have different staining characteristics, so we can help identify them by imparting a dye. In fact," she added, "that's why they're called chromosomes—from *chroma*, the Latin word for 'color.' And we can count them. That's how we can be sure if Down's is present: We can actually see an extra twenty-first chromosome."

Charlie shook his head, as if he were hearing for the first time of the amazing progress in medical diagnostic techniques. In fact, he knew all of this inside out from his trial preparation, but he wanted the jury to get the feeling that he and they were learning together.

"All these symptoms you described, Doctor, will they continue to get worse as Angel gets older?"

"Well, certainly her heart will continue to weaken, and her dementia—mental retardation—will become more pronounced. In Angel Walton's case, I would say that the disease will present progressive physical and neurological deterioration."

"And for how long will this deterioration go on?"

"Until the child dies." She would have preferred to use a clinical word like "expires" or "terminates," but Charlie had persuaded her to use the one word that the jurors could not possibly misunderstand.

"Dr. Caruso, do you have a medical opinion as to when that might be in Angel's case?"

"Yes, I do." Again she looked at the jury. "In my opinion, Angel Walton won't live beyond her tenth birthday, and it's quite possible that she won't survive past her sixth or seventh birthday."

"Could future medical advances—new technology— increase her life expectancy?" Charlie had a reason for the question. It would be more expensive to care for Angel for twenty years than for two, and the mere possibility of a longer life might help him squeeze a higher verdict out of the jury. A positive answer from Dr. Caruso would set the stage for a subsequent witness to testify to the possibility of Angel having a longer—and therefore more expensive—life than the earlier testimony had suggested.

"Indeed. We are learning new things every day. For example, new procedures for pediatric heart surgery may be available to repair Angel's heart, and this could prolong her life considerably."

"Thank you, Doctor, I have no further questions."

Horace Grubner looked toward the defendant's counsel table. "Mr. Beck?"

"No questions, Your Honor."

Dr. Kevin Harrison was a diminutive man who peered out at the courtroom through rimless spectacles. He was on the low side of forty, but looked older because of a salt-and-pepper beard that was neatly trimmed for his appearance in court. In response to Charlie's preliminary questions, Dr. Harrison told the jury that he was a geneticist—a medical doctor who specialized in the field of genetics. While he had no private practice, he taught at Northwestern University School of Medicine and had consulting contracts with a large pharmaceutical firm and a genetic counseling clinic.

"You say you specialize in genetics," Charlie said. "Could you tell us what that means?"

"It's the branch of medicine that deals with heredity."

Charlie had misgivings about putting a geneticist on the stand because the field was so complicated that it could easily confuse the jury, and he liked to keep his cases as simple as possible. But if he went without a geneticist, then sure as hell Beck would put one on, and Charlie would rather have the jury hear this mumbo jumbo from his own witness than from one partial to the defense.

"Are you familiar with Down's syndrome?"

"Trisomy twenty-one, yes. It's classified as one of the autosomal trisomy disorders."

Christ, Charlie thought, here we go. "Please tell the jury what that means, and try to do so in terms they, and I, can understand." Everyone in the courtroom except Dr. Harrison smiled.

"Every person normally has forty-six chromosomes in every cell. Forty-four of those are arranged in pairs—twenty-two pairs. These forty-four are known as auto-somes. In addition, every person has two nonpaired chromosomes. Those are the sex chromosomes designated as X and Y. A woman has two X chromosomes, and a man has one X and one Y. Occasionally, instead of a normal pair of chromosomes, we find a third chromosome. Sometimes it's attached to another, and sometimes it stands alone. We call that a trisomy. Trisomy twenty-one, or Down's syndrome, results when there is an extra twenty-first chromosome. If the trisomy is of a chromosome other than number twenty-one—"

"Let's just stick with number twenty-one," Charlie interrupted. "That's what we're dealing with in this case."

"Of course," the witness responded curtly. It wasn't clear whether he thought Charlie was an intellectual clod because he didn't want to know more about genetics or whether he felt robbed of the opportunity to deliver a lecture.

"Now, Dr. Harrison, please tell the jury and me how a person gets Down's syndrome. How does he or she happen to get this extra chromosome?"

"It can happen in one of two ways, either a translocation or a nondisjunction. A translocation can be either inherited or spontaneous. Let me explain the differences. An inherited translocation occurs when one of the parents has a balanced translocation—that is, when one of the twenty-first chromosomes—remember there are two of them—has attached itself to *another* chromosome. That's what we mean by translocation—that the chromosome is in the wrong place. But that parent still has the proper total amount of genetic material, even though it's misplaced, so we say the translocation is *balanced*. That parent, who has had the translocation since birth, is clinically normal in every way, but he or she is a carrier of Down's syndrome."

The witness paused to look at Charlie apologetically. "Is this getting too technical?"

Charlie smiled. "No, I think we're still hanging on."

"Okay. When the father produces sperm and the mother produces ova, their chromosomal pairs split so that each sperm cell and each ovum cell contain only *one* of each pair of chromosomes. So, at the moment of fertilization, the baby-to-be gets one of each pair from the mother and one of each pair from the father. Now, let's say the father has a balanced translocation, and that one of his twenty-first chromosomes is attached to one of his fourteenth chromosomes. It's possible that the baby will get the isolated twenty-one *and* the fourteen with the other twenty-one attached, *and* the mother's twenty-one. So the baby will have three twenty-ones—an *unbalanced* translocation—and he or she will have Down's syndrome."

"Wouldn't *every* baby born to that parent have Down's?" Charlie asked.

"No, not at all. If, for example, the father's *other* number fourteen chromosome—the one without the twenty-one attached—is passed on to the child, there will be only two twenty-ones, not three, and therefore no trisomy. In fact, studies show that when one parent is the carrier of a balanced translocation, the chance that the fetus will be abnormal is between four and twenty percent, and only about one-third of those abnormal fetuses will survive to birth. Consequently, we can have a relatively large number of carrier parents, but a low number of Down children."

"And if a child happens to receive a triple dose of some other chromosome, one other than number twenty-one, then that baby would have a different disease, right?"

"Not exactly. You see, no trisomy other than thirteen, eighteen, and twenty-one will allow a fetus to survive birth, and trisomies thirteen and eighteen won't allow a child to survive infancy. The only trisomy that *might* permit survival beyond infancy is twenty-one—Down's syndrome."

Charlie, who didn't refer to notes during the entire examination, paused long enough to amble toward the jury while he tugged at his ear. He hoped to give the impression that he was groping for another question to ask the witness. In fact he was covertly studying the jurors' reaction to all of this technical evidence, and what he saw was twelve people sitting on the edge of their chairs. I'll be damned, he thought to himself. They're actually following all this shit. Might as well give them a little more.

"You said something about a spontaneous transloca-

tion. How is that different from an inherited translocation?"

"At the moment of conception, a structural rearrangement of the chromosomes can occur. We don't know how
or why it happens; it's a new mutation that occurs for the
first time in that fetus. If this rearrangement still endows
the fetus with two twenty-ones, one of which is attached
to another chromosome, that child will have a balanced
translocation; he or she will be normal but will thereafter
be a carrier whose offspring may have the disease.
However, if the rearrangement produces a *third* twenty-
one—and that can happen—that child will have Down's
syndrome."

"Okay, Dr. Harrison, you said that there are *two* ways
a child can get Down's syndrome. Translocation, either
inherited or spontaneous, is one of them. What's the
other one?"

"Remember when I said that each parental pair of
chromosomes splits in the egg or the sperm cells? Well,
sometimes a parent has a chromosomal pair that somehow doesn't split when a sperm or egg cell is produced.
This is called a nondisjunction. If a sperm cell containing
an unsplit pair of twenty-first chromosomes fertilizes the
ovum, or if an ovum cell containing an unsplit pair of
twenty-first chromosomes is fertilized, we again end up
with a Down baby having three twenty-ones—two from
one parent and one from the other."

"What causes this nondisjunction?" Charlie asked.
"What causes the two chromosomes not to split?"

"We're not sure, Mr. Mayfield, even though we see
that it's more common in the ovum as the mother's age
increases. It's just another one of those accidents of
nature."

"Do you have an opinion, Doctor, as to whether Angel
Walton's condition came from a translocation or was the
result of a nondisjunction?"

"It was a spontaneous translocation."

"How do you know that?"

"Because, at your request, I analyzed the child's

chromosomes through a process called karyotyping. Karyotyping is——"

"You needn't explain it. Dr. Caruso already told the jury what karyotyping is. Just tell us what you found."

"We can easily see if a trisomy is the result of a translocation or a nondisjunction. In Angel Walton's case it's clearly a translocation because this child's extra twenty-first chromosome is attached to another of her chromosomes. This wouldn't be true in the case of a nondisjunction."

"But how do you know that it was spontaneous and not inherited from one of her parents?"

"Because, again at your request, I did a karyotyping on Mr. and Mrs. Walton. I found their chromosomal patterns to be perfectly normal. Neither of them has a balanced translocation. Therefore, the child's condition had to be the result of a new mutation developed when Angel was conceived. That would make it a *de novo,* or spontaneous, translocation."

Charlie felt the need to summarize what the witness had said, and he chose to do so by asking a few more questions while his eyes moved from juror to juror. "Okay, Dr. Harrison, let's see if I have this straight. It's normal for a baby to have two twenty-ones. If one of those twenty-ones is attached to another chromosome, the baby has a balanced translocation; he or she will not have Down's but will be a carrier. Right?"

"Right."

"Okay. But a baby with *three* twenty-ones *will* have Down's syndrome. And in this case we can tell if it's the result of an unbalanced translocation or a nondisjunction by determining whether the extra twenty-one is standing alone or is attached to another chromosome. But in either case the baby will have Down's. Is that right?"

"Yes, sir."

"And if the condition is the result of an unbalanced translocation, we can find out if it was spontaneous or inherited simply by seeing if one of the parents has a balanced translocation. Have I got it right?"

"Yes, Mr. Mayfield, you've got it right."

Charlie walked back to his counsel table, pulled four sheet of paper out of a folder, then returned to the witness. "Dr. Harrison, I am showing you four diagrams. Have you seen them before?"

"Yes, I prepared them myself."

"At my request?"

"Yes, sir."

"And what do these diagrams represent?"

"They represent four different chromosome patterns."

Since Judge Grubner had made a pretrial ruling that Charlie could use these diagrams to help explain this part of the case to the jury, Charlie now handed copies of them to each juror. Then he turned to Dr. Harrison.

"Now, Doctor, I've marked these diagrams as Exhibits A, B, C, and D. Would you please tell us what Exhibit A represents?"

"Exhibit A shows a normal pattern—that is, what we'd see in a person who does not have Down's syndrome and is not a carrier. And since we see both an X and a Y sex chromosome, we know this pattern belongs to a male."

"How about Exhibit B?"

"Exhibit B shows the chromosome pattern for a person with a balanced translocation. One of the twenty-first chromosomes is attached to chromosome number fourteen. This person would appear normal in every way but would be a Down carrier."

"And Exhibit C?"

"This individual has Down's syndrome because of an *unbalanced* translocation. There are two twenty-ones standing alone, and another attached to number fourteen." The witness looked at the jurors. "This would be the pattern for Angel Walton. And we know hers was a spontaneous mutation, not an inherited condition, because neither of her parents is a Down carrier. As I said earlier, we checked the patterns for Mr. and Mrs. Walton and found them to be perfectly normal, just as in Exhibit A."

EXHIBIT A
Normal Chromosome Pattern
(Male)

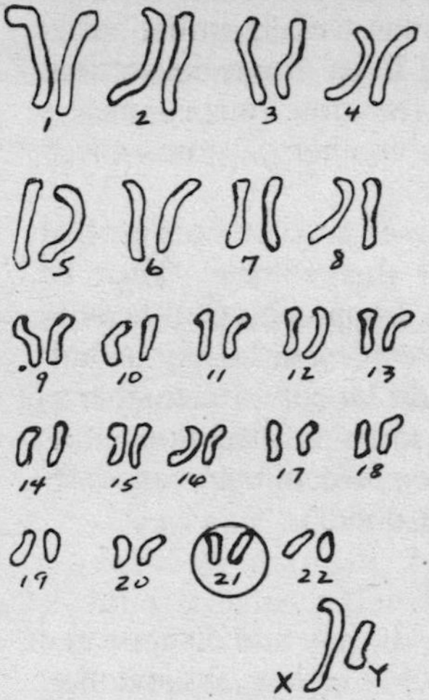

EXHIBIT B
Balanced Translocation #21
- Carrier (Male)

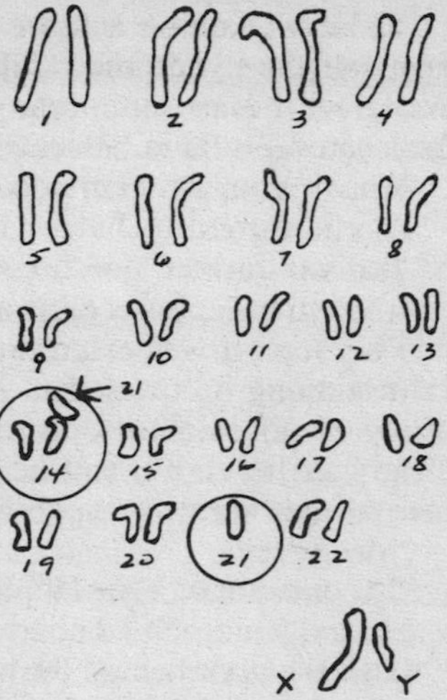

EXHIBIT C
Unbalanced Translocation #21
- Down's Syndrome (Female)

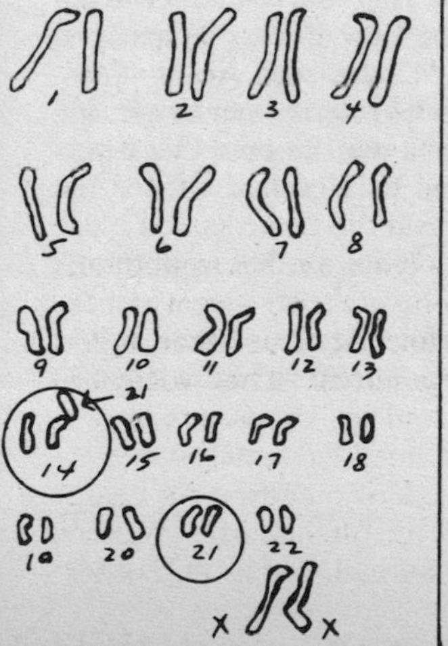

EXHIBIT D
Nondisjunction #21
- Down's Syndrome (Female)

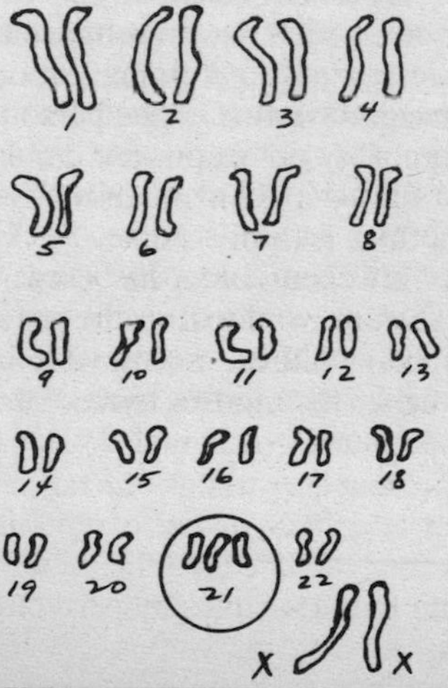

"And finally, Doctor, tell us about Exhibit D."

"Exhibit D shows another person with Down's, but in this case the syndrome resulted from a nondisjunction. We know this because none of the three twenty-ones is mislocated—that is, attached to another chromosome."

"Thank you, Dr. Harrison."

Charlie turned to Judge Grubner and announced that he had no further questions of this witness. Then he returned to his counsel table and dropped himself heavily into his seat. It was exhausting to present highly technical testimony in a way that would be comprehensible to a jury of nonscientists. But he knew he had done it as clearly as he could, and he promised himself an extra martini that night for a job well done.

"Mr. Beck?"

"No questions, Your Honor."

The judge adjourned court for the day and disappeared through the door behind the bench. The lawyers and their clients stood while the jury left the courtroom, and all noticed that some of the jurors smiled warmly at Tracey as they departed.

While Dr. Harrison was testifying, Steve had written a note, which he now handed to Lew Beck: "When you were cross-examining Mrs. W., she said she couldn't recall the name of the person who referred her to me. It's probably not important, but I just remembered that it was a former patient of mine." And then he had written the former patient's name. Beck read the note, leaned close to his client and whispered, "It's not all that important." Then he wadded up the note.

It would be a long time before Beck or Steve would realize the significance of the name Steve had written in that note.

FOURTEEN===

THE THIRD DAY of *Walton v. Sinclair* began at 9:30 A.M. sharp. Charlie Mayfield, in the same navy blue suit he had worn since opening arguments on Monday, called his first witness.

"Please tell us your name."

"Peter Barrington."

"And your occupation?"

"I'm a physician specializing in obstetrics."

"Where do you practice, Dr. Barrington?"

"Here in Chicago. The Pittsfield Building."

Dr. Peter Barrington testified that he had been a practicing obstetrician for twenty-eight years, that he lectured at Loyola University Medical School on the subject of prenatal diagnosis of fetal disorders, and that he had delivered several papers to the American Medical Association on that subject.

Barrington's voice and manner were confident and professional, Charlie noted with satisfaction. He chose each word carefully and enunciated it distinctly, and his warm smile and friendly tone provided a comfortable delivery for testimony that was sure to be technical. When he leaned back and crossed his legs easily, it occurred to Charlie that Peter Barrington could have been speaking from an easy chair in a cozy den instead of from a straight-backed seat in a sterile courtroom. While his black hair was beginning to turn gray at the temples, his thick mustache was the color of pitch. Though he looked more like a matinee idol than an obstetrician, Charlie had a hunch that no patient could help but feel secure in his care. Everyone in the court-room had to have sensed by now that Dr. Peter Bar-rington would be a powerful witness whose testimony would weigh heavily in the jury's final verdict.

Charlie Mayfield was set to take full advantage of this valuable resource. "Would you say that you're an expert on fetal disorders, Dr. Barrington?"

"Well, I believe my colleagues would say so," he answered modestly.

"And have other doctors consulted with you on their cases?"

"Yes, often."

"Are you familiar with Down's syndrome, Dr. Bar-rington?"

He nodded grimly, as if Charlie had mentioned a personal enemy instead of a disease. "I am."

"Tell us, Doctor, have you had occasion to diagnose Down's syndrome in the prenatal state—that is, before the baby was born?"

"Yes, I have."

"Are you able to explain how that is done? In terms we can understand?"

"Yes, I think so."

Charlie was pleased when Barrington spoke to the jurors as if they were a group of first-year medical students. His manner was authoritative but not conde-scending, and he gave them credit for having enough intelligence to grasp what he was telling them.

"We can accurately diagnose Down's syndrome through a process known as amniocentesis," the witness said. "Preferably, this is done at sixteen to eighteen weeks into the pregnancy. Amniocentesis involves the insertion of a needle into the amnionic sac and the withdrawal of a sample of amnionic fluid for analysis. I should point out that the procedure is painless because a local anesthetic is applied to the mother's abdominal wall."

Charlie posed a question that he thought the jurors

might be mentally asking. "Dr. Barrington, doesn't amnionic fluid *surround* the fetus—the baby?"

"Yes, that's correct."

"Then how is it that an analysis of the fluid can tell you what is happening inside the fetus? Aren't they two different things?"

Charlie knew all of this material backwards and forwards, but he was putting himself in the shoes of the jurors and asking the questions they might want to ask.

"Yes, they are two different things, to use your words, but they are interrelated, and what we find in the amnionic fluid tells us quite a bit about the fetus. You see, the fetus continuously sloughs off cells, especially skin cells, which end up in the amnionic fluid. We capture these cells during amniocentesis, and then we observe them through a microscope as they go through the stages of cellular division. In the stage known as metaphase, the chromosomes within the cell are microscopically visible. It's at this point that we stabilize the cells and photograph them."

"Amazing," Charlie said, shaking his head.

"Yes," Dr. Barrington agreed. "This is all new technology, and every day we learn more, especially in the field of genetics." Looking back to the jury, the witness said, "Through a process known as karyotyping—"

"We already know what karyotyping is, Doctor," Charlie said as he winked at the jury. "Other witnesses have explained it."

"Fine. Then I'll simply say this: If we see that these cells have an extra twenty-first chromosome, which is technically called trisomy twenty-one, we can safely diagnose Down's syndrome. Remember, the human body is made up of cells, and every single cell in that body has exactly the same chromosomal pattern. If one cell has an extra twenty-first chromosome, then so do all the others."

"I take it, Dr. Barrington, that you're familiar with a procedure known as the alpha-fetoprotein test."

"Certainly."

"And that involves testing the mother's blood?"

"Yes, although we can also determine the AFP level from the amnionic fluid."

"Can you explain to the jurors how the condition of the fetus can be determined by testing the mother's blood?"

"Fetal urine contains alpha-fetoprotein, and the fetus secretes urine into the amnionic sac. Traces of this alpha-fetoprotein are transferred through membranes into the mother's bloodstream. By measuring those levels we can approximate the levels of alpha-fetoprotein in the fetus. Although this test is not as precise as a test of the amnionic fluid, it's risk-free and serves as a useful tool in telling us whether we should take the next step and do the amniocentesis."

"Tell us, Doctor, is it important to know the gestational age—the age of the fetus—when measuring the alpha-fetoprotein?"

"Oh, absolutely," he replied, as if the answer were obvious.

"And why is that?"

"Because the concentration of alpha-fetoprotein changes during the pregnancy. It decreases rapidly in the fetal blood and in the amnionic fluid after about the thirteenth week, but it increases just as rapidly in the mother's blood during the entire pregnancy. It would therefore be impossible to know whether the concentration was high or low without knowing when the pregnancy began."

"And would a miscalculation of the gestational age of, say, three weeks be significant?"

"Indeed it would. As I said, the changes in the concentration are rapid, and over a three-week period the levels change dramatically."

"Assume, if you will, that a mother is eighteen weeks pregnant, but the person reading the AFP test results thinks that she's only fifteen weeks pregnant. Would that error cause a normal reading to appear abnormal, or vice versa?"

"Yes, it would. If we were reading the AFP levels in

the mother's blood, a low level might appear quite normal."

"And in that case," Charlie said, his arms widespread, "further testing that *should* be done might *not* be done. Is that correct?"

"Yes, that would be correct," Peter Barrington responded. "That's why, Mr. Mayfield, we always try to verify the age of the fetus—so as to avoid just that kind of mistake. It's not safe to rely solely on the mother's memory as to the date of her last period."

"How do you make this verification?"

"Several changes are constantly taking place in both the fetus and the mother during pregnancy, and by monitoring these changes we can make independent estimates as to the age of the fetus. For example, just the size, shape, feel, and position of the mother's uterus, which we examine by hand during office visits, help us calculate how far along the mother is. Then, too, we can accurately estimate the age of the fetus by using ultrasound."

"Thank you, Doctor. I'll ask you more about ultrasound in a few minutes."

Charlie walked over to stand next to the jury box before asking his next questions. He knew that Dr. Barrington's answers to these questions could nail Sinclair, and he wanted to be sure the witness was looking toward the jurors when he spoke.

"Doctor, have you seen the results of the alpha-fetoprotein test administered to Tracey Walton on October twentieth, 1987?"

"Yes, I personally checked the records of the lab where Mrs. Walton's blood was sent for analysis."

"And were the AFP levels in her blood normal?"

"As I said before, Mr. Mayfield, that would depend on how far along she was in her pregnancy. If she was in her fifteenth week, the levels would appear to be within normal limits. But if she had those same levels in her *eighteenth* week, they would be abnormally low—so low that further testing would be called for."

"And what would that further testing consist of?"

"When we see low AFP levels in the mother's blood at that stage of the pregnancy, two specific tests come to mind—amniocentesis and ultrasound."

"You already explained the amniocentesis, Dr. Barrington. Now tell us about the ultrasound."

"Ultrasound is rather like an X-ray, except that high-frequency sound waves are applied instead of radiation to produce pulse-echo images. The test is totally painless and risk-free, and can provide vital information about the development of a fetus. Sonography, or ultrasound, has become so advanced that multiple pulse-echo systems can be applied in sequence so we can actually observe fetal movement such as breathing and heart behavior."

"Can an ultrasound help detect Down's syndrome in a fetus?"

"Yes, indeed. It would allow us to measure the femur—that's the thighbone—and the fetal head. Both have unique characteristics in Down fetuses. Also, a fetus with this disease has thickened neck folds and digital—that is, finger and toe—abnormalities that are often visible on an ultrasonic image. And finally, up to fifty percent of Down fetuses have heart malformations, and these can often be seen during an ultrasound."

Charlie was shaking his head in feigned amazement as Peter Barrington finished the last answer. "That sure sounds like a remarkable procedure."

"It is, Mr. Mayfield. It's indispensable."

"And you say it's risk-free?"

"That's right."

"It doesn't even present a *minor* risk?" Charlie asked.

"No risk at all."

"Tell me, Dr. Barrington, do you use ultrasound on all your patients?"

"I certainly do, and I recommend that other obstetricians do likewise. But," he added, shaking his head, "some don't ultrasound their patients unless there are special circumstances."

Charlie hoped the jurors remembered Tracey testifying

that she hadn't had an ultrasound, but he would bring that point up again when he got Sinclair on the stand. For now he simply walked back to his counsel table to scan a few documents—a stalling tactic to give the jurors a short respite after hearing a half hour of technical testimony.

He mentally reviewed the three grounds on which he would later argue that Steve Sinclair had been negligent. First and foremost, he had misread the results of the alpha-fetoprotein test on Tracey's blood. Second, Charlie would argue that Sinclair was lax in not granting Tracey's request for amniocentesis, even though he was sure that Lew Beck would point out that the procedure involved a minor risk and that Sinclair was therefore justified in not doing it. And third, Charlie would argue that Sinclair was remiss in not doing a risk-free ultrasound. His negligence in any one of these areas could account for his failure to detect Angel's condition, and that was all Charlie needed to support a favorable verdict.

"I have just a few more questions, Doctor," Charlie said as he walked back toward the jury box.

The witness straightened in his seat. Charlie was aware that Barrington knew what was coming next and that he wanted his answers to be both clear and correct. Expert witnesses like this one were theoretically unbiased, but Charlie knew that they dearly wanted "their" side to win. A natural alliance, almost a bond, was formed among all of the people working on either the plaintiff's or the defendant's team, and everyone wanted to be part of a winning effort. Indeed, Charlie suspected that the expert witness often had an extra incentive, because his or her testimony could mean the difference between winning and losing. During his years as a lawyer, Charlie had often detected a kind of competition among expert witnesses who often went head to head against each other, and this rivalry produced a contest within a contest. A loss meant that the *other* expert was more credible, more persuasive, and that might translate into a dent in one's prestige as well as one's pride. Barrington, he knew, would do his best for his team.

"I'd like to go back to the alpha-fetoprotein test," Charlie said, resuming his examination. "First of all, how reliable is it when testing the mother's blood, as was done in this case?"

"First, Mr. Mayfield, you must remember that the AFP test is not used to diagnose any particular disease. We use it only to see if there is an abnormally high or low concentration of alpha-fetoprotein. If there is, then we do additional testing to find out exactly what the problem is. But to answer your question, the AFP test has about a seventy-five percent reliability, perhaps higher."

"But if you get a high or low reading, it's still a danger signal, isn't it?"

"Oh, yes. Very much so."

"What would, say, a very high reading tell you?" Although Tracey Walton had had a *low* concentration of alpha-fetoprotein in her blood, Charlie wanted to ask a few broad questions to remind the jurors that his witness was truly an expert in the field.

"A high reading would tell us that we might have any one of several problems and that we would have to do further testing. The problem could be severe kidney or liver disease, esophageal or intestinal blockage, urinary obstruction, osteogenesis imperfecta—that's a fragility of the baby's bones—or, most serious, a neural tube defect."

"What is a neural tube defect?"

"An abnormality in the spinal core, in the brain stem, or in the brain itself. One such abnormality is anencephaly—a marked defect in the development of the brain to the extent that there is only a rudimentary brain stem and only traces of basal ganglia present; there aren't even bones for the cranial vault. Another more common neural tube defect is spina bifida—an absence of the vertebral arches—which allows spinal membrane to protrude."

"Thank you, Doctor. Now I'd like to ask—"

"Excuse me, Mr. Mayfield, but I think I should add something to my answer."

"Of course."

"A high AFP concentration doesn't necessarily mean that any of these conditions exist. As I said earlier, it's only about seventy-five percent accurate. And a high reading might only mean that the mother is carrying twins or that the doctor reading the test results has miscalculated the age of the fetus. We never know until we do further testing."

"That's helpful, Doctor, thank you. Now, what would you think if you saw a *low* AFP concentration in the mother's blood?"

"Well, first I'd double-check the age of the fetus— overestimation of gestational age is one of the most common explanations of what appears to be an abnormally low reading. But if I had already verified the age, then I'd consider the possibility of a chromosomal trisomy such as Down's syndrome. Of course, a low AFP reading could also mean that the fetus is not alive, but that's easy enough to check and rule out right away."

"So what you're saying, if I understand you, is that if you had seen Tracey Walton's AFP, and if you believed her to be in her eighteenth week of pregnancy, you would immediately have suspected Down's syndrome. Is that correct?"

"Yes, that's correct."

"And then you'd have ordered an amniocentesis?"

"Certainly, right away."

"What about an ultrasound?"

Dr. Barrington smiled. "I routinely would have done an ultrasound before that time, in which case I might already have suspected Down's syndrome. As I said earlier, I order ultrasound for all my patients."

Charlie had known all along that Tracey and Sinclair would disagree on the answer to the most important question of all: Did Tracey tell him during that first visit that her last menstrual period started in mid-June, as *she* claimed, or did she say it began on July fifth, as *he*

claimed. If Charlie could bring out evidence that corroborated her version, he could ice the case. And now
was the time to do that.

"Dr. Barrington, did you, at my request, examine all of
the hospital and medical records relating to Tracey
Walton's pregnancy and the delivery of her child?"

"Yes, I did."

"And based upon that examination, did you form an
opinion as to the date of her last menstrual period?"

"Yes."

"What parts of the records did you examine to form
this opinion?"

"First, I checked the baby's birth weight. Angel
Walton weighed a shade under eight pounds—seven
pounds fourteen ounces to be exact. That's a good size,
especially for a Down child. That would be a strong
indication of a full-term baby. Since the date of birth was
March 16, 1988, I am led to believe that the date of conception—which we measure from the date the mother
started her last menses—was in mid-June 1987."

"Did you see anything else in those records, in
addition to the baby's weight, that supports that opinion?"

"Yes, I did. Because Angel was born with complications, she underwent extensive testing immediately after
her birth. I studied the results of those tests, which
described every aspect of her development. That development was entirely consistent with a full-term baby,
again suggesting that the mother's last menstrual period
was in mid-June 1987."

Charlie, like every other trial lawyer, always wanted
the favorable testimony to be stated in two or three
different ways so there was no chance the jury could miss
it. "And now I'd like to ask you, Dr. Barrington, if you
saw anything in those records to indicate that the date of
conception, measured from Tracey Walton's last menstrual period, could have been three weeks later? Specifically, July 5, 1987?"

"No, I saw nothing whatsoever to indicate that." He

leaned toward the jury to explain his unequivocal answer. "If Angel's conception had been measured from early July, then her birth in mid-March would have been three weeks premature. Based upon both her size and her development at birth, she clearly was not premature— and certainly not three weeks premature." Peter Barrington felt a twinge of regret for having to put that extra nail in Steve Sinclair's coffin. He had met Steve professionally on a few occasions and had no reason to doubt his competency. However, the truth was the truth, and he resented medical witnesses who modified their opinions to protect fellow doctors charged with malpractice.

Charlie gave a silent sigh of relief. Barrington's last answers were perfect. No way would the jury believe that Tracey's last period was in July, regardless of what Sinclair's records said—not after hearing Peter Barrington. But he figured it wouldn't hurt to gild the lily.

"One other question on this point, Doctor. Was there anything you would have *liked* to see to help verify the date of conception, but didn't see?"

"Yes, sir. An ultrasound. That would have given me a chance to see fetal development quite clearly, and there is probably no better tool than that for ascertaining gestational age."

"And why didn't you see an ultrasound?" Charlie asked while looking at the jurors.

"I was told that Tracey Walton never had an ultrasound during her entire pregnancy."

"Whose responsibility is it to order an ultrasound?"

"The obstetrician." For the first time since taking the stand, Peter Barrington looked at Steve Sinclair with an expression that said "I'm sorry, pal, but you screwed up."

"Let's take fifteen minutes," Judge Grubner announced.

Peter Barrington had been an outstanding witness so far. Charlie was sure the jury trusted him and accepted everything he was saying. Now, after the recess, he decided to deal with the issue of minor risk.

"Tell us, Doctor, what are the risks associated with amniocentesis?"

"First of all, while the risks can be serious, I must point out that problems develop only quite rarely, particularly when the procedure is done by someone with a great deal of experience. But to answer your question, there are three risks." He held up three fingers as if he were lecturing. "First, a misdirected needle could cause some damage to the fetus, the placenta, or, less often, the umbilical cord or the mother herself. Second, there is the chance of infection. And third, the procedure might precipitate premature labor and abort the pregnancy."

"Have any studies been conducted, Doctor, to determine the *percentage* of risk? In other words, how often does one of these things really happen?"

"I'm familiar with studies done here in the United States as well as in Canada and England. Based on those studies and on what I have seen with my own eyes, I would say that there is a less than one percent chance of something going wrong during amniocentesis."

Charlie looked incredulous. "Did you say *less than one percent?* That ninety-nine times out of a hundred everything is perfectly all right?"

"Yes, that's my opinion, and it's a generally accepted statistic."

"Do you order amniocentesis for all your patients?"

"No, I don't. The small risk I described earlier—less than one percent—is enough to negate amniocentesis as a routine procedure in all cases."

"Then let me ask you this, Doctor. Would *you* have prescribed amniocentesis for Tracey Walton?"

"Objection!" Lew Beck interjected before the witness could answer. "The question calls for speculation, Your Honor. Dr. Barrington was not Tracey Walton's doctor. How could he possibly know for certain what he would have done five years ago if he *had* been her doctor? His answer would be influenced by hindsight—hindsight that Dr. Sinclair could not have had at the time—and to allow it would be highly prejudicial to the defense."

"Not so, Judge," Charlie responded, waving his hand as if to brush aside Beck's objection. "My question would call for speculation only if the witness would be speculating. But I suggest to the court that the witness would *not* be speculating. He would not be speculating because he *knows* what he would have done." Charlie was suggesting the same test the judge had applied when Tracey was asked whether she would have had an abortion. "Ask him, Judge, if he knows."

Horace Grubner took the bait. He turned to the witness and asked, "Dr. Barrington, sitting here today, five years after Mrs. Walton's pregnancy, do you know—and I mean *know*, not *think* you know—whether or not you would have ordered an amniocentesis? Just answer yes or no."

"Yes, I know what I would have done."

"Objection overruled."

Charlie looked over to Lew Beck in time to see the defense lawyer brace himself for the question and answer that would inevitably follow.

"And what would you have done, Dr. Barrington?" Charlie asked. "Would you have ordered the amniocentesis?"

"Yes, I definitely would have."

Charlie could see that Beck was doing his best to act as if the answer meant nothing. But Steve Sinclair, apparently forgetting his attorney's instruction against making gestures, bolted upright, frowned, and shook his head from side to side. Lew Beck quickly nudged him.

"How can you be so sure?" Charlie said, turning back to his witness.

"Three reasons," he responded. "First, I would already have sonographed Mrs. Walton, as I do all my patients. The ultrasound alone might have told me that we had a possible Down fetus."

"Because of the shape of the head and the neck folds?" Charlie asked.

"Yes, and the short femurs and possibly other abnormalities. That would have persuaded me to do an amniocentesis."

"But isn't it a fact that the ultrasound will not reveal these symptoms in all Down fetuses?"

"That's correct. It could miss them. But—and this brings me to my second reason—the ultrasound gives us a very good indication of the age of the fetus. It would have told me that the fetus was considerably older than Dr. Sinclair's records showed—that the date of conception was closer to mid-June than early July. And I would have taken that into consideration when reviewing the alpha-fetoprotein test. Accordingly, I would have suspected that the AFP level was low, and that, too, would have told me to do an amniocentesis."

"And what's the third reason?" Charlie asked.

"Well, that's the most compelling reason of all. I understand that Mrs. Walton was terribly worried about having an imperfect baby and that she specifically requested an amniocentesis."

Lew Beck leaped to his feet. "Your Honor, with all deference to the witness and to Mr. Mayfield, this is an *outrage*. How could Dr. Barrington 'understand' that Mrs. Walton requested an amniocentesis? No such request appears in any of the hospital or medical records that the witness examined to *prepare* his testimony." Beck stressed "prepare" as if it were a dirty word. "That so-called request, which is flatly denied by Dr. Sinclair, exists only in the testimony of Mrs. Walton, and this witness was not even in the courtroom when Mrs. Walton testified. *This is a setup, Your Honor,*" Beck shouted with uncharacteristic emotion. "To permit this witness to proceed would be a travesty."

But his emotion was lost on Horace Grubner. "I'll allow it as a hypothetical question."

"But, Judge—"

"I've made my ruling, Mr. Beck. I'll ask the hypothetical question myself." Swiveling his chair to face the witness, the judge asked, "Dr. Barrington, assuming Mrs. Walton was your patient, and assuming further that she told you of her fear of having a child with birth defects and that she specifically requested an amniocentesis, would that have influenced your decision to prescribe that the test be done?"

"Yes," Peter Barrington replied. "Let me explain. When I treat a patient, I treat the *whole* patient—her psychological side as well as her physical side. A patient's state of mind is important to her, and it's important to me as her physician. But even more important, my experience has taught me that emotional anxieties can intensify—and can even cause—physical disorders. If I believed that Mrs. Walton had a special fear of having a defective child, and that we could alleviate that fear by doing a test that had less than a one percent risk of complication, then certainly I would have made sure that we did that test. And, at the risk of sounding immodest, in my own practice the risk of complication is far less than one percent."

Nothing that had occurred to this point in the trial had made such an impact, and had such a devastating effect on the defense, as Peter Barrington's last few answers. But Charlie Mayfield wanted one more ounce of blood.

He lumbered back to the counsel table, but before he sat down he turned to the witness and said, "So it's clear then, Dr. Barrington, that if Tracey Walton had been seeing you instead of Steven Sinclair, she would have known that she was carrying a child with Down's syndrome. Is that what you're telling us?"

"Objection!"

"Never mind, Judge, I'll withdraw the question."

To hell with the answer, Charlie was thinking as he sat down. It was the *question* I wanted the jury to hear.

FIFTEEN ====

PETER BARRINGTON'S DIRECT examination had taken all morning on this, the third day of *Walton v. Sinclair*. But as strong as his testimony had been, Charlie Mayfield couldn't afford to let up. He had been through too many trials where crucial witnesses performed beautifully, only to be torn apart on cross-examination. He himself had done his share of tearing apart in the past, and so, he knew, had Lew Beck. The fact that Beck had waived cross-examination with the other two doctors didn't mean a thing. Charlie knew he would come after Peter Barrington loaded for bear.

Beck's opponents—Charlie included—had learned that his low-key, textbook courtroom manner was not to be confused with apathy or indifference, especially when it came to cross-examination. His meticulous preparation, coupled with intelligence, experience, persistence, and a killer instinct, had nullified the testimony of many hostile witnesses. This wasn't apparent from his handling of Tracey Walton on the stand because she had testified to very little that he could challenge, and she was an aggrieved mother who had to be treated with tenderness. Not so with Dr. Peter Barrington. Charlie knew that if Beck wanted to score enough points to win the game, he would have to start now, and that meant he would go for Barrington's jugular.

Scoping out the situation, Charlie believed that his case would not get any stronger than it was at that very moment—*before* Peter Barrington's cross-examination.

And it followed that if there was ever going to be a settlement, this would be the ideal time to make it happen. "When I start to deal," he always told his clients, "I like to deal from strength, not from weakness." So, as they were preparing to break for lunch, he sidled over to Lew Beck who was writing on a yellow legal pad.

"Wanna talk, Lew?"

Beck said he'd like to but would have to invite the insurance man along.

Charlie understood.

Charlie, Lew, and Duane DeLuca stood together in front of the Cook County Courthouse near the famous Picasso sculpture that looked like a baboon to some, a prehistoric bird to others, and a tangle of rusty metal to most.

"Should we do this over lunch?" the ever-hungry DeLuca asked, relighting a half-smoked cigar.

"Nah," Charlie said quickly, "shouldn't take that long."

Beck, apparently hoping to reinstall himself as the negotiator for the defense team, grabbed the reins. "You called the meeting, Charlie. Does that mean you've decided to come down off your four and a half million?"

"Not really, Lew." Charlie tried not to sound too unyielding. While he would have preferred to stand pat, the Waltons had authorized him to settle for four million. They were the clients and they had the final say, and he was duty bound to try to settle at or near that figure regardless of his personal feelings. "But when I told my people that Duane here tossed another half million on the table yesterday, I sensed that they *might* be willing to consider something less than the four and a half. I don't think they'll move much, though," he added. "Tracey's already done her bit on the stand, so she doesn't have to worry about that anymore, and they're feeling damn good about the way things are going, especially Barrington's testimony."

"I suppose," Beck said, "but I've got a few things to

ask your Dr. Barrington this afternoon. Maybe they won't feel so good after the cross-examination."

"Now Lew," Charlie said playfully as he lightly cuffed his adversary's shoulder, "let's not rattle our sabers."

"All right, you're still at four-five, and we're at two-seven. Correct?"

"Correct," Charlie echoed.

"And we made the last move? In fact, the last two moves?"

"No, I made the last move by calling for this get-together."

"Aw, c'mon, Charlie," DeLuca pleaded. "You can't call that a move. Hell, you haven't even told us that your people *would* move, only that you sensed that they *might*."

"Which is telling you more than I had before. And anyway, Duane, you can read between the lines." The sentence came out a little different from what Charlie had intended, and Beck and DeLuca exchanged glances.

Beck decided to expand the metaphor. "And how much space is there between the lines, Charlie? Is the bottom line below four million?"

"Hell no. I said they might move a *little,* not come down like Humpty-Dumpty."

"So you're telling us that you won't come down more than half a million, but you expect us to come up by more than a million three—and that's on top of the half million that Duane threw in the pot yesterday."

"Yeah, Lew, that's what I'm saying. But don't try to make me sound like a hard-ass. I'm sitting on a realistic number, and you're not. You can't make me a shitty offer, then add a penny to it and claim that now it's my turn."

Beck held out his arms. "I'm not saying you're a hard-ass, Charlie. I'm just trying to figure out where you're standing. Can I assume from what you've said that you won't go below four, but that four might buy the case?"

The question put Charlie in a bind. If he said yes, that he could settle for four million, they might offer it on the spot. But if he said yes and then they *didn't* offer it, he'd be screwed. Then four would be the highest number he'd ever see, and he'd have gotten nothing for the concession. "Well," he hedged, "maybe not four, but maybe something closer to four than to four-point-five."

If this had been a wrestling match—and in a way it was—the referee would have shouted "Reversal" and awarded two points to Charlie. Now he knew that Beck and DeLuca had to make a decision. Would they try to wrap it up now for about four-point-two million, or would they try to get away with less? That had to be the question racing through their minds.

"Give us a minute to talk, Charlie," the insurance man said. "Wait here." He started to lead Beck a few feet off to the side.

Charlie hated these asinine settlement negotiations where each side moved by nickels and dimes. He wanted to end this thing over the lunch hour or else give it to the jury to decide, and the best way to do that was to let these two guys know that he was done with the foreplay. "Hey, take all the time you want," he said as he picked up his briefcase. "I'm going to have lunch. I'll see you back here at one-fifteen. If you have something for me then, fine; if not, we'll go back to work." He started to walk away, then turned and said, "Ya know, every time we talk, the price comes down, and a third of that comes out of my own pocket. So do me a favor this afternoon: Tell me we don't have a deal and that I should go fuck myself."

"And then I told them to do me a favor this afternoon and tell me to go screw myself." The Waltons and Bernard Benedict were in Charlie's office, and he had just finished telling them about his five-minute meeting with Beck and DeLuca. Although he offered a somewhat expurgated version, he accurately recapped the status of the settlement negotiations. "You should have seen 'em standing there with their fingers in their asses when I trotted off."

Tracey winced.

Charlie caught her reaction and turned his hands palms up in a gesture of apology. He suspected that she heard salty language from construction crews at job sites, but she apparently wasn't comfortable with it in a business or professional setting.

"So what do you think will happen?" Bernard Benedict asked. "Will they pay the four-point-two?"

"I hope not." Seeing their stunned expressions, Charlie explained, "Of course, when I say that I'm only speaking for myself. My big toe is still telling me that the jury'll give us more than that, but I'm still doing my best to settle for the four million you told me you'd take. You're the bosses."

"But," Larry said, "you've never told them we'd take four million. You never even said for sure that we'd take four-point-two."

Charlie might have let the comment go under other circumstances. But ever since he had learned of Larry's cynicism about personal injury litigation, and especially since he'd found out that Larry wasn't convinced that Steve Sinclair was responsible for his daughter's condition, Charlie'd had trouble accepting him as part of the team. In that light, he took the comment as a personal insult. "Listen, Larry," he said forcefully, "I know you don't think much of this lawsuit, and it's pretty clear that you don't think much of me. Well, I don't think much of architects, either, but if I hired one I'd either take his advice or get rid of him. Now, if you and Tracey want to fire me, go ahead, but until you do, this lawsuit is going to be run the way I want to run it. And that includes the settlement negotiations."

"Okay, okay, but I don't—"

"And I still don't know what in the hell I'm supposed to do with *you*. The jury expects me to put you on the stand, and it'll raise a lot of questions if I don't, but I'm scared to death to let you get up there. If you don't believe in this case—I mean, really believe that we're the good guys and Sinclair is a reckless quack—it'll show. Everyone in the courtroom will see it. You're not a good enough actor to fool the jury, especially with Beck cross-examining you. He'll jump all over you about the divorce, just like he did with Tracey. And what'll you tell him? That Tracey was never home? That she was too busy with her job to pay any attention to her husband and child? Or are you going to tell them that you split because it was too inconvenient having a sick kid around the house? One wrong answer out of you and they'll throw Angel out of court on her little ass."

"Are you finished?" Larry asked.

"Yeah," Charlie answered, "I'm finished." He popped the lid on a can of soda and leaned back in his chair.

"Then I'm going to tell you how I feel about this case and why I was against filing it. If you decide to use me as a witness after that, fine. It'll be up to you."

The lawyer took a swig of his soda. "Go ahead, I'm listening."

"First of all, Charlie, I have nothing against you personally. You're good at what you do, and I respect that. And I don't really have a problem with personal injury litigation in general. There are times when it's justified. If someone is injured because of someone else's negligence, that person *should* be compensated, at least for medical expenses and lost income. But I *do* have a problem when someone gets filthy rich from an injury, especially when the decision to award the money is based on nothing more than sympathy."

Larry took a deep breath. "And that's really what bothers me about this case, Charlie. Our daughter has Down's syndrome, and she'll have it after this case is over, regardless of the settlement or the jury verdict. Even if we get four million dollars—or, for that matter, *forty* million dollars—Angel will never walk or talk like other children. Her mind still won't work. And pretty soon she'll be dead and we'll have all that money.

"So we'll be making a profit—an actual *profit*—or at least Tracey will, because I've agreed that she can have the whole amount. I decided a long time ago that I don't want to get rich from this tragedy. My conscience wouldn't let me buy an expensive sports car or take a lavish vacation with money that came from Angel's suffering.''

Larry looked at Tracey and then continued. "And there's another thing: I've never been convinced that Dr. Sinclair did anything wrong. We know he didn't cause Angel to have Down's, and we know he couldn't have cured it. Okay, maybe he should have detected it. Who knows? But so what? I probably would've wanted to have Angel anyway. And if Lew Beck asks me that question, that's what I'll tell him. Tracey testified that we agreed we'd have an abortion if our baby had a serious birth defect, but I don't recall any discussions like that.''

He sighed and said, "So you see, Charlie, why I feel the way I do. I don't like asking for all this money—more than we'd ever need to take care of Angel, especially after what we're getting from our medical insurance. And I don't like trying to get it from Dr. Sinclair." He sat back, relieved to have that off his chest.

Tracey turned toward her ex-husband and said, almost apologetically, "Remember, Larry, we're not going after Dr. Sinclair personally. He has insurance for five million, and I already told Charlie and Daddy that we won't ask for more than that.''

"Makes no difference. Five million's more than we need, and in the meantime we'd be ruining the poor guy's reputation. And I'll bet his malpractice insurance premiums will triple because of this lawsuit. No, Tracey, I'm sorry, but I don't like it.''

Charlie clasped his hands behind his head. He wasn't the least bit moved by what Larry Walton had said. He had other things on his mind. "I'm glad we had that out, Larry," he said, "but I still have to decide whether to call you as a witness." He was already of the mind that he couldn't put Larry on the stand—especially after hearing how he planned to answer the abortion question. "May I ask you something?"

"Of course.''

"Why *did* you and Tracey get divorced?''

Larry fidgeted with his wristwatch for several seconds. Finally, without looking at Tracey, he said, "Well, at first everything was fine between us—at least I thought it was. Oh, sure, we had some disagreements, usually about the long hours and the weekends she worked, but I didn't think they amounted to anything. Then, about the time Tracey became pregnant with Angel, she began to act differently toward me. Kind of distant, not as affectionate. I chalked it up to the pregnancy and didn't worry much about it. I figured everything would be fine after the baby, but . . ." Larry stopped and glanced uncomfortably at his father-in-law.

"Go ahead," Charlie urged. "I have to hear this. Beck's going to ask you about it if I put you on the stand, and I don't need any surprises."

Larry took a deep breath and nodded. "It just got worse after Angel was born. I guess I'd describe Tracey's attitude toward me as . . . cordial, tolerant, something like that. Certainly not loving. And I don't think it had anything to do with Angel's sickness. That was tough on her, I'll be the first to admit that, but, hell, it was tough on both of us. She was obviously unhappy with *me,* and I was never able to figure out why. I'd ask her, but I'd get evasive answers like, 'Oh, nothing's the matter.'

"Then, after we were finally able to get full-time help for Angel—help that Tracey felt comfortable with   she began to spend more and more time at her job. She had always put in long hours, but now it became almost compulsive. I'm sure a lot of it had to do with the fact that the construction business was going through hard times, but I was beginning to resent spending more time with Angel's nurse than with my own wife." Larry paused to look at Tracey. "And I resented the fact that I spent more time with Angel than she did." He turned back to Charlie. "About a year ago, after I convinced myself that things weren't going to get any better, I brought up the subject of divorce. Tracey seemed almost relieved. I moved out, and that was that."

Charlie stood up and walked over to the window. With

his back to the room he put another question to Larry: "If Beck asked you, like he asked Tracey, why you got divorced, would you tell him all that? And would you tell him that you and Tracey never talked about abortion?"

"If he asks the questions, I'll have to answer them truthfully."

Charlie nodded.

Yeah, sure I'll call you as a witness, he thought to himself. When pigs whistle and chickens piss.

Lew Beck was beside himself. "Damn it, Duane," he said, "you just don't understand. Charlie's not like those personal injury shysters who'll grab any check you wave in front of them—the kind of guys *you're* used to dealing with. He's made more money than you and I will ever see, and he's done it by winning his cases, not settling them. I'm telling you, you can't bluff him."

"And I'm telling you, that's bullshit. I've negotiated with good lawyers and bad lawyers, rich lawyers and poor lawyers, and they all have the same goal in common—to grab the money and run. And your pal Charlie Mayfield is no different from the rest of those fuckin' ambulance chasers."

Several uncomfortable moments passed while Lew Beck picked at his salad and Duane DeLuca wolfed down a plate of lasagna.

"Look, Lew," the insurance man finally mumbled through a mouthful of food, "if Mayfield is so damn cocky about going to the jury, why in the hell did he ask to see us a little while ago? Answer me that. And why did he come down three hundred thousand?"

"He never came out and said for *sure* he'd take the four-point-two."

"But don't you understand? That's the way those plaintiff's guys talk. When they say they *might* be able to get their client to consider a certain figure, you can bet your sweet ass that they'd kill their mothers and sell their children to get it. Hell, Mayfield couldn't have been clearer about wanting the four-point-two if he tattooed it on his forehead, and I translate that to mean he'll take less.

"And there's something else you're missing," DeLuca added, holding up his fork to emphasize the point. "He's already put on his client and his three experts. His case'll never be stronger than it is right now. So why does good ol' Charlie pick *now* to come to us with a lower number? I'll tell you why. Because he's afraid of something. Maybe it's your cross-examination of this Barrington guy, or maybe it's Sinclair, but whatever it is, Lew, the guy's scared of *something*."

"Okay, Duane, let's assume, just for the sake of argument, that you're right, that Charlie'd take four-point-two right now and that he's got a weak spot we don't know about. What do you propose we do?"

"Nothing," DeLuca replied as he sat back and loosened his necktie. "Absolutely nothing."

Beck looked up in disbelief. "Are you out of your frigging mind?"

"Trust me, he'll come down before we go up."

"But you have authority from Boston to pay four-point-two if he'll take it, and you yourself just said that he *would* take it. So give it to him and we can all get the hell out of here."

The insurance man smiled as he dipped his napkin into his water glass and used it to wipe his hands. "That's not the way I do business, Lew. Maybe that's how those junior-level insurance adjusters work, which explains why they're given the two-bit fender-benders to settle. But I didn't get where I got by giving away company money. My job is to *save* money, not spend it. And when I fly back to Beantown, I'll not only have this case settled but I'll bring back some of that four-point-two for the boys in the front office."

"If you're so damn sure that Charlie's running scared, why in the hell did you chase him down the hall yesterday and offer him another half million? Is that the way you earn your brownie points back at headquarters?"

"Okay, maybe I screwed up with that half million, but

things were different yesterday. He was at four-point-five and showed no sign of budging. He seemed to think he couldn't lose. But everything changed an hour ago. Now *he* comes to *us,* and with a lower number. I tell ya, Lew, something's going on in their camp. Once you go to work on Barrington this afternoon, Charlie'll be back to us on his knees."

Beck was shaking his head. "I've known Charlie for more than twenty years, and I've never seen him on his knees."

"So maybe *he* isn't scared. Maybe his *clients* are starting to panic. Same difference. Either way he'll come crawling back."

"So what do we tell him at one-fifteen?"

"*Fuck* him. It's time we teach ol' Charlie a little humility. We're staying right here and having dessert."

Larry Walton had left the others at Charlie's office, telling them that he'd meet them in the courtroom at one-thirty. Charlie took advantage of his absence and explained to Tracey and her father that it would be too dangerous to allow Larry to testify. "If he said those things to the jury, Trace—especially that business about your work keeping you away from Angel—it'd kill us."

"I understand," Tracey said. Then she leaned forward and said earnestly, "But he's wrong about that. Maybe that's how he saw it, but it just isn't true. I hope both of you believe that."

Charlie and her father assured her that they did.

Then Tracey, seeing her lawyer looking over his morning's phone messages, said, "Oh, that reminds me, Charlie, I have to make a quick phone call before we go back to court. Do you have an extra office I can use?"

"Sure, just ask my secretary and she'll set you up."

"If it's business," Bernard Benedict said, "let it go. You've got enough on your mind as it is."

"It's no big deal, Daddy. I just want to call Dave Roberts to find out about that Civic Center bid."

"Hell, honey, that can wait. Call him later."

"I can't. He's leaving town this afternoon, and he won't be back in his office until Monday." She started toward the door. "I'll only be a few minutes."

Benedict glanced at his wristwatch and then spun around toward Charlie. "Hey, it's already past one! Hadn't you better get moving if you're going to meet those guys at one-fifteen?"

"To hell with 'em. If they have a good number for us, they'll let me know in court. In the meantime, let 'em wait around and try to figure out what that Picasso's supposed to be."

SIXTEEN ═══

DR. PETER BARRINGTON nodded when Judge Grubner reminded him that he was still under oath. He noticed that Lew Beck wore a tight smile as he stood up and spoke from behind his counsel table.

"My compliments, Dr. Barrington," he began. "You were an excellent witness."

"Thank you," Dr. Barrington said tentatively, not having expected the cross-examination to begin on a cordial note.

"I take it you've done this before?"

Now he knew where Beck was going. "Yes."

"How often, Doctor? In how many lawsuits have you performed as an expert witness?"

"Object to the word 'performed,'" Charlie Mayfield said from his chair.

Before the judge could rule, Beck turned to Charlie and said, "Oh, but it *was* a wonderful performance, Mr. Mayfield, and I should also compliment you for your part in it."

Horace Grubner banged his gavel before Charlie could respond. "Objection sustained. Just ask your questions, Mr. Beck. Save your editorializing for closing argument."

"Yes, Your Honor." Turning back to Barrington, Beck asked, "In how many lawsuits have you testified, Dr. Barrington?"

"Several."

"Can't you be more specific, Doctor? We can always check the records."

"Over twenty, perhaps as many as forty."

"And that does not include the cases in which you gave depositions but which were settled before trial, isn't that right?"

"Yes, that's right."

"So you may have participated in as many as a hundred cases. Would you agree with that?"

"Yes," he answered reluctantly, "I suppose that would be a fair estimate."

"And perhaps even more than that?" Beck prodded.

"Perhaps." The witness adjusted himself in his seat.

"And in how many cases have you testified for Mr. Mayfield?"

"Three or four, maybe five."

"But weren't there many more cases in which you advised him or gave depositions?"

"Yes."

"Tell us, Doctor, how much do you charge for your testimony in these cases?"

Peter Barrington had been in court often enough to expect these kinds of questions, and he knew it would be a mistake to fence with any lawyer asking them. Nevertheless, he found such questions distasteful, even insulting, and on more than one occasion he had lost his temper with lawyers who implied that his testimony was for sale. "Three hundred dollars an hour for preparation time," he answered, knowing it would sound like an enormous sum to the jurors, "and twenty-five hundred dollars for every day I testify."

"How many hours did you spend preparing for your testimony in this case, Doctor?"

"I'd have to check my records." He glared at Beck who remained silent, clearly not accepting that answer. After several uncomfortable seconds Barrington conceded. "Perhaps thirty hours, including the time I spent going over the medical records for Mrs. Walton and her daughter."

"And including the time you spent conferring with Mr. Mayfield?" No one missed the implication.

"Yes, including the time I spent with Mr. Mayfield."

"So by the end of today you will have earned nearly twelve thousand dollars on this case, correct?"

"About that."

"And you'd like to get *more* opportunities to earn twelve thousand dollars on Mr. Mayfield's cases. Isn't that right?"

"If you're suggesting that I tailored my testimony to suit Mr. Mayfield—"

"Oh, no, Dr. Barrington. Any suggestions here come from your answers, not from my questions."

Now that Beck had implied that maybe, just maybe, Peter Barrington was little more than a hired gun, he moved deliberately to the lectern, apparently intending to get to the substance of his cross-examination.

"Before you agreed to testify in this case, Doctor, had you known Dr. Sinclair?"

"We met professionally on a few occasions."

"And excluding this case, do you know of any instances in which Dr. Sinclair failed to exercise prudence in his practice of medicine?"

Technically, Barrington knew, the question was improper since Steve Sinclair's conduct in other cases was legally irrelevant, but Charlie clearly meant to let it pass, probably since he saw no need to dwell on the cases Sinclair had handled properly.

"No, I don't."

"Had you ever *heard* of any such accusation against Dr. Sinclair?"

"No."

"From *anyone*?"

"No."

"Now, Dr. Barrington, you told us this morning that you examined the lab report on the alpha-fetoprotein test, didn't you?"

"I did, yes." Peter Barrington relaxed a bit, relieved at the new line of questions.

Beck walked over to the witness stand and handed him a document. "Is this the lab report you examined?"

He studied it briefly and answered that it was.

The lawyer took back the document momentarily and pointed at something typed in the upper corner. "Tell the jury what this says."

" 'LMP, seven, five, eighty-seven.' "

"And what would you interpret that to mean, Dr. Barrington?"

"It means that, according to this report, Mrs. Walton's last menstrual period began on July 5, 1987. But as I testified, Mr. Beck, I don't agree with—"

"Just answer the questions, Doctor. We don't care whether you agree with the report; we only want to know what it says. Now, what is the date of that report?"

"October 20, 1987."

Beck walked back to the lectern before asking his next question. "How would the lab get the date of July fifth?"

"From the physician who sent the blood in for testing—in this case, Dr. Sinclair."

"So," Beck proclaimed, "way back in October of 1987 Dr. Sinclair believed that Tracey Walton's last menstrual period had begun on July fifth. Isn't that what you would understand from this report?"

"It would seem so, yes."

"Then wouldn't it be false to say that Dr. Sinclair altered his records to show the July fifth date *after* Angel was born in March of the following year?" Beck glared at Charlie while he asked the question.

"Yes, it would appear that he had that date in his records all along."

"And where would an obstetrician ordinarily get the date of his patient's last menstrual period?"

"From the patient."

"Thank you for acknowledging that, Doctor."

Beck moved to another area. "Didn't you testify this morning that you do ultrasounds on all your patients?"

"Only on the pregnant ones."

Lew Beck joined in the laughter. "Thank you for the

clarification. And didn't you say that all obstetricians should do likewise?"

"I did, yes. I firmly believe that ultrasounds should be standard procedure in all pregnancies."

"Sure, and my dentist believes that people should brush their teeth after every meal. But the issue in this case, Doctor, isn't what you think the standard procedure *should* be. It's what the standard procedure *is* among practicing obstetricians. So I'll put it to you point-blank: Is it the ordinary and customary practice among obstetricians in the city of Chicago, or anywhere else in the United States, to do ultrasounds on all their pregnant patients, even where there are no indications of medical complications?"

Barrington paused, formulating his answer.

"Well, Doctor, we're waiting. Would you like me to repeat the question?"

"No, that won't be necessary." Peter Barrington turned to face the jury, feeling the need to explain the testimony he had given that morning. "Even though the use of ultrasound is becoming more and more common, it is not yet considered a standard procedure for *all* doctors in *all* cases."

"It's not even covered by most medical insurance policies, is it?"

"No, not unless there are other indications of medical problems, in which case an ultrasound might be necessary for diagnosis or treatment. That's the only time that most insurance policies will cover it."

"I believe you said that you reviewed Dr. Sinclair's office records when you were preparing to testify in this case. Is that right?"

"Yes, I went over them quite carefully."

"And didn't those records indicate that he *tried* to order an ultrasound for Mrs. Walton, but that she never followed through to schedule it?"

"That's what his records say."

Beck didn't let him get away with the innuendo. "Do you have any reason to distrust his records, Doctor?"

"Well, no, I don't suppose so."

"Have you found any other entries in his records that you could point to as having been altered?"

"No."

"Even the date of Mrs. Walton's last menstrual period was *always* July fifth, right? Didn't we establish that from the information on the lab report?"

"Yes, that would appear to be the case."

"One more question about ultrasounds, Dr. Barrington, and I'd like to make it a hypothetical question. Assume an obstetrician recommends an ultrasound for a patient, but the patient is a busy career woman and she doesn't get around to scheduling the appointment to have it done in spite of her doctor reminding her to do so on at least one other occasion. Assume further that there are no indications of medical complications with the mother or the fetus, and that the mother is still in her twenties. In such a case, Dr. Barrington, do you know of any official or recognized obstetrical guidelines where it is recommended that the doctor in question take further steps to ensure that the patient has the ultrasound?"

"I know of no such guidelines."

"Thank you."

Lew Beck said, "And now, Dr. Barrington, I'd like to ask you a few questions about amniocentesis."

Peter Barrington nodded.

"You testified, as I recall, that there was about a one percent risk of something going wrong when that procedure is done. Is that correct?"

"I said *less* than one percent. And in all those that I did myself, the rate of complication was even lower."

"But when there *is* a complication from amniocentesis it can be very serious, can't it?"

"Indeed."

"It can cause permanent damage or even death to the fetus. Isn't that correct?"

"Yes, Mr. Beck, that's correct."

"And the mother can sustain serious injury?"

"Possibly."

Beck shuffled through his note cards for several seconds before finding the one he was looking for. He studied it, nodded to himself, and then looked up at the witness. "Isn't it a fact, Dr. Barrington, that a recent study concluded"—and here Beck enunciated each word for emphasis—"that the number of normal fetuses *lost* because of amniocentesis actually exceeds the number of abnormal fetuses *detected*?"

"Yes." Barrington sighed. "I'm familiar with that study."

"Do you agree with its conclusion?"

"I have no basis on which to disagree with it."

"Then I presume that a prudent obstetrician will not do an amniocentesis in the absence of some indication of special circumstances."

"That's correct. It should not be done indiscriminately."

"But you said this morning that if you had been Tracey Walton's doctor, and if she had asked you to do an amniocentesis because she was worried about the baby, you would have done it. Would you call *that* a special circumstance—special enough to jeopardize the health, and perhaps the life, of that same baby?"

Barrington knew he was trapped. If he said yes, he would sound like a quack who would take unnecessary risks just to appease a nervous mother; if he said no, he would be seen as having lied in his earlier testimony. "That's not exactly what I said this morning, Mr. Beck."

"It isn't? Well, let's find out." Beck nodded to the court reporter who, at his request, had already pinpointed the testimony in question. "Would you please read what Dr. Barrington said this morning?"

The reporter, in a monotone, read the testimony: "'If I believed that Mrs. Walton had a special fear of having a defective child, and that we could alleviate that fear by doing a test that had less than a one percent risk of complication, then certainly I would have made sure that we did that test.'"

"Now, Doctor, do you stand by your testimony from this morning, or would you care to correct it?"

Peter Barrington was sure everyone in the courtroom could see that he was shaken. "Well," he said, trying to brush away the inconsistencies in his testimony, "what I was trying to convey—"

"Never mind, Doctor. We all know what you were trying to convey. After all, isn't that why you're charging Mr. Mayfield twelve thousand dollars for your testimony?"

Good cross-examination!

SEVENTEEN

CHARLIE MAYFIELD HAD two missions. The first was to convince the jury that Steve Sinclair was liable to the plaintiffs—that is, that Sinclair did something wrong that caused damage to the plaintiffs. The second mission was to establish the *extent* of that damage. If Charlie did a good job on the first mission, his clients would win; if he did a good job on both, his clients would win *big*.

By the time Dr. Barrington stepped down from the witness stand, Charlie was satisfied that he had established liability. The jury should have no trouble believing that Sinclair had screwed up. Having the wrong date of conception in his records had caused a misreading of the alpha-fetoprotein test, and it was more likely that he wrote down the wrong date than that Tracey told him the wrong date. Her testimony on the dates had been very strong; she'd have had no reason to call Sinclair within a few days of being late with her early August period, especially with a history of irregular periods, which, fortunately, was confirmed by Sinclair's own records. And even if the jury wasn't convinced that he negligently wrote down the wrong date, they had plenty of reasons to think he was negligent in not *realizing* it was the wrong date, either then or shortly thereafter. He would have known that if had simply done an ultrasound, as Dr. Barrington said *he'd* have done. Even the shape and feel of Tracey's uterus, which he examined during her visits to his office, should have told him that.

Sure, Beck had done a good job of cross-examining

Tracey, and a great job of cross-examining Peter Barrington, but he'd done little more than chip away at the edges of rock-solid testimony. In fact, every one of Charlie's witnesses had done well and had made a strong impression on the jury. A hell of a lot stronger, he thought, than Sinclair would make. He recalled taking Sinclair's pretrial deposition and noticing how hesitant and unconvincing a witness he had been.

Charlie tended to his second mission—showing the *extent* of the damage resulting from Sinclair's negligence—by presenting witnesses who testified to the cost of caring for Angel for the rest of her life. The expenses, both past and projected, were for doctors, nurses, medicines, custodial care, and, if she could handle it, special schooling. The damage testimony took the better part of two days; no detail was too small to include.

Establishing Angel's life expectancy presented a special problem for Charlie. The longer she might live, the more the ongoing expenses of caring for her would accumulate and translate into a larger verdict. But her malformed and defective heart foretold a shorter life, and Charlie refused to concede, even to himself, that that added defect should mean a smaller verdict. He solved the problem by putting a pediatric cardiologist on the stand to expand on a point made earlier by Dr. Cynthia Caruso. Owing to new techniques, the cardiologist told the jury, a series of heart operations could conceivably prolong Angel's life—theoretically to middle age but more probably only into her teens or slightly beyond. This evidence had the extra benefit of allowing Charlie to add the cost of the heart surgery itself to the already staggering amount of other expenses.

"I have no further witnesses," he finally announced at three o'clock on Friday afternoon.

Horace Grubner raised his eyebrows. "May I presume, then, that you are resting your case?"

"Not quite, Your Honor. I'd like to have the jury meet Angel Walton. She won't be testifying, of course, but I thought the jurors might want to see her."

"Any objection, Mr. Beck?"

"No, sir," Beck replied, knowing that an objection would get shot down before it was out of his mouth.

With that, Charlie nodded to Larry Walton who quickly went to the rear of the courtroom and held the double doors open. A moment later a nurse, carefully guiding a wheelchair, entered the room and stopped in the aisle dividing the two halves of the spectators' section. Everyone's attention was riveted on the pathetic figure propped up in a corner of the wheelchair. Angel Walton's sad, drooping eyes seemed not to register anything around her, just as her open mouth seemed not to have anything to say. The crisp white bow pinned in her colorless hair seemed sadly out of place. For the first time since *Walton v. Sinclair* had begun, there was a noticeable absence of hostility in the courtroom. In the sudden silence the war games were temporarily suspended.

The nurse surrendered the wheelchair to Larry, who wheeled the child slowly down the aisle. Few in the courtroom missed the irony: This was surely the only aisle down which this father would ever escort this daughter. As they approached the counsel tables, Tracey came to meet them and lifted the almost lifeless body into her arms. If the child had any recognition of her mother it wasn't apparent. Tracey, gently patting and rocking her daughter, walked to the jury box and slowly passed before the twelve people who would soon be asked to decide what the small bundle in her arms was worth.

When the heartrending scene was over and Angel was wheeled from the courtroom, Lew Beck leaned over to whisper in Steve's ear: "Charlie surprised me."

"How so?"

"I know from studying Angel's records that she can't walk—hell, she can't even stand. She's got about as bad a case as she can have. But I figured that ol' Charlie would've tried to put the kid on her feet so she'd fall flat on her face right in front of the jury. Not like him to miss a trick like that."

Charlie Mayfield felt a surge of relief. He had taken a certain risk by bringing Angel into the courtroom because the jurors, once they saw her, might be unable to forgive Tracey for admitting that she would have had an abortion. But from the looks on their faces it was clear that they had seen Angel Walton as little more than a helpless burden. Charlie knew he'd been right to bring her into the courtroom.

He stood to announce that he rested his case. But even that he did with a sense of the dramatic. He slowly rose and let his eyes pass from juror to juror. Then he turned to Judge Grubner, held his arms wide, and rhetorically asked, "What could I possibly add to what we have just seen? The plaintiffs rest."

Lew Beck rose. "Your Honor?"

"I know, Mr. Beck," Judge Grubner said. "It's late on Friday afternoon and you'd prefer to begin your defense on Monday."

"Well, it's just that—"

"Quite all right," Horace Grubner assured him, knowing how unfair it would be to force Beck to fight for the jury's attention after what they'd just seen. "It's time for a break anyway, and that would take us almost to four o'clock. We'll give the jurors a chance to beat the Friday night traffic. Court's in recess until Monday morning, nine-thirty."

EIGHTEEN ═══

CHARLIE AND THE Waltons had already left the court-room. Lew Beck was sitting alone at the counsel table getting his papers together when a short, heavy body plopped into the chair next to him.

"Shit," Duane DeLuca said, "they damn near brought tears to *my* eyes."

"Yeah," Beck said sarcastically without looking up, "ol' Charlie sure does look like he's running scared."

"He tries a hell of a case, I'll give him that."

Beck still didn't look at the insurance man, but if he had, he would have seen a brow sweatier than at any time during the week.

When Beck was about to clamp his thick briefcase shut, DeLuca seized the moment to admit that the settlement negotiations were not going according to plan. "Listen, I know I'm reading this case right, and I know I'm reading Charlie right, but maybe what I'm not reading right is the way *he's* reading *me*."

Beck looked at the insurance man with an expression that said he had no idea what the man was talking about.

"Well, maybe I confused him, and he doesn't know how to come back to us."

Still Beck said nothing. Obviously DeLuca was having second thoughts about the way he had been handling things, and Beck wasn't about to make it easy for him. God, he thought, it's almost fun watching the son of a bitch squirm.

"What I mean is this," DeLuca explained. "First I tell

him that he's got a piss-poor case and that I wouldn't add more than a token amount to the two-point-two we had on the table. That was on Tuesday morning, over at his office. Then a couple of hours later, during the morning break, I come out of nowhere and throw another half million into the kitty. So he thinks I'm getting snakebit, just like he is, and he makes the grand gesture by coming back to us the next day, just before lunch, and drops down from four-five to four-two. What he's really doing, Lew, is saying, 'Okay, guys, now you know I'm willing to deal, so come back to me after lunch and let's wrap this mother up.' Now he runs back and tells his people that we're about to settle, maybe in the mid-threes, and he gets them to give him the go-ahead. He can't wait to see us—shit, Lew, he thinks he's about to pocket a huge fee, well over a million bucks—so he gulps down his lunch and breaks his ass running back to the courthouse to wrap it up. But guess what? We're not there. We're having dessert while he's pacing around that statue like a dog in heat. That's what I mean when I say he's confused."

"*Confused?*" Lew Beck threw back his head and laughed. "Charlie's not confused, Duane. He's *pissed*. He eats guys like you for breakfast, but he still made an effort to meet you halfway. And what did you do? You tried to jerk him around. Worse, you insulted him by not showing up. And by the way, if you think he's nervous about his fee, then you don't know Charlie Mayfield. He's probably got a stronger balance sheet than your company has, and if you ask me, he's being a hell of a lot more reasonable."

"Okay, maybe Charlie does think I'm an asshole, and maybe *you* think I'm an asshole, but the fact remains that this case can still be settled. All we gotta do is find the right number."

Beck rolled his chair back a foot or two from the table, then swiveled around to face the insurance man. "Listen, Duane, I'm sorry I unloaded on you, but I'm so damned frustrated and I can't do anything about it. The case isn't going well, the settlement talks are going worse, and I'm not in control of either. I want to see this thing settled more than you do. Hell, I've been trying to push you guys in the home office for months to give me something to work with. But it's slipping away from us, Duane, and fast."

"All right, pal, I've got a suggestion, and I think you're going to like it. The way I figure it, Charlie still wants out. Sure, his nose is out of joint because we stood him up after lunch on Wednesday, but we can fix that."

"How?"

"By my stepping out of the picture and leaving you in there to work it out with him. He likes you, Lew, and if you have to suck up a little to get him back to the table, well, you can blame me. Tell him I'm a prick if you have to, whatever you have to do to get this thing back on track."

Suddenly Beck had fire in his eyes. "You know, Duane, you *are* a prick."

"Now, wait a min—"

"No! *You* wait a minute. You think I can't see through this bullshit? You wanted to be the big hero, save the company some of the money they were willing to spend. So you come out here like a big shot from the East Coast to teach us shit-kickers a lesson. You probably thought you'd steal the case for about two and a half million. But now you see you can't do it, and you hear that big verdict roaring down the track. You're in way over your head, Duane, and now you see that your only way out of this mess—the mess *you* created—is to toss the hot potato to me. It's 'screw Lew' time. If I settle for a big number, you'll tell the boys in Boston that I got buck fever and caved in. And if I can't settle and the jury sticks it up our asses, you'll tell 'em I blew the settlement *and* the trial." Beck seized his briefcase and rose to leave. "Uh-uh, Duane, I'm not letting you off that easy."

DeLuca grabbed for his arm. "Wait, Lew, there's gotta be a way we can do this. And you said yourself that you wanted to be part of the settlement talks."

"That was before you screwed them up." Beck knew that he had the upper hand—and this was the first time all week that he'd had the upper hand in *anything*—and he had to play it right to preserve any hope of getting out of this mess. He was tempted just to walk out of the case altogether, but he had a responsibility to Steve, and anyway, Judge Grubner would never let him withdraw at this stage. More realistically, he admitted to himself, withdrawing would mean that he'd never handle another case for North American Casualty. He sat down again and rubbed his eyes. Finally he looked at the insurance man. "All right, Duane, but only on my terms."

"Which are?" the insurance man asked eagerly.

"We give it one shot, and we make it our *best* shot. No more pussyfooting around with a dollar here and a dollar there."

DeLuca obviously knew what was coming, but Beck figured he had asked for it.

Beck laid out his terms: "I'll call Charlie from the phone out in the hall—he should be back in his office any minute—and offer him four million. I'll tell him I had to go over your head—that I called your boss in Boston—to get that authority. He'll like that, thinking you might have your ass in a jam back at the home office. I know Charlie. If he's willing to take four million, he'll take it right on the spot. If he isn't, he'll make a counteroffer, and then I'll tell him to stay right there while I make another call to Boston. Then I'll wait a couple of minutes, call him back, tell him he outplayed us, and concede the four-point-two."

"Christ, Lew, can't you try to get out of this for a little less, something in the high threes?"

"No way, unless you want to try it yourself. And the longer we argue about it, the less chance we have. It's Friday night, and Charlie may be taking off for the weekend."

DeLuca dabbed at his forehead with a soiled handkerchief and shrugged. "Okay, Counselor, make your call."

• • •

Bernard Benedict looked at his daughter with more than ordinary concern. "Let's stop up at my place for a drink, Tracey, give you a chance to unwind a little, and then I'll drive you home. We can have dinner at the club."

"I have my car, Daddy."

"Forget it. I'll have one of my men run it out to your house first thing in the morning. The same guy who's taking Angel and the nurse home now."

Tracey knew one of the nurses was scheduled to stay with Angel all night, but she still took a moment to log other factors: What time was it now? Did she have any other plans? Would she need her car before tomorrow morning? Then she said, "Okay, Daddy, it's a deal." She stood on tiptoe and kissed her father on the cheek. "I'll just take a second to run into the drugstore here and make a call to break my date with a gentleman."

"Wait, pumpkin, don't do that. I didn't mean to—"

She laughed. "Just kidding. But I do have to call and leave a message for Dave Roberts about that bid."

"I thought he was going out of town."

"He is, but he left me a number."

Before he could tell her to use the phone at his place, she turned away and disappeared into the drugstore.

Steve Sinclair had checked in with his office, left some instructions, and then trekked the few short blocks over to the Prudential building. He hoped he could persuade Molly to leave work early—well, hell, it would already be four-thirty—and walk home with him. Heading east into the warm afternoon breeze blowing in from Lake Michigan, he still couldn't shake the image of Angel Walton. He hadn't seen her since he brought her into this world four years ago. Even though he would hardly have been a welcome caller at the Walton home, his failure to have followed her progress, or lack thereof, only added to his feelings of guilt.

He hadn't completely shaken these thoughts as he

walked off the elevator into the reception room of Molly's advertising agency. "Molly O'Connor, please," he said to the receptionist. "Tell her it's Steve Sinclair."

Waiting, Steve couldn't help but notice the contrast between a hospital and an advertising agency. Hospital walls were usually bare, but here they were covered with full-color ads of the well-known clients who came here to have their wares marketed throughout the world; hospital floors were vinyl, but these were covered with thick pastel carpets; hospital personnel were faceless bodies clad in white, all looking and acting alike, but here he saw jeans on women with short hair, earrings on men with long hair, and bizarre clothing on both. And here he heard the laughter and the banter that are alien to hospitals, and he felt the creativity and whimsy in the air. Then he thought about himself and Molly and smiled. Even though they got along marvelously they, like the two institutions, had little in common. While he couldn't possibly feel comfortable working in a place like this, Molly would rather rot in jail than work in a hospital or a doctor's office.

"Hey, Doc, don't they work till five down at the halls of justice?" She came bouncing into the reception area, all five-feet-one of her. "No wonder the taxpayers are revolting." She was wearing baggy pleated khaki slacks, an oversized, beige jacket that was cut like a man's sport coat and would have fit Steve—no wonder, since she had taken it from his closet that morning—and a floral necktie with an oversized knot.

"The other side finished their case about a half hour ago, and the judge gave us till Monday morning to start ours."

"Wanna join the group for Friday night happy hour?"

"Would you mind if we passed on it, Molly? Maybe just the two of us could go home and have a quick drink, then go out for dinner and a movie."

Steve hoped she could see that he wasn't in any mood to go drinking with a bunch of advertising crazies. She half closed her eyes and, doing a terrible imitation of

Greta Garbo, said, "I cannot stand these eembiciles for another meenut. I vant to be alone, and I vant to be alone weeth you."

A few minutes later they were walking up Michigan Avenue hand in hand. Short as Molly was, Steve knew they didn't look mismatched since he was only five-six and had a slight physique. "So what happened over at the House of Horrors today?" Molly asked.

"Mayfield spent the whole day on damages. If the jury believes *half* of what his witnesses were saying, they'll give that poor girl's family enough money to start a war. Then he finished with his best punch, a real haymaker."

"Oh, Lord, what'd he do now, get the kid's mother to take off her clothes and show the jury her stretch marks?"

"Worse, he brought the little girl in."

Molly cringed. "How'd the jury react?"

"Not a dry eye in the house." Steve described the scene in detail. "I tell you, Cecil B. DeMille couldn't have staged it better. It even got to me."

"What about the settlement?" Molly asked. "Any news from the front?"

Steve shook his head. "We're still about two million apart." He still hadn't been told that the Waltons might take four-point-two or that the insurance company would, if necessary, go that high. He, like Charlie, was unaware that there was already a figure acceptable to both sides.

They walked in silence for a while before Molly spoke. "Why don't those scuzzballs just go ahead and give them four and a half million and be done with it? They've got plenty of money. So they raise their premiums? Who cares?"

"Do you have any idea what we pay for malpractice insurance as it is, Molly? If the insurance companies kept paying what every plaintiff wants, it would only get worse. No," Steve added emphatically, "I've always believed that the insurance companies have to draw the line. I can't waffle now just because I'm the one being sued."

"But this time maybe they drew the line too low. From what you told me, four and a half million doesn't sound all that high." She stopped and looked up at him. "Now, that doesn't mean I think you did anything wrong, Doc. I just think—"

"I know what you think, Molly, and I love you for it. But just a few days ago you laughed at me when I said I was worried about having only five million dollars' worth of insurance. The jury would never go that high, you said. Now you think the insurance company is cheap because they won't ante up four and a half million." He put his arm around her, and they continued to walk. After a minute or two he said, "The toughest part of the whole thing is that I'm starting to doubt myself."

"What's that supposed to mean?"

"Well, maybe I *should* have realized that Tracey Walton was further along than six weeks when she first saw me, even though that was what she said. I knew she had irregular periods—that was already in her record—and if I'd thought about that when I felt her uterus, I might have realized she was further along than she thought. But no, I just took her word for it and didn't double-check. And if I'd have kept after her to have the ultrasound, then for sure I'd have seen that the fetus was older. Then I wouldn't have screwed up the alpha-fetoprotein test. Hell," he added angrily, "if I'd have done the ultrasound I might have suspected Down's syndrome even without the AFP."

"C'mon, Sinclair, don't go second-guessing yourself."

"I don't have to. Everyone else is doing it for me."

"Dave? . . . Hi, it's Tracey. . . . Yes, we finished our case just a little while ago, and court's recessed until Monday. . . . Oh, sure, everything went well. In fact, Charlie is feeling so good about the case that he's persuaded us to ask for more money to settle. . . . Five million. . . . No, Larry and I agreed that we won't ask for more than five. Anything higher would mean that Sinclair would have to pay, and we don't want to

bankrupt him. . . . Now you sound like Daddy, and
Charlie would agree with you. But I just wouldn't feel
right. . . . Good, I'm glad you understand. . . . Okay,
you guys behave yourselves. I have to run now, Daddy's
waiting to drive me home. . . . Thanks, that'll get me
through the weekend. Remember what I said about
behaving yourselves. Bye."

As Lew Beck came out of the phone booth, the
insurance man tried to read what happened from the
expression on his face. Good news, he thought at first,
Lew's smiling. But wait a minute, is that a smile or isn't
it? Yeah, it is, but it's kind of a weird smile.

"So, what's the scoop?"

"Charlie already left, but he gave his secretary a
message for me. I took it down word for word. Here, take
a look at it."

Lew,

 I figured you'd be calling about now. Wasn't
Angel an angel? We've withdrawn our offer to settle
for four and a half million. Our new demand is five
million. Regards to the fat-ass from Boston.

P.S. Sorry I stood you up after lunch on Wednesday.

NINETEEN ═══

"DO YOU SWEAR to tell the truth, the whole truth, and nothing but the truth, so help you God?"

"I do."

Lew noted that Steve Sinclair was wearing a dark blue suit—"Blue's sincere," Beck had told him—a white shirt with a button-down collar, and a muted paisley tie. Lew had seen no need to tell him not to wear a large ring or a showy wristwatch; he never wore either. Lew Beck knew that Steve had been dreading this moment since the case was set for trial, but like a sprinter waiting for the starting gun, an unexpected feeling of calm determination seemed to have enveloped him now that it was time.

After a few preliminary questions, Lew Beck asked how long Steve had been practicing gynecology and obstetrics.

"Thirteen years, not counting the years I spent in residency."

"I take it, Dr. Sinclair, that you're familiar with all the tests and procedures that were discussed here last week—alpha-fetoprotein tests, amniocentesis, ultrasound. Is that correct?"

"Yes, these are all very basic procedures. We couldn't do our job without knowing all about them."

"Have you ever had occasion to diagnose Down's syndrome in a fetus?"

"Yes, several times."

"And how did you do that?"

"By karyotyping, ultimately. But in each of those

cases I ordered the karyotyping because I already had some reason to suspect Down's, usually because of an abnormality in the alpha-fetoprotein count. Sometimes we discover the abnormality by testing the mother's blood, in which event I immediately order an amniocentesis to confirm it, but other times we learn of it during an amniocentesis without having first tested the mother's blood."

"Why would you do an amniocentesis if you didn't first get a low AFP reading from the mother's blood?"

"When the mother is over thirty-five, or if there is a history of birth defects in the family, I automatically do an amniocentesis. The higher chance of a problem in those cases justifies the slight risk."

"Did you ever diagnose a Down fetus from an ultrasound?"

"No, sir. Even in the clearest of cases, we wouldn't make a final diagnosis of Down's from an ultrasound. But we could *suspect* it from the image of the fetus, especially from the size and shape of the femur and head, digital abnormalities, and thick folds in the neck skin. In those cases, and I've had some, I ordered amniocentesis and karyotyping."

"Dr. Sinclair, I'd like you to think back to the first time you saw Mrs. Walton about her pregnancy. That was August 17, 1987, wasn't it?"

"Yes, that's right."

"Do you recall the things she told you on that date?"

"Most of them, yes. At least the relevant things."

"That was nearly five years ago. How is it that you can remember conversations that took place that far back?"

"For one thing, I take very detailed notes when I interview a patient—I never know what might become important, so I'd rather write down too much than not enough—and I've reviewed those notes a hundred times since Angel was born four years ago. Secondly, Angel's condition made such a profound impression on me that everything about that pregnancy and birth seemed to freeze in my mind."

"Do you remember asking Mrs. Walton, and her telling you, the date she had begun her last menstrual period?" Beck and Sinclair had spent considerable time discussing the best way to answer this question. Neither had suggested that an untruthful answer should be given, but there were several ways to state the truth.

"Not specifically," Steve replied. "What I mean by that, Mr. Beck, is that I can't actually recall asking the question, but I know that I *did* ask it because I *always* ask it. It would be unthinkable that I would interview a woman who suspected that she might be pregnant and yet *not* ask the date of her last period. It's so basic—everything that follows is keyed to that date. Also, my notes show the date she had begun her last period, which confirms that I asked her and she told me."

"And what was that date?"

"July 5, 1987."

"Is it your practice, Doctor, to write your notes directly into the patient's record during the visit, or do you write them down elsewhere and then later transcribe them into the record?"

"I write them directly into her record as we're talking. The only time that doesn't happen is when I see a patient in the hospital, in which case I enter my notes directly into the hospital record, and later, when I get back to my office, I make notations in my office record. I do the same thing if a patient calls me at home: I make notes and later transcribe them into her record at the office."

"Is it possible you might have misunderstood Mrs. Walton—that she told you a June date and you wrote down a July date?"

Steve shook his head. "I don't see how. I mean, I suppose it's *possible* to write 'July' instead of 'June,' but she's saying she told me it was sometime in mid-June, and I can't imagine that I could write down the wrong day as well as the wrong month." He held up a finger to make a point. "But there's another reason I know that I didn't write down the wrong date."

"What's that?"

"After a patient tells me the date she began her last period, it's only natural that I'd say something like 'Well, let's see, that means you're three weeks late.' If I misunderstood her, the patient would say, 'No, Doctor, I'm *six* weeks late.' And then we would try to calculate the expected delivery date. What I'm saying, Mr. Beck, is that it's very unlikely that I would write down the wrong date, and even if I did, we would catch the mistake in the ensuing conversation."

"So then it's your testimony that Mrs. Walton gave you the July fifth date. Is that right?"

"Yes, it is. There is no other way I could have gotten it."

"And was it that date—July 5, 1987—that you gave to the lab that measured the alpha-fetoprotein?"

"Yes, sir."

"If you had thought at the time that Mrs. Walton had begun her last period in mid-June, and if you had given *that* date to the lab, would anything have been different?"

"Certainly. That would have meant that Mrs. Walton was three weeks further along than we thought when we measured the alpha-fetoprotein, and in that case the concentration would have been low—so low that I would have immediately ordered an amniocentesis."

Lew Beck put his elbows on the lectern and leaned toward Steve when he asked his next question. "Dr. Sinclair, sitting here today, do you have an opinion as to when Mrs. Walton actually had her last period?"

"Yes, I believe it was in mid-June, as she testified last week."

There was a stirring among the jurors. Was the accused actually agreeing with the accuser?

"And when did you form that opinion?"

"When Angel was born. Her birth weight and state of development were consistent with that of a full-term baby. Counting backward from the date of delivery, I saw that her last period must have begun sometime in mid-June."

"Do you have any idea why Mrs. Walton would have given you the wrong date?"

"No, not at all. She must have made a mistake. Either that or I—"

"You *what*?" Lew Beck asked. He immediately realized he had spoken too quickly and too forcefully.

"Never mind," Steve mumbled.

"I object to this, Your Honor!" Charlie had obviously seen a chance to score, and Lew knew he wouldn't let it get away from him. "The witness was in the middle of saying something, and Mr. Beck stopped him. I think the jury is entitled to hear his complete answer."

Judge Grubner asked the court reporter to read back the answer that Beck had interrupted and then the question that preceded it. He pondered for a few moments, then asked the reporter to read the question and answer again. "Dr. Sinclair, it seems you wanted to qualify your statement that Mrs. Walton might have made a mistake. You may do so now."

Lew Beck was seething. First Steve had almost confessed that maybe he *did* write down the wrong date, and then, after Beck stopped him in mid-sentence, Grubner had the testimony read back to the jury *twice*. And if that wasn't enough, Grubner broadcast that Steve was about to qualify his statement that the error was Tracey's. Christ, Horace, Lew thought, why don't you just sit at the counsel table next to your ol' buddy Charlie and try the goddamned case for him?

"No, Your Honor," Steve said after a long pause. "I was not going to qualify my answer. The mistake in the date was definitely Mrs. Walton's." It was a good try, but by the time he said it, and the *way* he said it, the answer had about as much credibility as the Easter Bunny.

Beck knew that his next line of questioning could backfire on him, but it couldn't be skirted. The jury had heard Dr. Barrington say that he would have known the July fifth date was a mistake even if that was the date that Tracey had given, and that consequently he wouldn't have misread the alpha-fetoprotein test. Steve had to respond to that.

"Dr. Sinclair, you said a little while ago that you eventually figured out that Mrs. Walton must have started her last period in mid-June, and not on July fifth as she told you."

"Yes. As I said, I realized that after the baby was born."

"Why didn't you realize it earlier?"

"I most likely *would* have realized it earlier if we had done an ultrasound, but Mrs. Walton wouldn't cooperate with me in scheduling it. I tried to set it up twice, but both times she put me off by saying she had to check her calendar, and then she never got back to me."

"Why didn't you pursue it? Why didn't you *insist* she have it done?"

"In retrospect, I wish I had. But at the time there was no compelling reason to make an issue of it. Everything seemed quite normal. There was no family history of birth defects, she was feeling well, and she seemed to be in excellent health. Also, she was still in her twenties, and the higher-risk pregnancies are seen most often where the mothers are in their mid-thirties. I did bring it up one other time, but she said she'd just as soon let it go. She said it wouldn't be covered by her insurance and didn't see any reason to spend the money as long as everything seemed okay."

Lew Beck noticed that Tracey Walton, sitting at the defense counsel table, angrily shook her head from side to side, then leaned over to whisper something in Charlie's ear.

"Is all of that written in her record?" he asked his witness.

"Yes."

"And did you write those things in her record when they occurred?"

"Yes."

"You didn't add them to the record after Angel was born, did you?"

"Absolutely not!" Steve answered emphatically.

"At the time you were treating Mrs. Walton, was it your practice to recommend ultrasounds for all your pregnant patients?"

"Yes, and it still is, except in those rare cases where the patient objects to spending the money. But if I see any problems, or if the patient is thirty-five or older, I insist that it be done anyway, even if *I* have to pay for it."

"When Dr. Barrington testified, he said that the age of the fetus could be determined when a doctor examined the mother's uterus during a regular office visit. Do you recall that?"

"That's not exactly what he said. He said fetal age could be *estimated* by examining the uterus and, yes, I would agree with that. But that's not as accurate as knowing the date of the last period, especially when it's given by a woman who certainly seems as if she should know. And remember," Steve added, now looking directly at the jury, "in this case the discrepancy was only about three weeks, and that's too short to be disproved by uterine examination, especially early in the pregnancy."

"By the way, Doctor, did you confirm at or near the time of that first visit that Mrs. Walton was indeed pregnant?"

"Yes, I could feel that the cervix—the neck of the uterus—was softening, and that's something that we can usually tell by the sixth week. But I actually confirmed her pregnancy through blood and urine tests."

"And during that first visit on August seventeenth, did you ask Mrs. Walton a series of questions?"

"Oh, sure. We call that a history. It's critical that we know about prior pregnancies, health problems, and whether there's been a family history of birth defects. Naturally, I had taken a history when Mrs. Walton first became my patient, but now that she was pregnant it was important to go over these things again."

"What did you learn from taking Mrs. Walton's history?"

"As I already said, there was no reason to suspect

anything other than a normal pregnancy. She was in good health, she had never had a prior pregnancy, and neither she nor Mr. Walton had a birth defect show up in either of their families. And she was only twenty-seven."

"Do you recall her asking you to do an amniocentesis?"

"No, but it wouldn't have made any difference if she had."

Damn it, Steve, just answer my questions. Don't volunteer information unless I ask for it.

"Why wouldn't it have made a difference?"

"Because, based on her clean history, it would have been the wrong thing to do. Amniocentesis poses certain risks which, though rare, can be very serious. Unless there is already a reason to suspect a problem, it would have been careless to subject her to those risks. In fact, as we heard during Dr. Barrington's testimony, indiscriminate amniocentesis will cause the loss of more healthy fetuses than it will detect unhealthy ones."

"Thank you, Dr. Sinclair. I have no further questions."

TWENTY

STEVE SINCLAIR NOW knew that in every trial, as in every war and sporting event, there were shifts in momentum, some subtle and some dramatic. No one could see them coming, but everyone recognized them as soon as they happened. As Tom Andrews had explained to him, first one side moved ahead, then the other, and often the advantage kept swinging back and forth throughout the contest. The combatants sensed the shifts in momentum before the onlookers did, and this affected their confidence and, in turn, their performance, and that performance further drove the momentum.

In *Walton v. Sinclair* Steve had seen such a shift start to take place on Monday morning when he took the stand. It had begun with the mood of calm determination he felt even before he was sworn in at nine-thirty, and it continued to grow throughout his testimony as his voice became stronger, his answers more confident. He had stumbled only once—when he nearly admitted that he could have written down the wrong date of Tracey's last period—but apart from that, he knew he'd been an excellent witness, convincing and even likable. He believed in himself as a doctor, and the self-doubts he had expressed to Molly on Friday had disappeared. He had not screwed up when he treated Tracey Walton, damn it, and he wasn't going to let any jury think that he had.

By the time Beck finished his direct examination, Steve felt certain that no one in the courtroom believed he was a sloppy physician. Even if the jury decided that he had made a mistake in Tracey's case, they could see he wasn't a quack and they wouldn't be as likely to crucify him with a jumbo verdict.

Charlie Mayfield felt the vibrations. He had anticipated that Beck would score some points now that the defense had started, but he had never expected Sinclair to be such a strong witness. And in the back of his mind was the worry that maybe he had overplayed his hand by jumping his settlement figure to five million dollars. Now, c'mon, Charlie, he thought to himself, don't start second-guessing yourself.

The lunch recess was over, and it was time to start his cross-examination of the man he had been maligning for the past week. He had to get the jury back to thinking that Sinclair had been negligent—no, not negligent, reckless.

He walked slowly toward Steve and put his beefy hands on the railing in front of the witness stand. "*Doctor* Sinclair," he began in a voice that told the jury he wouldn't believe a word the witness said, "didn't your records show that Mrs. Walton had a history of irregular periods? And didn't you know that before she came to see you about her pregnancy?"

"The answer to both questions is yes."

"Now, is it your testimony that she told you she had her last period on July 5, 1987?"

"Yes, that's what she told me."

"So her next period, assuming she was regular, would have started somewhere around the first week of August, right?"

"Right."

"And she came in to see you on August seventeenth?"

"Yes, sir."

"Then she must have phoned your office for an appointment sometime *before* August seventeenth, right?"

"That's right."

"Didn't you think it was strange, Doctor, that she would have phoned in for the appointment when she was less than about two weeks late, considering that she had irregular periods to begin with? That's hardly enough time for her to suspect that she was pregnant."

Steve and Beck had anticipated the question, and Steve was ready for it. "I can't recall what specifically went through my mind, Mr. Mayfield, but when a patient comes to me and says that she might be pregnant, I don't turn her away. I test her to find out. It's very easy to do, and as it happened, she *was* pregnant. So whether or not her coming in that early was strange, to use your word, it turned out that she was right."

"According to your testimony this morning, you didn't realize until Angel was born that the pregnancy had begun earlier than you thought. But wasn't there some point in time, before she was born, that you suspected it?"

"Yes, based on my examinations of Mrs. Walton during the later months of her pregnancy I began to think that she might be further along than we thought. But I couldn't be sure, especially since she never went in for the ultrasound."

"When you thought that might be the case, did you do anything about it?"

"I recall going back to check the results of the alpha-fetoprotein test and thinking that if she *was* further along than we thought, then she would have had a low AFP count."

"And what did you do about that? Did you tell her she might have a problem? Or," Charlie added in a louder voice, "that her baby might have an abnormality?"

"No, sir. I didn't have that much to go on. First of all," Steve said, "I only suspected—I didn't *know*—that she was further along. Second, the AFP test isn't conclusive as a diagnostic tool; it merely raises an alert. And third, even if there was an abnormality, it was too late to do anything about it."

"Too late? What do you mean by too late?" Charlie, as shrewd and experienced as he was, broke a cardinal rule of cross-examination: Never ask a question if you don't know what the answer is going to be. But he was eager to challenge Steve and didn't see the door he was opening.

"We don't abort live babies in the seventh or eighth month, Mr. Mayfield, even if the mother wants us to."

TWENTY-ONE ====

LEW BECK WAS exhausted. He felt good about the way Steve had handled himself on the stand throughout the day, but now that it was over, he was physically and emotionally drained. All he could think about was going home, having an early dinner with his wife, watching the baseball game on television while reviewing his notes for the next day, and getting a good night's sleep.

He had just returned to his office and was about to call his wife when Duane DeLuca sauntered in as casually as if he were the regular occupant. "Sorry I didn't catch you after court, Lew, but I had to call Boston. It's an hour later out there, and I wanted to call before they all went home."

"No problem, Duane. I just stopped by to check my messages before I pack it in for the day. I'm beat."

"Hey, you must be. You did a hell of a job with the doc today, and Mayfield didn't even make a dent during cross."

"Thanks," Beck mumbled absentmindedly, his attention focused on which papers he would take home with him to help prepare for the next day's witnesses.

"I thought maybe we could have dinner together," DeLuca said. "I'd like to hear how you plan to handle the rest of the trial. Hell, the way things went today, we have a good chance to win this thing."

Not likely, Beck thought, and the idea of having dinner with Duane DeLuca was about as appealing as having a root canal. But when someone from the home office—

even a creep like DeLuca—wanted to have dinner, Beck knew that he would eat in a crowded restaurant with the creep and not at home with his wife.

"Charlie, I'm glad I was still able to reach you."

Charlie immediately recognized the voice on the other end of the line. It was Tracey Walton.

"Hi, Trace. Yeah, I stopped by the office to clean up a few things, maybe work a little on the closing argument. What's on your mind?"

"Well," she said, "we were just talking about the settlement, and I wonder—"

"We? Who's 'we'?" Charlie knew what was coming, and he wanted to know if it was coming from Larry or Benedict.

"I'm with a friend of mine; you don't know him."

"Tracey," he said with exasperation, "I've asked you not to talk about these things except with your father, Larry, or me. Other people don't know enough of the details of the case—the ins and outs—to be in a position to advise you. And a lot of them have big mouths. If it got back to Lew Beck—"

"Give me some credit, Charlie. My friend and I are very close. Whatever I tell him he'll keep to himself."

"Or he'll tell someone he trusts, who in turn will tell someone *he* trusts. Before we know it, Beck will know what our bottom number is."

"You already told him what it is—five million dollars."

"But I have a hunch you want us to come down. Isn't that why you're calling?"

Charlie heard Tracey take a deep breath before she answered. "Yes, it is. If we insist on five million, we're leaving the insurance company with no alternative but to forge ahead with the trial. They'd have no reason to pay five million to settle since that's all they could lose in any event." She hesitated for a moment, then said, "We have to give them a way out, a way to save a little face. Maybe if we tell them we'd still take the four and a half, or even—"

"You've got a good case," he interrupted, "a damn good case. You can't panic every time Beck scores a point. I've been doing this for a long time, and I can tell when a jury's on our side. This one is. Trust me. I can see it in their eyes, the way they look at me. I tell you, Trace, we got 'em."

"Just the same, Charlie, I'd like you to tell them we'd take less than the five million. We have to let them walk away with *something*."

If she could be stubborn, then so could he. "Okay, Tracey, I'll do it, but only if Larry agrees."

"Larry?" she blurted. "What does he have to do with this?"

"We're talking about money to take care of Angel, and Larry has as much to say about that as you do. Even though he agreed to let you take his share of the verdict, he's still her father and, like you, he's a plaintiff in the case."

She sighed. "All right, I'll have Larry confirm it with you. I'm sure he'll agree."

"And your father."

"*No!*" Tracey exploded.

Charlie knew that Bernard Benedict wanted to shoot for the moon and wouldn't lose a minute's sleep if the case bankrupted Sinclair. In fact, Charlie suspected that Benedict liked the idea that the young doctor might have to pay off his share of the liability over the next twenty years. He probably saw it as sweet revenge for the tragedy of his grandchild.

"Your father's in this thing as deep as you are, Tracey, and he's the one who's footing most of the bills. If you won't listen to me as your lawyer, then listen to me as your friend: Talk to him about this. You owe him that courtesy."

Charlie waited for her to admit that he was absolutely right. He felt sure that she knew it and was embarrassed at having to be reminded.

"All right, Counselor," she said finally. "You win. Let's get together in your office before court in the morning. Say about eight-thirty. I'll have Daddy and Larry there."

Steve had called Phil Ogden and Tom Andrews from the courthouse as soon as he got off the witness stand and insisted that they meet him and Molly for dinner. "I won't take no for an answer," he told them. They had agreed to meet at Arnie's, a popular restaurant on Rush Street known for its excellent steaks.

The two lawyers arrived a few minutes after Steve and Molly were seated. "What's the occasion?" Phil asked after Molly and Tom were introduced.

Molly giggled. "You sure know the doc, Phil. Any time *he* springs for a dinner, you can bet your seater there's gotta be an occasion."

Tom, who hadn't met Molly before, liked her instantly. Phil had told him on the way over that she was a five-foot stack of dynamite, and the description seemed accurate.

"The occasion," Steve explained, "is that I survived the witness stand. I walked into hell and lived to tell about it." He gave a play-by-play account of his testimony, stopping only when the waiter came over to take their drink orders, and then evaluated the impression he thought he'd made on the jury. "I know it's way too early to celebrate, but I thought my performance today earned me the right to a slab of cholesterol."

"I agree," Tom said, "but how did we get lucky enough to be invited?"

"You kiddin'?" said Molly, answering for Steve. "You guys are a big part of this. Dr. Sourpuss here would've stuck his head in the oven by now if he hadn't started talking to you. You explained more in just a few days than that insurance lawyer did in the last three years. And, Phil, you've called twice just to see how he's doing. The least he can do is feed you."

"Aw, hell," Phil said, "I thought we'd even things up by having him take care of me the next time I get sick."

Molly laughed. "Won't work, Phil. You don't have any of the things he fixes."

After the drinks were served and the meal orders taken, Tom asked Steve how he saw his chances for winning the case.

"Hard to say. By the time the plaintiffs rested last Friday, I didn't think I had a prayer. And I think Lew Beck would've agreed. But things got a little brighter today. Even the jurors stopped scowling at me."

"How are the back room negotiations going?" Tom inquired.

Steve shrugged. "From the little I hear, it doesn't look like they'll settle."

"What do you mean, 'from the little you hear'?"

"Well, I've never been around while they were talking, but Beck told me that they're far apart and not getting any closer." Steve recounted all he knew about their offers and Charlie Mayfield's demands.

"Are you telling us," Tom asked, "that the plaintiffs are willing to settle for a figure that would be covered by your five million dollar policy?"

"Yeah, I think so. Beck told me they were asking four and a half million." Steve still hadn't been told that Charlie had since moved down to four-point-two million or that he had more recently jumped clear up to five.

"And how much has the insurance company offered?"

"Something under three million, I think."

Tom looked at Phil. "I think Steve should preserve a bad faith claim."

"I agree."

"What are you guys talking about?" Steve asked.

Phil answered the question. "Insurance companies aren't allowed to throw the policyholder to the wolves just so they can try to save a few dollars for themselves. I'll give you an example. Suppose you're negligent and cause an auto accident that injures someone. Maybe the victim has a fractured skull and sues you, and you turn the case over to your insurance company. You have a hundred thousand dollar policy, and the man you injured says he'll settle for, say, ninety thousand. The insurance company says, 'To hell with it. Why should we pay ninety when the worst that can happen is that we lose a hundred? Better to take the gamble that we win.' The way they look at it, they'd only be risking ten thousand to save ninety thousand—good odds. So they go to trial, and the jury awards the guy a hundred and fifty thousand. The company gives him the hundred, which is only ten thousand more than they could've settled for, and you're stuck for the other fifty. In a case like that, you can sue the company for that extra fifty thousand."

Steve wrinkled his brow. "I'm not sure I understand. If the maximum coverage is only one hundred thousand dollars, how can the company get stuck for a hundred and fifty?"

"Because," Tom Andrews replied, "the law imposes a duty of good faith on the insurance company to protect you, and that includes the duty to offer up to the policy limit to settle if it's reasonable to do so."

"But what if the guy has only a broken finger instead of a fractured skull? Are you saying that the insurance company still has to offer him the hundred thousand?"

Tom laughed. "No, not in that case. The company isn't required to pay an unreasonable amount for the injury in question, and it's not reasonable to think that a broken finger could be worth a hundred thousand dollars. And we can't use hindsight. Even if the jury came back with a crazy verdict—like two hundred and fifty thousand— the company could still say that they were acting reasonably in not offering the hundred thousand to settle. In other words, they'd say, it wasn't *reasonable* to anticipate a verdict of over a hundred thousand for a broken finger."

Molly held up her hand to ask a question. "But what if the injured guy was a concert pianist? Wouldn't—"

"Aha!" Phil interjected. "In *that* case a broken finger could be worth a heck of a lot more than a hundred thousand, depending on how long the pianist was unable to play, how much money he lost by not being able to play, whether the finger healed well enough to let him play as well as he did before—all those things. So," he said, holding up the stir stick from his drink, "you can see that the question of whether the insurance company acted reasonably depends on the facts of each case."

"So what about Steve's case?" Molly asked the two lawyers. "He has a five million dollar policy. If Mayfield said he'd settle for four and a half million, is it reasonable for the company not to pay it?"

Tom answered. "That's the key question, Molly, and it's tougher than the one about the broken finger. What it boils down to is this: Considering the nature of that child's illness, and the likelihood that the jury could find that Steve was negligent in not diagnosing that illness, is four and a half million a reasonable settlement?"

"Well," she asked impatiently, "is it?"

"I'm not sure, but it isn't crucial that we know that—not yet, anyway. The important thing for now is to put Steve in a position so that, if the jury does come back with a verdict higher than five million, he can make a claim against the insurance company for the excess."

"How do we do that?" Steve asked.

"You should write a letter to the insurance company demanding that they offer whatever it takes to settle the case—up to the five million dollars if necessary. That will put them on notice that you intend to look to them if a higher verdict comes in."

"Okay, I'll write a letter like that."

"Like hell you will," Phil said firmly. "*We'll* write the letter, and you'll sign it. And we'll do it tonight back at our office after dinner. Then you can hand a copy to Lew Beck in the morning, and we'll send the original to the insurance company at their home office by certified mail. That way they can't deny they got it."

"Whew," Molly said, "you guys work fast."

"That's what we're paid for." Tom laughed, holding up the expensive menu.

"There's one more thing," Phil added. "I think Tom or I should be with you when you give the copy of the letter to Beck. Then he'll know you're serious, and it'll give us a chance to talk to him and find out exactly where the settlement negotiations stand.''

"Is that okay?" Steve asked. "I mean, is it okay for me to bring another lawyer with me to talk to him?"

"Not only is it okay, it's essential. Whenever there's a chance that a defendant can be hit for more than his insurance coverage, he *should* have his own lawyer. Most defendants don't, but that's only because they don't know any better."

TWENTY-TWO ===

LEWELLEN BECK WALKED into his office early Tuesday morning feeling no more rested than when he had trod back there from the courthouse the previous afternoon.

During the long dinner with DeLuca the evening before, he had convinced the insurance man that the trial was still an uphill battle. True, Steve Sinclair had been a surprisingly strong witness, but they still couldn't possibly win unless the jury believed that Tracey Walton was wrong about the date of her last period. And there was just no way to prove that. By the time they had finished dinner, DeLuca was sweating again; he urged Beck to try the gambit they had discussed the preceding Friday afternoon—offer four million and, if Charlie balked, offer the whole four-point-two. Beck thought it would be a waste of time, since Charlie was now up to five million, but he had been too tired to argue. And anyway, as DeLuca had said, there was no harm in trying.

Beck was still wondering what it was that Steve wanted to see him about in his office at eight-thirty in the morning. It wasn't unusual for a client to call him at home at night and ask to see him before court the next morning, but Lew had heard an uneasiness, an urgency, in Steve's voice that worried him. When he had asked Steve why he wanted to see him, the question was met with evasiveness, and that worried him even more.

At eight-thirty sharp Steve showed up with Phil Ogden. After the introductions Beck brought them each a cup of coffee.

Phil didn't waste any time getting to the point. "I've represented Steve for the past three years," he began. "I set up his professional corporation, and I'm the one he sees about his lease, estate plan, and anything else that calls for legal advice."

Beck nodded, beginning to get an idea of what the meeting was about. "I don't know if you're aware of it," he said, "but when I took this case I sent a letter to Steve to tell him that he was free to retain his own counsel. I make sure I do that in any case where the verdict could conceivably exceed the amount of coverage."

"I know you did that; Steve showed me your letter. He finally got around to taking your advice, and that's why I'm here."

Beck was actually relieved. When he had first learned from DeLuca how much North American Casualty thought the case was worth—about *twice* what they had offered—he was concerned that Steve was being put at risk without his knowledge. That concern had eased when Charlie indicated that the plaintiffs would come down to four-point-two, a figure that Beck knew North American was willing to pay if push came to shove. But then on Friday Charlie had jumped up to five, and Beck knew the company would never go that high—they had no reason to. So now Steve was at risk again, and Beck was relieved that he had someone to advise him.

"I'm glad Steve's bringing you into the case, Phil. Do you want to sit in on the rest of the trial? I'm sure Judge Grubner would permit it."

"No, thanks. Even though my partner does trial work, we think it would send the wrong signal to the jury if another lawyer all of a sudden showed up at the defense table. Steve has confidence in you and in the way you're trying the case." Phil sipped his coffee and added, "So you can relax, Lew. I'm not here to interfere with your trial."

"I see. Then I assume you're here because you want to know where we stand on settlement."

"Right. From the little Steve has been able to tell me,

you've offered something in the mid-two's, and the plaintiffs are somewhere over four. Is that correct?"

Beck nodded.

Phil put his elbows on the desk. "I have no way of knowing exactly what the case is worth, Lew, and neither does anyone else. We won't know that until a jury tells us. But it sure seems to me that you guys are being chintzy. You have a sick child who needs a lot of expensive care, a mother who's a strong witness, a lawyer who knows how to wring the last cent out of a jury, and a judge who'd love to help him do it."

He leaned back in his chair and crossed his legs. "So from where I stand, it doesn't sound like the plaintiffs are being all that unreasonable in asking for something over four million. Am I missing something?"

Beck could hardly argue with what Phil was saying. These were the same things he had been telling North American for two years, and Duane DeLuca for the past week. "The only thing you're missing," he said, "is that your client might not have been negligent. Maybe the jury will decide that he didn't do anything wrong and that we won't have to pay anything—not even a single red cent."

"I've thought about that," Phil assured the other lawyer. "In fact, from what Steve tells me—and I believe him—I don't think for a minute that he was negligent. But I'm not sure the jury will be that considerate of my friend here—especially if it means giving nothing to that poor little girl."

Beck heard his secretary, who had just arrived, moving things about in her cubicle just outside his office. He walked over to the door to let her know that he was in. Then he came back and stood behind his chair. He looked at Steve apologetically for what he was about to say, then turned to Phil Ogden. "I'll level with you, Phil. Last week the company told me that they were prepared to make a substantial increase in their offer. They started by going from two-two to two-seven early in the week. We thought that would get things rolling, and that the plaintiffs would make a corresponding move so that eventually we'd meet somewhere in the middle."

"What happened?"

"Well, last Wednesday Mayfield said that maybe—just maybe—his people would consider something around four-two. He tried to give the impression that he didn't much care one way or the other, but it was pretty clear that he'd have taken four-two on the spot and everyone could've gone home."

"But that was nearly a week ago," Phil pointed out. "Surely someone's moved since then. Both sides wouldn't just stand still and stare at each other—not this late in the game."

Beck sat down. "On Friday afternoon, after court adjourned, I called Charlie at his office to increase our offer, but he'd already gone for the weekend. He left a message for me saying that they now wanted *five* million."

Steve Sinclair slumped into his chair and covered his eyes for several moments. Then he looked at the two lawyers who had been carrying on as if he weren't even in the room. "You know," he said, "everyone has been pooh-poohing my fears about having only five million dollars of liability insurance. That would be more than enough, they all told me. But now I sit here with the Waltons asking for every dime of it. And if Mayfield's demanding five million just to settle, then he must think there's a good possibility of getting more than that if he takes his chances with the jury. And everything over five million comes right out of my own pocket." He paused as if calculating his net worth and obviously realized that it wouldn't take much beyond the five million to put him into bankruptcy.

His despair wasn't lost on Beck and Ogden who spent the next few minutes trying to convince him that things weren't as bleak as they seemed. The case might still settle for less than five million, the jury might return a verdict of less than five million, or—what the hell—the jury might even decide in his favor altogether.

Finally Phil Ogden brought the conversation back to the business at hand. "I think we have a right to know, Lew, just how high North American is willing to go. What's the top dollar they'd be willing to pay to settle?"

Beck shifted uncomfortably in his seat. There was no doubt that Ogden had the right to ask that question and that he had the obligation to answer it. A sleaze like DeLuca might try to b.s. his way out of it, but that wasn't Lew Beck's style. "The last I heard, and that was last week, was that they'd go to four million two hundred thousand."

"*What?*" Phil Ogden jumped out of his chair and nearly came clear across the desk at Beck. "What kind of sadistic motherfuckers are you guys? You admit that the case is worth four point two, and you knew last Wednesday that the plaintiffs would have taken it, but instead of paying it, you dick around and try to steal the case for less. And then, while you're standing there playing with yourselves, Mayfield's case gets better and he moves up to five million! Christ, Lew, you had it in your hand and you let it get away from you. All because you wanted to play hero, or was it because you wanted to get a couple of extra days of fees before you settled?" He fell back into his chair and reached over to put his hand on Steve's shoulder. "And in the meantime, this poor guy is like a butterfly pinned to a board, waiting to find out what you guys are going to do to him next."

Lew Beck wished he were anywhere else in the world. Everything Ogden had said was on target. It wouldn't have done any good to explain that he, Beck, hadn't even been told until last week how high the company would go, that they didn't trust him, and that they'd sent some schmuck out here from Boston to take over the negotiations. In his own defense he was about to explain that he had planned to increase the offer to four or even four-point-two this morning as soon as he saw Charlie at the courthouse, but before he could do it he saw a white envelope sliding across his desk toward him.

"I'll be amending this letter," Phil Ogden was saying,

"in light of what you've told me. It'll be stronger. But in the meantime I think you should have this so you'll know our position."

As Beck unfolded the letter, his eye caught the last short paragraph and signature:

> Therefore, as a result of the Company's failure to exercise good faith in attempting to settle the claim within the policy limit, and thereby breaching its duty to me as the insured, I intend to look to the Company for payment of any judgment entered in *Walton v. Sinclair*, including any portion of said judgment that may exceed the sum of five million dollars, plus interest, and plus any attorneys' fees, court costs, and expenses I may incur to enforce said payment.
>
> Steven Sinclair, M.D.

• • •

"All right," Charlie Mayfield was saying, "I'll recap." He took a sip of coffee and looked across his desk at the Waltons and Bernard Benedict. "As soon as we get to the courthouse I'll get a message to the judge and ask if we can have a conference in his chambers. Just him, Beck, and me. When we get in there I'll tell Beck—right there in front of the judge—that I still think five million is a fair settlement. But then I'll tell him you two are eager to put this thing behind you, that you prefer not to wait out a verdict and the appeals, and that you just might bite at a lower number. If I play it right, he won't know how much less you'll take. It might get them to come back with their best shot, and it still doesn't commit us to anything less than the five."

Bernard Benedict had a question. "Why do you want to do this in the judge's chambers, Charlie? Why don't you just talk to Beck directly?"

"Two reasons. First, I know Horace Grubner and I know how he thinks. He's one of those judges who like to help lawyers settle cases, and he'll think Beck's being too stingy by sitting on two-point-seven million. Remember, he used to be a plaintiffs' lawyer, and all plaintiffs' lawyers think insurance guys are tightwads. I figure he'll put a lot of pressure on Lew to give us his top dollar, and it's gotta be higher than two-seven."

"What's the other reason?"

"Well, this is a little tricky, but I have an idea how we might get *more* than five million and still not take anything from the good doctor. It's a long shot, but I might be able to pull it off."

Charlie then explained about the insurance company's duty to protect the insured—in this case Sinclair—by making every reasonable attempt to settle within the policy limit. "If we don't settle, and the jury gives us more than five million, I think Sinclair might have a bad faith claim against the company. If I can help him make that claim stick, then it would be the company, not Sinclair, who'd have to come up with the difference. That'd make Tracey and Larry happy."

He looked around to make sure everyone was following him. "Now, in order for Sinclair to succeed on the bad faith claim, he'd have to prove that we were willing to settle for five million or less. There are only three witnesses to that—me, Beck, and that guy from the insurance company. But"—Charlie grinned—"once I move the negotiations into the judge's chambers, I'm giving our good doctor an additional witness—none other than the Honorable Horace Grubner himself—who'll know we were willing to settle for less than five million. That would give Sinclair a real leg up if he ever went against the insurance company."

Charlie leaned back in his chair. "Okay, then, are we in agreement? And if I can push Beck up to four and a half million, I have your permission to take it? Isn't that what we agreed to a little while ago?" Charlie hadn't been happy about coming down from his five million dollar perch, but Tracey had been adamant after talking to her friend. And she was the client.

Tracey nodded and then looked at her father, who had earlier wanted them to hold out for more.

"I'm not sure I have an official vote," Benedict said, "but I'll go along with whatever Tracey wants to do. However," he added, "if we don't settle and then the jury gives us more than the five million, I like your idea of trying to stick the insurance company for the whole ball of wax."

All eyes turned to Larry Walton. "I won't stand in the way of whatever Tracey decides," he said, "even though you all know I think we're milking this lawsuit for too much. I'll still support Tracey on this. She's the one who has to live with Angel every day. But as Mr. Beck said during his opening statement, this was an act of God, and the jury giving us money—no matter how much—won't make Angel well." Looking at Charlie, he added, "And the fact that the money will come from an insurance company doesn't change my opinion."

He studied his hands for a few seconds, then, without looking up, said, "I agree that maybe Dr. Sinclair should have done this, or maybe he shouldn't have done that, but when it's all said and done, I can't see where he's done anything that should haunt him the rest of his life." He paused again, then added, "If he's guilty of anything, it's having bad luck—just like us."

TWENTY-THREE

HORACE GRUBNER HAD already put on his robe when his bailiff brought him word that Mr. Mayfield would like a short conference with the judge and Lew Beck.

"What's on your mind, Charlie?" Judge Grubner asked when the two lawyers were ushered into his chambers.

"Well, Judge, we're about to start our seventh day of trial, and I'd guess that we'll be done by the end of the week." Charlie Mayfield turned to Beck. "You agree with that, Lew?"

Beck nodded, still not sure why the conference had been called. He had assumed Charlie wanted to go over a few of the perfunctory details that surround all trials—verifying exhibit numbers, scheduling witnesses, that sort of thing—but until he knew for certain, he decided to say as little as possible.

"But I'm not satisfied that Lew and I have exhausted all settlement options," Charlie went on. "I'm not saying the Waltons are eager to settle, Judge, but it's always been my practice to turn over every stone to see if there might be a figure that's agreeable to both sides."

"And you thought I might be able to help?"

"I was hoping that would be the case. We all know that a bad settlement is often better than a good lawsuit," Charlie said, repeating an old saying that really didn't say very much, "but you know how we lawyers are—we're never able to be up front with each other. Sometimes we need a judge to come in and beat our heads together."

"What do you think, Lew?" Grubner asked.

189

Beck hesitated. Now that he knew what the meeting was about, he had to decide whether to bring DeLuca in. It was customary to have a representative from the insurance company in chambers at these times, but DeLuca could be so repulsive that his presence might do more harm than good. On the other hand if Lew didn't invite him into the meeting, the bastard could later make him the scapegoat in the event of a high settlement or, worse, no settlement and a higher verdict. He had to make a decision. One way might be better for the case; the other would surely be safer for him. He chose the safe route. "I'd welcome your help, Judge, but with your permission I'd like to bring in a representative from North American Casualty. He's out in the courtroom."

"By all means," said Grubner. He took off his robe while Beck stepped out of the room to get DeLuca.

Once the insurance man was in the room and introduced to the judge, Grubner reached for a file sitting on the corner of his desk. "Let's see, if I remember correctly, we had a pretrial conference to discuss settlement several weeks ago. Is that right?"

The two lawyers nodded and said that was correct. Each knew that Horace Grubner recalled very vividly the meeting in his chambers the previous month. Cases of this size, and with Charlie Mayfield, weren't everyday occurrences.

"Ah, yes, here are my notes." Grubner paused long enough to scan what he had written when they met before the trial. "According to this," he said without looking up, "the plaintiffs were asking for four million five hundred thousand dollars, and the defendant was willing to pay two million two hundred thousand." He looked up. "Are my notes correct as of that time?"

Again the two lawyers nodded.

"So you were two million three hundred thousand dollars apart. How much closer together are you now?"

Beck jumped in with the answer. He had a message he wanted to deliver, and he couldn't deliver it if Charlie did the talking. "Unfortunately, Judge, we're *still* two million three hundred thousand apart."

Horace Grubner looked genuinely startled. "How could that be? The positions of the parties before trial are often nothing more than ceremonial chest thumping, but I would expect more realistic thinking once the trial starts, and certainly when it's nearing its conclusion."

"And I would agree, Your Honor," Beck said. "In fact, after the trial began we increased our offer to two-point-seven million."

The judge looked at Charlie. "And how did you respond?"

Beck quickly answered for his opponent. "He responded, Judge, by increasing his demand to five million dollars."

"Now, wait a minute," Charlie said, "let's be fair about this. Shortly after they came up to two-point-seven, we came down. I admit that I wasn't very specific, but I clearly implied that we'd take four-point-two."

"So," Grubner said, as if making sure he was tracking the negotiations, "they went up five hundred thousand, and you came down three hundred thousand?"

"Right," Charlie continued, "and it wasn't until they ignored my four-point-two for over two days that we went up to five million, and that was because our case got better during those two days."

Now Lew Beck wanted to make a correction. "You indicated you'd take four-point-two just before lunch last Wednesday, and we agreed to meet before the afternoon session to talk further. But you never showed up." Beck didn't really misrepresent the truth—Charlie *hadn't* shown up for the meeting outside the courthouse and had so admitted in the note he had his secretary read to Beck on Friday afternoon. Of course, Beck and DeLuca didn't show up either, but Charlie didn't know that.

Horace Grubner looked over to DeLuca who had agreed just before coming into chambers that Beck would do most of the talking for their side. "May I ask about the policy limit?" Although jurors were not allowed to know how much insurance was available in a case, or even that there *was* insurance, since that knowledge could influence their verdict, Beck knew it was legitimate information for a judge who had been asked to help facilitate a settlement.

"Five million dollars," DeLuca replied.

Grubner smiled at Charlie. "That doesn't leave the insurance company with much incentive to pay you five million, does it? No matter what the jury does, that's the total extent of their risk." He paused for a moment and then said, "Perhaps we should invite Dr. Sinclair in here. It looks like he could be in jeopardy if we can't settle."

It was Charlie who replied to that suggestion. "I don't think that'll be necessary, Judge, not if we can wrap it up right here and now."

"All right, Charlie," the judge said, "you called the meeting. Can I assume from what you just said that your people are willing to lower their figure?"

Charlie hesitated for several seconds before answering. "That's a fair assumption, Judge. We're very confident that we'd win this case and win it big. In fact, I smell a verdict of well *over* five million, but the Waltons are willing to take less to end it now and not wait for posttrial motions, appeals, and all the other delays. They'd like to get on with their lives. It's already been four long years—"

"A number," the judge said impatiently. "Give us a number."

Beck was relieved that the judge kept the pressure on Charlie to make the first move. Finally Charlie answered: "Four million seven hundred and fifty thousand dollars," he said, clearly trying to make it sound like a huge concession. "That still leaves Mr. DeLuca here with a quarter of a million to take back to Boston with him."

The insurance man couldn't keep his silence. "Big deal! We'd be better off losing five million to the jury. We could stall the appeals so it would still take you two or three years to collect, and in the meantime we could earn more than a million in interest on the money. That beats saving a quarter of a million now."

Asshole! Lew Beck thought, wanting to crawl under the judge's desk out of embarrassment.

Charlie was gloating about the remark, but Horace Grubner was not. "I'm not surprised, Mr. DeLuca, that your company thinks that way. I've dealt with insurance companies my entire professional life, from both sides of the bench, and nothing they do surprises me anymore. But what does surprise me is that you would have the audacity to make such an outrageous and odious statement out loud—openly threatening to exploit the judicial system just to collect interest on other people's money, without caring a whit about the Waltons and Dr. Sinclair."

Duane DeLuca obviously didn't know when to leave bad enough alone. "I'm just being honest, Judge, and explaining why we couldn't even consider Mr. Mayfield's offer. I realize we'd have to pay interest on a judgment, but that would still be a lot less than we could earn with that money during the appeals."

"I see." The judge nodded. "Then what you're telling me is that the plaintiffs would have to come down to somewhere under four million to make a settlement worthwhile for you. Is that correct?"

"Yes, Your Honor, *considerably* under four million. But," he added with bravado that no one took seriously, "we're not afraid to take our chances with the jury. Mr. Mayfield has already rested his case, and we don't believe he proved that Dr. Sinclair was negligent."

Lew Beck was beside himself. He couldn't very well contradict DeLuca, but he'd be damned if he'd let a settlement get away from him just because of the man's stupidity. "Would it be all right, Judge, if Mr. DeLuca and I stepped outside to confer for a minute or two?"

"Yes, Lew, I think that would be a good idea. Meanwhile, I'll have my bailiff tell the jury that we'll be a little longer."

• • •

"Are you out of your frigging mind?" Beck said as soon as they shut the door to the judge's chambers. "We agreed to offer four million right out of the chute and go to four-point-two if need be. And now you have us locked down there in the mid-threes."

"Lew, can't you see what's going on here?" DeLuca said. "Something happened in Mayfield's camp and they want to bail out."

"Sure, just like last Wednesday when you said he was running scared. Then he went up, not down."

"But that was then and this is now. Trust me, Lew, we're gonna get out of this thing for about three and a half, three-seven-five tops."

"You can level with me, Charlie. How close are you?"

"I'm not sure, Judge. I know where *we* are, but I don't know where *they* are." Charlie Mayfield could be devious when he had to be, but he had learned long ago to be absolutely honest in private conversations with judges. One misstatement, one half-truth, and his word would forever be mud with the entire judiciary in Chicago. He explained that he would prefer to go for broke, but that Tracey would accept four and half million and that Larry would go along with whatever she decided. He even mentioned that Tracey's father would like to see them hold out, but that he, like Larry, was leaving the final decision to her. And he explained that the family, while financially comfortable, didn't have the unlimited resources to provide the care Angel would need—not without this case.

"Then why isn't Mrs. Walton willing to go along with your recommendation? You obviously told her that you were confident of a high verdict. Just how confident are you, Charlie?"

The lawyer laughed out loud. "Judge, you and I have tried a hell of a lot of cases. How many times have we thought that we could tell what a jury was going to do, and how many times have they surprised us?"

Grubner smiled. "Fortunately, the surprises balanced out. Sometimes I lost when I thought I was riding a sure winner, and other times I won when I figured I had a lost cause."

"But on this one," Charlie said, "I think the jury likes Mrs. Walton, and I think they believe her. The doctor's testimony wasn't strong enough to overcome that."

"And you haven't been able to convince her of that?"

"On the contrary, I think I have, but she has a soft spot in her heart for Sinclair. So does Mr. Walton. They really don't want him to have to pay anything out of his own pocket, so they have no interest in risking a good settlement for a verdict higher than the five million dollar policy limit."

"The curse of every plaintiff's lawyer—a compassionate client."

"Right," Charlie nodded, "but I might have an ace up my sleeve on this one." He told Grubner about his idea of helping Steve Sinclair make a bad faith claim against the insurance company in the event of a high verdict, and how that could stick the company with the entire amount.

The judge listened intently, clearly intrigued with any scheme that could work against an insurance company. And Charlie knew that this one was especially appetizing to Grubner in view of Duane DeLuca's offensive statements a few minutes earlier. "So," the judge said when Charlie was done, "you had an ulterior motive for calling this meeting. You wanted me to be a witness to their bad faith."

Charlie shrugged his shoulders. "Only if we can't get a decent number out of them when they come back in here."

Just then there was a knock at the door.

"All right, gentlemen," Horace Grubner said to Beck and DeLuca after they had resumed their seats, "where do we stand? What's your response to Charlie's opening bid of four-point-seven-five million?"

Lew Beck tilted his head toward the insurance man.

You want to carry the ball, meathead, so go ahead and carry it.

"Three and a half." DeLuca undoubtedly had intended to sound confident, but he overplayed it and it came out cocky.

The judge pursed his lips while he made a few notes. Then he looked up. "While you two were out in the anteroom, I had a chance to probe Mr. Mayfield's position. Perhaps it would be a good idea if he now stepped out of the room so I could explore yours."

As soon as Charlie left the room the judge turned to Beck, ignoring the insurance man. "Lew," he said, "I'm afraid you might not be realistic about the way you're assessing this case."

So much for letting DeLuca carry the ball, Lew thought. "There's always that possibility, Judge, but in my heart I don't believe that Steve Sinclair is guilty of malpractice."

"But the jurors can't see or hear your heart. They see and hear an attractive, convincing mother who is struggling with a terrible ordeal. Maybe, they think, Dr. Sinclair didn't do anything wrong, but then again, maybe—just maybe—he did. They're not sure about Sinclair. But they *are* sure that Mr. and Mrs. Walton didn't do anything wrong. So whose side will they be on, Lew? The Waltons, who for sure did nothing wrong, or Sinclair, who just *might have* done something wrong?"

Beck didn't reply to the judge's question. He didn't have to.

But DeLuca, true to form, couldn't keep his mouth shut. "You miss the point, Judge. Even if we *knew* the jury would hold in favor of the Waltons, we *still* wouldn't offer more than three and a half million to settle. Like I said before, anything more than that would be worse for us than getting hit with a high verdict and paying five million two or three years later."

Beck had learned long ago that something happened to a man who became a judge and wore the robes of office. He might not be able to shed completely his prejudices and biases, but his respect for justice sharpened his sense of fairness. His vision might be blurred by prior experiences, but he nevertheless saw more clearly than most people. So Lew was sure it wasn't Horace Grubner's partiality to plaintiffs' causes, or his lifelong battle with insurance companies, that inflamed him when Duane DeLuca smugly repeated his position.

"Mr. DeLuca," he said sharply, "your entire logic to settlement is based on float. You measure your duty to Dr. Sinclair and your obligation to the Waltons in terms of how long you can hang on to your money and earn interest on it. You even admit that you will use delaying tactics to prolong the appeals for at least two years if you lose." Judge Grubner pointed a finger at the insurance man. "I ask you, Mr. DeLuca, did your company give Dr. Sinclair a two-year grace period for the payment of his premiums? Did the Waltons have a two-year grace period for the payment of their child's bills?"

The judge threw down his pen and watched it skip haphazardly across the desktop and then onto the floor. "As I said before, I'm not surprised that your company thinks that way. But since you insist on bringing your position out into the open and making it a part of your sales pitch, then I must ask you a question that has been on my mind for years: How can you people live with yourselves? Aren't you ashamed of what you're doing?"

Before DeLuca had a chance to answer, the judge had other questions for him. "This case was filed over three years ago. How long must this family wait for recompense? Isn't three years long enough? Must they wait two *more* years? Must they wait until their daughter is dead before they get the money they need to keep her alive?"

DeLuca pulled a handkerchief from his pocket to dab at his glistening forehead. "Your Honor—"

"Never mind. I'm not interested in your answers. I only want you to think about the questions. And I want you to think about the enormous risk you're putting on Dr. Sinclair's head because of your contemptuous attitude."

Horace Grubner made a fuss about rearranging the papers on his desk and then stood up and started to put on his robe. "We're nowhere near a settlement, gentlemen. I won't tell you what I learned from Mr. Mayfield, just as I won't tell him what we've been talking about. But I know his bottom number, and in my opinion he and his clients are being very reasonable."

He looked in his mirror to be sure his robe was hanging straight, poked his head out of the door to say something to his bailiff, and then turned back to the two men who were still sitting in front of his desk. "We're going back into the courtroom now to continue the trial. Before five o'clock this afternoon I expect you to give me a piece of paper, and I want only two things written on that piece of paper. One will be the top figure—the absolute top figure—you'd be willing to pay to settle this case. Not a negotiating figure, and not a let's-test-the-water figure, but your drop-dead absolute maximum figure. The top dollar. And the other thing on that piece of paper will be Lew Beck's signature. That's all I want, your top number and Lew's signature."

He started to walk out of the room, but at the last second turned to say one more thing. "I frankly don't give a damn if you settle or if you don't. That's between you and Charlie. But if I ever find out that you settled for a figure higher than the one written on that piece of paper, Lew, I'll never want to see you in my courtroom again. Because then I'll know that you lied to me about how high you'd go, and if you lie to me once, I'll never trust you again, so help me God."

The last thing Lew saw was a black robe flowing through the doorway, and the last thing he heard was the door slamming.

TWENTY-FOUR ═══

IT WAS NEARLY eleven o'clock when the trial resumed.
Lew Beck went through the motions, but his mind was
elsewhere—about a thousand miles to the east. He had
decided to call North American Casualty's headquarters
in Boston during the lunch hour and explain the disaster
that was unfolding here in Chicago. He knew they'd hear
about it soon enough, but he wanted them to hear about
it from him, not from that horse's ass they had sent out.

The only witness he called that Tuesday morning was
a distinguished obstetrician who corroborated much of
what Steve had testified to during his direct examination.
Yes, it was accepted practice to estimate fetal age from
the mother's statement as to the date of her last period—
especially an intelligent mother who seemed confident
about the date. Yes, there were other methods, but they
were not as reliable during the earlier stages of pregnancy. No, amniocentesis was not a routine procedure; it
should be used only when special circumstances warrant
it. No, there were no such special circumstances in this
case—at least none that Dr. Sinclair should have been
expected to know about. Yes, ultrasound was becoming
more and more common, but no, it was not mandated as
a standard procedure in all cases. No, based upon his
review of all the records in this case, he would have done
nothing different from what Dr. Sinclair had done.

Beck had noticed that DeLuca wasn't in the courtroom
during the examination. Just as well, he thought. I hope
the son of a bitch is on his way to the airport. After he

199

finished, and after Charlie asked the witness a few questions for clarification, the judge announced a two-hour break for lunch. Sure, Lew thought, give me plenty of time to come up with the magic number. By the way, Horace, is it okay for me to sign your little piece of paper with ink, or do you want it in blood?

DeLuca was waiting for him in the corridor. "Hey, Lew, we gotta get together on that number."

"Get out of my sight," Beck said, not even slowing down as he strode toward the elevator.

As soon as he got to his office he put in a call to Jerry Michaels, the chief claims manager at North American Casualty, a man he had known and worked with for years. He didn't like going over DeLuca's head, but the son of a bitch hadn't left him with an alternative.

Fifteen minutes later Beck was still fuming over the phone call, thinking, I should have known that the home office would back DeLuca up, damn it. His thoughts were interrupted by the buzzing of his intercom. "I know you asked me to hold your calls, Lew, but Mr. DeLuca is on the phone. He said he was sure you'd want to talk to him."

He rubbed his eyes with one hand and picked up the receiver with the other. "Hello, Duane."

"I understand you just talked to Jerry."

Beck decided to play it straight. "Yes, I did. You and I aren't reading Charlie the same way, and I thought the company should have the benefit of my thinking. I told Jerry what I thought, but he's still in favor of letting you call the shots."

"That's what he told me, too. Now, the first thing we have to do is give the judge that number."

"I assume you think the number should be four-point-two, but if that's the number we give him, Duane, we're stuck with it as our top figure. Remember what he said: If we end up paying more than the number on that piece of paper, he'll have my ass in a sling. So you have to be up front with me on this one and tell me the absolute max we'd pay if things got as bad as they could get."

"Our top figure has nothing to do with this. The only thing we have to decide now is what to put on that piece of paper."

Beck couldn't believe his ears. "But it's the same thing. Grubner specifically said—"

"You're too goddamned worried about Grubner. Can't you see what's happening, Lew? He and Mayfield are too chummy. I don't know what the hell they were talking about while you and I stepped out of chambers this morning, but when we got back in there that fucking judge wanted to rip our throats out. If we tell him our top number is four-point-two, he'll run to tell Mayfield and then they'll try to get us higher than that. Our top number will then be our bottom number."

"What about me, Duane? What do I tell Grubner if we ever offer more than the number we write down on that piece of paper?"

"Tell him we changed our mind. Blame it on me." DeLuca laughed. "What's he gonna do—fly out to Boston and spank me?"

Beck let out a long, audible sigh. He had enough on his mind just trying a lawsuit, and he wasn't in the mood for moronic humor. "A minute ago you said that I couldn't see what was happening. Well, I think I can, and I'll tell you what it is. You ran out of Grubner's chambers this morning and headed straight for the phone. You read the tea leaves and saw we were in trouble, and you couldn't wait to start covering your own ass. 'Beck's pissing in his pants,' you told Jerry, 'and he wants to bail out.' Then you said that Charlie and the judge had picked up on this and now they were leaning on us for too much money.

"Now you've covered yourself, Duane, regardless of what happens. If we settle cheap, you're the hero; if we settle high, it's because I gave the wrong signals; and if we don't settle and then get nailed, it's because I screwed up the trial. But you've put yourself in a box, and you don't even know it. In order to make me the heavy, you had to tell Jerry that the case isn't worth as much as I think we should offer. So now you've locked yourself into a low number with the boys in Boston, and you can't ever get back to where we should be without looking like a fool. Isn't that right?"

"I don't have to answer that," DeLuca said, "and I don't have to justify my conduct to you or anyone else."

"You will if Sinclair ever hits us with a bad faith claim. And you'll have to do it from the witness stand."

"I'll worry about that when the time comes. In the meantime, we'll meet during the afternoon recess. I'll have a number on a piece of paper, and you can sign it."

TWENTY-FIVE

BECK STARTED THE afternoon session with another obstetrician who basically made the same points as the first one had that morning. It went quickly. The idea was not to give the jurors a course in obstetrics but to let them know that other doctors would have handled Tracey Walton's pregnancy just as Steve Sinclair had handled it. Sinclair was to be judged by the standard of medicine practiced by other obstetricians in like circumstances, so it was that standard—and not the way chromosomes split or didn't split—that the jurors had to know about.

Beck knew that if he was to win the case, he'd do it by showing that Sinclair wasn't negligent. Technically, it was the plaintiffs who had the burden of proof. The law required that they prove that the defendant was negligent, not that the defendant *disprove* it. But that was classroom stuff; it didn't recognize the major role played by sympathy and by the deep-seated biases the jurors brought with them into the jury room. In fact, experience had taught Lew that the jurors were more likely to find negligence when they just plain *liked* the plaintiff more than the defendant. So, while the jury was theoretically concerned with the presence or absence of negligence, a trial was often little more than a popularity contest. And Lew knew that the defense lawyer who thought too defensively and concentrated only on throwing up legal roadblocks in front of the plaintiff's case was destined for hard times.

Beck had a tougher decision to make on the question

of damages. In most negligence cases the lawyers for the defense would happily accept a low verdict for the plaintiffs. Never mind that the scorekeepers would put it down in the loss column; that was a small price to pay if the verdict was less than the amount the plaintiff expected, or less than the defense offered.

But, in a case like *Walton v. Sinclair,* fighting over the damage issue could easily backfire on Beck. For one thing, challenging the amount the Waltons were asking invited the inference that they were entitled to *something,* and that in turn could be construed as a tacit admission that Sinclair did something wrong. Moreover, Beck could not very well prance around and whine that Angel Walton didn't really need nurses or special care. And would it really have served his purpose to argue that the jury should award only a small amount of expense money since Angel wouldn't live very long? What was he supposed to say? "No need to give her money for special schooling, folks—she won't be alive long enough to need it"?

He elected, therefore, to concentrate on the negligence issue and put damages aside until his closing argument when he could make a few careful statements. He'd kick himself if the jury came back with a big verdict, but that was a normal risk in his business.

Meanwhile, Charlie Mayfield was trying to be as inconspicuous as possible for a man of his size and presence. He'd raised hardly any objections to Beck's questions and asked hardly any questions of Beck's witnesses. He obviously wanted his own evidence to be fresh in the jurors' minds when they finally made their decision. To prolong the case now would only add to the burden of their memory. It was far better strategy, he had learned, to sit there looking bored while the defense was trying to put points up on the board. "If *I* don't look like it's important enough to worry about," he had explained to Tracey, "then maybe the jury won't think it's important enough for *them* to worry about."

Owing to the long lunch recess, it was midafternoon when the witness finally stepped down from the stand.

"We'll have a twenty-minute recess," Judge Grubner announced. Then he looked over toward the defense table. "Mr. Beck?"

"Yes, Your Honor?"

"If you have anything for me you can give it to my bailiff. He'll be in the courtroom throughout the recess."

"Waddya mean, you're not gonna sign it? You forget who you're workin' for, goddammit!"

"No, Duane, I haven't forgotten who I'm working for: I'm working for Steve Sinclair. You might be paying me, and you might think you own me, but I'm working for him."

This had started out as a hushed conversation at the far end of the corridor, but now, less than a minute later, passersby would have thought they were at ringside in Madison Square Garden.

". . . and I refuse to give Grubner a bullshit number," Lew Beck was repeating for the upteenth time.

"Oh, excuse me," the insurance man said sarcastically. "We mustn't take a chance of irritating His Royal Highness, Lord of the Realm and Protector of Sir Charlie."

A few minutes later, Beck approached the bailiff. "Fred, could I trouble you to take this note back to the judge?" The bailiff eyed the folded piece of paper suspiciously. "It's okay, he's expecting it," Beck said, "and I assure you that Charlie won't mind."

Horace Grubner had not even tried to guess the number that would be written on the note, and it was just as well:

Your Honor,
    I have decided to give you no number rather than take a chance of giving you the wrong one.
    There is no way I can be sure—absolutely

sure—that whatever figure I give you will not
eventually be exceeded by the insurance carrier. Mr.
DeLuca will handle any further settlement discussions. I'll be limiting myself to the trial itself.

Lew

Beck felt himself growing tense as the rest of the
defense went in fast. With him sticking with his decision
not to offer damage evidence, and Charlie sticking with
his decision to remain as quiet as possible, Beck could
see that the defense would rest by five o'clock that same
Tuesday afternoon. Ordinarily, this would have pleased
Beck. He preferred short, snappy defenses and hoped he
wouldn't be remembered as one of those lawyers who
never knew when to quit—the doth-protest-too-muchers.
But this time he knew that resting his case would bring
him that much closer to a disaster. He had no illusions
about what the jury could do to him, and the prospect of
settlement had, as far as he was concerned, evaporated.

After the last witness for the defense stepped down
from the stand a few minutes before five, Beck formally
announced for the record that he rested his case.

"Will you have any additional evidence, Mr. Mayfield?" Judge Grubner asked.

"I don't believe so, Your Honor."

If Charlie and the judge were surprised that the case
wound down so early, they didn't show it. "Very well,"
the judge said, pulling his calendar closer. "Let's see,
today is Tuesday. We'll use tomorrow to hear motions, go
over jury instructions, and take care of any other unfin-
ished business, and we'll have closing arguments on
Thursday." Then he turned to the jury. "You will be
excused tomorrow. Tend to any business you have and
then be here by nine-thirty Thursday morning. But get
some rest—you'll need it. And, as I've already instructed you, you won't discuss this case with anyone
until after your verdict is in."

TWENTY-SIX ===

AS SOON AS the judge adjourned court, Lew Beck leaned toward Steve. "I called Phil Ogden during the afternoon recess and asked if he could meet us in my office about five-thirty. Can you make it?"

"Sure." Before Steve could ask what the meeting was all about, Duane DeLuca came over to the counsel table and started talking to Beck as if Steve weren't even there.

"Hey, Lew, let's see if we can catch Mayfield before he leaves."

"I don't have anything to talk to Charlie about."

"C'mon, I can't talk to him alone."

Beck snapped his briefcase shut and sighed. "Look, Duane, we've been all over this before. If you have anything to say to him, go ahead. I'm staying out of it."

Steve, feeling out of place, asked if he should leave.

"Yeah," the insurance man said, "would you mind?"

But Beck quickly reached for Steve's arm. "No, stay here. You have every right to know what's going on." Then he turned to DeLuca. "Charlie's about to leave, so you'd better hurry."

"At least go over there with me. I don't want him thinking that we're not together on this thing. I'll do all the talking, and you won't have to say a word. C'mon, whaddya say?"

"Good luck, Duane." With that Beck tapped Steve's shoulder and the two of them walked out of the courtroom.

• • •

Charlie and the Waltons were halfway to the elevator when DeLuca caught up with them. "Excuse me, Mr. and Mrs. Walton, would you mind if I had a word with Charlie?"

Tracey and Larry had never met the insurance man, but they knew who he was—Charlie had pointed him out to them earlier. They looked at their lawyer, who nodded, then moved to the other side of the corridor.

"What's on your mind?" Charlie asked, sounding as if he really didn't care.

"Now that all the evidence is in," came the reply, "let's get realistic with each other. We don't have enough time to keep playing games."

"Okay, you be realistic first."

Duane DeLuca knew that this had better be good. He had only one chance to set the hook or his fish would get away. "Here's the deal, Charlie. I have a little flexibility, but when I get back to Boston I gotta have a little change in my pocket."

Charlie, knowing that the policy limit was five million dollars, misread that to mean that the company would settle for something in the high fours. He let his relief show. "Well, that's better, because I have a little flexibility too."

As soon as DeLuca heard the sigh of relief and Charlie's comment about being flexible, he leaped to the conclusion that Charlie was more eager to settle than was actually so. That, coupled with his never-ending quest to save every single penny he could, led him to blow it. "Great," he said, "I think I may be able to get the company to move up—maybe up to the high threes."

"Let's go," Charlie called across the corridor to Tracey and Larry. The three of them were already halfway to the elevator before the insurance man saw what was happening.

"Wait," he shouted after them desperately. "The *very* high threes."

They didn't even slow down.

• • •

Lew Beck was looking across his desk at Steve
Sinclair and Phil Ogden. He had already apologized for
not having kept Steve better informed about the settlement discussions before and during the trial. "I know it
won't be much consolation to you, Steve, but the fact is
that even I wasn't sure what the hell was going on."

Beck was obviously embarrassed by the way the
insurance company was treating him, but this was not the
time for commiserating. Ogden came right to the point.
"I have two questions I have to ask you, Lew."

"Shoot."

"First, do you think the case will settle?"

Beck pondered the question for a moment. "No. It
should, but I don't think it will." He explained that the
company wouldn't consider anything over the four-
point-two, and that DeLuca, trying to be a hero to the
Boston crowd, wouldn't even offer that. And the plaintiffs, he predicted, were prepared to go for broke.

"But," Ogden asked, "doesn't the company realize that
the jury could come back with a killer verdict?"

Beck was well aware of the consequences of his
answer, but right was right. "I can only tell you what I
think, and what I think is that the insurance people just
don't give a damn. As far as they're concerned, a ten
million dollar verdict is no worse than one for five
million. And paying out five million dollars after a
couple of years of delays and appeals wouldn't be any
worse than paying four million now. So why pay more
than four now? That's the way they look at it, and that's
why they're sitting back."

"And that," Ogden said, "leads me to my next question. If what you say is true, then it's a classic case of bad
faith by an insurance carrier. And if we can prove it,
they'll have to pay the entire verdict, even if it's over five
million, and Steve'll be off the hook. So my question is:
Will you help us prove it?"

Beck had known he would have to deal with this
question eventually. From the moment he'd learned that

Ogden intended to press a bad faith claim, if necessary, he had known he would be called upon to tell what he knew. "Do you have any idea what that would do to me, Phil? I make my living defending cases for insurance companies. If they found out that I played ball with you on this I'd be out of business."

"But if I called you as a witness you'd have no choice. You'd *have* to tell what you know. You can't hide behind the attorney-client privilege to keep information from Steve—he's your client. And any conversation with Mayfield wouldn't be privileged anyway."

Beck stood up, took off his suit jacket, and carefully hung it on a coat rack in the corner. Then he loosened his tie and came back to his chair. "Can I make a proposal?"

Ogden glanced at Steve. "I'm listening."

"You can prove your bad faith case by showing that the plaintiffs were willing to settle for less than five million dollars, that the figure they wanted was a reasonable one, and that the insurance company knew it but acted in their own interest to the detriment of Steve's—in this case by subjecting him to great risk in order for them to save a little. Do you agree with that?"

"It sounds right."

"Okay. If subpoenaed, I'd have to testify to those things, but I'd like a favor of you in return. First, see if you can get the information you need from Charlie Mayfield and Judge Grubner. If you can't get it from them, then I'll give it to you."

"Mayfield? Grubner? I can understand how they'd know what the plaintiffs would settle for, but how would they know the company's motives for not paying it?"

"Because DeLuca—that imbecile—came right out and admitted it this morning in chambers. He even threatened to stall the appeals so the company could hang on to the money longer and earn interest on it. Can you imagine that? I thought Grubner was going to drag his ass up to the roof and throw him off."

"It's an interesting proposition," Ogden said, "and I

might take you up on it. But I have an even better suggestion."

"What's that?"

"Win the case. Then we won't have a verdict to worry about."

It had been ten minutes since Ogden and Sinclair had left his office, and Lew Beck was feeling better than he had felt during the past ten days. Cleansing his conscience about the settlement was a catharsis, and now he could get back to focusing on the jury instructions and his closing argument. Ogden's suggestion that he win the case was offered in jest, but it was a reminder, damn it, that he *could* win it. He had never believed that Steve Sinclair was negligent, and he had thought before the trial started that they had a good chance of winning. And really, nothing in the trial had changed that; Charlie's evidence included nothing that Beck hadn't anticipated, and Steve turned out to be a better witness than anyone expected. Beck had felt depressed only because of the botched-up settlement, and he couldn't afford to let that affect his attitude toward the trial itself.

He was about to start making notes for his closing argument when his secretary buzzed to say that he had a phone call.

It was from Jerry Michaels in Boston, asking him to be a good soldier and work with DeLuca on the settlement.

"No way, Jerry."

"We can't negotiate without your help, Lew. What'll it take to get it?"

"First, get that fat slob out of Chicago. And second, give me authority to pay four-point-seven-five. I think I can settle for four and a half, maybe a little less, but I'll want to know that the higher number is there if I need it. We still have a good shot at winning the case, Jerry, but a settlement within the policy limit still makes sense. We owe that to Dr. Sinclair."

"You're asking the impossible. If I yank Duane off this thing and let you settle it for anything *close* to five million, he'll tell everyone we sold out for too much. He'll say he could have had it for three and a half."

"How's he going to take potshots at you, for crissakes? You're his boss."

"You might know a lot about the law, Counselor, but you don't know shit about corporations."

TWENTY-SEVEN ════

TELEPHONES. IF THE legal system were a machine, telephones would be the lubricant. They were used to strike deals, issue threats, make demands, give instructions, confirm appointments, and transmit the information needed to make things happen. But as far as *Walton v. Sinclair* was concerned, there could have been a universal telephone shutdown on Wednesday morning and it wouldn't have meant a thing. At a time when serious communications were called for, the players were silent.

Phil Ogden didn't call Lew Beck. Ogden had already made his position clear, and he would have nothing further to do unless and until a verdict came in over five million dollars.

Duane DeLuca didn't call Charlie Mayfield. Simple men see things in simple ways, and in Duane DeLuca's mind it was Charlie's turn to make a move. That was all the rationalization he needed to dig in his heels and wait. Anyway, he sensed deep down that the two sides were too far apart to settle; he'd have had to offer well over four million just to get things moving, but he had only four-point-two to play with. And how could he ask the home office for more money after what he had already told them?

Jerry from Boston didn't call DeLuca or Beck. He sensed an impending disaster in Chicago and he didn't want to leave any more of his fingerprints at the scene of the crime.

Lew Beck didn't call anyone. He was sticking with his resolve to stay out of the settlement talks, except on his terms, and he had enough to do with preparing jury instructions and his closing argument.

Charlie Mayfield didn't call anyone either. As he saw it, he held a good hand and could afford to stand on it. If there was going to be a settlement, they'd have to come to him. In the meantime he, like Beck, had work to do.

The jury instruction conference began in Judge Grubner's chambers that Wednesday afternoon at two.

People watching a trial were always either impressed or bored when they heard the judge's charge—the reading of instructions—to the jury. The charge usually took anywhere from five or ten minutes to two or three hours, and consisted of a recitation of the legal rules, which the jurors were to keep in mind when they reviewed the evidence. Some of these rules were general and applied to all cases—"When I say that the plaintiff has the burden of proof, what I mean is . . ." Others were specifically related to the case at hand—"If you believe from all of the evidence that Dr. Steven Sinclair, in his treatment of Tracey Walton, failed to exercise the standard of care ordinarily exercised by physicians in similar circumstances . . ."

Cases were sometimes won or lost at the jury instruction conference. The judge did not assemble or create the instructions on his own, but instead picked and chose from between the two sets submitted by the opposing lawyers. Each lawyer argued that his or her instruction on a given issue was the better of the two, either because it was more understandable to the jury or because it was a more accurate statement of the law. And the lawyer whose instructions were accepted had the benefit of a jury that would hear most of what he or she wanted them to hear.

The conference in *Walton v. Sinclair* went quickly. The laws that applied to the case were not complicated and not in dispute, and therefore the instructions submitted by Charlie Mayfield and Lew Beck were not, for the most part, at variance. Their dispute concerned the facts, not the law, and those facts were for the jury to decide. The lawyers' conflicting versions of the facts would be debated during closing arguments, not during the instruction conference.

When the conference was over and the two lawyers were preparing to leave, Horace Grubner leaned back in his chair. "Has there been any progress on settlement?" he asked.

All judges wanted to see their cases settled. Then they didn't have to worry about an appellate court saying they were wrong. Even in a jury case a judge had to make rulings that could be appealed. Grubner was looking at Beck when he asked the question, a sign that he thought it was the defense that was being stubborn.

"I wouldn't know," Beck replied. "If there's anything going on, it's between Charlie and Mr. DeLuca from the insurance company. I'm out of it."

"By your choice?"

"Yes, as a matter of fact." Beck was tempted to leave it at that, but then decided that an explanation was in order. "After you asked me yesterday, Judge, to sign my name to our highest number, I went back to the insurance company. I can't tell you everything that was said—that wouldn't be right—but I walked away thinking that maybe they were holding back a few dollars. Now, I'm not accusing them of anything improper, but I'm the guy who will have to deal with you when this is all over. And because I couldn't be sure that the number was their top one, I wouldn't sign that piece of paper."

"But that doesn't mean that you can't continue to negotiate with Charlie," the judge pointed out.

"The company people prefer to handle that themselves, Your Honor."

Grubner turned to Charlie. "Are you and the company talking?"

"Not since yesterday," Charlie answered. "They're

still in the high threes, and we're still in the high fours. That leaves a hell of a lot of space."

The judge nodded slowly as he thought through the arithmetic. "Well," he said finally, "I can't force them to come up any more than I can force you to come down. My only interest is in seeing that you communicate, and it doesn't look to me as if you're doing so. I blame both sides for that."

"May I ask you a question, Judge?" This from Lew Beck.

"Certainly, Lew."

"It's a little off the wall, and I'll understand if you won't answer it, but I'd like to ask what you think the jury will do. Not the figure, but who do you think is going to win?"

Horace Grubner's eyebrows arched. "That's an interesting question. It's also a tough one. Would my answer be important?"

"Yes, I think it would. You can see the evidence more objectively than Charlie and I can. If you thought the Waltons were going to win, I would have something to tell the company. Maybe that would shake a few more dollars out of them. And if you thought Sinclair was going to come out on top, Charlie might persuade his clients to come down a little."

The judge took off his glasses and rubbed his eyes. "I guess there's nothing wrong with my making such a prediction. Judges do it privately all the time in jury cases. Of course," he added with a grin, "we're usually dead wrong, but the fear of being wrong has never stopped a judge."

He replaced his glasses and, speaking more seriously, said, "The problem is, I don't have a strong feeling either way as to how the jury will go. At the end of the opening statements I would have been hard pressed to predict the eventual winner. Maybe that's because I don't pay too much attention to openings—that's just lawyers talking, not evidence. Oh, sure, Charlie made a couple of points that made me think Dr. Sinclair could have been negligent, misreading one test and not doing the others, but then Lew did a good job of explaining those things.

"But, after I heard Mrs. Walton testify, I began to see the plaintiffs getting out ahead—way out ahead. I could tell that the jurors liked her, and her testimony about the date of her last period was very convincing. I started to think at that point that the doctor must have dropped the ball—that putting the wrong date in the record was his mistake—and that's what led to the wrong diagnosis. It even occurred to me that he might have had another patient in his office at the same time, maybe in the next examining room, and that he somehow confused their dates of conception. My feelings became even stronger when I heard the plaintiffs' expert witnesses. I got the feeling that Dr. Sinclair should have insisted on the ultrasound, even if Mrs. Walton was lax in scheduling the appointment, and that maybe he should have done the amniocentesis regardless of whether she requested it." He looked at Beck and, nodding grimly, said, "What I'm saying, Lew, is that I had the feeling he didn't know as much about that baby as he should have."

The judge paused to pour himself a cup of coffee from the carafe on his desk. "But then Lew did a masterful job cross-examining Dr. Barrington, and I finally saw that not doing those tests was perfectly understandable. In fact, it might have been a mistake on the doctor's part to have *done* the amniocentesis in the absence of other circumstances. By the time you rested your case, Charlie, I had serious reservations, but I still would've bet that you were ahead in the jurors' minds. But then Dr. Sinclair got on the stand and went a long way toward evening things up. His answers and the way he handled himself helped his case a great deal. So did the other doctors that Lew put on the stand.

"So what do I think?" He shrugged his shoulders. "Well, gentlemen, I think you could flip a coin and get just about as good an answer as I could give you." Then he pointed a finger at Charlie and said, "But you have a bigger problem here than just proving liability."

"What's that, Judge?"

"Figuring out how to get a big award. As I see it, you've got two problems. First, whenever a plaintiff gets a verdict in a close case—and I regard this as a close case—the jury tends to compromise on the damage question. They go back in the jury room to deliberate, and the seven or eight of them who want to go with the plaintiff can't convince the four or five who are holding out for the defendant. So they make a deal, and the holdouts vote for the plaintiff in return for a concession on the damages. Then they all go home happy, the plaintiff gets a verdict, and the defendant can afford to pay it. A perfect compromise—a little something for everyone. That can happen here, Charlie, and it would leave you with a shallow victory."

Charlie knew all about jury compromises, but that thought didn't bother him a bit. Sure, it happened in close cases, but he didn't think this case was that close. And even if there was some horse trading in the jury room, he counted on enough jurors wanting to give the Waltons the moon that a compromise would still end up in the neighborhood of five million, maybe more. Rather than debate the point he asked, "You said I had two problems, Judge. What's the other one?"

"It's that damned abortion issue."

"What do you mean?"

"Your whole case on damages is based on the premise that Mrs. Walton would have had an abortion if she had known that her child would have Down's syndrome."

"She would have, Judge. She testified to that."

"Yes, but she equivocated a bit on cross-examination. Remember, Lew asked her what she'd have done if she had known that the baby would live for at least four or five years. She said she wasn't sure."

Charlie smiled. "I'll take my chances on that one. The jury saw that little girl, and they heard about the kind of life she's living and all the care she needs. Hell, Judge, every one of 'em would run to have an abortion if they were in the Waltons' shoes."

"You're betting a lot of money on that, Charlie—nearly four million dollars. If even one juror takes a hard line on abortion or sees anything redeeming in that child, you'll end up with a hung jury. Then you'd have to start all over."

"I covered that during the *voir dire*. I asked them if they agreed that abortion is acceptable in certain cases, and each one said yes."

"And we both know that prospective jurors don't always tell the truth. Or maybe some of them think that this is not one of those special cases where it's okay to abort. What then?"

"Well, Judge, if that's what happens, then I guess I'll just have to kick myself in the ass for not taking the insurance company's offer."

TWENTY-EIGHT ═══

CHARLIE TURNED AROUND to survey the courtroom. It was Thursday morning and both sides were at their respective counsel tables a few minutes before closing arguments were to begin. The bailiff had just told Charlie and Beck that the judge would like to see them before the arguments, but at Charlie's request they had agreed to wait for about five minutes before going back into chambers. When he spotted the person he was looking for, he started to walk quickly toward the spectator section. As he reached the row where Duane DeLuca had just taken a seat, he motioned for the portly man to follow him out into the corridor.

"Morning, Charlie," the insurance man said as soon as they were out of the courtroom. "Looks like everyone's—"

"I only have a minute," Charlie said brusquely, "so I'll make this fast. My people will take four and a half million. Tell me right now that you'll pay it and we have a deal. Otherwise all bets are off."

"For crissakes, Charlie, you're askin' for too damn much." Tiny beads were already starting to show on DeLuca's upper lip and forehead.

"I want an answer, not a critique. Will you pay four and a half million? Yes or no."

"But that's way over my authority. The company—"

"Then forget it."

Charlie already had his hand on the door when he heard DeLuca over his shoulder. "I think it's too much,

220

but I'll call Boston and see what they want to do. It'll take a few minutes.''

"That might be too late, but go ahead and give it a try."

Charlie was smiling to himself as he came back into the courtroom and nodded at the bailiff to indicate that he was ready to see the judge. The timing was perfect. He suspected that the insurance company still had some more money to throw into the pot, and this last-minute take-it-or-leave-it strategy might suck it out of them. DeLuca's nerves were showing, and that would help.

He knew that DeLuca would have a new number for him before the morning was over. If it was four and a half million, terrific, they'd have a deal. If it was less, Charlie would tell DeLuca to cram it.

"I take it that you have nothing further to report on a settlement?" Judge Grubner's question was directed to both lawyers.

"I threw a new figure on the table this morning," Charlie replied, "and I'm waiting for the insurance company to get back to me."

"Are you proposing that we wait for them, or should we go ahead with the arguments?"

"Oh, we should go ahead, by all means. We'll still have plenty of opportunity to talk. Hell, Judge, we can settle anytime before a verdict comes in, and sometimes those damn insurance companies don't get serious until the jury starts to vote."

"And that's agreeable with you, Lew?"

"Yes, Judge."

"All right, then, let's agree on the ground rules. I'd like to give each of you one hour for your closing statement. That way we can finish around noon. Then we'll break for lunch, and when we get back, I'll give the jury their instructions and they can start their deliberations. Do you have a problem with that?"

"Can I break up my hour any way I want?" Charlie asked.

"I have no problem with that. You can open and close,

and Lew can go in the middle. As long as your total time doesn't exceed an hour—"

"Excuse me, Judge," Beck interrupted. "It wouldn't be fair if he spent only five minutes to open, and then saved fifty-five minutes for closing. He's the plaintiff, and I have a right to hear what he tells the jury before I respond."

"No problem," Charlie assured him. "As far as my case is concerned, I'll say all I want to say in the beginning. That'll take most of my time—at least forty-five minutes. I'll save ten or fifteen minutes for the end to rebut things you bring up."

A few other points were discussed—major matters such as deciding when to have a twenty-minute bladder recess, what to do if either lawyer was in the middle of his argument at that time, and whether the jurors should have their meals brought in to them during deliberations.

"All right, gentlemen, we'll start in five minutes."

Coming back into the courtroom, Charlie saw Duane DeLuca frantically trying to get his attention. Thirty seconds later they were in the corridor.

"What do you have for me?" Charlie asked.

"Four-point-one. And listen, Charlie, you don't know what I had to go through—"

"Cram it, Duane."

The closing arguments were predictable and typical of the two lawyers who made them. Each did a superb job of highlighting the evidence that favored his side and belittling the evidence favoring the other side.

Charlie said: "Tracey Walton is a woman who would know that the date of her last period was in mid-June 1987, and that's the date she gave to Steven Sinclair. She'd have no reason to give him a different date."

Beck said: "Steven Sinclair is a doctor who makes careful notes of what his patients tell him, and if he wrote down that Mrs. Walton's last period was on July fifth, then that's what she told him. He'd have no reason to write down a different date."

Charlie asked: "Would Tracey have gone in for an ultrasound if her doctor thought she should have it? Of *course* she would have, and to suggest that she didn't is *ridiculous*."

Beck asked: "Wouldn't Steven Sinclair recommend an ultrasound for Mrs. Walton, just as he did for all of his patients? Of *course* he would have, and to suggest that he didn't is *ridiculous*."

Both lawyers were compassionate when they talked about Angel and about the care she required. Charlie implied that the burdens and expenses of that care could go on for years and years. Beck ever so delicately reminded the jury that according to the medical testimony they'd heard, Angel and the burdens and expenses of her care were not expected to last for more than a few years at the most.

There was an inexplicable similarity between trials and weddings: At weddings the bride's friends and relatives tended to sit on one side of the room while the groom's gravitated toward the other. And at trials those supporting a particular party, whether they were friends, relatives, or colleagues, tended to congregate on the side of the courtroom behind that party's counsel table. That explained why, whenever Charlie or Beck made a strong point, nodding heads were seen on one side of the courtroom while sober faces were seen on the other. When the arguments were concluded and the jury left the courtroom for the noon recess, those same supporters rushed forward to compliment Charlie or Beck for a job well done. They might have been in a locker room after the big game judging from the handshakes, backslaps and "attaboys."

Court reconvened at two o'clock.

The instructions were read to the jury, and then, by three, the twelve men and women were led out of the courtroom to begin their deliberations. As soon as the door had shut behind them, each of the two lawyers let out a long-held breath and slumped into his chair. Their job was done, at least for the time being. After years of preparation, long sessions with clients and witnesses, endless hours poring over law books and, in this case, medical books as well, and sleepless nights worrying about whether some obscure but vital point had been overlooked, they could relax — assuming there could be anything relaxing about waiting for a jury verdict. They shook hands warmly and each told the other what a tough opponent he had been.

Now the waiting would begin. After leaving phone numbers with the bailiff, both lawyers departed, Beck heading for his office to busy himself with work that had backed up during the trial, and Charlie zeroing in on his favorite watering hole. Each planned to spend the evening at home.

The jurors, however, were scheduled to work that evening. Judge Grubner had told them that their first assignment was to elect a foreman or forewoman. At six, he said, he would have sandwiches sent in from Berghoff's. Then they were to deliberate until nine, when they would break for the night. Those without cars would be driven home, and deliberations would resume at nine the next morning. It was now Thursday, and while no one expected a verdict before noon on Friday, everyone would be relieved if one could be rendered before the weekend.

There were no further settlement negotiations. The insurance company hadn't authorized DeLuca to pay more than the four-point-two million he had in his pocket when he flew to Chicago the previous week, and he couldn't bring himself to offer more than the four-point-one that he'd been told to cram that morning. He had to keep something in reserve, even if it was only a hundred thousand, so he could counter in the event that Charlie came back to him.

Charlie, however, had no intention of coming back to him. He and Tracey had agreed to stand pat. If they were offered four-point-five anytime before the jury returned a verdict, they'd take it, otherwise they were prepared to take their chances.

TWENTY-NINE ═══

WHILE THE JURORS were finally doing the job they had been summoned to do, everyone connected with the case was speculating on how they would do it.

"Did you see how the lady in the back row—the skinny one on the left—looked at Tracey just before they went out? It was as if she were saying, 'Don't worry, dear, I'll take care of you.'"

"Yeah, but that old guy sitting in front of her, he kept nodding when Lew was making his closing argument. He's on Sinclair's side, no question about it."

"Makes no difference. This is a savvy jury, and they figure there's a ton of insurance. Even if they think Sinclair did nothing wrong, they'd rather give that money to the kid than let an insurance company keep it."

Lew Beck left his office and headed home at six-thirty. He knew it was crazy to think that the jury could make a decision before their six-o'clock dinner break, but he was nevertheless disappointed when that time came and went and he hadn't received a call from the bailiff. He knew that every once in a while a jury would go back into the jury room, elect a foreman or forewoman, take a quick vote before any discussion and—eureka!—they would all agree. And when that happened, it almost always meant a victory for the defense. It took longer to bring back a plaintiff's verdict because that entailed an agreement on damages—an agreement that could be reached only after reviewing, predicting, discussing, and calculating past and future expenses.

And it was for these same reasons that Charlie Mayfield breathed a sigh of relief when he didn't get a call from the bailiff that Thursday evening.

When the two lawyers finally bedded down for the night, they did so knowing that they would spend the next day going through their daily routine but accomplishing nothing. They would relive the trial and think of things they should have done differently, and all the while their attention would be glued to the telephone. Tomorrow promised to be a long day. Since the jury hadn't reached a verdict in the first few hours, they most likely wouldn't have one until late Friday at the earliest.

Both lawyers were astounded when the calls came at ten o'clock Friday morning.

Lew Beck felt the tingle of excitement. Even a pessimistic defense lawyer would construe a verdict this early, and in a case of this complexity, to be a good sign. He and Steve Sinclair had already agreed that Steve would not be in court when the verdict was returned. The trial had already interrupted his practice immeasurably, forcing him to turn over a number of appointments, and even some deliveries, to colleagues. But he had committed himself to seeing his patients personally once the jury had retired.

Charlie Mayfield, however, was crestfallen. *They didn't even take the time to look at my damage evidence, the bastards,* he thought. *How could I have read 'em so wrong?*

He took a few minutes to compose himself and then called Tracey to report the news. "Don't bother to come down to the courthouse, Trace. . . . Well, it might not be good, coming this early, and there's no reason for you to be there. . . . Sure, I promise I'll call you the minute I know." He hung up the phone and buried his head in his hands. *And yesterday I turned down over four million dollars. Shit!*

•   •   •

The jurors' expressions revealed nothing as they filed into the courtroom and took their seats in the jury box. A few glanced toward one of the counsel tables, but a like number stole a peek at the other one. And if any of them noticed that Steve Sinclair or Tracey Walton was absent, they gave no indication.

For the record, Judge Grubner inquired whether the jury had reached a verdict. One of the jurors, a tall middle-aged man, stood and said that they had. In response to more questions from the judge, he gave his name, said that he had been elected foreman, and assured the judge that the verdict he held in his hand was freely and voluntarily signed by all twelve jurors.

In sequence, the foreman handed the verdict to the judge's clerk, the clerk handed it to the judge, the judge looked at it and then handed it back to the clerk.

"The clerk will please read the verdict."

The clerk cleared her throat and read in a strong voice: "We the jury find in favor of the plaintiffs, Lawrence Walton, Tracey Walton, and Angela Walton, and against the defendant, Steven Sinclair, and we assess damages in the sum of eight million dollars."

PART TWO

THE AFTERMATH

THIRTY

THE MOST COMMON complaint against lawyers was that they failed miserably in communicating with their clients—they just didn't keep in touch. But that was never the case when a lawyer had good news to deliver. As soon as the verdict was given and the obligatory handshakes were made, Charlie dashed to the nearest phone.

"We did it, Trace! We hit 'em right between the eyes. Eight million smackeroos."

He could tell that Tracey Walton was dumbstruck. "Oh, my God," she finally whispered when the number apparently registered. "I had no idea . . ." Then she was silent.

"Hey, you're a millionaire. You're supposed to be excited, but you—"

"Charlie, it's incredible, but it's—it's too much."

"Too much? How in the hell can it be too much?"

Then he realized what she meant. "Listen, Trace," he said, searching for a conciliatory tone. "I know how you feel about taking money from Sinclair, but we can talk about that when I see you. Remember what we talked about the other day? There may be a way we can collect the whole eight million from the insurance company, and Sinclair won't have to come up with a cent."

She obviously wasn't listening. "Oh, that poor man. Can I call him, Charlie, just to tell him—"

"No!" he replied sharply, "absolutely not. I don't think he even knows about this yet. He wasn't in court, and I doubt that Beck is in as big a hurry to call him as I was to call you. And he should hear about it from Beck, not you. You'll have plenty of time to talk to him later if you want to. All right?"

"All right, Charlie," she replied compliantly, "whatever you say."

The lawyer was shaking his head when he came out of the phone booth. Crissakes, he said to himself. Break your ass to win a case, and your client gives you a guilty conscience. Go figure.

Charlie was still trying to catch his breath after rushing back to his office from the courthouse. He had called Tracey because he wanted to; now he was calling her father because he had to.

Bernard Benedict's booming voice came over the line. He sounded ecstatic. "Charlie! Tracey told me the good news. You hit the jackpot, you old fox, and you read the tea leaves just right. Thank God you didn't let us settle."

"Thanks, Bernie, but it took a lot of help from you. And that's why I'm calling. I need some more help."

"From me?"

"From you. Tracey listens to you, Bernie, and you've got to talk to her. She's got these crazy guilt feelings about taking money from Sinclair."

"I guess I did too good a job raising her. I taught her to be a forgiving person, but I never intended for her to give away three million bucks."

Charlie laughed. "You were a hell of a teacher, but it's not really her money to give away."

"I don't understand."

"I didn't get a chance to give her the details when I called from the courthouse, but the jury awarded most of the verdict to Angel—seven million dollars to be exact. Technically, since she's a minor, the money goes to Tracey and Larry as her guardians, and it can be spent only for her care. The rest of the money goes to Tracey and Larry personally—half a million for each of them."

"Now, wait a minute, Charlie, you'll have to explain that."

"Okay. Let's take the easy part first. What Tracey and Larry get for themselves is theirs. They can do whatever they want with it. Larry already agreed to give Tracey anything awarded to him—that was part of the divorce settlement—so she'll get his half million. That leaves a million for her and seven million for Angel, minus my legal fee."

"But I don't understand that guardian thing," Benedict said. "How does that work?"

"Nothing complicated about it. Larry'll probably let Tracey be the sole guardian, and nobody will complain about that. Then she'll invest the money, not in her name but as Angel's guardian or trustee. There are very few restrictions on what she does with it, and it's really no different than if the money belonged to her outright. For example, she can reimburse herself and you for money the two of you already spent because of Angel's condition. And if she decides she needs a bigger car to cart Angel around, or a bigger house for live-in help, she can use some of that money. All she'll have to do is report it to the court, maybe get permission in advance for the bigger expenditures, but no one will object as long as she can show that somehow Angel will benefit."

"Well, that sounds . . . Oh, Christ, Charlie, what happens if Angel dies? What happens to the rest of that money?"

"It would ordinarily go to Tracey and Larry as Angel's closest heirs, but the divorce decree covered that too. It provides that anything left at Angel's death goes only to Tracey."

"Okay, I think I understand. Now what is it that you want me to say to her?"

"First of all, tell her that she can't give Sinclair a pass because that would be the same as her giving away Angel's money, and the court wouldn't let her do that. Hell, the judge could throw her in jail for doing something like that. And secondly," Charlie said, tapping the phone with his pencil for emphasis, "remind her about legal fees. One-third of that eight million is mine, and that comes to two and two-thirds million."

"And you don't want her giving that away either, do you?" Benedict chuckled.

"Damn right I don't, and I won't let her. Now listen, Bernie, if she gives you any trouble about this, remember there's a good chance that we can collect the whole eight million from the insurance company. They screwed Sinclair on the settlement, and he could have a claim against them for the entire amount. If Tracey doesn't let her heart get in the way of her head, I'll do everything I can to help Sinclair go after those bastards."

"So," Benedict repeated to be sure he understood, "I'll tell her that she can't give Sinclair a pass because one-third of that money is yours and most of the balance actually belongs to Angel. But Sinclair might be off the hook anyway if the insurance company can be forced to pay his share. Is that right?"

"You got it. And, Bernie, there's one other thing. She told me she wanted to call Sinclair. I don't know what she has in mind, but I don't want her calling him. Whatever she says to him, he'll run and tell Beck or the insurance company, and that could hurt us. If they see that she's sympathetic toward Sinclair, they'll play on that. This case isn't over until the appellate court affirms the verdict."

"Okay, Charlie, you're still the boss. You haven't steered us wrong yet and Tracey knows that."

Lew Beck dreaded making the phone call. He was half hoping that Steve Sinclair would be unavailable, but he knew better. Steve surely would have left word that if Lew Beck called he was to be interrupted.

"They brought back a verdict," the lawyer said bluntly when his client got on the line.

Beck had already told Steve that an early verdict would be a good sign, but he knew that the tone of his voice told a different story.

"You don't sound very happy, Lew."

"I'm not." He took a deep breath and then said the ugly words: "They think the Waltons are entitled to eight million dollars."

"Eight million! Are you serious? My God, Lew, what happened?"

"I have no idea. Chicago has a history of high jury verdicts, but I would never have predicted anything like this. Sure, during the first few days of the trial I had some concerns about a runaway verdict, but then we started to put a lot of points up on the board. Even the judge told us near the end of the trial that he thought it was a close case and that any verdict in favor of the plaintiffs would be low. He said that was the only way that those jurors leaning your way would go along with it."

"But," Steve asked, "even during those first few days, when things looked the worst, you could have settled by paying four-point-two million, isn't that right? In fact, I think you told Phil Ogden and me that Mayfield indicated he'd have agreed to that. Isn't that right?"

Beck admitted that it was.

"Now what am I supposed to do, Lew? Where in the hell am I going to get three million dollars?"

"We're not there yet, Steve. I plan to file a motion for a new trial, and we still have the appellate court. In the meantime, I'll call Ogden."

"Would you mind waiting a few minutes before you call him?"

"No, but why?"

"Because *I* plan to call him—and right now. I need help, Lew, more help than I think I've been getting from you or my insurance company."

The last ten minutes left Tracey's head spinning. First Charlie had called her about the verdict. Then her father had come into her office to pass on the warnings from Charlie. She was still mulling over that conversation when her phone rang. It was Dave Roberts.

"I just got back to the office and found your message

about the jury," he said. "Is it bad news? I mean, with them coming back so soon?"

"They gave us eight million dollars."

"Eight million? My God, Tracey, that's fantastic! Do you realize what that means?"

"It means Charlie did too good a job."

THIRTY-ONE ====

PHIL OGDEN WASTED no time getting into the case. Within an hour after Steve's depressing call to tell him about the verdict, he drafted and mailed to Lew Beck, Charlie Mayfield, and the court a formal notice that the firm of Ogden & Andrews would thereafter be serving as additional counsel for the defendant, Steven Sinclair.

Then, knowing that Charlie could verify the history of the settlement negotiations and therefore back up the bad faith claim against the insurance company, he called the lawyer he had known only by reputation. Sure enough, the older lawyer was cooperative, and why not? He told Phil he suspected that Steve Sinclair wouldn't be able to pay his share of the verdict, and it would therefore be to his advantage to help stick North American with the whole eight million.

Within two days Charlie furnished him with a letter describing each instance in which he had told Lew Beck or Duane DeLuca that the Waltons were willing to settle for five million dollars or less. The details, which included dates and places, made it obvious that Charlie had kept a careful log of all these conversations.

Then, attaching Charlie's letter to one of his own, Phil made a formal demand on the insurance company to pay the entire eight million dollars plus interest, court costs, and even his own fees "because of your failure to exercise good faith and reasonable judgment in attempting to settle the litigation, thereby subjecting Dr. Sinclair to unnecessary and unwarranted risk, which risk did in fact result in a three million dollar liability on his part."

Within a week the insurance company flatly denied any liability beyond the policy limit. And they did so in a computer-generated form letter.

Judge Horace Grubner entered the formal judgment for eight million dollars against Steve Sinclair on the Wednesday following the jury verdict. That started the clock running for the filing of a motion for a new trial and, should the motion be unsuccessful, for the appeal to the Illinois Appellate Court. It soon became painfully clear to Charlie Mayfield and his clients that North American Casualty was doing just what Duane DeLuca threatened that they would do—stall. Through Lew Beck the company asked for an extension of time within which to file a motion for a new trial and a supporting brief. Charlie had resisted, but Judge Grubner couldn't very well deny the request of a defendant saddled with an eight million dollar liability. He granted a short extension, but warned Beck that he would not be so accommodating if subsequent requests were made.

"Those damned insurance companies," Charlie explained to the Waltons, "they do this every time. They just love to hang on to their money as long as they can. And they have another motive, too: They figure that any plaintiff who wins a case needs the money and will eventually give up and settle for less than the full judgment just to get his hands on *something*. That's why so many cases are settled even after they're won. Insurance men are a bunch of heartless bastards," he said, shaking his head. "Our only consolation is that they'll have to pay us some interest from the date of judgment until final payment, but it'll be a hell of a lot less than *they'll* be earning on the money in the meantime."

Lew Beck and Phil Ogden worked out an accommodation for handling the motion for a new trial and, if necessary, the appeal. Since Beck was more familiar with the evidence, it was agreed that he would be in charge and that Phil and Tom would share second chair by making suggestions, doing most of the legal research, and in general playing the devil's advocate.

Ever since his divorce from his first wife, Phil had made it a rule not to let anything interfere with his relationship with his two sons. Fortunately Sally, unlike some of the divorced mothers he knew, did nothing to undermine the boys' love and respect for their father, not even after he married Maggie.

The first weekend in May, which was the weekend following entry of the judgment, was unseasonably warm, and Phil decided to spend it camping with the boys at Starved Rock State Park. He had left the office early enough on Friday to shop for all the things he would need before picking up the boys after school, and he didn't return to Chicago until after dark on Sunday.

Worn out from pitching tents, hiking, cooking, cleaning up, and breaking camp, and from all the fun and fresh air, Phil slept in an extra hour on Monday morning. Arriving at the office at ten, he found piled high on his already cluttered desk seven large file boxes stacked to within inches of the ceiling. Taped to the middle box was a note in Tom's handwriting: "Welcome to *Walton v. Sinclair*."

"This is from your colleague and co-counsel, Lew Beck," Tom explained as he entered Phil's office.

"But we just asked him to send us—"

"And that's just what he did. He sent over—let's see, each box is labeled—copies of all the depositions and interrogatories, the trial transcript, medical and hospital records, correspondence, pleadings and pretrial briefs, his research notes, and the documents introduced by both sides at the trial. He even sent over a box marked 'Miscellaneous Documents.' I guess he wants to make sure we can't accuse him of not cooperating."

"My God," Phil said, "are we supposed to read all this?"

"Read it and know it," his partner replied. "And the motion for a new trial is due in only six weeks. Sounds like a long time, but it isn't, not with all this," he added, gesturing toward the stack of boxes, "*and* having to write a brief."

Phil walked behind his desk, found his calendar, and leafed through the pages covering the next few weeks. Then he looked up at Tom with a forlorn expression.

"Yeah, me too," Tom said, "and my drug case goes to trial next Monday. It'll last better than a week, and I'll have to spend some time this week getting ready."

"Any ideas?" Phil asked.

"Well, we can ask Judge Grubner for another extension, but I don't think we'll get it, not after what he said last time. Let's just plan on working nights. If we split this stuff up between us, we should be able to digest it well enough to give Beck a hand."

They began that same night. They called their wives, Maggie and Alice, to say they'd be working late, called out for sandwiches, and prepared to dig in.

"You've worked on more litigation than I have," Phil said. "What do you think's the best way to divide this mess up?"

"By subject matter," Tom answered quickly. "That's the only way we can do it without overlapping. I'll take all the medical parts—expert testimony, hospital records, that kind of thing. Since Alice is a nurse, she might be able to help me understand the technical stuff."

"But that's the whole case," Phil protested. "It doesn't leave anything for me."

"Wrong. You'll have plenty to do. For openers, you'll have to analyze Mrs. Walton's testimony—every word of it. Look for inconsistencies. Compare what she said in court with what she said at her pretrial depositions. Here, I'll show you the best way to do that."

Tom reached for a yellow legal pad, tore off the top sheet, and printed, "Tracey Walton" at the top. Then he drew a line down the center to make two columns. At the top of the left-hand column he wrote "Deposition" and at the top of the right-hand column he wrote "Trial."

"Start with her deposition," he said. "Read through it carefully and condense everything she said on every subject into a sentence or two, and write that down in the left-hand column, and mark down the page where you found it. Then do the same thing for her trial testimony. After you've done that, do a cut-and-paste job on what you've written down so you end up with a line-by-line comparison of what she said both times on each subject. Then look for inconsistencies—even little things. Did she describe things—especially her conversations with Steve—exactly the same way on both occasions? And if she answered yes to a question at the trial, but answered 'I think so' to the same question at her deposition, it could be important."

"But that wouldn't be grounds for a new trial, would it?"

"No, but it could give us a clue that she was fudging about something, and that might lead us somewhere. Remember, Phil, when you're drowning, you grab at straws. Now, after you've done that, do the same thing with Larry Walton's testimony. And then compare hers with his, subject by subject."

"Steve told me that Tracey's husband never testified at the trial."

Tom looked up. "He didn't? That's strange."

"Maybe he didn't have anything to add to what his wife testified to. I understand she was a terrific witness."

"All the same, he's a plaintiff, and it's unusual not to put a plaintiff on the stand. You'd think that Mayfield would have stuck him up there if for no other reason than to have him corroborate his wife's testimony. More important, you'd think Mayfield would want the jurors to see and hear him. After all, he's the father of that child, and he was asking those twelve people to give him money."

"Well, it's pretty hard to fault Mayfield's strategy. He won the case, didn't he?"

Tom didn't reply. His mind seemed to be elsewhere. Finally he held up a pencil and said, "Mayfield had a reason not to put Larry Walton on the stand. Keep that in mind while you're reading all those transcripts."

"Maybe he just didn't know anything."

"Or maybe," Tom said softly, "he knew too much."

THIRTY-TWO ═══

STEVE SINCLAIR WAS relieved to find that his medical practice didn't suffer as a result of his having been found guilty of malpractice. He supposed that Molly, Phil, and Tom were right when they assured him that very few people outside of the legal circles knew about these cases, and those who knew didn't seem to care. Only a litigious society could be that indifferent to an eight million dollar malpractice verdict.

But if his practice wasn't suffering, his mind was. In the days following the verdict he became even more withdrawn and, worse, he became uncharacteristically abrupt with his office staff. Even Molly was not immune to his moods, which reflected a combination of depression, hostility, and paranoia. He felt that he had been slandered by a former patient, short-changed by the legal system, and cheated by his insurance company.

He began to second-guess himself about his competence, and he started to practice medicine more defensively than he knew was necessary. He saw every new case as a potential lawsuit, and every new patient as a potential plaintiff. He ordered tests that he knew weren't required, and sought useless second opinions from other doctors. He even considered giving up obstetrics and limiting his practice to gynecology. He didn't think he could survive another malpractice trial, and he would do everything in his power to avoid it. He was getting dangerously close to the point where he was more concerned with protecting himself than with protecting his patients. He even doubled the amount of his malpractice insurance, which carried an exorbitant premium because of the verdict. And he had to write it with a new company, since North American Casualty had canceled his policy three days after the trial ended.

It was during this period of turmoil and indecision that a former patient whom Steve Sinclair hadn't seen in over four years called his office for an appointment. She was the woman who had recommended him to Tracey Walton several years earlier.

By the third week following the verdict, Tom Andrews was devoting full time to Steve Sinclair's appeal.

"It's all in those damn dates," he said as he walked into Phil Ogden's office and sat in the one chair that wasn't covered with files. He threw his feet up onto Phil's desk and held up a thick folder.

Phil recognized the folder as the one that held all of his notes on the testimony in *Walton v. Sinclair*. *"What's* in the dates?"

"The key to everything. Let me explain. After I finished going through all the expert testimony and medical records, and did a little research on my own, I could see that the only glitch in the whole case was that alpha-fetoprotein test. If that test hadn't been misread, Steve would have ordered an amniocentesis, and that would have led to a karyotyping, which would have told him that Mrs. Walton was carrying a Down fetus. Everything that went wrong could be traced to that damn test, and he misread the results for only one reason: because he had the wrong date of conception."

"What about the ultrasound?"

"That's a red herring," Tom said, waving his hand to show that it was an issue that could be dismissed. "By the time Beck finished cross-examining Dr. Barrington, the ultrasound issue was out of the case. Barrington admitted that it wasn't a standard procedure, and anyway, Steve's records showed that he tried to schedule the test but Mrs. Walton never showed up. Steve even testified to that, and she never took the stand again to rebut it. Then Beck sewed it up by putting on a couple of other obstetricians near the end of the trial who said they often didn't do ultrasound in the absence of special circumstances and saw no reason to do it in this case. Mayfield didn't even cross-examine them. No," he said, shaking his head, "it all goes back to the AFP test, and to the screwup on the date of conception.

"One possible explanation for that screwup," Tom added, "is that Steve might have had another patient, also newly pregnant, in his office at about the same time that Tracey was there on that first day. Maybe that other patient gave him the July fifth date, and Steve accidentally wrote it in Tracey's record."

Phil shook his head. "According to Beck, Judge Grubner raised the same possibility in his chambers after all the evidence was in. So I had Steve check his schedule for that day, August 17, 1987. None of his other patients that day was pregnant."

"But," Tom remarked, "if that possibility occurred to me and to the judge, then you can bet it occurred to some of the jurors—and that it came up during their deliberations. Hell, that could've been their reason for finding that Steve was negligent. If Beck had been on his toes he would've covered it when he had Steve on the stand."

He waved the folder he had been carrying when he came into Phil's office. "This is the comparison you made of all the testimony. I've spent hours and hours studying it. Once you get around the ultrasound issue—and, as I said, I don't believe it was all that important—the only discrepancy is in the dates. Mrs. Walton swore she told Steve she had her last period in mid-June, and he swore she told him it was in early July." Tom looked at his partner and said, "One of them had to be lying, Phil. Our job is to prove it was her."

"It *was* her."

"What makes you so sure, other than the fact that Steve's your friend and you can't believe he'd lie?"

"He *didn't* lie, damn it. He wrote July fifth in his

records when Tracey was in his office, and that's the date that appeared on the lab report for the AFP test. He had no reason to lie at that point; it was before anyone could even know she was carrying a Down child."

"And by the same token," Tom countered, "*she* had no reason to lie during that first visit. So maybe it boils down to an honest mistake—either her mistake in telling him the wrong date or his mistake in writing down the wrong date."

"But that doesn't figure either," Phil said, running his hands through his uncombed dark hair. "It's unlikely she wouldn't know the date of her last period, and it's just as unlikely Steve would write down both the wrong month and the wrong day. That leaves us with only one explanation: She knew the date but deliberately misstated it. So, as I said, she lied."

"Okay," Tom conceded, "let's assume she lied. Then we have to find her motive. People don't lie for the hell of it. They have reasons, and we have to find out what hers was."

THIRTY-THREE ═══

"I HOPE YOU'RE willing to take me on again as a patient."

"Of course I am, Linda. Why wouldn't I be?"

"Well, I was the one who referred Tracey Walton to you, and I know how much trouble that's caused you."

Steve Sinclair, sitting behind the small desk in the office he used for conferences and patient interviews, smiled politely. "You had no way of knowing what would happen. None of us did."

"All the same, I want you to know that I still think you're a fine doctor. That's why I'm back."

Steve fiddled with his ballpoint pen for a few moments, then looked the woman squarely in the eye. "May I ask you a personal question, Linda?"

The woman laughed. "I can't imagine any question too personal for a gynecologist to ask a patient."

"It has nothing to do with your health," he explained. "It's just that I'd like to talk to Tracey to tell her how bad I feel about what she's going through, and to tell her that I don't bear any grudges about the lawsuit. But my lawyer—I guess I should say 'lawyers' because I now have three of them—they tell me I shouldn't call her until all this is behind us. I thought maybe you could deliver the message for me."

"Actually, I haven't seen or talked to Tracey during the past few years, and I really never knew her very well before that. My husband is the one who knew Tracey and her husband through his business. When they were still married, the four of us went out to dinner a few times, and that's when I gave her your name. Since their divorce I haven't had any contact with her at all, but if you'd like, I suppose I could call her and—"

"Oh, no," Steve said, holding up his hand. "I made the suggestion only because I thought you and Tracey were close friends. You stopped coming to me about the time she filed the lawsuit, so I naturally assumed that you and she were pals."

"It wasn't *my* idea to stop seeing you, Dr. Sinclair. It was my husband's. Shortly after Tracey had the baby, he insisted that I find another doctor. He thought . . . well, you know."

"Sure I do. He thought I had botched Tracey's case, and he didn't want me treating his wife."

"Something like that."

"Then tell me, Linda, why are you here now? Did he have a change of heart?"

"I wouldn't know. We separated a year ago, and now I make my own decisions. One of them was to rehire you as my doctor."

"I'm sorry to hear that—I mean, about the separation."

"Don't be. I'm happier than I've been for the past five years, since our marriage started to fall apart."

Phil poked his head into his partner's office. "Don't forget we're meeting Steve for a drink at six," he said. It was just past five on Friday; their secretaries had already gone home, but with only three weeks remaining before the brief and motion for a new trial were due, Phil and Tom were devoting as much time as possible—including evenings and weekends—to the case.

Tom Andrews sighed without even looking up. "Yeah, I remember."

"Hey, what's the problem? You look like you just lost the farm."

"Aw, I thought I had this great idea for Steve's case, but it didn't work out."

"What was it?"

"I was over at the title company this afternoon checking for liens on a client's real estate. I had the tract book out, and I started to get engrossed with all the entries. I can't get over how every single parcel of land has its own history, and it's all reflected right there in one place, usually on a single page. Every transaction affecting the parcel, whether it was a deed in 1880 or a mortgage in 1980, has been carefully recorded in someone's handwriting."

"What does *that* have to do with Steve's case?" Phil said impatiently.

"That's where I got my brainstorm. I was looking at all those dated entries when it hit me: Tracey Walton's calendar. You remember, Phil, how she kept referring to it during her testimony? She has a calendar for each year, and she records all of her appointments, both personal and business, in there."

"I remember, but I don't know what you're getting at."

"Well, if she really did tell Steve that she had her last period in July, like his records show, and if she was deliberately lying when she said it, then she must have lied because she didn't want him to know that her period was actually in mid-June, which is the time that everyone now agrees on. And that would mean she actually conceived sometime around late June or early July. Remember, doctors measure pregnancies from the date of the last period, but in fact the pregnancy doesn't begin until the actual date of conception, and that's a couple of weeks later. So the question is, why didn't Tracey want her doctor to know that she'd conceived her child in late June or early July—three weeks earlier than she led him to believe?"

"I give up. Why?"

"I have no idea, but I thought maybe her calendar would tell me. Those calendars are like diaries, and they give a pretty good picture of how people spend their lives—where they go, what they do, and who they're with. If she didn't want Steve to know she conceived in late June or early July, she must've had a reason, and I hoped the pages of her calendar for that time might give me a clue to what it was. So I dashed back to the office to dig through all the boxes Lew Beck sent us to get my hands on the damn thing."

"I don't think it's in there," Phil said. "I've already gone through all the evidence, and the calendar was never introduced."

"No, but when Beck took Mrs. Walton's deposition and heard her refer to her 1987 calendar, he served a notice on Mayfield to produce copies for him. Mayfield complied. They never got into evidence, but I found them in the box marked 'Miscellaneous Documents.'"

"And?"

"And nothing," Tom said dejectedly. "I went through all the pages covering late June and early July and I couldn't find anything out of the ordinary. The entries were the same as they were for other times—meetings with auditors, job site inspections, tennis matches, beauty shop appointments. And every day was chock full. Nothing suspicious, and certainly nothing she'd want to cover up. And naturally," Tom added with a wry grin, "her diary didn't show the dates of her periods or, for that matter, the dates she got laid. That would have been asking too much."

"I still say she lied," Phil said with determination. "I'll take the copy of her calendar home with me over the weekend and go through it. Who knows? Maybe I'll stumble onto something."

Harry Caray's restaurant has one of the great bars in Chicago. Housed in a renovated building on the corner of Kinzie and Dearborn just north of the Loop, the establishment, named for the popular announcer of the Chicago Cubs baseball games, is the nightly watering hole for crowds of beautiful young people. When Phil and Tom arrived, they saw Steve waving from the small round table he'd been able to capture in the far corner. The tables were high enough so that the patrons either stood at them or sat on tall stools if they were lucky enough to find any available.

"Are we late?" Phil asked, glancing at his watch.

"No, not at all," Steve replied. "I got here a few minutes early to grab a table. It was like taking a strategic hill in a war zone, and just as hard to hold, especially on a Friday night. But Molly told me this was *the* place to go." Steve had been saving two stools for them by putting his suit jacket on one and his briefcase on another.

By the time their drinks arrived, the two lawyers had brought their client up to date on the status of the motion for a new trial. "We have two main arguments," Tom explained. "One is that the judge made mistakes in some of his rulings, but I don't give that a lot of hope. A mistake has to be damned serious before it'll justify a retrial of the whole case. The other argument we'll make is that the verdict was so high, probably because of sympathy, that it can't be justified by the damage evidence. We have a few additional points, but they're mostly for window dressing."

"The point about the high verdict?" Steve said. "I didn't know that could be a reason for getting a new trial."

"It seldom is, but if the judge agrees that the verdict is beyond all reason—say, if a jury awards a million dollars for a little scratch—he or she has the power to reduce it. If the plaintiff doesn't accept the lower figure, then the judge will award a new trial."

Just as Steve was about to ask another question, he heard a familiar voice coming from behind him. "You gonna buy me a drink, Doc, or do I have to go over to the bar and start begging?"

He jumped up, kissed Molly on the cheek, and offered her his stool. "Hope you guys don't mind, but I told Molly we'd be here after work, and her office is only a couple of blocks away."

She exchanged hellos with Phil and Tom while Steve searched for a waitress and another stool. Molly took advantage of his absence. "I don't know what Sinclair needs more," she told them, "two good lawyers or one good psychiatrist. He hasn't been doing well since that jury clobbered him, and I'm starting to worry about him." She was about to explain his depression and how his confidence was fading, but Steve's reappearance at the table caused her to change the subject abruptly: "So I told the jerk, 'If you don't like my bloody ads go find another agency. Did it ever occur to you,' I told him, 'that your product isn't any good and *that's* why nobody's buying it?'"

"Nice try, Molly," Steve said as he pulled a fourth stool up to the table. "Listen," he announced to all three, "I know I've been a basket case since the trial ended, but I just can't help it. It so damned *unfair.* But starting right now I'm turning over a new leaf." He grinned and added, "I'll be my old self—witty, jolly, and the life of every party."

This prompted a laugh and another round of drinks. Phil and Tom did their best to reassure Steve and Molly that they shouldn't give up hope of a new trial either from Judge Grubner or from the appellate court. "And we're convinced the Walton woman lied," Phil said. "Now we're trying to figure out how to prove it."

"Oh," Steve blurted, "that reminds me—one of her old friends was in my office today."

"To do what," Molly asked sarcastically, "serve you with a summons?"

"No, nothing like that. She came to see me as a patient." He told them about the woman who had been a patient some years earlier, then had stopped seeing him after Angel Walton was born, but had now come back. "In fact, she was the one who originally referred Tracey to me."

"Why did she leave you?" Molly inquired. "And why did she come back all of a sudden?"

"She left because her husband insisted on it. He knew the Waltons because he'd done business with Benedict Construction, and like them, he blamed me for their baby's condition. But this woman and her husband separated a year ago, and now she feels free to do what she wants. So she's back."

Steve was careful not to mention the name of the patient. He was always offended when he heard doctors reveal their patients' names and problems, and he believed that he, as a gynecologist and obstetrician involved with the most personal aspects of a patient's health, had an even greater obligation to be discreet.

"If she and her husband are separated," Phil joked, "I don't suppose she's seeing you because she's having a baby."

Steve smiled. "No," he said, "just a regular gynecological checkup. But I'm being super-careful with her."

"Worried that she'll sue you too?" Molly asked.

"No, but she has had some problems, and I want her to know that I'm cautious and that she made the right choice to come back."

"Well," Molly joked, "it would be a shame if she and her husband got back together. He'd probably tell her to stop seeing you again."

"No danger of that. She told me that their marriage could never have survived, and she claims to be getting along just fine. The problem, she said, was that she couldn't compete with the fish."

"The fish?" Phil wasn't sure that he had heard that correctly.

"Yeah, the fish. Apparently he has a small house on a lake somewhere in Wisconsin. He flies his own plane, and just about every weekend during the spring, summer, and fall he goes up there with his buddies to fish. His wife saw the place only twice, she said, and that was six or seven years ago when he first bought it. In any event, she admitted to me that she hated his going up there so often and leaving her alone on all those weekends, and she resented him for it. She even said she was jealous of the place."

Molly pointed a finger at Steve. "If I ever get you to the altar, Buster, you'd better not plan on leaving *me* alone every weekend. I'd get the meanest divorce lawyer in Chicago, and when we got done with you you'd think that malpractice case of yours was a tea party."

Steve and Phil laughed, but Tom, who hadn't even been listening to her, suddenly hopped off his stool and picked up his briefcase. "I just thought of something I have to check out at the office. See you later." And with that he disappeared into the crowd.

"Hope it was nothing I said."

"No, Molly," Phil said. "That's just the way Tom is. If he happens to think about something that he has to do, he can't rest unless he takes care of it."

But Phil knew that Tom was too polite to run back to the office without an explanation. He had thought of something, and it had to be something important.

THIRTY-FOUR

"WHAT THE HELL was that all about?" Phil Ogden asked from the doorway to Tom's office an hour later. "It's not like you to run off and leave half a glass of beer on the table."

"I should've stayed and finished it," Tom replied, tossing his pencil on the mess of papers strewn across his desk. "Steve said something back at the bar that turned on a light bulb, but it led to another dead end—just like the calendar this afternoon."

"What was it?"

"I'm almost embarrassed to tell you, it was such a long shot."

"Hey, at this point we don't have anything left but long shots. Let's hear it."

"Well, Steve was telling us tonight about that patient he saw today, the one who knew Tracey Walton."

"Sure, the one who sent Tracey to see him in the first place."

"Right. And her husband had done work with Benedict Construction. Well, she told Steve that she and her husband separated about a year ago, and that would be about the time the Waltons got divorced. So I'm sitting there thinking how cozy that could have been for Tracey and that woman's husband."

"Jesus, Tom, that's more than a long shot. Just because Tracey's divorced and this guy's separated doesn't mean there's anything cozy going on between them. And anyway, what if there is? I would *expect* Tracey to be seeing other men. What's that got to do with the case?"

"If that's all I thought there was to it," Tom explained, "I'd still be back at Harry Caray's. But according to Steve, this patient said her husband flies up to Wisconsin on weekends to go fishing. He's been doing it for years, and he went up there without her."

"I still don't see the connection."

Tom shook his head. "That's just it, damn it, there isn't any connection. I learned *that* when I got back to the office. But when Steve mentioned this business about Wisconsin, something clicked—something I remembered stumbling across last week. I had been going over Tracey Walton's case history, the one Steve took down when she was in his office, and something stuck in my mind. It was during that very first visit when she thought she might be pregnant. I must've read Steve's notes of that interview a dozen times, but until tonight I never paid any attention to something I saw in there."

"What was it?" Phil prodded.

"Well, Steve must've noticed that she had a recent injury to her leg—either that or she brought it up on her own—but in any event his notes mention the injury and that she'd had a tetanus shot. I remembered that, according to Steve's notes, she got the tetanus shot somewhere up north, probably near the place where she had the accident, only I couldn't recall exactly where that was."

"I still don't see what—"

"Man, I'm looking for anything I can find. Our only hope is to find out that she lied to Steve about those dates. Remember, if we can prove that she lied about them, we could have the verdict thrown out"—he snapped his fingers—"just like that. Well, she'd have no reason to lie unless she was covering something up. So my mind has been working backwards to find something in her life that she'd want to cover up, and naturally I thought about whether she was cheating on her husband. Then when I heard about this guy having a hideaway in Wisconsin, and her having been up north somewhere getting a tetanus shot—well, hell, it was too tempting to pass up."

"So what are you so pissed off about? What did you find out when you got back to the office?"

"That she had the shot in *Michigan*," Tom said, throwing his hands up in frustration, "not Wisconsin, and I doubt that she swam across Lake Michigan for a quick roll in the hay." He looked whipped.

"Don't take it so hard," his partner said sympathetically. "It was a good try."

"Maybe, and what the hell, the real key to this case isn't whether Tracey Walton sleeps around; it's whether she's a liar, whether she lied about something that did or didn't take place in June or July of 1987, and that damn calendar of hers shows nothing out of the ordinary during that time. I've checked it a dozen times, and it indicates that she was right here in Chicago, all day every day, running a construction company."

THIRTY-FIVE ===

PHIL HAD BEEN telling his wife, Maggie, how Tom had run back to the office hoping to discover from Tracey Walton's diary that she'd had a tetanus shot in Wisconsin, but that it turned out to have been in Michigan.

"However," Phil explained, sitting on the side of the bed and kicking off his shoes, "it wouldn't have made any difference anyway. If Tracey had been covering up anything, it would've been something that occurred between late June and early July of 1987, but her calendar proved that she wasn't in Wisconsin *or* Michigan at that time. She was right here in Chicago, conducting business as usual."

"Maybe her calendar was phonied up," Maggie suggested as she slipped into bed. "Maybe she wrote down a lot of false entries just to throw you off." Maggie herself was a lawyer in a large Chicago firm, and she knew how documents should not necessarily be taken at face value, especially the calendar of someone who might want to cover up her tracks. She yawned and then said, "If there's nothing about a trip to Michigan in her calendar, then something's wrong. She had to have gone up there *sometime* if that's where she got a tetanus shot."

"Oh, my *God*," Phil Ogden said, slapping his forehead. "How could we have been so *stupid*?" He couldn't believe that he and Tom had overlooked the possibility of phony entries. They had been so intent on searching for the needle that they hadn't looked for the haystack. The words were hardly out of Maggie's mouth before he reached for the bedside phone to call his partner.

The next morning Phil and Tom pored over their copy of Tracey Walton's calendar. The first thing they checked was the most obvious: Were the entries for any dates during the critical time period written in a different way from those for the other dates? Different ink or different handwriting, for example, could mean that they had been written down out of sequence. That would support the premise that Tracey was covering up something—something important enough to cause her to lie about the date of her last period. *Why* she might have lied wasn't the critical issue; the question now was *whether* she lied.

Tom and Phil were disappointed to see that the entries were consistent and orderly, all of them presumably in Tracey's neat handwriting and all with the same type of pen. There were, to be sure, several changes in the calendar, but this was to be expected; people constantly changed their schedules to accommodate emergencies or last-minute appointments. One couldn't assume that these changes were made after the fact, in preparation for trial, and for the nefarious purpose of covering up something that took place—or did not take place—five years earlier, especially since the original entries, when changed, had a single line drawn through them and were still legible—hardly the practice of one who wanted to destroy evidence of what he or she was doing on a certain day.

And there was the mystery of the tetanus shot. Steve's records indicated that Tracey had suffered a "recent" injury, and the fact that he wrote that in her record on August seventeenth suggested that the injury requiring the shot occurred during the previous two or three months. But they examined her calendar for the entire year and saw no evidence that she had been in Michigan. This only heightened Phil's and Tom's suspicion that something was fishy. But *what*?

Having no luck in finding altered entries, the two

lawyers pursued the more laborious method of discrediting the calendar. They carefully wrote down every single entry from June 20 to July 10, 1987, using a separate page for each date. They knew that Tracey had to have become pregnant during that time, and they knew—because of the absence of a Michigan entry—that the calendar was suspect. If, as they believed, Tracey was covering something up, then some of these entries had to be bogus. Finding out that *any* entry was phony would be a signal that further investigation into that day's activities might be worthwhile. They realized they would be looking into events that were five years old, but they had no alternative. Digging, digging, and more digging—Tom and Phil both knew that that was the not-so-glorious-but-all-too-common task of a lawyer in search of facts.

After writing down each listed appointment, they went over them to decide which would be the easiest to verify. A beauty shop appointment, for example, could be double-checked by calling the beauty shop, although that could be problematic. Did beauty shops keep appointment records for five years? And if so, would they release them? Meetings with people could be verified by checking with those other people, who in turn would have to check their own calendars for those dates. Would they still have them? Would they show them to Phil and Tom?

And how long would all this take? The two lawyers surely couldn't divert their attention from the motion for a new trial and brief; they were already behind on the things they were doing to help Lew Beck prepare those papers. They decided that Tom should concentrate on verifying the calendar entries while Phil would put in double time on the motion and brief.

That afternoon Tom Andrews began his arduous assignment. He could see that Tracey had been a busy woman, averaging about four appointments for each of those twenty-odd days in 1987. Even if he tried to confirm only one on each day—since one would be sufficient to establish that she was in Chicago and tending to business—the task could take weeks. So he began looking for a constant, something she did regularly, where it would be easy to see if there had been a break in her routine. That would make more sense than trying to validate many unrelated appointments and meetings.

An idea came to him near the end of the day: her car! Did she drive to her office each day? If so, could Tom find out whether her car was in fact *not* driven during any days in the critical time period when her calendar indicated she had gone to her office? Damn! Tom thought to himself. This could be the key to everything.

He knew it would be easy enough to find out if she generally used her car to commute, but how could he find out if she drove it on specific dates five years earlier? The more he thought about it, the more impossible it seemed. He continued to wrestle with the problem until nearly six o'clock when he glanced at his watch—and remembered that he'd promised his wife that he'd meet her at her parents' home for an early dinner.

He hurriedly threw his notes into his briefcase, grabbed his jacket, and ran into his partner's office. "I gotta get out of here, Phil, or Alice'll kill me. I'm taking all of the Walton woman's appointments home with me. I'll work on them tonight." Then he dashed the two blocks to his parking garage, took the steps two at a time up to the second level, climbed into his three-year-old BMW, and navigated the circular exit ramp down to the street level. The line of waiting cars backed up at the cashier's booth wasn't a problem—he took the special lane for those regular customers who used electronic pass cards to open the gate whenever they entered or left the garage. Instead of paying each time they left, they received a monthly bill. Just as Tom was about to insert his pass card into the slot that would register his leaving and raise the barrier—*Oh, shit!*

He slammed on his brakes, checked the rearview mirror, threw his car into reverse, and with tires shrieking, backed up into an empty parking place. He sat in the car for a few moments concocting a plan to get the information he wanted, then got out and walked past the cashier's window to a door labeled OFFICE. He knocked.

"Come on in. It's open," said a pleasant voice.

He went in and saw a middle-aged black woman sitting at a desk and writing numbers on a spreadsheet. No one else was in the room. "Hi," he said cheerfully, "is the manager in?"

"At six o'clock on a Saturday? You gotta be kiddin'." She didn't even look up at the tall black lawyer.

"Well, then," Tom said, tossing a ten dollar bill on her desk, "this is for you." The woman looked at the bill and then at Tom. "And if you can tell me what I want to know, I just might be able to find another one."

"Hey," she protested, offering to return the bill, "I don't tell no stories. If you want to find somethin' out about someone, you go look someplace else, hear?"

Tom himself slipped into the rhythmic lingo of the streets, thinking that this would help gain the woman's cooperation. "No, sister, I don't need to know about nobody else; I have to know somethin' about *me*."

"You?"

"Yeah, me. Y'see, the police have someone who said they saw a car like mine take off from a robbery at a 7-Eleven. But I know I was downtown workin' at the time, and I had my car parked right here. I need you to help me prove it."

"Now how could I do that?"

Tom held up his garage pass card, "I use this when I bring my car in here. Doesn't that machine out there keep a record to tell you when I come and go?"

The woman suddenly smiled. "Well, child, why didn't you just come in here and ask me that in the first place? You coulda saved yourself twenty bucks." She took his pass card and studied it. "This here your name? Thomas Andrews?"

"Yes, ma'am."

She pulled out a scratch pad and wrote down his name

and some numbers from the card. "Now, what day you want me to look at?" she said, shifting her chair around to face a computer terminal.

Christ, Tom thought to himself, everyone in the world but me uses those things. "It was—uh, let's see—last December tenth." He had only been parking in the garage since last fall, so he couldn't ask her to check earlier than that, and he selected December tenth because that was his birthday and he remembered that it had fallen on a weekday when he was at work. "Can you go back that far?"

"You kiddin' me?" she answered. "We can go back years." Her fingers danced across the keyboard for what seemed like only a few seconds. "Here! Here it is," she announced triumphantly. "Let's see, you came in here at eight forty-two that morning, and you didn't leave until five fifty-five that night. Your car was here all day, unless that robber took it out without using your card." She looked up. "That help?"

"You bet it does," Tom replied, grinning. "That 7-Eleven was knocked off at three in the afternoon."

"I'll make you a printout."

"No, sister, that won't be necessary." He tossed another ten dollar bill on the desk and started for the door.

"But don't you need somethin' to show the police?"

He was already halfway to his car.

It was all Tom could do to sit through dinner at his in-laws' place that night. When he and his wife finally got home, he unlocked the front door and said, "Alice, honey, you go on in. I have an errand to run, but I'll be back in half an hour."

"What kind of errand? It's almost ten o'clock."

He simultaneously kissed her on the cheek and swatted her on the rump. "I'll tell you about it when I get home. Now get ready for bed and keep your fingers crossed."

Having already checked out the address, he wasted no

time driving to the offices of Benedict Construction Company. All evening he had been trying to predict whether Benedict Construction was near a parking garage or lot that utilized an electronic pass card system. If so, was the lot there in the summer of 1987? And was it likely that Tracey parked there? Maybe she had a private stall on the company's own property.

The Benedict Construction Company offices were located on Polk Street, a little more than a mile southwest of the Loop in an industrial park that had been developed about ten years earlier. The property had been a slum until a pilot urban renewal program converted the area into a complex of office buildings, medium-cost housing, and a Chicago campus for the University of Illinois. The generous lighting along the wide streets revealed a clean neighborhood that was anything but run-down. As Tom turned onto the block he wanted, his heart sank: There was no sign of a commercial parking lot. Then as he got closer he noticed—right next door to Benedict Construction but set farther back from the street—a modern, two-story parking structure. As he inched closer, he prayed that he'd see—*There it was!* A gate that could be automatically raised to allow a car to enter, and in front of it was a yellow post supporting an orange metal box.

Tom parked in the driveway and walked over to look closely at the box. He was hoping it was similar to the one at his garage downtown, and not one that would allow any driver to activate the gate simply by pushing a button and taking a ticket to be used to pay the fee when leaving. When he finally got close enough to inspect the box, he saw that it accommodated both types of drivers— the regular customers who used pass cards and those who took a ticket and paid each time they left. Perfect! A regular customer—and he prayed that Tracey Walton was a regular customer—would surely use a pass card for which a record was kept.

Before he left the garage, which was deserted that late at night, he walked over to the unoccupied cashier's booth and saw a small sign below the window: Thank You for Parking with Us—Peerless Parking, Inc.

Now Tom had to find out if both buildings—the parking garage and the building that housed the Benedict Construction offices—were there in 1987. If not, his efforts and hopes over the past few hours would turn out to be an exercise in futility. He couldn't tell the age of the buildings from his own observation, but he knew he could find out when the building permits were issued by checking with the city building department on Monday morning. In fact, as he thought about it, there was an even easier way.

With a glimmer of optimism that he had not felt since he got involved in *Walton v. Sinclair,* Tom returned to his car and headed for home.

THIRTY-SIX

TOM WANTED TO tell Phil about his idea first thing Monday morning, but his partner was at a real estate closing in the suburbs and wasn't expected in the office until noon. Tom couldn't wait. He went into his office and dialed the phone.

"Benedict Construction."

"Good morning. May I please speak with the office manager?"

"One moment, please."

Tom drummed his fingers to the music that came through the phone while he was on hold. He was thinking that he should have come up with a better excuse for the call when the music was replaced by a woman's voice.

"Hello."

"Is this the office manager?"

"Yes, it is," the woman replied in the impatient voice of someone accustomed to fending off unsolicited sales pitches.

"I need only a second of your time, ma'am. I'm with the Chicago Census Department, and we'd like to know how long Benedict Construction has been at its present location." Tom didn't even know if Chicago had a census department, but he was confident that the person on the other end of the line wouldn't know either.

"Do you mean our offices? We do have some other property where we keep our trucks and heavy equipment."

"We're asking about your offices, ma'am. On Polk Street."

"Well, let's see. We moved in here in the fall of 1985. And then we took some additional space in the building. That was in—"

"That's all right. We're only interested in the date you first moved in." Tom sat back in his chair and silently sighed with relief. One down and one to go. "By the way, ma'am, maybe you could save me a phone call."

"Surely, if I can."

"Our records show that there's a parking garage next door to your offices, to the west. Is that correct?"

"Yes, I park there myself."

"Would you happen to know how long it's been there?"

"Not really. All I can tell you is that it was there when we moved into our offices. So it must have been there since at least 1985."

Bull's-eye!

Tom Andrews immediately made another trip to the neighborhood—this time in daylight—and was now reasonably sure that Tracey would have parked at the garage next door. He saw no other places where she could have parked as conveniently. There were no reserved stalls for executives near the front entrance or behind her office building, and there was no curbside parking available on the street.

When Phil returned to the office just before noon, Tom was waiting to tell him about his plan to use Tracey's parking log to cross-check her calendar. He was disappointed to see that his partner didn't share his enthusiasm for the idea.

"I suppose it might work," Phil said as he unpacked his briefcase. "But if Tracey Walton was up to something back in the summer of eighty-seven—something that she didn't want anyone to know about—it was probably something she did on a weekend and not during her working schedule. And if I'm right about that, the records from the parking garage next to her office won't help."

"You could be right about that," Tom admitted, "but that sure doesn't mean that we shouldn't give it a try. Now my problem is to figure out how to get that garage record," he said. "I can't very well just walk in there and ask, the way I did yesterday at my own garage."

"Why not?"

"Because at my garage I was asking about my own car, not someone else's. There's no way the staff at her garage will go back five years into their records to give a complete stranger information about one of their customers— not without her permission."

Phil grinned as he made a notation on a file he had just removed from his briefcase. "I know you, Tom. You'll think of a way." Then he stopped writing and looked up. "Hey, where'd you say that garage was?"

Tom told him.

Phil thought for a moment and then nodded to himself. "That's in the First Ward, Alderman Kelly's ward. Maybe he can help. I'll give him a call."

Tom raised his eyebrows. "You?" he asked. He couldn't believe that Phil knew the name of the First Ward alderman, let alone that he knew him well enough to call him.

"Sure," Phil said, "Maggie and Kelly's daughter were sorority sisters in college, and they stayed close. In fact, Maggie was a bridesmaid at her wedding, and we've been to Kelly's home a few times. He's always throwing an arm around my shoulder and asking me to call him if he can ever do me a favor. No reason I shouldn't take him up on it."

"That's one of Harry Weintraub's lots," Alderman Kelly said as soon as he heard the location of the garage. Phil hadn't even had a chance to mention the Peerless Parking sign Tom had spotted.

"You knew that off the top of your head?" Phil asked, surprised.

"It's my job to know who owns what in my ward, and Harry's a hard guy to forget. He's always suckin' up to the political guys—makes him feel like a big shot, and he thinks it'll give him an edge if he ever needs something."

Phil explained what he and his partner were looking for. "If we could just see the printouts for June and July of 1987, we might be able to find out if this woman was lying to us about what she was doing back then."

"Before I can agree to help you, Phil, I'll have to know this woman's name. I want to be sure I'm not checking up on the mayor's wife."

Phil laughed. "Her name is Tracey Walton."

"Isn't that Bernie Benedict's daughter?"

"Uh-huh," Phil replied cautiously, afraid he was about to lose the alderman's cooperation. "Is that a problem?"

"Hell, no! That son of a bitch made a campaign contribution to the guy who ran against me in my last election. After all we've done for Benedict in this city, he should've known better."

Harry Weintraub took pride in the fact that he had come out of the streets of Chicago to claim his piece of the pie. Starting with neither money nor education, he had not followed an easy road to success. But success, he knew, was a relative term, and Harry was aware that he was not in line for the Horatio Alger award. Nonetheless, he was proud of the position he'd earned among Chicago's middle class, and he protected it zealously. He worked hard, lived within his means, paid his taxes, thanked the Almighty every day, and remained faithful to his wife of forty-one years.

One way to protect one's business in Chicago, Harry Weintraub had learned long ago, was to play ball with "the city." When he was a street kid, "the city" had meant the cop on the beat, but more recently he had come to understand that the man in blue could only do, or not do, so much. Now it was the ward heelers, the tax assessors, and the rest of the gang at City Hall who had to be coddled. Harry wasn't the only businessman in Chicago who had figured that out, but while political kowtowing was a form of insurance for most businesses, it was a downright necessity for Harry Weintraub, because he owned Peerless Parking, Inc., and Peerless Parking owned or managed no less than twenty parking lots and garages throughout the city.

Hardly a day went by that Harry didn't have to deal with "the city." He'd call them for a real estate tax reduction; they'd call him for a political contribution. He'd call them for extra police protection when cars in his lots were stolen or broken into; they'd call him for free parking passes for friends and relatives. He'd call them for a building permit or a zoning variation; they'd call him to seek a job for someone's kid. Harry didn't complain. "Hey," he'd say, "that's life in the big city." Actually, Harry Weintraub liked the system. It took good care of him, and if the truth were known, he liked to brag that he was a regular at the mayor's thousand-dollar-a-plate fund-raisers.

Harry's office was on the third floor of an old office building on South Wells Street. All of the office windows had an unfortunate view of Chicago's famous el tracks, and they rattled in strange harmony every few minutes when the el thundered noisily by. It was hardly a showplace, but the rent was right. "What the hell do I need a fancy office for?" he'd ask. "This ain't where my customers come."

It was Harry Weintraub's practice never to answer his office phone. There were just too many calls from irate customers complaining about a scratched bumper or a dented fender or a package stolen from the back seat or the trunk. He was the boss and bosses didn't deal with that sort of thing.

"Harry," one of the clerks shouted through the open door to his office, "pick up line two."

"Who is it?"

"Says he's Alderman Kelly."

Harry hesitated just long enough to fix in his mind the alderman's first name and ward, and whether he owed Harry or Harry owed him. Then he kicked his door shut and picked up the phone. "Patrick, m'boy, how're things in the First Ward?"

After the obligatory pleasantries, Alderman Kelly got down to business. "Harry, I'd like to ask a favor from you. It's something the mayor would really appreciate."

In Chicagoese, such a statement was not intended to mean, nor was it taken to mean, that the mayor had any idea that the favor was being asked. What it really meant, coming from an alderman in the mayor's political party, was that it was important to the *alderman* and that if Harry turned him down, everyone in City Hall, including the mayor, would hear that Harry Weintraub wasn't a team player. Conversely, if Harry granted the favor, then everyone, including the mayor, would be reminded that Harry *was* a team player. More important, he would hold the alderman's marker for a return favor. If there was anything Harry Weintraub coveted, it was a reputation in City Hall of being a team player. That and an alderman's marker.

"Name it, Pat, and you got it."

"There's a parking lot in my ward on Polk between Desplaines and Halsted. I understand it's one of your lots, Harry. Is that right?"

"Yeah, that's one of mine. It's an indoor garage. I don't own it, but I've managed it since it was built. Anything wrong?"

"No, nothing wrong at all. It's just that there's a little investigation going on, and it's important to find out if a certain car was parked there at a certain time."

Weintraub noticed that Alderman Kelly was careful not to say who was doing the investigation, what it was all about, or whether it was a criminal investigation, a background check into an applicant for a liquor license, or a little political espionage.

"I can help you out, Pat, if the car was owned by a

monthly charge customer. Those customers are given cards to use when they come and go, and—"

"Yeah, Harry, I know about that. That's why I'm calling. If I give you a name and dates for, say, five years ago, can you get me a printout to show when that card was used?"

"Sure, no problem. We used cards at that garage back then. But I have to ask you, Pat, is this on the up and up? I mean, is this person you're looking into some kind of big shot, and will he shit all over me when he finds out that I gave out this information?"

"Nothing to worry about there, Harry. We're just interested in some woman who we think parks in your lot."

"Oh, hell," Harry said, now assuming he was involved in nothing more sinister than a domestic problem between a husband and wife, "why didn't you say so? Just give me her name and the dates. All that stuff is right here in my office, and my computer can spit it out in no time."

"Thanks, Harry. And by the way, let's keep this in the family, okay? I wouldn't want the lady to know I'm doing this."

Less than half an hour later, Alderman Kelly's secretary told him that Harry Weintraub was calling.

Kelly instinctively looked at his watch as he picked up the phone. "Harry!" he exclaimed. "You work fast."

"It's those computers. Don't ever piss one of those things off, Pat. They got great memories."

"That's what I'm counting on. Were you able to get what we're looking for?"

"Got it right here in my hand. Want me to bring it down to your office?"

"No, thanks, Harry. You've already done more than enough. I'll have someone come over to your office right away and pick it up. That way you can explain to him how to read it if he has any questions."

"Tell him to ask for me. I'll go over it with him personally."

"Great. His name's Ogden—Phil Ogden."

"Got it."

"And, Harry?"

"Yeah, Pat?"

"I owe you one."

THIRTY-SEVEN ═══

PHIL BROUGHT THE printout back to his office, and within minutes he and Tom were carefully cross-checking Tracey Walton's parking log against her calendar entries.

Two hours later they were ready to throw in the towel.

"Shit," Tom said dejectedly as he pushed his chair back from the table on which they had spread their papers, "everything jibes."

And everything did. On June 23, for example, when Tracey's calendar reflected a lunch date in the Loop at noon, the parking log showed her leaving the garage at 11:38 A.M. and returning at 2:26 P.M. Whenever the calendar indicated a meeting or date outside the office in the middle of the day, she left the garage just in time to make it and returned soon after it was over. When she had something scheduled in her office, her car was in the garage next door, and when she was shown to be somewhere else, the log showed her car was gone. And that pattern was consistent throughout the critical period from June 20 to July 10, 1987.

"It was still a good idea," Phil said to console his partner. "Maybe we should try the same thing with the garage in her apartment building. We could see if her night and weekend parking schedule coincided with the calendar entries for her personal life."

"She doesn't live in an apartment," Tom said. "She has a home in the suburbs. In Burr Ridge, remember?"

"She does now, but she didn't five years ago. She testified that she bought the house after she learned she was pregnant. According to Steve's records, Tracey and Larry were living in the city, up on Lincoln Park West, in the summer of eighty-seven."

"I don't think it's worth the effort," Tom replied. "On nights and weekends she was probably with her husband, and that's not when she'd have been doing something she'd want to cover up. Uh-uh." He stood up and stretched, then tilted his head toward the calendar and parking log. "Pack it up, Phil. We're not going to find anything in those. We just have to face the possibility that she was telling the truth and that Steve screwed up and wrote down the wrong date."

While Tom went out to the reception room to see if he had any phone messages, Phil casually picked up the calendar. His intuition that she was lying was as strong as ever. But, damn it, he thought, she was never out of the office long enough to do anything she'd want to hide. And Tom was right—every entry that could be corroborated by the parking log *was* corroborated. But what about that damned tetanus shot? She had to have been in Michigan *sometime*, even if her calendar didn't show it.

Phil pondered for a few more minutes. Then he went back to the parking log to see if there were days when her car was gone—and therefore when she was out of the office—for unusually long periods of time. Only two days out of the twenty seemed to fit that test: On June 26 and June 29, the log showed that she had not been at the office at all. Then Phil turned to the calendar to see that both days had the same entry: "Checking job sites."

Phil recalled passing over those two entries each time he went through the calendar—there was nothing unusual about a construction company executive visiting job sites. But now, seeing from the log that she didn't get to the office *at all* on those two days, he began to wonder.

He put the calendar on his lap, threw his feet onto the corner of the table, and flipped through the pages for the entire year, day by day.

That was where Phil discovered the first inconsistencies. At no other time had Tracey Walton spent more than a couple of hours on job sites. And at no other time had she failed to show in her calendar the specific sites to be visited. But here, on the two dates that drew Phil's attention, she was gone all day and she curiously didn't identify the sites.

Could there be something there? He was wrestling with the problem when Tom came back into the room. Phil explained what he had discovered about Tracey's job site visits—on the two days in question and at other times. "Think there's any way we could prove she was somewhere else on those two days?"

Tom thought for just a moment. "Impossible." He handed the calendar back to Phil and put a hand on his partner's shoulder. "Give up, pal. We'll be better off spending our time on the motion and brief than worrying about two unrelated days back in 1987."

He had started to walk out of the room when Phil said, "But maybe they're *not* unrelated. Look here." He showed Tom the calendar. "These two dates—June twenty-sixth and twenty-ninth—are a Friday and Monday, so instead of two unconnected days, this could indicate one connected four-day period. And that would include a weekend." Phil looked at his partner and added, "A lot can happen in four days that she might want to hide."

Tom turned at the door. "Unless she had been with her husband on the intervening Saturday and Sunday."

"Well, if that was the case it sure must have been a boring two days. She doesn't have one thing written in her calendar for the entire weekend, and that's unusual because all other Saturdays and Sundays were full of golf and tennis dates, dinner dates, and beauty shop appointments."

Tom stared at his partner for a moment and then came back and took a seat at the other side of the table. "Now you've got my attention. Trial lawyers never trust coincidences. And that last thing you just said rang a bell for me—there were just too many coincidences in Tracey Walton's life during those few days in 1987. It was the only time all year she spent two whole days visiting job sites, it was the only time she didn't write down the addresses of the sites in her calendar, and it was the only weekend that she and her husband didn't have any social engagements." He rubbed his palms together, like a man about to eat his favorite dessert. "You're on to something, Phil. I can feel it in my bones. There's something out of kilter about those few days, and somehow we have to figure out what it is."

"Well," Phil said, "that could be the weekend when the Waltons made their baby."

Tom laughed. "Yeah, it figures. They had no golf or tennis games and didn't have anything else to do."

"Seriously," Phil said, "maybe they took the weekend off, took a short trip to get out of the city for a couple of—" Phil snapped his fingers. "Michigan! Shit, Tom, that has to be when she got that tetanus shot."

"Maybe, but that doesn't explain that business about the job site visits on Friday and Monday." Tom put his hands behind his head and leaned back. "And anyway, if they decided to take a few days off and go to Ironwood, why wouldn't she put that in her calendar?"

"How in the hell would I— *What! What did you say?*" Phil looked incredulous at what he had just heard. "Did you say Ironwood?"

"Yeah, that's where she told Steve she had her tetanus shot. I already told you that."

"No, you only said it was in Michigan. That night you ran back here from Harry Caray's, you only said Michigan, not Ironwood."

"What the hell's the difference?"

"The difference, you jag-off, is that Ironwood isn't in the main part of Michigan. It's in the Upper Peninsula, the part of the state that hangs over Lake Michigan and borders on Wisconsin. And Ironwood is right on the state line."

THIRTY-EIGHT ===

PHIL OGDEN AND Tom Andrews had reviewed what they had so far, and they were now willing to bank everything on the hypothesis that Tracey Walton was in the vicinity of Ironwood, Michigan, between June 26 and June 29, 1987, and that it was then and there she became pregnant. Unfortunately, proving that alone wouldn't mean a thing. But there was something *else* about that weekend, something Tracey didn't want to put in her calendar or testify about in court. Both lawyers now believed that delving into those four days might explain the mystery of why Tracey had misled Steven Sinclair about the date of Angel's conception.

Clearly, the key was whether Tracey was with her husband during those fateful four days. Not likely. The curious entries in her calendar hinted that she was up to something out of the ordinary, and both lawyers figured that she was probably with someone other than her husband.

Tom, in fact, was ready to bet money that his earlier hunch—the one that had prompted him to dash out of Harry Caray's—was correct: Tracey had been with another man, and that man was the husband of the woman who referred her to Steve Sinclair. At the time it had been a wild hunch, but now it was starting to look more realistic.

They decided once again to split their investigation. Tom would look into whatever had happened at Ironwood while Phil, who still had work to do on the motion for a new trial and brief, would keep looking into the Chicago side of the puzzle. Each had something critical to investigate, but neither had any idea as to how to go about it.

While they were tossing ideas back and forth, Phil thought about calling Lew Beck to tell him what they had learned. "No way," Tom cautioned him. "He still represents the insurance company first and Steve second. If we come up with something that helps, let's use it to negotiate a better deal for Steve. To hell with the insurance company."

"It just doesn't seem right not to share everything."

"Which is why you'd never make it as a litigator. You're too nice a guy. And I'll tell you something else, partner: Your friend Beck had this case for nearly four years before the trial, and he didn't come up with diddly. Here we've been on it for less than four weeks and we may have found the answer—and *we* never had the same chance he did to put the Waltons under oath and ask them questions about those four crucial days. Screw Beck."

"Tom Andrews here."

"Tom, it's Molly O'Connor, Steve Sinclair's—"

"I remember you, Molly." Tom smiled, sat back, and shifted the phone to his other ear. He had met Molly only a couple of times, but couldn't forget her free-swinging, uninhibited personality. "To what do I owe the pleasure?"

"Steve told me about your phone call yesterday, when you asked him for that patient's name."

Tom, playing his hunch for all it was worth, had been stymied without some information about the man he suspected of having been with Tracey. When he had called Steve the day before to ask the name of the man's wife, Steve had balked. He wasn't comfortable divulging the patient's name, especially since he had already revealed something about her health and her marital problems. But Tom had assured him that he needed her name only to identify her husband and that he would never disclose anything about her health or her personal life. "And Steve," he had said, "it could be important for the case. Damned important." After he had explained his hunch and some of the evidence to support it—Tracey Walton's knowing the man, his frequent trips to Wisconsin and her being near Wisconsin around the time she became pregnant, and the oddities of her calendar entries for that weekend—Steve had decided to cooperate. He not only had given Tom the name of the patient but also the name of her husband and his work number—information he kept for all patients.

"And," Molly was saying, "Steve also told me about your theory."

"What do you think of it?"

"I think you're right on, Counselor. Which brings me to the reason for my call. I want to help. I want to help you find out what that broad was up to that weekend." She was virtually pleading, which was uncharacteristic for Molly O'Connor. "It would mean a lot to me, and to my relationship with Steve, if I could help him beat this thing. It's killing him, Tom, and so far all I've been able to do is pat him on the butt and tell him not to worry."

Tom said nothing while he thought about her offer.

"Please," she begged. She explained that she had purposely been acting like a cartoon character in Steve's presence since the trial had begun in April. "It makes me feel like an idiot," she said, "but it was the only way I knew to offset the funk he's been in. But now I have a chance to help—*really* help—and you have to let me."

"Molly, this involves more than making a few phone calls. I've given it a lot of thought, and I've decided that the only way to do this right is to go up to Ironwood and snoop around."

"That's just what I thought, too," she said with excitement in her voice. "I have vacation time coming, and things are a little slow at the agency. It's a good time for me to get away for a few days."

"What does Steve have to say about this?"

"He doesn't know about it, and I don't want him

to—not yet. He'd feel guilty if he knew I was taking time off work to help him, and he'd try to talk me out of it. He's one of those martyrs who'd rather suffer than accept help from someone."

"And how do you propose to do this without him knowing about it?"

"I'll leave him a note. He'll find it after we're gone."

Tom still wasn't sure. "Listen, Molly, he's liable to be furious, if not with you, then with me. He might not look kindly at my taking his girlfriend up to the North Woods for a few days."

"Hey, you're a happily married man, and I want to be a happily married woman. Maybe this will help me be one."

"All right," Tom sighed, "you're on."

"Fabulous, and I promise you won't regret it. Can we leave in the morning?"

"No, but maybe the day after. I have to clean up a few things in the office, and I have to get some information about the mystery man."

"Do you know his name?"

"Yes, Steve gave it to me. It's David Roberts."

THIRTY-NINE ═══

PHIL OGDEN'S END of the investigation into the puzzling weekend in 1987 presented a moral problem for him: There was no way he could get the information he wanted without lying or getting someone else to lie for him. Finally he rationalized that if it took a thief to catch a thief, then it would also take a liar to catch a liar.

The plan he eventually settled on required an ally, and he had the perfect one in mind.

Stanley Goodman was pacing back and forth across his cramped office at the Internal Revenue Service headquarters in Chicago. "Jesus, Phil, I'm not sure I can pull this off."

"Sure you could, Stan. You've been telling me for years about the scams you pull to trick people."

"Not people—*taxpayers*. But that's what we're *supposed* to do when we audit someone's tax return. It's part of the procedure. Hell's bells, this guy isn't even under audit."

"All the better. He's not at risk, and after you talk to him he'll forget all about it. He'll never give it another thought."

"Well . . ."

"C'mon, Stan, go for it. You do this one thing and I'll be in your debt forever."

"Horseshit, you've never paid me back for the times I had to lie to save your ass with all your old girlfriends."

"That was in college, and as I recall you married one of them."

"Some payback."

"Ryder, Ruther and Walton."

"Lawrence Walton, please."

"And your name?"

"Goodman. I'm with Internal Revenue." Stan had thought about using a fake name, but chose to go with his own when he realized that Walton might not have the information handy and would have to call him back. Still, he'd try to get the job done with one phone call, and he'd mention his name as seldom as possible.

Within a few seconds he heard the usual apprehensive voice of someone being called by a revenue agent. "Hello, this is Larry Walton."

"Mr. Walton, I'm with Internal Revenue. Thanks for taking the time to talk to me." Goodman had learned long ago that the best way for a revenue agent to gain people's cooperation was to tell them that it was someone else who was under investigation. "And by the way, Mr. Walton, this inquiry has nothing to do with your taxes. We're auditing another taxpayer's return, and you may be able to give us some information that will help us."

Stanley Goodman could hear the sigh of relief. "Sure, if I can."

"Great. The taxpayer in question is claiming a business entertainment deduction for a large dinner party he threw. He's given us your name and Mrs. Walton's as two of the guests. If you can just tell me whether you were at that party I won't have to bother you any further."

Larry Walton then asked the question that Goodman had heard a thousand times. "Is it okay for me to be doing this? I mean, I'd hate to get someone in trouble if—"

"This is just a routine inquiry, Mr. Walton. Of course, if you'd prefer not to cooperate, we could serve you with a subpoena to appear before a grand jury."

"Oh, Jesus! No, I wouldn't want that. Who's the person who threw the party?"

Goodman made a circle with his index finger and thumb, and winked at Phil Ogden, who was sitting nervously across his desk. "His name is Herbert L. Bookman, and he does business as Bookman Builders."

"Herbert Bookman," Walton repeated. "The name doesn't ring a bell."

No wonder, Goodman thought, since he had made up the name just a few minutes earlier. "Well, maybe you've forgotten. The party was five years ago, in 1987."

"But still, I should remember the name, especially if he invited me to a big party."

"Maybe he didn't. Remember, Mr. Walton, that's why I'm calling. Maybe Mr. Bookman came up with your name later because he needed it to claim the party as a business expense. If it's not too much trouble, is there a way you could double-check? Perhaps if you have a date book or calendar for 1987?"

"I'm sure I have my eighty-seven calendar around here someplace. My secretary always hangs on to those things, but it'll take us a little while to dig it up. Can I call you back?"

Goodman didn't want to give Walton his name. "Tell you what, Mr. Walton. I'm out of the office right now on another audit. Can I call you back in ten or fifteen minutes?"

"Sure, that'll be fine. By the way, what was the date of that party?"

"June 27, 1987. It was a Saturday night."

"And where was it?"

"At Bookman's home, an apartment on North Sheridan Road."

It was the longest ten minutes that Phil Ogden ever spent, and it gave him plenty of time to think of all the things that could go wrong: What if Walton couldn't find his 1987 calendar? What if he wasn't there when Stan called back? What if he realized the whole thing was a ruse?

Finally Goodman placed the second call, and it was answered by the same woman who answered before. "It's Internal Revenue again," he said, "for Mr. Walton. . . . Hello again," he said when Walton came on the line. "Any luck finding the calendar?"

"Well, yes," the answer came back tentatively, "but there's something really strange about this whole thing."

Stanley Goodman held his breath. "Strange? What's so strange?"

Phil sensed that something had gone wrong. He jumped up and started to pace around the office.

"Well, after we spoke a few minutes ago, I asked around the office and no one around here ever heard of this Bookman guy or his company. And then I checked the phone book. There were several Bookmans, but no Herbert L. or Bookman Builders."

Goodman had anticipated something like this. "I'd be surprised if he *was* in the phone book, Mr. Walton. He went out of business in eighty-nine. Lost his shirt. Just liquidated his assets and moved to Florida. You'd have to look in an old phone book to find him in Chicago."

"That explains the phone book," Walton said, "but it still doesn't explain that business about the party."

"What do you mean?"

"If Bookman had a party on Saturday, June twenty-seventh, I assure you that I wasn't there."

"And how do you know that?"

"I was out of town."

Shit! He was in Michigan with his wife.

"In fact, I went to an architectural conference in London the previous Wednesday and stayed out of the country until the following week."

FORTY

MOLLY DIALED THE number and then drummed her fingers nervously while she waited for someone to answer. In her quest to play a role in Steve's defense, she had persuaded Tom to let her have a crack at Dave Roberts. But how? She couldn't very well come right out and ask him if he and Tracey Walton had been carrying on an affair five years ago. And what if they were? Would that be enough to undo an eight million dollar verdict? No, Tom had convinced her that they had to find something more solid than that, it had to be something more ominous, more threatening, than Roberts would be willing to admit over the phone to a stranger. In fact, it had to be something that he and Tracey would do their best to conceal—something that would have to be dug out. If only she—

"David Roberts and Associates."

"Mr. Roberts, please."

"I'm sorry, he's out to lunch."

Whew! Tom was right. He had told her to make the call a few minutes after one, banking on Roberts still being at lunch while his secretary would already have returned. Although Molly would have spoken to him if he'd been there, she wasn't sure she could have pulled it off.

"May I speak with his secretary?"

"One moment, please."

Shortly a young, bubbly voice came on the line. "Mr. Roberts's office."

"Hi," Molly said in a friendly tone, "is Dave in?"

"No, but he should be back soon. May I have him call you?"

"Oh, heck," she responded, trying to sound disappointed. "I have to run, and I won't be where he can reach me."

"Can I do anything to help?"

"Well, maybe." Molly hesitated as if she hadn't anticipated the question, and then said, "The thing is, my husband and I met Dave a few weeks ago. We keep our planes at the same place, and he gave us his card. That's how I got this number. Anyway, he told us about his place in Wisconsin and how beautiful it was up there this time of the year. When he mentioned the fishing, Sam—that's my husband—Sam got all excited, and now he wants to fly up and try his luck. The problem is, we can't remember the name of the lake. Would you happen to know what it is?"

"Gosh, I'm not sure, but I think he fishes *several* of the lakes around Hurley. If you could hold on for a minute, I might be able to find out from—"

"Oh, no," Molly interjected, "I wouldn't want to inconvenience you. I'll call Dave later. By the way, you did say Hurley, didn't you?"

"Yes, ma'am, and if you'll give me your name I'll be sure to tell Dave—"

But the line was already dead.

Carrying a huge atlas under her arm, Molly came crashing into the office of Ogden & Andrews. She poked her head through the reception window in the waiting room and, before the two secretaries even saw her, hurriedly said, "I have to see Tom or Phil. Are they in?"

"They're both in the conference room. Who shall I say—"

"Never mind, it's a surprise," Molly said, already heading toward the door that led to the lawyers' private offices.

"But—"

"It's okay. I promise." She disappeared through the

swinging door, bellowing, "Relax, you guys! Molly O'Connor has come to the rescue."

"Hurley?" Tom asked, looking at his partner. "Where the hell is Hurley?"

Phil shrugged his shoulders. "Beats me. I never heard of it."

"I didn't know either," Molly replied, "but dig this." She dropped the atlas on the conference room table and opened it to a full-page map of the state of Wisconsin. And there, within a tiny circle she had made with a red felt pen, were the towns of Hurley, Wisconsin, and Ironwood, Michigan.

They were less than five miles apart.

"I'll be a monkey's uncle," Tom said half to himself. "You could damn near throw a stone from one town to the other." He looked up at Tom and Molly. "This is just what we needed."

"It sure is," Molly said proudly. "That's why I didn't waste time calling before I ran over here. I haven't even called Steve. I'd better do that right now." She looked around for a phone.

"No, just wait a second," Phil cautioned both of them. "Before we get too excited, let's just stop and see what we have, then figure out what we still need." He grabbed a fresh yellow legal pad and a pen. "One," he said aloud as he began to scribble, "we know Tracey Walton actually conceived her child in late June 1987. Two, she was in Ironwood getting a tetanus shot sometime around then."

"And three," Tom chimed in, "on the weekend when she set up the alibi to go up there—you know, that business about visiting unspecified job sites—her husband was in England."

"Okay, that's good," Phil said, nodding while he wrote. "We also know this Roberts guy has a place within five miles of Ironwood and that he flies up there pretty regularly. That's point number four."

Molly held up her hand. "But we don't know that he was going up there back in eighty-seven, do we?"

"Sure we do," Tom said confidently. "Linda Roberts told Steve that her husband bought the place six or seven years ago. That's what Steve told us that night at Harry Caray's. And that's one of the reasons I left my beer on the table and high-tailed it back to the office."

"Okay," Phil said after making another notation on his pad, "that makes five points to suspect that Tracey and this Roberts guy had a tryst in the North Woods about the time she became pregnant. Anything else?"

Both lawyers pondered the question, each wearing a frown.

Molly's elation began to fade. "God, you guys, I thought you'd turn somersaults when I showed you that bloody map. But now you're looking like—"

"Wait, Molly," Phil interrupted, reaching over and putting his hand on her shoulder. "The information you got about Roberts going to Hurley, and about Hurley being next to Ironwood, is pure gold. It's just that we have to tie up all the possible loose ends. We can't leave them with a way to wiggle out."

"That's right," Tom added. "Remember, Molly, we're dealing with a pretty slick lady there. If she's as good a liar as we think she is, we have to box her in so tight that she can't fib her way out of this."

"It would've been a lot easier for Lew Beck to trap her," Phil said, "if he'd known this stuff at the time of the trial. He could've grilled her on the witness stand about all these things—her trip up north that wasn't in her calendar, her friendship with Roberts. No telling what she'd have said."

He tossed the legal pad on the table. "But we lost that opportunity. Now we need something definite—and something *big*—to attack the verdict. It doesn't take much, Molly, to sway a jury, but it takes something colossal to get a court to throw out the jurors' verdict after they've voted."

"Is this enough? This stuff with Roberts and Ironwood and Hurley?"

"It could be," Tom said, "but only if we can fit all the pieces together to make the picture we're looking for. That means we have to be able to prove, actually *prove*, that Tracey Walton and Dave Roberts were up there together when she became pregnant. And we have to do it without asking them."

FORTY-ONE ===

THE NEXT EVENING Steve Sinclair came home from the office to an empty apartment. Assuming that Molly was working late, he decided to call her at the agency and suggest meeting her later for a bite to eat. But when he went into the kitchen to fix a drink and make the call, he spotted her note on the refrigerator door:

> Doc—Left town with another man for a few days. Didn't tell you earlier 'cause I thought you'd try to stop me. I'll call you tonight. If you're nervous, call Phil. He'll explain.

Tom had picked Molly up at nine that morning.

"Don't let me forget to call the doc tonight," she said after she tossed her bag into the trunk and jumped into the front seat. "He'll be wondering what I'm up to."

They settled in for the long drive that would take them north across the entire state of Wisconsin. "We should be up there by dinnertime," Tom said, "and that'll leave us time to get settled in and map out our plan of attack for tomorrow."

"Have you thought more about how we'll go about this?"

"We'll start with the Ironwood phone book and make a list of all the doctors and hospitals. Maybe we'll find the place where Tracey got that tetanus shot. That should lock her into being up there that weekend."

"How are we going to find out if Roberts was up there at the same time?" she asked.

"Remember, he flies his own plane. I made a couple of calls last night and found out that there are only two airports in the Hurley-Ironwood area, and one of those is pretty far away. I'm hoping that both airports keep a record of the planes that land and take off and also of the ones they service. If so, it'll be easy to find out if he was there that weekend."

Molly thought about that, then said, "But don't we have to show that they were together?"

"Listen, Molly," Tom said without taking his eyes off the road, "it'll be a home run if we can just prove they were both in the area that weekend. I'd love to hear them try to explain it away as a coincidence, especially with her husband out of the country and her calendar saying nothing about her going out of town for the weekend."

Ironwood was only a few miles east of Hurley, with the Wisconsin-Michigan border between them but slightly closer to Hurley. Molly and Tom were both struck with the beauty of the area—the clean, fresh air, the tall stands of dense trees, and the hilly, almost mountainous, terrain that explained the popularity of nearby ski lodges such as Big Powderhorn and Blackjack. And if they hadn't already known that the region had a rich history associated with the mining of iron ore, the names on the signposts would have told them as much. Hurley, the seat of Iron County, lay between Iron Belt, Wisconsin, and Ironwood, Michigan. And while one of its main streets was understandably named Iron Street, another was curiously named Silver Street.

Although they hadn't made reservations, they had no trouble finding rooms in early June, since the bulk of the area's tourism focused on the winter sports of skiing and snowmobiling. They checked into Davey's Motel on the eastern edge of Ironwood and agreed to meet at the car in fifteen minutes so they could go to dinner and solidify their game plan.

• • •

"Did you remember to bring the phone book?" Tom asked when he came out of his room and found Molly waiting for him at the car.

"Sure did." She lifted her purse and patted it. "Can you imagine getting a Chicago phone book in here? If I had a few more minutes, I could have memorized the darn thing."

Tom pulled out onto the highway and headed west. "The guy at the front desk told me we might want to try a place called Bell Chalet. It's over in Hurley."

Although it was a Wednesday night, he noticed that the large parking lot at Bell Chalet was about three-quarters filled with cars, pickup trucks, vans, and campers. "Would you look at that crowd?" he said. "It's barely six o'clock."

"But you're not in Chicago," Molly reminded him. "Up here people get up earlier, they eat earlier, and they go to bed earlier."

"And they probably look better and live longer."

Tom smiled when he saw that the building resembled a Swiss chalet, as its name implied. It had a peaked shingled roof, wooden shutters, flower boxes, and dormers, and inside, the restaurant was charming. The walls, like the front door, were of knotty pine, and the furnishings and lighting gave the place a warm, rustic appearance. Just off to the right was a cozy curved bar with a copper countertop.

Tom noticed that a few heads turned to check them out, so he assumed that racially mixed couples probably weren't common in that part of the world. But the gawkers soon went back to their drinks, food, and conversation.

The hostess led them to a corner table at the far end of the dining room. In the center of the polished wood table was a flickering candle in an amber jar.

"This is really neat," Molly said as she unfolded her napkin, "and I'll bet the food beats anything we have in Chicago."

"If not the taste," Tom observed as he looked at some of the other tables, "then certainly the portions."

After they were served their drinks, Molly pulled out the Ironwood phone book and a small notepad while they waited to be served. "It shouldn't take long to make a list of all the places where someone could get a tetanus shot around here," she said.

"Let's look first to see if there's a hospital," Tom suggested. "People usually get tetanus shots when they've had an accident, like a deep cut or a puncture wound. If that's what happened, then Tracey Walton probably went to a hospital rather than a doctor's office, especially on a weekend."

"Right," she said, flipping through the Yellow Pages. "It should be . . . Okay, here we are. There's only one hospital listed in Ironwood. It's called Grand View."

A thought crossed Tom's mind. "I hope she was right about having that shot in Ironwood, and that she didn't mean it was somewhere *near* Ironwood. Anyway, we'll try Grand View Hospital first thing in the morning."

"Why wait till morning? The records we're looking for are probably in the emergency room—that's where she'd have gone if she had an accident—and there's always someone on duty in an emergency room." She looked back at the Yellow Pages. "Sure, take a look at this." She pointed to an advertisement: "Grand View Hospital Emergency Department, Physician-staffed 24 hrs."

Tom gave a courtly bow of his head. "I knew it was a good idea to insist that you come along. We'll go over there right after dinner."

After dinner, as Tom and Molly drove east through the center of Ironwood on their way to the hospital, they saw the town's famous landmark, a fifty-two-foot statue of Hiawatha holding a peace pipe and wearing a full-feathered headdress, and heralded as the World's Tallest Indian.

Molly shook her head and said, "There must be a hell of a big cigar store around here somewhere."

They found Grand View Hospital, a modern two-story brick building, just east of town. Tom parked near the emergency room entrance and Molly hopped out. They had already agreed, at her urging, that she would handle this particular mission while Tom waited outside.

The reception area was empty, but Molly spotted a small office where a nurse was busy filling out forms. "Excuse me," she said politely. "I wonder if you might be able to give me some information."

The nurse looked up. "Certainly, if I can." She was middle-aged and carried an air of such strict professionalism that Molly worried that she might not be able to pull this off.

It would have been easy to ask if their records showed whether they gave a tetanus shot to a Tracey Walton in June of 1987, but Tom had warned her that that wouldn't work. Hospital personnel, he explained, were trained to treat patients' records as confidential. Moreover, he'd said that owing to the number of claims filed by disgruntled patients, hospitals turned defensive when asked to give out information that might eventually be used against them. Consequently, he and Molly had concocted a story that they hoped would not set off defense alarms or suggest a breach of confidentiality.

"Well, first of all, I know this might not be a good time, and if you prefer I can come back in the morning."

"No, ma'am, it's quite all right. How can I help you?"

Molly hoped that her nerves weren't showing. "I know it doesn't look like it from the way I'm dressed," she said, "but I work at a bank in Chicago. I'm in the trust department. Anyway, one of the vice presidents in the department is working on a large trust, and when he heard that I was going to be up here this week he asked if I could do him a favor."

The nurse was nodding, but her expression gave no hint as to whether she was buying Molly's story.

"Well, it seems that Mr. Briggs—that's the vice

president's name—has a wealthy client who's setting up this trust to make charitable contributions."

Tom had said that whereas lawyers made hospitals defensive and uncooperative, the thought of charitable contributions had the opposite effect. The nurse, who up till then had been all business, smiled. "By the way," she said, "my name's Betty. Betty Erickson."

"And I'm Molly O'Connor," Molly replied, then immediately realized she'd forgotten to use an alias as Tom had instructed her. They shook hands.

"So, as I was saying, Grand View might be on our client's list for a possible gift."

"Might be?"

"Well, that's why I'm here. You see, our client's daughter vacationed up here a few years ago. She had a minor accident and received such nice care and attention at the hospital she went to that her mother wants to include it for a donation. The thing is," and here Molly spread her arms out in a gesture of frustration, "she isn't sure if this is the right place. You see, the accident was five years ago, and the daughter can't remember the name of the hospital where she was treated. Only that it was in Ironwood."

"But this is the only hospital in Ironwood."

"Yes," Molly replied, "I saw that from the phone book. But still, Mr. Briggs insisted that I make sure. There are other hospitals in the area."

"Well," Nurse Erickson said confidently, "we should be able to find out easily enough. All we have to do is check our records to see if her daughter was a patient."

"Oh, that would be wonderful," Molly exclaimed. "But if it's too much trouble—"

"No trouble at all. I can pull her record up on my computer." Turning her chair to face a keyboard at the side of her desk, she asked, "Can I have her name?"

"Yes, it's Walton. Tracey Walton. And she would have been here in late June 1987, sometime between the twenty-sixth and the twenty-ninth."

Molly kept her fingers crossed while Betty Erickson

punched out commands. After a minute or two the nurse turned and asked, "You did say 'Walton,' didn't you? With a *W*?"

"Yes, that's right, W-a-l-t-o-n."

"I'm awfully sorry, but I find no record of a Walton except for Archie Walton who was in here last year. But I know Archie. He lives up the road from me, and believe me, Miss O'Connor, Archie's mother wouldn't be making any gifts to this place."

"If Tracey Walton came into the emergency room for only a shot, or to get a dressing for a wound, would it still show up on your computer? Even if she was here only for a few minutes?"

"Absolutely," the nurse assured her. "We can't do a thing—not even take out a sliver—without getting a name and entering it in our records."

Remembering that Tracey was trying to conceal her whereabouts during those few days, Molly asked, "What if she used a different name?"

"Wouldn't work," the nurse replied. "We ask for identification even if the treatment is not charged to insurance."

It's not fair, Molly thought to herself. Everything was falling into place, and now our best lead turns into a dead end.

After asking the helpful nurse to double check one more time, which produced no results, Molly thanked her and left.

It was hard to tell which of the two women felt worse.

"C'mon, Molly, don't feel bad," Tom said as they drove away from the hospital. "You did beautifully. Hell, it's not your fault that Tracey got her shot somewhere else."

"I know that, Tom, but it's still so disappointing. When I went in there I was scared to death that I'd screw it up, but I was *great*. I had the nurse eating out of my hand. She'd have told me anything I wanted to know."

"Don't worry about it. We just got started, and you

can't expect to score a touchdown on the first play. Tomorrow we'll go to work on our list of doctors.''

"Oh, Lord," Molly groaned, "that'll be a nightmare. Did you see that phone book? There are three pages of doctors, and if it takes as long with each one as it took at the hospital, we'll be here for a month."

"It won't be that bad," he said. "After we take out the doctors who specialize in eyes, ears, and feet and the dermatologists and radiologists and all the rest of the doctors you wouldn't go to for a tetanus shot, the list will be pretty manageable."

The words did little to ease Molly's depression. She gazed out of the car window for a few minutes, and then said, "I guess I'm not cut out to be a private eye."

"Listen," Tom said, "we have a lot of work to do and I don't want you pissin' and moanin' every time we come up empty. Hell, that's what investigating is all about— patience, patience, and more patience. There are fifty blind leads and a hundred hours of wasted time for every fact that you eventually uncover, so you'd better get used to it."

She looked at him with a sheepish smile. "Sorry, Tom. I don't want to be a drag. I promise to be a good trooper tomorrow."

He returned the smile. "Okay, let's stop for a drink and then call it a night. We have a busy day ahead of us."

FORTY-TWO ═══

TOM AND MOLLY worked independently throughout the next day, Thursday, but met every two hours to compare their progress. In spite of Tom's lecture on patience and his own perseverance, even he was ready to call it quits by the end of the day.

Finding out if any of the doctors in town had given Tracey the tetanus shot five years ago was turning into an impossible task. It wasn't that they or their office staffs weren't cooperative—on the contrary, it was surprising how helpful they tried to be. But their recordkeeping just wasn't up to the task.

For one thing, only a few of their offices were equipped with computerized filing systems, especially systems that held data from five years earlier. The rest of them had all of their records on paper, and after five years they were generally stashed away in cardboard boxes and stored in attics or basements. In these cases the best Molly and Tom could get was a promise that the doctor or a staff member would check and get back to them if anything was found. This led to their early decision to abandon guile and come right out and ask for the information. As long as they had to leave their names and phone numbers, they thought it best not to advance phony reasons for wanting to know about Tracey Walton and her mysterious tetanus shot. And, as it happened, the straightforward approach worked just fine: The doctors were eager to help anyone who was trying to overturn a medical malpractice verdict against a fellow doctor.

By midmorning it had occurred to Tom that many of the doctors wouldn't even have kept a record of the shot. Tracey, not wanting a record of her trip for her own reasons, most likely paid for it with cash, and in that event the doctor might have pocketed the fee and not kept a record of it.

They finished canvassing the doctors' offices by four in the afternoon but still had not established that Tracey was in Ironwood—or, for that matter, anywhere other than Chicago—on that last weekend of June 1987.

"Maybe she got that shot in one of the other towns around here," Molly speculated when she and Tom finally rendezvoused at the car.

"Possibly," Tom sighed, "but there are at least twenty towns in the area, some in Michigan and some in Wisconsin. It would take a miracle to find out where she got that shot."

"Is all of this really necessary?" Molly asked. "After all, Tracey herself told Steve that she had a tetanus shot in Ironwood. Isn't that enough to prove that she was here?"

"Are you kidding? She'd never admit that, and if we showed her where Steve had written it down, she and her lawyer would say that Steve had altered his records— just like they did before. Anyway, she never told him exactly when she had that shot. His records only said that it was 'recently,' and he wrote that in August."

"So what are we going to do now?"

Tom, who had preached about patience the night before, was losing his. "Pray that one of those doctors we saw today comes through," he mumbled. "In the meantime, let's drive over to the airport."

"With our luck," Molly said as she slid into the car, "it won't be the airport Roberts uses."

"It's his airport all right. I checked this morning."

She looked at Tom. "Really? How?"

"Easy." He shrugged. "While I was at one of those doctors' offices this morning, I had a few minutes to kill, so I called the closest airport, the one just outside of

Ironwood. I just said, 'I'm a friend of Dave Roberts from Chicago,' I said. 'Could you tell me if this is the airport he uses when he comes up here?' The guy who answered said, 'Yeah, he flies in and out on weekends all the time.' He even knew that Roberts flies a Cessna."

"Sounds too easy, considering all the trouble we've had learning anything since we got here. Now keep your fingers crossed and pray that Roberts was up here *that* weekend."

The Gogebic County Airport was just east of Ironwood. Tom parked in the near-deserted lot and asked Molly to wait for him in the car.

"Why can't I go in with you? Maybe I'll be able—"

But Tom had already gotten out of the car and slammed the door.

"Another dead end," he snapped as he slipped back into the driver's seat ten minutes later. "It's not a controlled airport. All they do is give clearance to land and take off. They don't even write down the pilots' names or the tail numbers of their planes. They do keep records of fuel purchases, but only for a few weeks."

"Damn," Molly groaned as Tom started the engine.

Tom was beside himself. He *knew* that Tracey Walton had to have been in Ironwood during that weekend in 1987. But until he could prove it, he was nowhere, and the fact that he couldn't prove it was testing his patience past the breaking point. The thought of expanding the search into all of the small towns around Ironwood was just too impractical to pursue. All they had left was the dim hope that one of the doctors' offices they'd visited would call to say they had followed up and found that Tracey Walton was indeed in to get a tetanus shot in late June of 1987. Fat chance.

They agreed to go back to Davey's Motel and get freshened up, and then decide over dinner whether to fold camp and go home.

• • •

Molly had already showered and was toweling her short hair dry when she spotted the blinking message light on her phone. She put on her robe and called the motel operator to find out that a Mrs. Erickson had called a few minutes earlier, evidently while she was in the shower. There had been so many other names and introductions during her exhausting day that "Mrs. Erickson" didn't ring a bell.

She dialed the number that was left with the message, and lit a cigarette while she waited for someone to answer.

"Emergency room."

It still didn't register. "I have a message to call this number. It was left by a Mrs. Erickson."

"Is this Miss O'Connor?"

"Yes, but I—"

"This is Betty Erickson from Grand View Hospital. You were here at the E.R. last night."

Christ! "Oh, of course, Mrs. Erickson. I'm so sorry, but it's been a long day and I just wasn't thinking."

"I have those days myself. Anyway, I hope you don't mind my calling you."

"No," Molly replied quickly, her heart starting to pound, "not at all. How did you know how to reach me?"

Betty Erickson giggled. "This is a small town, Miss O'Connor, and it doesn't take much to get attention around here. I overheard a couple of the doctors at the hospital this afternoon when I came in—I'm on the three-to-eleven shift—and they were talking about a lawyer who was in their offices earlier today asking about a woman named Walton who might have had a tetanus inoculation some years ago. Then a little while ago another doctor was in here, and he mentioned that a woman had been in his office this afternoon asking the same question."

"Yes, that was us. That lawyer and I are working together."

"Well, I wasn't sure. I mean, last night you said that

lady—the daughter of your client—was treated at the hospital, not in a private office.''

"That's right," Molly said quickly, "but as I told you, we weren't *sure* where she was treated. That's why we began checking with doctors today."

Molly was afraid the explanation would make no sense to Nurse Erickson in view of yesterday's story about a charitable gift to a hospital, but she was relieved when the nurse let it pass.

"You didn't say anything about a tetanus inoculation," Mrs. Erickson reminded her.

"Well, after you said that she had never been at your hospital, I didn't think it was important to mention the tetanus shot."

"I understand," the nurse said, not really sounding as if she did.

"I still don't know how you knew where to reach me," Molly said.

"Oh, that. Well, that doctor who was here a while ago—he said you left word at his office to call you if he found anything. So I called his office, and Irma—that's his receptionist—told me you were staying at the motel. She also gave me your Chicago number."

"But why did you want to call me, Mrs. Erickson?"

"Well, you seemed so desperate last night that I took another look after you left."

Molly inhaled deeply on her cigarette. "And did you find a record of Mrs. Walton being at the hospital?" she asked hopefully.

"No, not really. At least I couldn't find anything for Walton—"

Then why in the hell—

"—but then I pulled up those dates you mentioned, and I saw something I missed the first time."

Uh-oh. "And what was that, Mrs. Erickson?"

"I remembered you saying that Mrs. Walton's first name was Tracey, and when I checked back to June 28, 1987, I happened to notice that we treated another woman whose first name was Tracey. It's the kind of name that sticks out. Just the same, I still didn't give it much thought until I heard today that you were asking about a tetanus inoculation. That's what we gave that woman named Tracey."

Okay, say a prayer and ask the question. "And what was the last name of the Tracey who got the shot on June twenty-eighth?"

"I'm not sure I—"

"Please!" Molly wasn't about to let this get away from her. To hell with playing it cool. "Betty, it's terribly important. And I know you want to help. That's why you called me, and that's why I'm so grateful to you. So *please,* Betty, tell me that last name."

There was an awkward silence, which was finally broken by Betty Erickson's half whisper: "Roberts. Her name was Tracey Roberts."

Thank you, God!

"Miss O'Connor?"

"Yes?"

"We won't really be getting a donation, will we?"

Molly threw on a pair of jeans and a sweatshirt and raced over to Tom's room with the news. After the self-congratulatory hugs, Tom placed a call to Phil Ogden.

"Well," Phil asked, "how are the two sleuths doing up there?"

"We might not be the greatest detectives in the country," Tom kidded as he winked at Molly, "but we found out who's been dickin' Tracey."

Then he related the good news from Grand View Hospital. "I have to tell you that Molly was fantastic," he said to his partner. "To think that she made enough of an impression on that nurse so that she'd go to the trouble of double-checking the dates, and then track Molly down here at the motel—well, it's unbelievable."

Listening, Molly wondered what good fortune had caused her to give Betty Erickson her real name instead of an alias, as she had intended.

After Tom hung up the phone he told her that there was still one more thing to button up at the hospital, and that he and Phil agreed that it was now time to bring Steve up to date. They agreed that Molly had earned the right to call him and break the good news.

Twenty minutes later they were in the car, their first destination being a store where they could pick up a box of candy, and the second being Grand View Hospital.

"Were you able to reach Steve?" Tom asked.

"Sure was. Luckily he wasn't in the middle of delivering a baby."

"How'd he take the news?"

"Just as I expected." She lowered her voice to imitate Steve's: " 'But what does it mean, Molly? Do you think it'll help? Maybe there's a *real* Tracey Roberts, and *that's* who was in the hospital that day.' " She shook her head. "He's a perfect example of the guy who sees the hole and not the doughnut."

"I know what you mean," Tom said, his eyes still on the road. "Phil's a little like that, and it drives me crazy. He can be the most upbeat, optimistic guy in the world when things look bad, and then when everything looks great he starts to worry about what can go wrong."

After a short silence, Molly turned in her seat to face Tom. "So what are you going to do with all of this when we get back to Chicago?"

"Well, a little depends on what we find when we go back to the hospital, but an idea came to me back at the motel while you were on the phone with Steve. I haven't even mentioned it to Phil. It's a gamble, but if we pull it off, Steve could be a winner—a *big* winner. This could be even better than getting the verdict thrown out."

"Tell me about it," she asked eagerly.

Tom didn't say a word.

"C'mon, you brute, I'm part of the team."

"And if you want to stay on it," he grinned, "you'll have to learn to be patient. Isn't that what I told you last night?"

• • •

Molly glanced around at the emergency room. It was nothing like the ones she'd seen on television dramas. Here there were no burly policemen taking statements, no stretchers stacked up with victims of knife fights and shoot-outs. And instead of the wailing of hysterical mothers and the beeping of portable monitoring equipment, the only sound in the Grand View emergency room was soft piped-in music.

"Hi, Mrs. Erickson."

"Oh, Miss O'Connor. I didn't think I'd be seeing you again." Betty Erickson glanced back and forth between Molly and the tall black man standing next to her. "Is everything all right?"

"Better than all right. This is Tom Andrews. We work together. Tom, this is Betty Erickson."

Tom shook the nurse's hand. "Here," he said, handing her a small gift-wrapped package. "It isn't much, but the candy shop was the only place open."

"Oh, you didn't have to—"

"We wanted to. You've been very helpful."

Molly took the nurse's hand in both of hers. "There's one other thing we'd like to find out—that is, if we could."

"And what's that?"

"When this woman—this Tracey Roberts—came into the hospital in 1987, was she with someone?"

Betty Erickson smiled and reached for a thin folder on the corner of her desk. "Naturally I was confused by the different name," she said. "After all, people can't very well walk in here and give us any old name, because we insist on seeing identification, usually an insurance card. I think I told you that yesterday. So, after I spoke with you a little while ago, I dug up the forms we filled out the day she was here."

She held up the folder. "And after I looked in here, it all became very clear."

"What became clear?" Molly asked.

"That you had made a mistake, Miss O'Connor. You

were asking about a woman named Walton, but you didn't know that back in 1987 she was married to someone named Roberts, and that was the name she was using at the time.''

"And what makes you think she was really married to someone named Roberts?"

"Because of this." The nurse pulled a sheet of paper from the folder and showed it to Molly and Tom. "The admission form was signed by her husband. His signature's right here: David Roberts. And he put an X in the box that says 'Husband.' See? And it was *his* identification we saw.''

Nurse Erickson, obviously pleased with herself for solving the mystery of the names, said, "So to answer your question, Miss O'Connor, yes, she came into the emergency room with her husband. They were together.''

FORTY-THREE ═══

ALTHOUGH STEVE SINCLAIR had sounded skeptical when Molly called him on Thursday night, his subsequent reflections, and a call from Phil Ogden, convinced him of the importance of what Molly and Tom had learned in Ironwood. They would be getting back to Chicago the next afternoon, and he wanted to give Molly the welcome she deserved.

First thing on Friday morning he bought her an engagement ring, and presented it to her that evening at Spiaggia, a superb Italian restaurant on Chicago's Magnificent Mile.

Steve sat down with Phil and Tom in the offices of Ogden & Andrews the next morning. It was Saturday, but time was running out. The brief and motion for a new trial were due in less than two weeks, and they had to settle on a strategy in light of the discoveries Tom and Molly had made in Ironwood.

"Here's the problem," Tom explained to Steve. "I'm certain that we have enough to convince Judge Grubner to give us a new trial. Hell, he might even give us a judgment n.o.v."

"What's that?" Steve asked.

"Technically, n.o.v. stands for *non obstante veridicto*, which is Latin for 'notwithstanding the verdict.' Whenever it would be a grave injustice to enforce a jury's verdict, the judge can throw that verdict out and enter a judgment for the other side. It's called a judgment notwithstanding the verdict—or a judgment n.o.v. It's rare, but this would be a perfect case for it because it would be so unfair for this verdict to stand. On that very first day in Steve's office, Tracey Walton lied about the most critical issue in the trial—the date she got pregnant. The whole case turned on that. And now we can prove that she lied and prove why she lied."

"And," Phil chimed in, "she also lied about who the father is."

"It would seem so," Tom said with a grin. He looked back at Steve. "But our problem is whether to mention all this in the motion and brief. The law is quite clear on this: If we know we have grounds for a new trial or a judgment n.o.v., then we have to say what those grounds are at the time we file our motion. Otherwise, the judge can say we waived them—that we were too late. And if he did that, then we couldn't even bring up the lies on the appeal. In other words, it's 'speak now or forever hold your peace.'"

Steve looked puzzled. "Then what's the problem? It doesn't seem we have a choice—we *have* to mention that Ironwood business when we file those things, don't we? Isn't that what you just said?"

"Yeah," Tom replied, "we'd be taking too big a chance if we held the information back. The problem is, we're working with Lew Beck on the motion and brief, and there's no way we could put that stuff in and still keep it a secret from him."

Phil, seeing the bewildered expression on Steve's face, laughed. "Relax, Steve. We know we're going to win this case. No question about it, especially with what Tom and Molly found in Ironwood. You'll never have to pay that three million dollars."

"Well, that's what I gathered after you explained everything to me Thursday night. But—"

"The 'but' is this: Tom and I aren't satisfied with just saving you three million dollars. We have something bigger in mind for you, and for that we have to keep our ace in the hole a little longer."

• • •

Phil was impressed with what he saw when he got to Lew Beck's office the following Monday afternoon. The two lawyers had been in constant communication over the past weeks, exchanging drafts, research notes, and ideas, but this was the first time he'd been in the law library of the twenty-seven-lawyer firm. The room was spacious—about the size of the entire suite of offices occupied by Ogden & Andrews—but divided into five separate work areas by four-foot partitions.

The table at which Phil and Beck were seated, in the largest of the five areas, was impressive. The highly polished and beautifully grained oak surface was at least sixteen feet long and nearly half as wide. It was surrounded by a dozen large, comfortable chairs, each upholstered in tufted maroon leather.

All of the walls and partitions were lined with enough complete sets of law books and reference materials to ensure that Beck and his associates would never have to fight for a seat among the crowd of lawyers at the Cook County Law Library, where the treatise one needed was invariably checked out, stolen, or misshelved.

Beck had apparently noticed the way Phil was taking in the room. "I know it seems a bit pretentious," he said defensively, "but as I told my wife, most of us spend more time here than we do at home. Might as well be comfortable."

"I thought only plaintiffs' lawyers could afford a setup like this," Phil remarked.

"The successful ones, the guys like Charlie, can afford a lot better. But those of us on the defense side can do okay. We don't get the big contingent fees, but we get paid for every case, even when we lose." He shrugged self-consciously, apparently realizing they were meeting for that very reason—because Lew had lost *Walton v. Sinclair*.

Deciding that Beck's comment was a good cue to get to the business at hand, Phil asked, "How do you feel about the motion for a new trial? Think Judge Grubner'll buy it?''

"I doubt it," Beck answered, shaking his head. Obviously aware that Phil was not a seasoned trial lawyer, he explained: "There was clearly enough evidence to justify the jurors' belief in Mrs. Walton. So we're left with having to argue that Grubner committed prejudicial error—that is, that he made a mistake in one or more of his rulings—and because of that the jury went the wrong way. That's a tough one, asking a judge to admit he made a mistake, especially one that would mean he has to take eight million dollars away from the Waltons and try the case all over again." He leaned back in his chair and clasped his hands behind his neck. "I'm sure Grubner has doubts about some of his rulings, but he'll never give us a new trial because of them. He'll leave that for the appellate court."

"Any chance he'll lower the verdict?" Phil asked. "It sure seems excessive, especially with the little girl being expected to live for only a couple of more years."

"Not a chance. Remember, Judge Grubner was a plaintiffs' lawyer before he went on the bench. He's never seen a verdict he thought was too high."

Time to play the first card, Phil thought to himself. "Doesn't sound like you have your heart in this, Lew."

"Oh, I wouldn't say that. By the time I go in there to argue the motion, I'll be all charged up and ready to go. I don't think Grubner'll buy it, but it won't be for my lack of trying."

"Personally I think you'd do a good job, but Steve's really upset about the way everything's been handled. That's what I want to talk to you about, Lew."

"I don't understand."

"Well, you already know that Steve thinks you and the insurance company screwed him during the settlement talks. He doesn't think you used good faith in trying to settle, and frankly I agree with him. That's why we're looking to you guys for the excess three million dollars if we can't get the verdict set aside." Phil knew it was

North American Casualty, not Beck, who had acted in bad faith, but the plan was to cast Beck as a co-culprit. That would be the best way to ensure he would react as they hoped. "And after all," Phil added, "you were the guy who tried the case, and who lost it. So you can see why Steve's pissed."

"What are you getting at?" Beck sounded uncomfortable.

Phil looked him straight in the eye. "Steve doesn't trust you, Lew. He doesn't want you to argue the posttrial motion. Or the appeal. He wants me to handle things from here on out at the insurance company's expense, or else he wants them to hire another lawyer—one who is acceptable to him."

Phil could tell that Beck was shaken by this unexpected turn of events. He could imagine Lew's mind racing through the personal ramifications. The litigation bar, even in a large city like Chicago, was a close-knit group, and everyone would know he was being dumped. It would also hurt him with North American Casualty; Phil suspected that they were already distressed over his feud with DeLuca. Finally, he would lose the substantial fees he could have earned for the posttrial motion and the appeal, and for the new trial if it was granted.

"And there's another thing, Lew," Phil said. "If Steve does get stuck for that three million, he intends to do more than go after the insurance company on a bad faith claim. He's going to sue you for malpractice."

"What?" Lew Beck sounded as if he couldn't believe his ears. "I can see why he's teed off at North American, but why me? I broke my ass for the guy." He looked almost desperate. "You've reviewed the case, Phil, and you know I didn't make any mistakes. So how in the hell can he sue me for malpractice?"

"Well, *Steve* didn't make any mistakes when he treated Tracey Walton, either, but that didn't stop *her* from suing *him* for malpractice. And as I recall, she won." Phil was tempted to add that if Beck had investigated the facts before the trial as thoroughly as he and Tom had after it was over, he would have won and wouldn't have to be worried about defending his own malpractice suit; however, the success of their plan depended on Beck not yet knowing what they had learned in Ironwood.

"What if North American insists that I stay on the case?" Beck said. "They have five million dollars riding on the outcome, so they should have the right to pick their own lawyer."

"And Steve Sinclair has three million riding on it, which means a hell of a lot more to him than five million does to North American. So, if you don't bow out of the case gracefully, we'll have to go before Judge Grubner and tell him Steve doesn't want you representing him any longer. That means we'll have to tell him all about the bad faith claim, and that Steve intends to go after you for malpractice."

Beck stared at the papers spread out on the library table. Finally he looked at Phil and said, "I'll need to think it over. In the meantime, I'll have to call North American and tell them about this."

Phil felt a tinge of guilt for putting Beck through this, especially since the discoveries in Ironwood could put a quick end to the case and relieve him of his pain, but guilt had no place in the plan.

It was time to play the second card. "As long as you're planning to call the insurance company, Lew, I have another proposal you may want to run by them."

"What kind of proposal?"

"Well, as I see it, the company stands a pretty good chance of losing eight million on the case—five under the policy and three because of our bad faith claim. You yourself said a few minutes ago that we probably won't be able to throw the verdict out, and you virtually admitted back in April that the company was guilty of disregarding Steve's risk during the settlement talks. You told me back then that North American could've settled for less than five million, but refused. Am I right so far?"

"Go ahead," Beck said, clearly reluctant to admit anything further until he heard what Phil had to say.

"I'll get right to the point. I want to make a deal with the company: They pay the five million directly to Steve, and in return he'll release you guys completely. He'll waive his claim against the company for the excess three million, and he'll waive the malpractice claim against you. What do you think?"

Lew frowned as he analyzed the proposal. "And what about the posttrial motions? And the appeal?"

"My partner and I will take over," Phil replied. "If we somehow win and are able to get the verdict set aside, then Steve's ahead by the five million you give him. But if we're not successful, then he gets stuck for the entire eight million—the five he will have gotten from the company plus three million of his own."

Beck thought about the offer for a few moments. "And you think that North American will pay the five just to get off the hook for the other three?"

"They will if they're smart. As I see it," Phil explained, "they were willing to pay more than four *before* the verdict, so why in the hell wouldn't they pay five now, especially since they could get stuck for eight?"

Phil knew the offer made sense; Beck would have to admit that. The company should gladly pay five million to end the thing. In spite of their bravado, Phil was sure they were really worried about the bad faith claim. The only thing the company would be giving up was the possibility of winning the case and paying nothing, and that just wasn't a realistic possibility. Phil also knew that the most enticing part of the deal, for Beck, was that it would allow him to avoid a malpractice suit. He was probably wondering why Steve would take such a risk. After all, the possibility that he'd end up keeping the five million was virtually nonexistent—and certainly not worth giving up the bad faith claim for three million. And on top of that he was taking on Ogden & Andrews's legal fees and the risk of having to pay interest on the verdict.

Phil guessed what Lew was thinking: *These guys are crazy.*

Beck looked at his watch. "I'll call Boston and get back to you."

"Please do it as soon as you can," Phil said as he rose to leave. "We're running out of time."

Phil was grinning when he poked his head into Tom's office fifteen minutes later. Tom looked up and burst into a bright smile. "He bought it? He honest to God bought it?"

"Bought it? Hell, the poor guy nearly went into cardiac arrest when I mentioned a malpractice suit."

"All *right*!" Tom clapped his hands like a kid at the circus. "Give me the whole thing, and start from the beginning. I want it from the minute you walked into his office."

After Phil finished replaying his visit with Lew Beck, Tom reached over his desk to shake his partner's hand. "Good goin', my man. You just passed your first test as a litigator. You bullshitted another lawyer and got away with it."

"Well, I didn't really lie; I just held back some of the truth. I was having a little trouble at first, mostly because I felt sorry for Lew. But then he started to tell me what a good job he did for Steve, and I said to myself, 'Screw you, buddy. If you had done a good job you would've won, and Steve would've been sleeping like a baby during the past month.' It was easy after that."

"What do you think he'll do?"

"Do? He's probably already done it. I'll bet I wasn't down the elevator before he had Boston on the phone, and I'll also bet he's pushing as hard as he can to get them to come up with the five million. Believe me, he wants to put this case behind him." Phil fell into one of Tom's chairs. "Just picture what the guy's going through. First he gets hit in the face with an eight million dollar verdict, which he knows will piss off the insurance company. Then he finds out that Steve won't let him argue the posttrial motions or the appeal. And after all *that* the poor guy finds out he's about to be hit with a malpractice suit. Shit, Tom, he wants out, and the deal we offered is just the ticket. He wants it as badly as we do."

"Let's hope so."

The grand plan that had taken seed in Tom's mind in Ironwood was now under way. Step one was to make the deal with the insurance company. If that worked, step two would be to drop the bomb on Charlie Mayfield.

"But," Phil reminded his partner, "for now we have to sit back and wait for Beck."

Waiting for Lew Beck to get back to them involved yet another deception. There was still work to be done on the brief and the motion for a new trial, but Phil and Tom knew those papers would never be filed. They were holding the aces that would win the case, but they couldn't tell that to Beck, not yet, or the boys from Boston would put away their checkbook. So they had no alternative but to go through the charade of working on the papers.

Although everything was falling into place, Phil wasn't used to deception, and it made him uncomfortable. And the deception of Beck was only one more added to so many others: the scam at the parking lot downtown and the lie to induce the cooperation of Harry Weintraub of Peerless Parking; the ploy to get the office manager at Benedict Construction to tell how long the company had been on Polk Street; the ruse to find out that Larry Walton was in London on the last weekend in June of 1987; the story about the charitable trust to suck information out of Betty Erickson at Grand View Hospital; and the threatened malpractice suit against Lew Beck—a suit they had never even discussed with Steve.

But, Phil reasoned, all of these lies were necessary just to trap Tracey Walton with a single lie of her own. And that was justification enough.

FORTY-FOUR

BY WEDNESDAY MORNING Phil was starting to panic.

"How the hell long should it take for the guy to call Boston, get an answer, and then call us to tell us what it is?" he asked as he walked into Tom's office carrying a cup of coffee. "It's been nearly two days."

Tom looked up from one of the thick volumes of the Illinois Revised Statutes. "You're too antsy. I doubt if we'll hear from Beck before Friday. Tomorrow at the earliest."

"But—"

"C'mon, Phil, think about it. When Beck calls his contact at the insurance company and tells him about our offer, the guy isn't going to say, 'Sure thing, Lew baby, how should I make out the check?' No way! If we're lucky, the guy won't reject it out of hand. If it makes any sense at all to him, he'll tell Lew to sit tight while he takes it up with someone else—maybe his boss or some friggin' committee. A dozen people will probably have to be consulted before someone cuts a check for five million bucks, and one of 'em will most likely be that guy they sent out here during the trial—you know, the one who made an ass of himself."

In spite of his anxiety, Phil had to chuckle when he thought of Duane DeLuca. He'd never met him but he remembered Lew Beck's description of him.

"So actually," Tom said, "no news is good news. It would've taken them only a minute to say no, but it has to take a few days to say yes."

317

As Phil was turning to go back to his own office, his secretary, Carol, came into the room. "Oh, there you are. Dr. Sinclair is on the phone, and he wants to know if you'll be around for a while. He'd like to come in and see you—both of you."

Steve, dressed in light gray slacks and a navy blue blazer accented with a somewhat outdated narrow red and blue striped tie, was sitting on the small couch in Phil's office drinking a cup of coffee. Phil was sitting on the corner of his desk, and Tom had just walked in and was standing in the doorway.

"Well, look who's here," Tom remarked. "Shouldn't you be over at your office listening for little heartbeats?"

Steve smiled. He had heard people describe the daily routine of an obstetrician-gynecologist in many ways, but none as kindly as Tom just had. "I don't have office hours on Wednesdays. I came here after making my hospital rounds." Then he motioned toward an empty chair. "You may want to sit down, Tom, when you hear what I came up here to tell you guys."

Tom glanced at Phil, who simply shrugged his shoulders. "Let me guess," he said as he took a seat. "You've had seconds thoughts about marrying Molly and you want us to get you out of it."

"No, nothing like that." Steve laughed. He took a sip of coffee and said, "This has to do with Dave and Linda Roberts. I learned something that might be useful to us."

"Useful?" Phil asked in a surprised voice. "What you told us that night at Harry Caray's was enough to turn the whole case around."

"Well," Steve said, setting his coffee cup down, "there's more. Linda Roberts had had a miscarriage when she was my patient the first time, but there really wasn't anything unusual about that. A single miscarriage, by itself, doesn't mean too much. But then, when she came back to see me a couple of weeks ago, she told me she had miscarried three more times before she and her husband separated last year." He paused to take another sip of coffee. "Now, this might not mean anything to you, but it means a hell of a lot to an obstetrician. Most important, multiple miscarriages tell us that there's a possible chromosomal problem."

Phil wasn't sure what was coming, but he sensed it could be important. He paid close attention to what Steve was about to tell them.

"So when I heard this, I decided to have a karyotyping done on Linda Roberts's cells. I had to take a blood sample anyway, as part of her physical exam, so I asked the lab to run a chromosome check at the same time. I figured that if she had a problem she should be told about it, even though she's separated and probably not planning to have a child in the near future. I didn't give it too much thought at the time, but after Tom and Molly got back from Ironwood I began to put two and two together. So this morning I checked with the lab and found out that her chromosomal pattern is perfectly normal."

Phil looked at Tom, wondering if he missed anything. Then he looked back to Steve. "So what's the big deal?"

"Maybe nothing, but if Linda Roberts is normal and still has multiple miscarriages, then there's a pretty good chance that her husband has a chromosomal imbalance that was passed on to their fetuses. See what I'm getting at?"

Tom slapped his forehead. "Oh, sure! If Dave Roberts is Angel's father, then maybe she got Down's syndrome from *him*."

"Right," Steve said. "If he has a balanced translocation of his twenty-first chromosome, he'd be a Down carrier, and that could tie everything up in a neat package. It would be like his fingerprints on Angel—literally."

"Absolutely!" Phil said. "It would be almost as good as his signing the admission form at the hospital in Ironwood."

Tom got out of his chair and began pacing back and forth across the office. "That was good thinking, Steve," he said. "But just to lock it up, do you think there's a way we could actually find out if Roberts has one of those balanced translocations?"

"We don't have to find out," Steve replied with a grin. "I already know: He *does* have it."

"He *does?*" Tom exclaimed. "How do you know that?"

"I called Linda Roberts from the hospital this morning. I told her I had suspected a chromosomal problem when I learned of her miscarriages, but that the lab confirmed that she was normal. Then I asked her if her previous doctor had looked into this as well. She said yes. She and her husband had been checked after they lost their last baby, and her husband did in fact have a chromosomal problem. Of course, she never realized the significance of that, as it relates to our case, because she has no idea he had anything going with Tracey. Anyway, after I spoke with her I called her previous doctor's office. They checked the lab reports for me and confirmed that Mr. Roberts has a balanced translocation of the twenty-first chromosome."

Tom slapped Phil's desk with the palm of his hand. "We got 'em, guys. We got 'em right where we want 'em."

"Wait a minute," Phil said, frowning. "Didn't that one witness at the trial say Angel got Down's from a spontaneous translocation—a new mutation—and not from a parent with a translocation?"

"That's what he said, all right," Steve confirmed, "because that was the only possibility, since neither Tracey nor Larry Walton had a translocation. But," he added with a grin, "they checked the chromosomes of the wrong father."

FORTY-FIVE ===

LEW BECK'S CALL came only a few hours later.

Since Tom had predicted that it would take another day or two for Beck to get all the approvals he'd need to make the deal, Phil's first thought was that Beck was calling with bad news. Nonetheless, he felt a rush of adrenaline when he picked up the phone.

Beck got right to the point. "The people at North American Casualty have some interest in your proposal, Phil, but they'd like to put off a final decision until Grubner rules on the motion for a new trial."

Shit! Nothing's easy in this business. "No, Lew. Either we make the deal before the ruling or we don't make it at all."

"I don't see that it makes any difference."

You would if you knew what we know. "It makes all the difference in the world. Right now Steve is willing to let you guys off the hook on the bad faith claim in return for your paying him five million dollars. Then he'd take on the risk of the entire eight million himself, but he'd have two bites at the apple—the first at the motion for a new trial and the second at the appeal. However, if Grubner should rule against us—and you think he will—then Steve would have only one chance left to get out from under the three million dollar liability. He's willing to waive his bad faith claim for both bites but not for one.

"And remember," Phil added, "interest is running on the verdict. That could come close to another million. If you take our deal, North American won't have to worry about that interest; it'll be Steve's problem. But you can't expect him to pay the interest while you guys hold the money. He'll have to invest the money to offset his risk."

"Excuse me for asking, but where the hell is Sinclair going to get the extra three million if you lose?"

"Don't worry about it. Steve's considered that and he's prepared to deal with it."

There was a long pause before Beck spoke, and Phil knew exactly what he was thinking: If North American gave the five million to Sinclair, he'd have to make sure it would be kept available to pay the Waltons if the verdict stood up; otherwise the company could still be on the hook for it.

"All right, Phil," Beck said finally, "let's assume we take the deal. How much time would we have to pay Sinclair the five million?"

"The money has to be in Steve's hands before we argue the motion—that's a week from Friday—or the deal's off. Considering the way he was treated during the trial, you can understand why he doesn't exactly trust the crowd from Boston."

Phil could hear a sigh coming through the phone. "Okay," Beck said, "I'll get back to you."

Got him! Phil thought. Now don't let him off the hook. "When? Remember, Lew, if you nix the deal we'll have to figure out who's going to argue the motion. Steve still doesn't want you doing it, and if you or the company gives us any trouble on that . . . well, we'll have to get over to see Judge Grubner right away for a ruling."

"It's nearly five o'clock in Boston," Beck replied. His tone was clearly one of resignation. "I'll see if I can get an answer for you before the day's out. Otherwise first thing in the morning."

Phil dashed into his partner's office and repeated his conversation with Lew Beck. "I think they're taking the bait, Tom."

"Sounds like it. I'll bet the company already told Lew they'd make the deal but that he should try to delay as long as possible. That way they could play with their money a little longer."

"Sure," Phil said, "and they probably told him to try to get off by paying something less than the five million— maybe four or four and a half—but Lew wouldn't have the stomach to try that, not after what they put him through with their nickeling-and-diming during the trial."

"And you were absolutely right to insist they pay the money now instead of later. If they knew what we had up our sleeve, they'd be screaming bloody murder and saying we should've told them. Then we'd have another fight on our hands."

"They're still going to raise hell," Tom said, "but there won't be a thing they can do about it. I've researched it—we'll be safe as long as we get the right language in the releases."

Twenty minutes later Beck was on the phone again.

"Okay, Phil, we're in business. I thought we might have a problem with an attorney's lien, but Charlie Mayfield never served us with one. I guess he knows the Waltons well enough to trust them not to welsh on his fees. Anyway, since that means we don't have to protect Charlie's fees, North American can wire the money as soon as you and I can draw up an agreement. We'll need Sinclair's release of the bad faith claim, and also a release of any claim against me."

"No problem. I'll draw something up tonight and have it in your office in the morning. And, Lew?"

"Yes?"

"I'm going to put some language in to guarantee that once we make the deal and you pay Steve the five million, you don't get it back."

"Certainly, that's the agreement."

"I know, but if we somehow save the case and Steve ends up winning, I don't want you guys coming after us for a refund."

Lew Beck laughed. "You pull off something like that and I'll be the first one to shake your hand."

•   •   •

By the following Tuesday afternoon the papers were signed and the five million dollars was safely in an interest-bearing account in Steve's name. Lew Beck and North American Casualty were out of the case.

The first step of the grand plan was a success. Now it was time to get on to step two: Charlie Mayfield.

FORTY-SIX=====

CHARLIE MAYFIELD AND and Phil Ogden were at the Metropolitan Club, their corner table offering a panoramic view of the city. "It doesn't seem fair," Phil was saying. "I called to invite you for a drink, and here we are at your club where they won't take my money."

"Don't give it a thought," the older lawyer said graciously. "They make martinis here just the way I like 'em. Anyway, I have to meet some people here later for dinner."

"Then you probably don't have a lot of time, so I'd better get right to the point."

"Fire away, Counselor," Charlie said as he beckoned to a waiter.

"Well, there's been a new wrinkle in our case, and I thought I should discuss it with you in person before I raise it in our posttrial motion."

"A new wrinkle?"

"Yes. For one thing, Lew Beck is withdrawing from the case. My partner and I will handle it alone from here on in."

"I don't understand," Charlie said, obviously surprised. "Why would North American agree to anything like that? I mean, with all respect, you aren't exactly a seasoned litigator, and they have five million bucks riding on the outcome—in fact, eight million if you can pull off your bad faith claim against them. And that's another thing: Why would they hire you to do the posttrial work *for* them at the same time you're threatening a three million dollar suit *against* them? Insurance companies aren't that broad-minded."

"We've worked all of that out, and I think you'll understand when I explain everything to you."

After the waiter took their drink orders, Phil told Charlie that the insurance company had paid Steve five million dollars and walked away from the case, and that in return Steve had waived his bad faith claim.

Charlie raised an eyebrow. "Seems to me that you and your client are taking a hell of a risk," he said. "That verdict is going to stick, Phil—I'm sure of it—so your doctor friend will have to give us the five million plus three of his own. Hell, I don't know if he even *has* three million, and he'd be giving up the chance to lay it off on the company. That doesn't make sense."

"But the verdict isn't going to stick, Charlie. Your case isn't worth ten cents."

Charlie Mayfield sat back in his chair and eyed the brash young lawyer. "Is that what you brought me over here for? To tell me I don't have a good case? You sound like that fat slob they sent out here from Boston. He tried to tell me the same thing, and I sent him back to Massachusetts with an eight million dollar banana stuck up his ass."

Phil had to laugh at the way Charlie described his conquest of the insurance company and, specifically, Duane DeLuca. "I know all about that guy and the job you did on him. But he was just blowing smoke. He didn't know what a lousy case you had. We do."

Charlie took a sip from the martini the waiter had just placed in front of him. Something in Phil's manner and tone of voice—a confidence that the senior lawyer wouldn't have expected—had set off one of the alarm buttons that rest deep within the brain of every litigator. "And just exactly what is so lousy about my case?" he asked, obviously trying to act unconcerned. "What did you see in just a few weeks that the rest of us haven't been able to see in four years?"

Phil studied the beer the waiter had brought him. "I

think you should ask Tracey Walton. Let her tell you. If she won't, then I will, and I'll be able to back it up with proof."

"And what should I ask her?" Charlie inquired cautiously.

"Well, before you talk to her, you might ask Larry where he was on the last weekend of June 1987. We did. He was in London, England. And that's the weekend that Angel Walton was actually conceived; your own witnesses testified to that."

Phil let Charlie digest that tidbit for a moment before he continued. "And then you might ask Tracey where *she* was that same weekend. I think she'll tell you that she was in Hurley, Wisconsin, and that while she was there she had a little accident and was treated at Grand View Hospital in Ironwood, Michigan."

Charlie Mayfield said nothing. His only reaction was a slight, almost imperceptible, nodding of his head, as if to indicate that there had always been something too clean, too neat, about Tracey's story. As if maybe this would explain the previously inexplicable conflict between her testimony and Dr. Sinclair's.

"Finally," Phil continued, "you could ask Tracey who she was with up there. If she says she can't remember, you might mention the name David Roberts—that should refresh her memory. She was with Roberts at his cabin that weekend."

Phil took a long swallow of his beer and then added, "By the way, Dave Roberts is a carrier of Down's syndrome."

FORTY-SEVEN ═══

NO TRIAL LAWYER could win as many cases as Charlie Mayfield had over the years without losing some along the way, but in recent years his losses had been few and far between. Of course, some cases were weak to begin with, but lawyers of Charlie's caliber didn't take weak cases—they didn't have to. Those were for the young-sters just starting out or for the lackluster guys on the fringe, that element of the bar that had to take the leftovers. When Charlie took a case, it wasn't a question of whether he would win—it was a question of how much he would win. Oh, he gambled now and then on an iffy case, but only if it offered a good chance for a quick settlement and an easy fee, or if the doubtful verdict could be enormous.

Walton v. Sinclair wasn't one of those iffy cases. Charlie had taken it because he knew he would win it and because the anticipated verdict was sure to provide a substantial fee, given his customary arrangement of one-third for him and two-thirds for his client. And while no loss was easy to take, an unforeseeable loss was simply not acceptable. He had said a thousand times, "I wish to hell I could practice law without clients; they're the ones who fuck me up. I can handle my opponents and the judges and juries, but I can't handle my own clients—not when they double-cross me."

Charlie was angry—damned angry—and the object of his anger was at the moment sitting in his reception room.

"They're all here now," his secretary announced over his intercom.

"Send 'em in." Showdown time, he thought to himself. This might not be the most delicate way to handle the problem, but so what? His client had made a fool of ol' Charlie, and she would pay for it—right in front of her daddy and her ex-husband.

Charlie didn't get up when they came in, but simply nodded toward the three chairs facing him. Tracey took the middle one and her father and Larry sat on either side of her.

"You don't look too happy," Bernard Benedict said. "What happened? Did the judge give them another extension?"

"No, Bernie, there won't be any more extensions. In fact, there won't be any motion for a new trial."

"I don't understand. Are they giving up?"

"Hardly. But before I answer any more questions, I'd like to ask a few of my own." He trained his eyes directly on Tracey, but now they weren't those sad eyes that said, "Trust me." They were piercing lasers. "Who the hell is Dave Roberts?"

Charlie could see that the question hit Tracey Walton like a blind shot to the side of the head. "Dave Roberts? He's an engineer, a consultant to the city. Daddy and I work with him once in a while. Why?"

"I'm asking the questions, remember?" Then Charlie looked at Larry. "Do you know him, Larry?"

Larry Walton looked confused. "Yes, but not well."

"Do you have any idea how he figures into this whole mess?"

"Mess?" Larry asked. "What mess?"

Charlie looked at Tracey. "Do you want to tell him or shall I?"

She simply closed her eyes, saying nothing.

Bernard Benedict leaned forward and put his hands on Charlie's desk. "Charlie, I know you're the one who's supposed to be asking the questions, but what the hell's going on?"

Charlie looked at his friend, and his eyes were sad again. "The fact that you don't know what's going on is the only good news I've heard in the last twenty-four hours. I've always considered you an honorable man, Bernie, and it would have broken my heart to learn that you were in on this swindle."

"*Swindle?* What in God's name are you talking about?"

"Well, it looks as if your little girl here is trying to pull a sting operation, and apparently she doesn't care who she tramples in the process."

Benedict jumped to his feet so quickly that his chair tipped over behind him. "I demand to know what this is all about! Charlie, if you don't—"

"All right, all right," Charlie said, holding up his hands. "You're entitled to know, and so is Larry. That's why I wanted you both here." He looked at Tracey. "Well?"

Tracey, who hadn't said a word since answering Charlie's first question about Dave Roberts, looked like a cornered animal. In less than a minute her beauty had transformed itself into a distorted collage of features that didn't seem to belong on the same face. Her cheeks were flushed, but at the same time she looked strangely pale. Her bottom lip was trembling. And in an effort to dab her tears away with a tissue, she had smeared her expertly applied mascara into two ugly blotches.

"Let me make it easy for you," Charlie said, suddenly sympathetic. Then, just as he had done when she was on the witness stand struggling with the more difficult parts of her testimony, he put questions to her that called for simple answers. Wasn't Angel conceived during the last weekend of June 1987? Wasn't that in Hurley, Wisconsin? Didn't you have a little accident and injure your leg during that weekend, and weren't you treated at a hospital in Ironwood, Michigan? Weren't you up there with Dave Roberts, and weren't you both staying at his place? And wasn't Larry in England on business at the time? And finally, isn't Dave Roberts Angel's father?

Each time Charlie asked a question, two things happened. Tracey, whose eyes and lips were tightly shut, conceded the answers with a slight, reluctant nod of her head, and Bernard Benedict, whose eyes were wide open and staring at her, flinched with each nod. He apparently hoped that she would shake her head and scream denials, but she only nodded.

Larry looked dumbfounded. His eyes darted back and forth between Charlie and Tracey during the questioning as he obviously tried to register the enormous significance of what was being said. His ex-wife had lived a lie for five years, and for four of those years she had shared Larry's bed. She had been unfaithful, and the sick child he loved and had helped to raise belonged to another man. He seemed unable to believe that all this could be happening.

There was a long, painful silence when the questions mercifully stopped. Then Tracey lifted her head and, avoiding Larry, looked pleadingly at her father, the one person she knew would understand. "Daddy, I *had* to give Dr. Sinclair the wrong date. Otherwise Larry would have known. . . . And I just couldn't tell you—"

"You couldn't tell me *what*?" Bernard Benedict barked. "That you're a liar? An adulteress? That you cheated your husband out of a marriage? And out of a child? That you tried to cheat a doctor out of his reputation, and an insurance company out of millions of dollars? That you lied to *me*? Is that what you couldn't tell me?"

Charlie saw that Tracey couldn't believe her ears. He knew that her father had never failed to come to her defense. Now he was not only refusing to defend her, he was *attacking* her!

"But the *expenses*, Daddy. The nurses, the doctors, the medicines—everything cost so much. And the business— we have the bank loans and all those other bills. Daddy, we needed the money!"

"We needed the money? Are you telling me *you* lied and cheated because *I* couldn't pay my bills and because *I* couldn't afford to take care of my grandchild? That *I'm* responsible for this?" He put his hands on the arms of her chair and leaned over so that his face was only inches from hers. "And I suppose *I'm* responsible for your climbing into bed with that political suck-ass Roberts. I suppose you'll tell me that it all started with those goddamn complimentary bids you gave him—and that you did that for *my* sake."

He started to walk over to the window at the far side of the room, but spun around and pointed a finger at his daughter's back. "And speaking of that no good son of a bitch, where in the hell has *he* been through all of this? What has *he* done about all these expenses you're so worried about—worried enough to lie and cheat and steal? He's a big hotshot man-about-town with money to spend in all the right places. He can even afford his own love nest in the woods and his own airplane to fly around in. I'll tell you what *he's* done: He's coached his girlfriend on the fine art of screwing the system, all the while hiding in the background while Larry and I foot the bills. When was he going to come out into the open, Tracey? After you got the eight million dollars?"

Bernard Benedict stood there breathing heavily for several seconds and then sighed and righted the chair he had knocked over earlier. When he sat down he looked ten years older.

In a voice barely loud enough for anyone to hear, Tracey said, "But, Daddy, it was *your* idea to file the lawsuit. You were the one who brought me to Charlie."

Benedict looked at her and slowly shook his head, not even bothering to explain that four years earlier he'd had no reason to suspect that his daughter was a fraud. Then he looked at his former son-in-law. "You were right all along, Larry—we shouldn't have filed the suit. The only consolation in all of this is that if we had listened to you we might never have learned the truth. Now you, at least, have no further responsibility for Angel."

Larry Walton, still reeling from the crushing revelations, could say nothing.

Then Bernard Benedict looked at Charlie and slowly

shook his head. "I'm sorry for getting you involved in this mess."

The lawyer with the sad eyes wanted to cry for his friend. "Hey, don't feel sorry for ol' Charlie. My mortgage is paid off and I'll still have my martini tonight." Then he added, "Maybe you'd better have a couple yourself, Bernie. You look as if you'll need them."

FORTY-EIGHT ═══

ALTHOUGH HARRY CARAY'S would have been the obvious choice, Steve wanted something different, something more unusual than the casual, free-swinging bistro just north of the Loop. He selected the *Odyssey,* a triple-decked ship that sailed from Navy Pier onto Lake Michigan each evening for three hours, catering to diners who wanted a dazzling view of Chicago's skyline while they enjoyed an elegant dinner. The food and wines were excellent, but they were upstaged by Molly's magnificent engagement ring. Maggie and Alice were still clucking over the ring, and Phil and Tom were still rehashing the case, when Steve suggested they go to the moonlit upper deck for after-dinner drinks.

The view was spectacular. "Say what you want about this city," Tom remarked, "it's still got the greatest skyline in the United States." The splendid glistening of the million city lights to the west was balanced perfectly by the single glowing moon to the east. Chicago had never been noted for either its scenery or its weather, but on this balmy June night, seen from the top deck of the *Odyssey,* it was second to no place on earth.

After they had savored the stirring view and the night breezes, Alice Andrews drew Phil aside to ask about Charlie Mayfield's reaction to the turn of events.

"He was a gentleman," Phil replied, "an absolutely wonderful gentleman. Here was a guy who worked his tail off for four years on a tough case, tried it beautifully, and won an eight million dollar verdict. With interest on

334

the judgment, he would've walked away with a fee of nearly three million bucks, and it was right there in his pocket until Tom and Molly clicked with that nurse in Ironwood. But you know what Charlie did today, Alice? He patted me on the back and congratulated me. 'Phil,' he said, 'you and that partner of yours whipped my butt. You taught ol' Charlie a thing or two about practicing law, and my hat's off to you both.' Can you imagine that, Alice? Charlie Mayfield saying that to *us*?"

Phil and Alice were standing at the stern of the *Odyssey,* staring at the wash from the giant propellers, when the others moved closer.

"The one thing Lew could never figure out during the trial," Steve remarked to no one in particular, "was why Larry Walton never testified and why he seemed so disinterested, almost negative, about the case. Do you think he had any idea that he wasn't Angel's father?"

"No," Phil said. "According to Charlie, Larry was shocked when Charlie broke the news. He was dazed— just sat there shaking his head. In fact, Charlie's been trying to call him for the past few days to see how he's getting along—I guess Charlie was pretty hard on him during the trial—but he can't get through. The poor guy's apparently devastated. And it's ironic because he was opposed to the lawsuit all along."

"Why?" Maggie asked.

"According to Charlie, Larry thought they should have settled early on, and when Tracey and Charlie turned down the offers from the insurance company, well, Larry thought they were being greedy. On top of that, he never believed that Steve was to blame for the kid's condition."

"But he still could have testified," Maggie pointed out.

Phil held up a finger. "Charlie couldn't take the chance. Larry had told him that he and Tracey never discussed abortion, and that information would have been inconsistent with Tracey's testimony. He also would have contradicted her about the amount of time she spent at work and away from the baby. Those things, along with his other misgivings about the case, scared Charlie too much to put him on the stand."

"So," Steve remarked, "Tracey tried to screw me all by herself."

"But you have to remember," Phil said, "that she didn't really *set out* to screw you. According to Charlie—and he got this from Tracey just yesterday—Tracey lied that first day in your office to hide the fact that she had been cheating on her husband. She knew damn well that Larry was out of the country when she conceived, and she was afraid he'd figure it out. So, in order to protect their marriage, she came up with a different date for her last period, a date that would be consistent with getting pregnant after Larry got back from London. That way she figured he'd never know the truth, and when the baby was finally born she'd simply say it was a few weeks premature. So yes, she lied to you, Steve, but not to set you up for a malpractice suit. She lied only to save her marriage, which at the time she probably thought was still worth saving. She had no idea back then that her baby would have Down's syndrome or that there would ever be a lawsuit. And she sure didn't know that giving you the wrong date for her last period would cause you to misread the alpha-fetoprotein test. Once she started with a few lies, she got sucked in and couldn't get out."

"But why didn't she ever go in for the ultrasound?" Maggie Ogden asked. "If she had done that, she might've learned that she was carrying a Down baby."

Alice, who was a nurse, said, "I think I can answer that. An ultrasound would have shown the size and development of the baby. If she'd had the test, Steve would've known that the pregnancy was a few weeks further along than he had thought. That would've blown her secret, so she kept ducking the test by telling Steve she was too busy and that she didn't have insurance."

"Right," Phil said, "but at the trial she knew those would be lame excuses—what pregnant woman is too busy or too cheap to have an ultrasound? So she testified that Steve never even suggested it, and that made him look even worse in front of the jury."

Steve put his arm around Molly, who had been uncharacteristically quiet all evening. "Are you all right, honey?" he whispered.

"Sure I am," she replied. "But what's the official word on the case? I mean, is it all over?"

"It sure is." Steve looked over to Phil. "Phil, tell Molly what happened today."

"They formally capitulated. Charlie called this morning to say he'd convinced Tracey that they didn't have a chance—not with all the things we'd learned in the past couple of weeks. So they agreed to throw in the towel. We went over to the courthouse this afternoon, and Judge Grubner entered a formal judgment in our favor—a judgment notwithstanding the verdict. It's all over. Steve won." Phil tossed the ice cubes from his empty glass over the side of the *Odyssey* and then asked the group, "And you know who's taking it the hardest?"

"Tracey?" Alice asked.

"Charlie Mayfield?" Maggie asked.

"Neither," Phil answered. "It's Tracey's father, Bernard Benedict. He's always despised Dave Roberts, and Tracey, even after she was divorced and Roberts was separated, was afraid to tell her father that she was seeing the guy. Also, Charlie told me that Benedict is a very moral person—you know the type: honor, duty, and country—and he was crushed beyond belief to learn about all the things his daughter had done.

"Tracey must have a vestige of conscience, though. She kept telling Charlie that she'd never take any money from Steve. It seems she was willing to lie to get money out of an insurance company, but she drew the line when it came to hitting Steve in his own wallet."

They passed a sailboat coming from the opposite direction and saw that its passengers were waving to them with drinks in their hands. They returned the greeting and stood silently as the small craft disappeared into the darkness.

Then Phil said, "You know, in a way I feel for Tracey, not just because she has a sick little girl but because she more or less got pulled into this whole thing."

"How can you say that?" Maggie asked. "This whole thing was her doing."

"Not according to Charlie," Phil explained. "He told me that she was reluctant to file the suit in the first place. It was her father who took her to Charlie and encouraged her to go ahead with it. To his way of thinking, Steve had botched up his daughter's pregnancy and therefore should have been made to face the consequences. So Tracey was in a bind: She couldn't refuse to go ahead with the suit without telling her father and Larry the truth, and she never had the courage to do that." Phil thought for a moment and then added, "Well, maybe she could've told Larry later, after their marriage was on the rocks, but she couldn't let her dad find out."

"And in the meantime," Tom said, "this Roberts guy was probably whispering in her ear to go ahead with the suit—that is, if they were still seeing each other."

Phil nodded. "They were, and still are."

"By the way," Alice Andrews asked, "did Roberts know all along that Angel was his daughter?"

"Yes," Phil answered. "Tracey admitted to Charlie that she told Roberts he was the father as soon as she learned she was pregnant."

"Then I assume he's going to bear the expenses for Angel from here on out?"

"That's what Charlie thinks," Phil said. "Roberts is pretty well heeled. Anyway, he and Tracey were planning to get married as soon as the case was over—and as soon as they could screw up the courage to tell her father. At least that was the plan while he was smelling a big check from the insurance company. But until then they wanted to keep their romance a secret because it could have messed up the case. Moreover, if people knew they were an item, someone might have put two and two together, just as Tom did, and figured out that Roberts was really Angel's father."

"Sure," Steve said. "Linda Roberts would certainly have put it together. She knew her husband was a Down carrier. If she'd known that he was seeing Tracey and that Tracey had a Down child, she would have realized in a flash that Dave was the father."

Tom laughed. "If they don't get married, I'll volunteer my services to Tracey to file a paternity suit against the son of a bitch." Then, in a more serious tone, he added, "But I hope they do get married."

"Why?" his wife asked.

"Because they deserve each other."

Half an hour later, as the night air grew chilly and the *Odyssey* was nearing the end of its short voyage, Molly snuggled up to Steve. "I want you to know how happy I am, Doc. It was only a few weeks ago that the jury dropped that bomb on us. Now here we are celebrating, and everything's absolutely wonderful."

Steve glanced over to Phil, who smiled and winked at him. Then Steve leaned back against the railing. "I'd like to make an announcement," he said.

"Oh, no!" Tom exclaimed, glancing at Molly's stomach.

"No," Steve laughed, "nothing like that. My announcement—and Molly doesn't even know this yet—is that Molly and I are going to take a little trip in about ten days."

Molly looked at him quizzically.

"You all know that the scheme Phil and Tom worked out means that I end up with five million dollars. Phil told me I'll have to pay taxes on it, and I suppose"—he put his fingers in his ears as if waiting for an explosion—"I'll be getting a bill from Ogden and Andrews, so I don't know exactly how much I'll have left, but I know it'll be more than I ever thought I'd have.

"So I figured out a way to spend some of it. On the weekend after next, Molly and I are going to a little lodge I heard about in Michigan's Upper Peninsula, and while we're up there, we're going over to Ironwood to have dinner with the head people from Grand View Hospital. And we're going to give them a check for one million dollars in honor of Betty Erickson."

Molly threw her arms around him. And although her voice was muffled against his chest, everyone heard her say, "For cryin' out loud, Doc, Tom and I already *bought* her a box of *candy*."

As the *Odyssey* settled into its mooring at Navy Pier and its passengers were preparing to disembark, Phil pulled Tom aside. "You know, Tom, we won the case and everybody's happy. But there's one thing I learned these past few weeks that really bothers me."

"What's that?"

"Well, people can be pretty rotten. Take Tracey Walton, for example. Here's an otherwise intelligent, respectable person, and yet she had no qualms about lying just to get five million dollars out of an insurance company."

Tom put his arm around him. "Neither did we, partner. Neither did we."